KEEPING MUM

Kate Lawson was born on the edge of the Fens and is perfectly placed to write about the vagaries of life in East Anglia. In between raising a family, singing in a choir, walking the dog, working in the garden, taking endless photos and cooking, Kate is also a scriptwriter, originating and developing a soap opera for BBC radio, along with a pantomime for the town in which she lives. As Sue Welfare, Kate published 6 novels, two of which are currently under development for TV.

For more information on Kate go to www.katelawson.co.uk.

Praise for Kate Lawson:

'Wonderfully warm and funny and a great lesson about finding answers to life's troubles in the unlikeliest of places.'   *Closer*

'A wonderful witty novel.'   *Woman's Weekly*

'Delightful.'   *Daily Telegraph*

By the same author:

Mum's the Word
Lessons in Love

KATE LAWSON

Keeping Mum

AVON

This novel is entirely a work of fiction.
The names, characters and incidents portrayed in it are
the work of the author's imagination. Any resemblance to
actual persons, living or dead, events or localities is
entirely coincidental.

AVON

A division of HarperCollins*Publishers*
77–85 Fulham Palace Road,
London W6 8JB

www.harpercollins.co.uk

A Paperback Original 2009

1

First published in Great Britain by
HarperCollins*Publishers* 2009

Copyright © Kate Lawson 2009

Kate Lawson asserts the moral right to
be identified as the author of this work

A catalogue record for this book is
available from the British Library

ISBN: 978-1-84756-053-7

Set in Minion by Palimpsest Book Production Limited,
Grangemouth, Stirlingshire

Printed and bound in Great Britain by
Clays Ltd, St Ives plc

Mixed Sources
Product group from well-managed
forests and other controlled sources
www.fsc.org Cert no. SW-COC-1806
© 1996 Forest Stewardship Council

FSC

FSC is a non-profit international organisation established
to promote the responsible management of the world's forests.
Products carrying the FSC label are independently certified
to assure consumers that they come from forests that are managed
to meet the social, economic and ecological needs
of present and future generations.

Find out more about HarperCollins and the environment at
www.harpercollins.co.uk/green

I'd like to thank my agent, Maggie Phillips, for her ongoing wisdom, insight, humour and kindness, not to mention buying me my first anti-wrinkle serum, and also Mary at Ed Victor for scouring the shops for bottom butter . . .

Huge thanks too, to Maxine Hitchcock, Keshini Naidoo and Sammia Rafique at HarperCollins for their ideas, their skilful editing, organising, support and encouragement.

And a special thanks to Lawrence and Maureen – sadly missed – and their daughter Danielle at Lewks in Downham Market, who year after year provide me with a place to launch and sell my books.

To my lovely man, Phil, my beautiful boys, Ben, James, Joe and Sam, and my dog Beau, and also the Fabulous Fish ladies on Downham Market's market.

Chapter One

'Blonde wig, sunglasses . . .' Cass tucked a stray lock of hair behind her ear and looked herself up and down in the ornate mirror currently leaning up against the wall in the spare room. She turned left and right to gauge the full effect and then shook her head. 'Fiona, I can't go out dressed in this. I look like a hooker.'

'No, you don't. Of course you don't,' Fiona said briskly, tugging Cass's wig down at the back. 'You look . . .' She hesitated. It was obvious that it was a struggle to find the right words.

'Conspicuous and very dodgy?' suggested Cass. 'Let's be honest, Fee, that's the last thing you want from a spy.'

Fiona's expression hardened. 'Spy is a very emotive word,' she snapped, handing Cass a trench coat and rolled black umbrella.

'Oh, and these are meant to help me blend in, are they? I don't think this is a good idea at all.' Cass dropped the umbrella onto the bed. 'And besides, I barely know Andy. I've only seen him a couple of times since you moved back.'

'Exactly.'

'What do you mean *exactly*?'

1

'Well, if you knew him you could hardly spy on him, could you? He'd get suspicious, but this is fine. You know Andy well enough to recognise him in a crowd or pick him out in a bar, but not well enough for him to come rushing over or, worse still, go rushing off.' As she spoke Fiona flicked Cass's collar up and fluffed the wig so it looked a little more tousled.

'There we are,' she said. 'That's absolutely perfect.'

'It's not perfect. Remember the sixth leavers do? Vamps and tramps? You made me wear a corset and nearly got us both arrested?'

Fiona sniffed. 'You always say that, but it was fine. I *told* the policeman we weren't soliciting.'

Cass nodded. 'Uh-huh – well all I need now are the fishnets.'

'Don't be so silly,' said Fiona. 'You look great.'

Cass wasn't convinced.

From an overstuffed chair out on the landing, Mungo the resident ginger tom and Buster, Cass's matching mongrel, watched proceedings with interest. They didn't look convinced either.

'It's not like I'm asking you to bug him or anything,' protested Fiona into what was proving quite a tricky silence. 'All you have to do is watch, take a few photos and possibly notes, and let me know exactly what he is up to. And with who . . .' Fiona paused. 'I know he's up to something.' But if Fiona was hoping that Cass was going to leap into the breach, she was sadly mistaken.

'I wouldn't ask, Cass, but I can't afford a private detective and I don't know what else to do. Does your mobile phone have a camera with a zoom lens?' Fiona asked, as she buttoned Cass into the trench coat.

2

This wasn't exactly how Cass had imagined the evening going at all. She'd been thinking more in terms of a DVD, a bottle of wine and a takeaway, along with a bit of girlie chat, while the cat and dog mugged them for prawns.

Cass had known Fiona since they were eleven years old, and at school together – which in some ways felt like yesterday and in others a lifetime ago. After sixth form they had drifted apart, separated by college, boys, careers. And then a couple of years ago, Cass had had a phone call out of the blue:

'Cass, this is Fee, just wanted to let you know we're moving back to the area – isn't that great? God, I'm so excited, maybe we could catch up sometime? I feel a bit like salmon coming home to spawn.'

Which was probably too much information. It obviously hadn't occurred to Fiona that Cass wouldn't remember who she was, not that Cass had forgotten – who could forget someone like Fiona?

Time smoothes away the raw edges of memory and Cass had forgotten a lot of things about Fee. What Cass had forgotten was that when she was on a mission, Fiona could be a grade A pain in the arse. These last two years of having Fee back in her life had brought all those annoying little qualities to light in glorious Technicolor. They hadn't spoken very much in the years since leaving school but in that first conversation it all came flooding back.

'When I saw this job in the paper I said to Andy it was fate. I can't remember if you met Andy – he comes from Cambridge. You'll have to come to dinner sometime once we've settled in. He can still commute; I know it's a bit of a drag but we'll get real quality of life in Norfolk. Or at least I will, he'll be spending most of his life on the train,' she giggled. 'And I've found this great house. In Barwell Road? Those really lovely old Edwardian houses overlooking the park – four bedrooms, big bay windows … It's going to be just perfect. I mean we want kids and London's no place for a family, at least not for a country girl like me. *So* what are you up to these days?' It had taken Fiona the best part of twenty minutes to get around to asking Cass anything about her life.

'Working mostly, you know I bought a shop? And bringing the boys up.'

'God, there's you nearly done and me just starting,' Fee had said. 'Doesn't that make you feel old?'

Cass hadn't known how to answer that and so instead said, 'Oh, and I sing in a choir.' It had been a throwaway line.

'Really?' said Fiona. 'You know I've always wanted to join a choir. Remember when we used to sing in the school choir? God – that was such a giggle.'

Which was why Fiona, the week after she moved in, had turned up to join Cass at Mrs Althorpe's All Stars – Beckthorn's community choir, which was a lot sexier and loads more fun than it sounded. When she saw Fiona waving and hurrying over to her, Cass groaned and wished she'd kept her mouth shut. Two years on and she hadn't changed her mind.

'God,' Fiona had said, as she slipped in alongside Cass. 'Isn't this great? Just like the good old days.'

Cass hadn't said anything.

As a lady bass and occasional tenor, Cass did a lot of well-synchronised do-be-do-be-doooos, dms, and finger snapping that made up the heartbeat of the doo-wop and blues numbers the band was famous for.

4

Originally Cass had joined the choir because she couldn't get a place on the garden design course, hated aerobics, and had always wanted to sing. She'd also thought it might be a good place to meet men, which it was – although as it turned out almost all of them were well over 50 and mad as haddock. It was fun though, because there was no need to be anything other than yourself with them.

For the choir's performances, which took place everywhere from church halls to street corners, the All Stars wore full evening dress, men in black tie and occasionally tails, the women shimmying and swaying in gowns of every colour under the sun, all glitzy and glamorous and very over the top with lots of diamante, feathers, sequins, tiaras and an ocean of bugle beads. It certainly beat workout Lycra into a cocked hat.

After Tuesday evening rehearsal, the choir traditionally went on to the pub. Which was how Cass and Fiona came to find themselves squeezed into the end of a pew behind a long table in the snug bar of the Old Grey Whippet, alongside Ray, Phil and Welsh Alf, whose voice came straight from the heart of the Rhondda – which didn't quite compensate for the fact that he often forgot the tune and occasionally the words – and Norman, who only came because his wife had an evening class across the road on Tuesday nights and didn't drive.

Cass hadn't intended to sing bass when she joined. But when she signed up there'd only been one man, Welsh Alf, and so, Alan – their musical director – had suggested that some of the female altos sing the bass parts an octave higher. (Which at that point meant nothing to Cass, who hadn't sung a note anywhere other than in the bath since leaving Beckthorn County High.)

Four and a half years on, there were half a dozen men and around the same number of women in the bass section, with a sprinkling of men in the tenors and of course Gordon in the sopranos, who sang falsetto, plucked his eyebrows and occasionally wore blue eyeliner, although he was the exception rather than the rule.

Her only real gripe was that while the sopranos got the tune and the altos had the harmony, the tenors grabbed the twiddly bits, and so nine times out of ten all the basses got were the notes left over and they didn't always make much sense musically. There certainly wasn't much in the way of a catchy little tune to hum while making toast.

So, after choir on Tuesday evening, everyone was just finishing a blow-by-blow dissection of how the evening's rehearsal had gone, and Gordon was perched on a stool at the bar, halfway down his second Babycham, when Fiona, who was sipping a bitter lemon said, 'I was wondering – could you do me a favour?'

Cass looked round. Fiona said it casually, in a way that suggested she wanted Cass to pick up a few bits from Tesco on her way home from work or maybe pop round to let the gasman in, and so, halfway down a glass of house red, Cass nodded. 'Sure. What would you like me to do?'

But before she could answer, Bert, the big chunky tenor, an ex-rugby player who sang like an angel, drank like a fish and was tight as new elastic, bellowed, 'Anyone fancy a top-up, only it's m'birthday t'day, so I'm in the chair.' Fiona's reply was lost in the furore.

'Maybe it would be easier if I popped round some time?' Fiona shouted above the general hullaballoo as people fought their way to the bar to put their orders in. 'Make an evening of it?'

'Okay,' said Cass, easing her way to the front. 'Why don't you come round for supper one night next week?'

Which was why they were now standing in Cass's spare room with a suitcase full of props and the remains of a bottle of Archers which Fiona had brought round – probably, Cass now realised, as a liquid inducement. It had slipped down a treat. Unlike Fiona's little favour.

It had taken Fiona a couple of glasses, a lot of idle chitchat and much admiring of Cass's home before she managed to get around to what she had in mind. What Fiona wanted was a little light surveillance. More specifically, she wanted Cass to follow Andy, and find out what he was up to, where, when and with whom – although so far the reasons behind it all were a little hazy.

'So tell me again what exactly has brought this on?' asked Cass. 'If I'm going to go the full Mata Hari, at least I should really know what I'm getting myself into.'

'Andy's seeing someone,' said Fiona, gazing past her into the mirror, presumably trying to gauge the effectiveness of Cass's disguise.

'How can you be so certain?'

The questions seemed to take Fiona by surprise. 'Because he's been acting very strangely over the last few weeks. He's changed the password on his email account.'

'And you know this *because*?'

'Well, when I was on his computer I couldn't get into his email,' said Fiona, casually.

'You read his email?'

At least Fiona had the decency to look a bit sheepish. 'Of course I do, I mean, doesn't everyone? We're practically married—'

'And that makes it all right, does it?' Cass couldn't

imagine anything worse than having someone nosing through her private life.

'What on earth has right got to do with anything?' said Fiona indignantly. 'He shouldn't need to hide things from me.'

'So presumably Andy's got your password too?' asked Cass.

Fiona looked outraged. 'No, of course he hasn't, but that's different – I mean, I'm not up to anything.'

'Changing your password is hardly proof of being up to something though, is it?'

'He keeps getting texts . . .'

'Oh for goodness sake, Fee, we all get texts.'

'Which he erases,' Fiona countered. 'I know because I've looked while he's in the shower. His inbox is always empty – you've got to admit that that is suspicious?'

Cass wasn't sure there was any sane answer. Experience told her that if you think someone is up to something, then your mind is only too happy to fill in the gaps, and everything the other person does only conspires to make them look even more guilty. And while Fiona's plan all sounded pretty crazy from this side of the fence, no doubt inside Fiona's head it sounded just fine. When it struck, jealously, insecurity and uncertainty could be a destructive and all-engulfing madness.

'How long have you two been together?' asked Cass, adjusting the wig and adding a bit more lipstick. She'd always wondered how she'd look as a blonde. Cass turned to catch a look at her profile; realistically she probably needed something a little less Barbie.

'Nearly four years. I read somewhere that four years is the new seven-year itch. And besides, if Andy's got nothing to hide, then why does he keep wiping the inbox on his phone, why does he have a new password on his email account and why does he sneak about? Did I tell you he's been sneaking about—'

'Have you thought it might be because you're trying to break into his email account, read his phone messages and are currently setting someone up to stalk him?' asked Cass.

Fiona considered the possibility for a few seconds then shook her head. 'Don't be ridiculous. Andy's got no idea he's going to be stalked. And besides, he *is* up to something, I know it – and I want you to find out exactly what it is.'

'Because?'

'Well, because we're friends, and I'd do the same for you.'

Cass stared at her. 'Really?'

'Oh God yes,' said Fiona. Which wasn't exactly how Cass remembered it. She did remember lots of things about being Fiona's friend, like being left at the bus stop in the pouring rain, in her gym kit, because Fee had persuaded her mum to give the school hunk, Alan Hall, a lift home instead of Cass, the same friend who had refused point-blank to lend Cass a tenner when they were at a gig and Cass found she'd left her handbag backstage.

None of which suggested to Cass that Fiona would be running to her rescue if she ever needed a bit of on-the-side spying.

'I don't think blonde's really my colour, do you?' asked Cass, narrowing her eyes, trying to gauge the effect of the wig and hoping to lighten the mood. 'Maybe something with a bit more caramel?'

'Can we please concentrate? I don't think you're taking this seriously,' snapped Fiona. 'Andy's going to be at Sam's

Place, Saturday night, at eight. I've brought my camera with me just in case yours doesn't have a zoom.'

Cass looked at her. 'Sam's Place?'

'Uh-huh you know, the trendy new bar, opposite the Corn Exchange.'

Cass shook her head.

'Oh, come on, Cass, you must have seen it. It's been all over the local papers. They did a double-page spread in the Argos and Echo, and a thing on local TV. Some guy off the telly is one of the partners in it. He used to be in *The Bill* – not that I watch that kind of thing, obviously. Anyway, there's a cocktail bar and restaurant, and a coffee shop, all retro and very Casablanca, with a nightclub upstairs. I've been trying to persuade Andy to take me there for weeks.' Fiona paused for effect. 'Do you know what he said?'

Cass decided it would probably be wiser not to offer any suggestions, so pulled an *I have no idea* face instead.

'He said, "Fee, what in god's name do you want to go there for? Clubbing – at our age? It's ridiculous." That's what he said, Cass, "*Ridiculous*". It was horrible. It made me sound like some sort of desperate pensioner . . .'

Fiona was wearing a skirt that was bang on trend – if you happened to be eighteen – a pair of Christian Louboutin knock-offs and a haircut that probably cost more than Cass's sofa, and Fiona had made Cass swear that she'd never mention the Botox or the fillers in front of anyone. Maybe 'pensioner' was a bit cruel, but 'desperate' wasn't far short of the mark.

'So you haven't been there?'

Fiona shook her head. 'No, of course I haven't been there, although now it looks as if he's going to be going without me. There was a message on the pad in his office

– "Sam's Place, 8 o'clock", and what looked like next Saturday's date. I was going to bring it with me to prove that I wasn't imagining it . . .'

'Did you ask Andy about it? I mean, surely if he left the note on his desk he meant you to see it,' asked Cass cautiously.

'He would think I was mad . . .'

Cass decided not to comment. 'Maybe he's planning to surprise you? You said you wanted to go – maybe he's going to take you as a treat.'

Fiona didn't look convinced.

'Why don't you just ask him, Fee? He left you a note – in plain sight . . .'

'It wasn't actually the note I saw,' Fiona said, after a few seconds. 'And Andy didn't leave it out on the desk for me to see. It was more of an impression on the pad underneath. I could see that it had something written on it, but I couldn't really make out what it said . . .'

'Right,' murmured Cass in an undertone. This was getting weirder by the second.

'Anyway, I saw this thing on a film once, where you get a soft pencil and then very lightly shade over the indentations.' Fiona mimed the action.

Cass had heard enough. 'Uh-huh, okay, look, I think we should stop right there, Fiona – this is nuts. You need to talk to Andy, not me. And as for the stalking? I think it's crazy and I'm not doing it.' As she spoke, Cass pulled off the wig and dropped it onto the bed. 'I really don't think it's a good idea. Do you want to stay with Andy?'

Fiona stared at Cass as if the question hadn't crossed her mind. 'Well of course I want to stay with Andy,' she snapped. 'Why on earth would I go to all this trouble if I

11

didn't want to be with him? For god's sake Cass – have you got any idea how hard it is to get your hands on a decent blonde wig? It's taken me ages to get all this stuff together . . .'

'Well in that case you need to talk to him, not go creeping around spying on him.' Cass slipped off the trench coat. 'I'm really sorry, Fee. I'd be glad to help but not like this.'

Fiona looked as if she was about to speak, and then she bit her lip, her eyes filling up with tears. She started stuffing the wig and the brolly into her holdall.

Cass sighed, feeling guilty. 'Oh for goodness sake Fee—' she began.

'Don't say anything,' she sniffed. 'I thought you'd understand.' Between sobs, Fiona rolled the trench coat into a ball and crammed it into the bag. 'I thought you were my friend.'

'I am your friend, and I do understand,' said Cass. 'Really, I do – but this isn't going to help anything.'

'How do you know unless we try?' cried Fiona. 'I don't know what else to do,' she wailed, still gathering things up as she made for the door.

'Fee, wait, let's talk about this,' said Cass, but it was too late. The last thing Cass saw was Fiona heading down the stairs with the holdall clutched tight to her chest.

'Oh bugger,' said Cass in frustration. The Chinese takeaway they had ordered arrived half an hour later. Mungo and Buster waited by the kitchen door, trying hard not to look too eager, although realistically there was no way Cass was going to manage all those chicken balls on her own.

Chapter Two

'Excuse me, Miss, Miss?'

Cass glanced up from her book and looked at the man framed in the shop doorway.

'I was wondering if you could help me? Is that record player in the window Chippendale?'

The guy was six two, maybe six three, tanned, with great teeth and an Armani jacket worn dressed down over good jeans and a black tee shirt. He had just the hint of a transatlantic twang somewhere in his voice. He had shoulders broad enough to make a grown woman weep and the biggest brownest eyes. If he were a spaniel, women would arm-wrestle each other to take him home.

Cass closed her book and nodded, 'Uh-huh, it most certainly is, and you see that cocktail cabinet in the back there? The cream one with the stainless-steel knobs?' She pointed off into the shadows, between a bentwood hat stand and the little painted pine chiffonier that she'd sold earlier in the day.

The man looked around. 'Which? Oh right – oh yes, that's very nice.'

'Hepplewhite. Genuine George III,' she said.

'No?' said the man, extending the oooo sound to express

his incredulity. 'My god, really? I'd imagine they are just so hard to find.'

'In that kind of condition,' Cass said, 'rare as hen's teeth.'

'Oh my god this is just too wonderful. Do you take credit cards? Do you think we can maybe do a deal on the two pieces?'

'There's been a lot of interest in them.'

'I'd imagine there has been. What's your best price?'

Cass considered for a few moments. 'Give me your best shot . . .'

'You're a hard woman, Cass.'

Cass broke into a broad grin. 'So Rocco, how's life treating you?'

He didn't answer, instead making a lunge for the biscuit tin, which initially Cass mistook for an attempt at hugging.

'Are those Fox's Cream Crunch?' he asked.

Cass whisked the tin away an instant before he could grab it. 'Still not quite fast enough, eh? Never mind, maybe another time. What are you doing out here in the boondocks anyway?'

'Come on, you're a legend. Cass's place – great gear, reasonable prices, you've always got such lovely things.' He paused. 'Actually I'm on the lookout for Christmas presents for your mother.' He started patting himself down. 'You want me to tell you how many shopping days we got left? The PalmPilot your mum bought me last year has got this feature—'

Cass shook her head. 'No, it would so only depress me,' she said. 'I'm never organised.'

'Maybe I could get your mum to buy you one—' Rocco began.

'No,' snapped Cass more forcefully as Rocco continued,

'I adore those repro radios and turntables you've got in the window. Nice chaise by the way,' he tipped a nod towards the dark green brocade number she had recently finished re-upholstering, which was also currently sitting in the shop's bay window. 'That won't be there very long.'

Cass smiled. 'I've already had a couple of decent offers.'

Rocco grinned mischievously. 'Really? And you're still here selling tut – I'd have been long gone by now, if I were you.'

'What and leave all this behind?' she said, heavy on irony. 'Besides one man's old tut is another man's design classic. Talking of which, how is my mother?'

He grinned. 'Gorgeous as ever. Did you get the post-card from Madeira?'

Cass nodded. 'Uh-huh, and Rome – and where else was it you went?'

'I could email you the full itinerary if you like.'

Cass laughed, 'What, when I've already had the post-cards. Anyway, what is it you're looking for?'

'Peace on earth and goodwill to all men?' Rocco suggested, as he thumbed through the pile of antique greetings cards she had arranged in a basket on the desk.

'And besides that?'

'I'm on the hunt for a couple of bedside cabinets, art deco, 1930s. Walnut veneer would be good. Your mother is such a slave driver . . .'

Not rising to the bait, Cass said, 'I might be able to help.'

'You've got bedside cabinets?'

'Might have.'

Rocco's eyes lit up.

Cass grinned. 'You'd never make a poker player.'

'What are they like?'

'Nice actually, cylindrical, still got both shelves. You mind the shop, I'll go and put the kettle on.'

'Jacko not in today?'

'No,' said Cass. 'He hates the cold. He keeps telling me he's not getting any younger. He's hanging on till I find someone else, but he can only do the odd hour here and there. . . . So if you know anyone wants a part-time job . . .'

Rocco held up his hands in surrender.

Cass laughed. 'Not you – that wasn't an offer.'

'Thank god. Working for your mother is hard enough. Have you got the cabinets here?'

'No, but there are some pictures on the computer. Take a look. They should be in the file marked "stock, warehouse". Under bedside cabinets?'

'Bit obvious – I think I'd rather look in the one marked this year's diary,' Rocco called after her as Cass made her way into the back of the shop.

Cass laughed. 'Knock yourself out, Rocco. My social highlights at the moment are dental appointments, haircuts and choir stuff.'

'I was hoping there'd be a few stars in the margin. How are the boys?'

'Last time I heard from them they were fine. Joe was hungover and Daniel was in debt, but that's university for you.'

'So okay then? Will they be home for Christmas?'

Cass laughed. 'It's obvious you've never had kids Rocco. I'm their mother, I'll be the last one to find out.'

Cass went back to making the tea, wondering how it was that her mother had ended up with a guy like Rocco and she was all on her own. Life was strange at times. She could hear him fiddling about, tapping on the keyboard and then he said, 'Oh they're nice. Are those the original handles?'

'Yup, and they're not bad, few nicks and dents and there's been a repair to the veneer, just general wear and tear really. Overall they're not bad for their age.'

'We are still talking about bedside cabinets here, are we?' he asked. Cass could hear the humour in his voice.

Rocco and Cass went back a long, long way, to the dim distant days when Rocco had been her boss, and Cass had been married to Neil, and Rocco hadn't been married to her mother, Nita.

Cass had introduced them at a cheese and wine party at the local college where she'd been teaching interior design part-time. Rocco had been her head of department, Nita had been happy but lonely, and Cass had got Rocco down as gay.

Cass had assumed they would get on, but she *hadn't* assumed they would get on quite so well as they did. Twelve years on, and Rocco and Nita were still getting on well. The fact he was around fifteen years younger and fit as a butcher's whippet seemed to present no problems at all to either of them.

Cass brought in a tray of tea and the biscuits. 'So, what are you up to?'

'At the moment? Work-wise we've got some corporate stuff and we've just taken on a complete makeover for some media type, art deco mad, hence the cabinets. She's bought one of the apartments in Vancouver House.'

'Down on the old wharf?'

'S'right. Cold Harbour. You'd have thought the marketing guys would have come up with something a little cheerier – Cold Harbour. I mean, what does that sound like?'

Cass grinned. 'Nice conversion, though. I remember the days when it was full of junkies and rats down there.'

'Cynics might say it still is, they're just driving Porsches and Beamers these days. How about you? You busy?'

'Ish – why, have you got something for me?'

Rocco grinned. 'Might have, there's a nice little job in Cambridge coming up in the New Year that I thought might be right up your street.' He glanced at the computer screen. 'And the cabinets are cute.'

'They certainly are. As I said, very nice.'

'Presumably that means you'll be doubling the price if I say I'm really interested?'

Cass grinned. 'What else are family for? I'm sure we can do a deal . . . So, how's Mum?'

Rocco took the mug of tea she handed him. 'Fine form, although she's still trying to persuade me that we should sell up and buy a fucking barge. I've told her I get seasick in the bath but she won't have it. Anyway, we're going over to Amsterdam to look at a Tjalk some time soon. And before you ask, it's some kind of huge bloody canal boat. She's arranged for us to go sailing with these two gay guys who own it. She's thinking "party". I'm thinking Kwells. How about you?'

'Nothing so exciting. Choir trip in few weeks, which should be fun – we're going to Cyprus. Oh and we've got a concert-cum-dress rehearsal before we leave. Can I put you and Mum down for a couple of tickets?'

'Don't see why not. And how's what's-his-name?'

'Gone but not forgotten.'

18

'What *was* his name, help me out here?'

Cass shrugged. 'No idea, he came, he went – you know what men are like.'

'You're making it up,' said Rocco, helping himself out of the biscuit tin. 'Oh – oh, wait – it's on the tip of my tongue. Jack, Sam—'

'Gareth.'

'That's it,' he said, with a mouth full of crumbs. 'I thought you were quite keen?'

Cass dunked a custard cream. 'Which just confirms what kind of judge of character I am. Bottom line? Once the initial lust had cooled down, it took me about two days to work out that we had nothing in common. Worse, he was picky and undermining. He was always making little jokes about my weight or my hair and stuff, and then when we were out spent most of his time ogling other women . . . And then he got blind drunk at Lucy's wedding – you know Lucy, from across the road? Makes silver jewellery? Anyway, he tried to pick a fight with the best man and he kept calling his ex-wife a brainless muppet, and I just knew that one day that brainless muppet would be me.'

'So you jumped ship?'

Cass nodded. 'I most certainly did.'

'And how did he take it?'

'Well, he was hurt and then he was weepy and then he was angry. And then a couple of weeks later I was talking to a mutual acquaintance and sure enough, I'm the muppet now.'

Rocco pulled a sympathetic face, no mean feat with a mouthful of custard cream. 'Not in my book. Anyone else on the horizon?'

19

Cass laughed. 'What is this, *Mastermind*? No, there is no one on the horizon at this particular moment. But to be honest, at the moment I'm that not fussed.'

Rocco looked horrified. 'What do you mean *not that fussed*? You're fit, you're gorgeous, talented, great company . . .' He grinned. 'Your mother worries about you. How am I doing?'

'So far, so good. Maybe I should get you to write my lonely hearts ad. The problem is, Neil's a hard act to follow. I keep picking idiots.'

'Is that all?' said Rocco. 'Realistically, if you kiss enough frogs one of them is bound to turn into a prince. It's purely a numbers thing.'

Cass sighed. 'To be honest, Rocco, I'm all frogged out.'

He looked pained. 'How about coming to Amsterdam with us?' he said. 'There's plenty of room. You'd be doing me a favour. Your mother can play at pirates with the beautifully buffed Hans and Bruno while we go shopping or do the markets and the museums. It'd be fun.'

Cass laughed. 'With two poofs, my mum and her toy boy? I don't think my ego could take it.'

'In that case, how about coming round to supper instead? We could talk about this job in Cambridge – your mum'll cook you something yummy. Nita would love to see you, and we'll go through our list, see if we can't fit you up with someone.'

Cass fixed him with a stare.

'What?' he protested. 'I owe you one.'

Cass laughed. 'My mother doesn't count – and besides, I've been on some of your blind dates before. I don't want anyone over sixty, and no one without teeth need apply.'

'Harry was a good bloke.'

'He was sixty-eight.'

'He was kind.'

'He had dentures that clicked.'

'You can be so picky. He was loaded. What about Fabian?'

'Anyone who left their wife the previous evening is right out. Okay?'

'Be fair – we didn't know about that.'

'He cried all the way through dinner.'

Rocco shrugged. 'Maybe it was your mother's cooking – who knows? I promise you that this new man is gorgeous.'

'You've already picked me one out?'

'Your mother always says it's good to have something tucked away for a rainy day – and besides, she's worried about you.'

'So what's new?'

'Well, the one she's got in mind is bright, the right size, right age, requisite number of teeth. Say yes, you know your mum's dying to take you on a guided tour of the new kitchen – did I tell you we've got to have the roof off the bloody house now? Anyway, she'll cook and while she's in there griddling and steaming away I'll show off, get horribly drunk and make a complete fool of myself. Remember last Christmas? It'll be just like that, only with less advocaat.'

Cass laughed. 'How could anyone possibly resist an invitation like that?'

Rocco grinned. 'How's Saturday night sound? Nita's threatening to drag me off to see some peculiar foreign film with subtitles and bicycle baskets full of sardines.'

Cass hesitated. Rocco pulled his puppy face.

21

'You'd be doing me a favour – honestly. And we could go with the fish theme for supper. There's this great stall on the Saturday market we've just discovered, I could pick something up first thing – your mother does this amazing thing with halibut and Gruyère?'

Cass pulled a face. 'Do I want to hear about this?'

'And you could dig something or pull something up out of your allotment, something trendy and seasonal and Gordon Ramsay for the resident chef. Now how about you go and fish these cabinets out of storage, and while you're gone I'll mind the shop and ring your mum to let her know about Saturday. Oh, and I'll get her to email you the brief over for the job in Cambridge.'

Cass sighed; it sounded like a done deal.

Wanting to pour oil on troubled waters, Cass tried ringing Fiona when she'd finished work, but got the answer machine. She had a feeling that Fiona was probably there listening, screening the calls. Whether Fiona was right or wrong about Andy playing away, Cass decided to be careful what she said in case he picked up the message. The last thing she wanted to do was add fuel to the fire, real or imaginary.

Cass sighed. She felt guilty about Fiona walking out. Although it had to be said that Fee had a talent for making her feel bad. When they were thirteen it had been because Mr Elliot – their art teacher, six feet tall and gorgeous – had told Cass that she was very talented, at fifteen because Cass had thrashed Fee in the mocks, and at sixteen because she had been the first one to get her hands on Justin Green, if Cass remembered rightly. Cass getting married, having two sons and being happy – even if it

22

hadn't lasted that long – had been the ultimate insult, and Cass had an odd sense that Fee had never quite forgiven her for any of it. When Fiona had walked back into her life, Cass had hoped they could start over; after all, they were grown-ups. Unfortunately two years on it was increasingly obvious that actually only one of them had made it through to adulthood.

So, after the beep Cass said, 'Hi Fiona, hope you're well. Be great to hear from you if you've got a minute. See you at choir on Tuesday if not,' making a real effort to sound warm and cheery.

A few mornings later, Cass heard a phone ringing somewhere in the darkness. Dragged from sleep and a complicated dream about Amsterdam, rats and a blonde wig, she felt around by the bed, found the handset, pressed a button and mumbled, 'Hello, who is it?'

'Oh hi Cass, it's me.' The voice belonged to someone wide awake and unnaturally cheerful. 'I'd got you down as an early bird, I thought you'd be up and about by now.'

'Rocco, it's the middle of the night.'

'No, it's not,' he said defensively.

Cass peered at the bedside clock. 'No, you're right. It's worse than the middle of the night, it's six o'clock in the morning. What on earth are you doing ringing me at six in the bloody morning? I don't open the shop until ten – I lie in. Like heads of state.' She paused. Rocco said nothing, at which point Cass's imagination fired up and filled in the gaps. 'Oh god, is everything all right. What's happened? Is Mum okay? Are you all right?'

'It's about the fish.'

'Fish? What fish? Oh for god's sake, Rocco, you're doing

23

too many drugs. Go back to bed and sleep it off. I'll call you later.'

'No, no listen, I'm serious. We've got to drive down to pick up the people from next door from Heathrow this morning, I'd totally forgotten about it. You are still on for tonight, aren't you?'

'As far as I'm concerned it still is the night.'

'Just listen to me and stop whining, will you? Could you nip down to the market and pick up the halibut for tonight? Four nice steaks and some prawns? Problem is, if you're not there early it all goes.'

Cass, totally awake now, groaned and rolled out of bed. 'Halibut?'

'Uh-huh, halibut and a pint of prawns. Only you really need to be there first thing when they open or it will all be gone. I'm not joking.'

'What constitutes first thing?'

'Half seven, eight – if you leave it any later—' he began.

'It's all gone. I got that the first time round, Rocco,' growled Cass. As she pulled on her dressing gown, phone tucked up between ear and shoulder, Cass couldn't help wondering who these people were who got out of bed at the crack of dawn to rush out and buy bloody halibut. 'Can't I nip in and get a bag of frozen fish from the supermarket? You know, if I don't make it to the market in time?'

There was a little pause and then Rocco said, 'Cass, you are such a philistine. And no, you can't, we need fresh. I've already got the Gruyère.'

'Well, good for you. What if the fish has all gone by the time I get there?'

There was another longer weighty pause. 'Then you didn't hear me right . . .'

'Okay, okay, I'm getting up now. You're such a bully.'

'Wait till you taste it, Nita does this—'

'Rocco, shut up, go and pick up your neighbours and leave me in peace.'

'Before eight.'

'Bugger off.'

Which was why at around seven forty-five, two mugs of tea and a short, sharp shower later, Cass found herself walking up the High Lane into town, wrapped up against the rain, with Buster tugging at the lead, amazed that he was out that early and desperate to wee up every lamppost by way of celebration. Early or not, it was a very grim morning.

Cass could think of innumerable other places she would rather be, although she did remind herself all this was for a purpose. Her mother's cooking was truly sublime, the apartment she shared with Rocco was breathtaking and, when they were on form, Rocco and Nita were the best company you could wish for. Rocco also found her work. The clients for their interior design business always paid top dollar, Cambridge was almost local and Cass needed the money.

So maybe it was worth it, Cass decided, sticking her hands deep into the pockets of her coat and hunkering down against horizontal drizzle. Buster didn't seem to mind. He wagged and sniffed and panted cheerfully, rooting out discarded kebab innards, greasy pencil sharpenings of cold meat, curled up in the gutter. Whoever said it was a dog's life?

Cass turned the corner into Market Street and down past the Corn Exchange.

Rocco was right; it might be early but the market was

already teeming with life. Most of the stalls were open and trading hard, with just a few latecomers still putting their stock out. Ready or not, everyone was open for business, including the parade of cafes and bars around the edge of the square. Every stall was lit, fighting off the gloom, and there was the smell of fried onions, fresh coffee and bacon hanging in the damp morning air.

'Nice dog, missus,' said a man laden down with bags as he hurried past clutching a bacon roll. It was a sad state of affairs when your dog got more compliments than you did, thought Cass grimly. Buster, meanwhile, tracked the man's progress with an accuracy worthy of NASA, while the man headed between the stalls, all shopped out.

'Maybe we'll get one of those on the way home,' said Cass conversationally. The dog wagged his tail.

The punters were four deep at the fish stall in the next aisle. Behind the spotless white counter, two middle-aged ladies were working the queue with a deft touch and a nifty line in helpful hints and off-the-cuff recipes. In front of the counter the broad chiller cabinet was full of the most amazing things – scallops, smoked haddock and rock, Nile perch, red mullet, unnamed things with fins and dark glassy eyes, mussels and lobsters glittering like bizarre jewels – all snuggled down amongst great drifts of diamond-like crushed ice, their hard edges a contrast to the soft flesh of the peeled pink prawns and cockles and shrimps, moist and shiny under the bright overhead lights.

Cass took her place in line and settled down to the slow shuffle towards the front, letting her mind idle over what wine to pick up from the offie at the bottom of the road, and whether she should just take along a big pan of home-made carrot and coriander soup to Nita's instead of taking vegetables. All this and half a dozen other thoughts were percolating randomly through her head as Cass looked around, just passing the time. As she idly gazed across the faces of the people at the stalls, she caught sight of Fiona's live-in boyfriend, Andy.

She'd seen him once or twice at concerts, although barely ever spoken to him despite Fiona's sporadic insistence that they should all get together for a meal sometime. He was loping across the road towards the market, dressed in a battered leather jacket, and he was smiling. Instinctively Cass looked in the direction he was looking, scanning the little groups of people, trying to pick out who he might be smiling at, wondering if it might be Fiona – and then Cass saw that it wasn't Fiona.

Picking out the recipient of the smile gave her an odd feeling, a little shiver that made Cass feel uneasy. Andy was smiling at a girl, a girl who smiled right back in a way that said she was more than pleased to see him. She waved and hurried towards him, all smiles.

'Hi,' the girl mouthed. 'How are you?'

As Andy and the young girl embraced and then held each other at arms' length, looking each other up and down, a million and one thoughts tumbled through Cass's head. First of all, she tried to tell herself it could be anyone, that it was silly to jump to conclusions. She could be a friend, a work colleague, god it could even be his sister – but there was another, stronger voice that was busy telling her that Fiona was right. Andy was seeing someone else. Someone significant, someone he was keeping away from Fiona, someone who he cared enough about to come out to meet first thing in the morning – in the rain.

As Cass watched, the girl tipped her head up towards

him and Andy kissed her on the cheek. Tenderly. And then he smiled. As he pulled away, Andy scanned the faces of the people around them, left and right. Everything about the way he moved suggested that he didn't want to be seen, not here, not now, not with this girl. Cass and Andy's gaze met for a split second and Cass felt the hairs on the back of her neck prickle as they made a connection. A nanosecond later and it was over, as Andy guided the girl between the stalls, away from the early morning shoppers.

The girl was small and blonde and slim, and very, very beautiful. She was in her early twenties, wearing a ginger wool jacket and a mustard coloured scarf. The outfit looked bold and stylish and youthful and for an instant Cass's heart ached, as if the breath was being pressed out of her chest.

Cass and Fiona were beautiful in the way that women over thirty are beautiful; they were women who had learned what suited them and how to wear clothes well, and what lipstick works with what and how to make the best of what nature gave you – but this girl, this girl had that other thing, the thing that only happens when you are young, the thing that means throwing on whatever you find on the floor from the night before, the thing that lets you scrape you hair up into a topknot with tendrils tumbling out and that still lets you end up looking gorgeous and stylish and desirable. Whatever it was, that youthful thing, the girl with whom Andy was currently walking across the market square, had it in spades.

Cass couldn't take her eyes off them. The pair of them drew her like a magnet. Their body language was a peculiar mixture of familiarity and reticence – maybe they were afraid of being seen, maybe Andy was afraid of looking silly with someone so young, maybe the girl wasn't sure of him or quite what to do. Whatever it was, it was obvious to even the most casual observer that they were together. Cass kept on staring. There was an instant when the girl tried to slip her arm through his. Andy artfully avoided it. Cass was mesmerised.

'S'cuse me, can I help you?' said a voice from somewhere behind her.

It took Cass a few seconds to realise the question was being directed at her, and even longer for her to get her thoughts back on track. 'Oh I'm so sorry. I'd like some – some . . .' Her mouth worked up and down. The word was somewhere there in the back of her head; it was just a case of finding it.

The woman smiled her encouragement.

'I'd like some fish,' said Cass, trying to buy herself some time.

The woman nodded. 'Righty-oh. Well, you've come to the right place, love. What do you fancy? We've got some smashing cod or then there's Nile perch, nice bit of tuna, or red snapper if you fancy something a little bit more exotic . . .' She managed to make it sound like a night in a lap-dancing club, but Cass couldn't quite tear her mind away from Andy and the girl, which must have shown on her face.

'Would you like me to give you a bit more time?' the woman said. 'Maybe you'd just like to take a little look and I'll come back to you?'

'No, it's fine,' said Cass. 'I'd like . . .' What the hell was it she wanted? Cass's brain rolled over and played dead. She looked up in desperation. Behind her the queue was getting restless.

'It begins with H . . .' she said miserably. 'And it goes early, which is why I'm here. I was sent by my mother's husband, my stepfather, although he's a lot younger so I don't call him that . . .' Cass cringed: her brain might be dead but her mouth was alive and kicking and just kept on going.

'And he sent you to buy a fish that begins with H?' The woman said helpfully, as if playing I-Spy was something she did on a regular basis.

Cass nodded.

'Haddock?' suggested the woman. She managed to make it sound like an insult.

Cass shook her head. 'No, I'm sure it wasn't haddock.'

'You sure? Only it's not dyed, and we do sell a lot of it – and we've got some lovely thick fillets. That's very popular. Smoked. That always goes real quick on a Saturday.'

'Or there's hake? Or what about herring?' suggested the other woman who was working behind the counter, as she plopped a couple of nice plaice fillets onto the scale. 'Have you got any idea what he was going to do with it?'

Someone in the queue behind Cass made a fairly graphic suggestion. Cass began to sweat, Buster began to whimper. Just exactly how many fish were there that began with H?

'Huss?'

Cass shook her head again.

'How about halibut?'

'Halibut,' Cass said, with a genuine sense of relief. 'That's it. I'd like some halibut. Please.'

'Righty-oh, we've got a bit left; it always goes early, you know.'

Cass nodded. 'So I've been told. Have you got four nice pieces, please?'

'Certainly have,' said the woman, holding out a snow-white piece of fish towards her. 'Four like that?'

Cass nodded. 'That will be great. And a pint of prawns please,' she said, although try as she might to concentrate on the fish, Cass's mind kept being pulled back towards Andy and the young woman. She couldn't see them now, but she guessed where they would be heading. They would be in Sam's Place.

Above the market square, the town clock was just chiming the hour. It was eight o'clock. Wasn't that what the note Fiona found had said, 'Saturday eight o'clock?' The only difference was that Fiona had assumed it was eight o'clock in the evening, not eight o'clock on a cold wet windy early autumn morning.

Walking home, Cass mulled over what she should do. Should she ring Fiona and tell her? Fiona *had* asked for her help. Or was it one of those things best left alone? Cass hunched against the wind, Buster tucking in behind, slipstreaming out of the weather.

Fiona didn't take bad news well. Cass could remember the time when she'd seen Peter Bailey – the boy whose children Fiona planned to bear when they were both about fifteen – in town with Alison Wickham. They had been holding hands. When Cass had told her, Fiona had accused Cass of lying and then of being jealous and, finally, when the two of them had caught Mr Bailey and Ms Wickham in a sweaty clinch behind the groundsman's hut after double games, of gloating – immediately before she sent Cass to Coventry.

The bottom line was that what went on between Fiona

and Andy was none of her business. *Even though they were friends*, asked her conscience? Especially because they were friends, countered Cass. And even if Cass had known about the girl *before* Fiona came round, her advice would have been that Fiona and Andy needed to talk about what was going on between themselves first, before they involved anyone else, particularly if that anyone else was likely to get mashed in the middle.

Cass sighed. The halibut weighed heavy as an albatross, the drizzle finally broke loose into a full-scale downpour, and even Buster was keen to beat a retreat as they hurried home.

As she slid the key into the shop doorway, Cass decided that the best course of action really was to say nothing. Maybe seeing Andy and the girl together was just a co-incidence, or completely innocent. Maybe Fiona coming round had planted a seed in her imagination; maybe she had imagined the little buzz between Andy and the girl. Maybe Fiona and Andy had already sorted it out, talked it through, made everything right. Maybe today was the day that Andy was going to tell the little blonde that it was over for good. If she said anything, Cass might put her foot right in it and break something that wasn't broken or cracked, something that was nine parts mended.

Who was she kidding? Cass sighed, wondering who'd died and made her Claire Rayner.

Meanwhile in an alcove in the back of Sam's Place, at one of the smallest tables, furthest away from the large plate-glass windows, Andy watched as Amelia's fingers knitted tightly around a tall thin mug of hot chocolate. She was hunched over it, apparently frozen, blowing away the steam as well as warming her hands, occasionally glancing up at him from under those long, perfectly mascara-ed lashes. She was wearing pink fingerless gloves.

The bar at Sam's Place had an old colonial feel to it, with an overhead fan, lots of dark wood, ochre-coloured rag-rolled plaster and rattan furniture arranged around a central bar, and at this time of the morning it was practically empty. The guys from the market were over in the Nag's Head if they wanted a beer and at Bennie's on the corner or one of the stalls if they wanted coffee, tea or bacon butties. Behind the servery, a couple of staff were busy fiddling with the coffee machine; other than Andy and Amelia, their only other customer was an elderly man reading his newspaper and drinking coffee. He hadn't looked up since the two of them had walked in.

'You look rough,' Amelia said, blowing over the top of the mug.

Andy, who hadn't been sure exactly which way this conversation was going to go, smiled. 'Well, thanks for that. I'd like to return the compliment but you look great.'

She had the good grace to blush. Last time they'd met Amelia had cried and shouted and stormed off, because he couldn't think of anything to say that could help her with the pain, so he'd said nothing and been left standing in the middle of the beach at Holkham on his own, with people staring at him.

When he had got back to the car, Andy had had to make sure there was no sand in his shoes in case Fiona found it. He'd showered as soon as he got home, rinsing the fine grit from his hair, feeling it rasp under his fingertips as he rubbed in shampoo, although in the pocket of his leather jacket he still had a little white shell Amelia had given him.

'You know, Andy, I could learn to really love you,' Amelia had said, as she pressed it into his hand, before all the crying and the shouting and the running away had started.

Andy looked across the table at her now; she was watching his face intently. 'So, how are things going?'

Amelia shrugged. 'Okay.'

'So . . . ?' He waited for a second.

Amelia looked up at him from under long, mascara-covered lashes. 'I know that you said not to ring you at home, but I didn't know what else to do. I've missed you,' she said, pausing as if trying to gauge his mood. 'I was worried that you might not come.' And as she spoke, Amelia began to spoon whipped cream, dusted with chocolate, into her mouth. 'I wanted us to talk.'

Andy had ordered an espresso; the coffee was as hot as it was bitter and left an unpleasant residue over his tongue and teeth.

'I can't stay very long,' he said, glancing round, tipping his wrist to indicate his watch and time passing, hoping to create some sense of urgency that would persuade her to come to the point.

Over the last few months he'd discovered that Amelia wasn't very good at getting to the point. She preferred to meander through unrelated backwaters, telling Andy silly things or exciting things or secret things, sometimes things that he would rather not know, sometimes things that took his breath away. When they first met he'd thought it was charming and amusing, but now he found it frustrating, and he felt bad for feeling that about her. She was beautiful and young and every time they met he promised himself that he wouldn't be bewitched or sidetracked by those things.

'I can't be long,' he pressed.

Amelia nodded, scooping up more whipped cream. There was a tiny blob of it on her chin and he fought the temptation to lean across and wipe it away.

'It's all right,' she said, still watching his face. 'I know, you have to get back to Fiona. Who are you trying to fool here, Andy? We both know you're not happy with her. You don't have to be a genius to work it out. It's not like you have got any kids or anything. Why don't you just say something – or just leave? For god's sake, it's not rocket science. Start over . . .' She stared at him, waiting for a reply. 'You're not happy, are you?'

Andy opened his mouth to say something but there were no words there. What could he say?

'Why don't you just tell her straight about me, about us?' she asked. 'Get it over and done with.'

Andy wasn't sure what the answer was, and so said nothing. He felt at a loss for not having the right answer, or any kind of answer, come to that. This wasn't the kind of man he was. The trouble was that, since meeting Amelia, it seemed to be the man he had become – meeting her had changed him forever.

Amelia took his silence for some kind of tacit agreement. 'Why don't you leave her, Andy? You know you want to.'

He winced, wishing that he'd never told Amelia that he was unhappy. *My girlfriend doesn't understand me* was hardly the most original line he'd ever come up with, and completely stupid really, particularly as Amelia would never have noticed how unhappy he was if he hadn't told her. She was far too self-obsessed to notice what was going on in anyone's life but her own.

Across the table, Amelia licked her lips and then rootled through her handbag so that she could check them in a little mirror, adding more gloss from a clear glittery tube, smoothing away the fleck of cream. She ran a finger over her eyebrows, first one and then the other, and Andy noticed as he always did what beautiful hands she had; those long fingers with French-manicured nails. Her component parts constantly caught his attention and enchanted him. She caught him looking at her and smiled slyly. 'So why don't you just leave her?' she asked.

Andy pushed his hands back through his hair; he had no idea now why he had even mentioned it to her. Confession and complaining had never really been his style. But then again he had never lied to Fiona before, nor gone behind her back. *This was such a mess.*

'Look Amelia, it's good to see you, but if there is something you want to say – I mean – I really have got to get back.'

Amelia's mouth tightened into a little *moue* of displeasure. 'I thought that we could talk. I haven't seen you all week . . .'

'Well, we *can* talk,' said Andy, hoping that she wasn't planning to make a scene like the one on the beach. 'Just not for long. I did say I couldn't be long today.' And then he made himself be quiet, because he didn't want to promise her that they would meet again soon and talk then, because she would want to know where and when and for how long, and her demands made him increasingly uncomfortable. He'd only met her this morning because he was afraid that if he held her off for too long she might turn up at their house, or ring when he wasn't home. She was unpredictable and she made him uneasy.

Meeting her had shaken his life to the core. Fiona wasn't the only person that he really should deal with.

And, even as he was thinking it, Amelia looked up at him, her chin resting on her knuckles, and Andy could see how vulnerable she was, how lost, and hated himself for trying to hold her at arms' length and for being afraid of her. Of course she was right, he really should tell Fiona. About her. About them. About how much he loved her.

'I'm listening, just tell me what you want to say,' Andy said, leaning forwards across the table, craning closer so that he could catch every word, his voice soft with compassion.

'I'm pregnant,' Amelia said.

Chapter Three

'Right, so has everyone got their starting notes? And is everyone happy with the arrangement for this?' asked Alan, before rapidly running through the flight plan for a little gospel number the choir were polishing for the *All Stars On Tour* show. It was also the opening number for the 'Bon Voyage' concert they were staging in the Corn Exchange before they left and it really needed to go with a zing.

Alan tapped his baton on the music stand. 'Mellow – nice and bluesy. Basses in first, twice through the intro and then altos you come in, along with the tenors and finally sopranos. We do the whole thing through a couple of times and then head on home for a big finish? Okay, just watch where I'm going with this – now relax, breathe – and let's really go for it. Lots of life, plenty of swing,' said Alan enthusiastically. Standing out in front of the choir, who were currently arranged in concert formation, he looked around the faces to ensure he had everyone's attention.

'Right. Here we go. One, two, one two three four . . .' and brought the bass section in with a crisp flick of his hands. At least, that was the idea – except that that wasn't quite what happened. For some reason, things weren't going well tonight, and the whole number rapidly dissolved into total chaos. The normally crisp dm, dm dm-dm, dm dm – a percussive, plucky snap without a vowel sound, created by the bass section and meant to resemble the sharp rhythmic slap of a well-tuned bass, and a staple part of a lot of 'a cappella' choral numbers, which anchored everyone else – sounded like a bag of spanners being dropped down a flight of concrete stairs.

Welsh Alf's attempts to recover the timing made the whole thing far worse – a lot worse. Within a few bars, the song sounded like a broken engine, mistimed, misfiring and gradually tearing itself apart, while behind it the dm, dm dm-dm, dm dms slowed, stalled and finally faded.

'Whoa, whoa, there cowboy,' said Alan, face contorted into a grin as he pulled an imaginary horse to a standstill. 'Let's try that again then, shall we folks? Just relax, feel the beat. Let's be honest, if you don't know it by now, really there isn't a lot of hope. Basses, would you like me to run through your part one more time with feeling?'

There was a faint murmuring, which Alan took for a yes, at which point he began to go over their part line by line. Given that most of it was dms, it wasn't so much a case of checking the words as the pattern. Cass looked around the rest of her section, wondering what the problem was. Fiona had barely said a word all evening, although everyone looked a bit down in the mouth tonight; surely they weren't all keeping mum?

Cass closed her eyes and reminded herself that she wasn't planning on saying anything about Andy, not one word, and that what happened between Fiona and Andy was none of her business. In fact, she had arrived a few minutes later than normal, and had to squeeze herself into place amongst the rest of the section, just so she couldn't do any pre-match bonding with Fiona, and she planned to leave before the last note had stopped vibrating round the hall, so she wouldn't slip up and nothing would slip out.

'Righty-oh,' said Alan, clapping his hands after they'd dm-ed the song through a few times. 'I really don't know what the problem was there, guys, but my advice is, you know it, you just need to relax and go with it. Right, let's go from the top. And don't worry, it's pre-match nerves. Not long now and we'll be on the road in Cyprus, on stage, on the terrace drinking pina coladas, groupies and sugar daddies hanging around wherever we go, clamouring for our bodies.'

'For god's sake don't tell my missus that,' said Welsh Alf, looking all flummoxed and anxious. 'I've had a hard enough job getting her to let me go as it is.'

There was a lot of laughter.

'You all set?' asked Fiona, as everyone settled down.

Cass nodded. 'For the trip? Oh yes, really looking forward to it,' she answered brightly, making sure there was no room for any other questions.

'Me too,' said Fiona.

Across the hall, one of the sopranos stuck her hand up and waved it about like a schoolgirl keen to answer a question. 'Alan? Alan?' she called in a tinkling voice, trying hard to grab his attention.

Taking advantage of the hiatus, Fiona said, 'Actually, Cass, I was hoping to have a word with you. Are you going to the pub afterwards? I wanted to talk to you about the other night.'

Cass felt her heart sink. After all, she could so easily be wrong about Andy and the girl, which was exactly what Rocco and her mum had said on Saturday evening, while eating a superb supper of halibut and prawns baked under a crust of Gruyère crumble, served with Cass's home-grown spinach, pan-fried courgettes and sauté potatoes – along with a spare man called Mike who they had invited along to make up the numbers.

'My advice? Snout out,' Rocco had said, tapping the side of his nose by way of a visual aid. 'You're damned if you do and you'll be buggered if you don't in a situation like that. God only knows the bucket of worms you'll be wading through.' He pulled a face. 'Blast, I just mixed my metaphors, didn't I?'

'Well and truly mixed, diced, and deep fried,' said Nita, tucking a strand of bleached blonde hair back behind her ear. 'Best to leave that one alone, Cass my darling. I remember what she was like when you were at school. She was always difficult. You did the right thing, told her to talk to him, and now it's up to them to sort it out for themselves. Do you want some more fish – there's plenty?'

'So what's your connection to the woman with the wayward husband?' asked Mike conversationally, offering up his plate for seconds. 'Nita said that you were in antiques – do you do counselling on the side?'

Cass glanced across at him. Mike was around five ten with grey-blonde hair and bright blue eyes with enough wrinkles around them to suggest he probably smiled a lot more than he frowned. Sadly, that was not enough to make him her type or fanciable. And, truth be told, he was prob-ably nice, except that tonight romance wasn't what was on her mind. So far he'd done little but listen and fiddle

41

with things in his jacket pocket and she was torn between feeling sorry for him and being annoyed. Her mum and Rocco always did this, invite along some poor sucker, hoping to play matchmaker, when really all she wanted was to gossip with the pair of them.

'We sing together,' she began. 'And we used to go to school together. She moved back to the area a couple of years ago.'

'Oh right – yes – in the choir, Rocco was telling me about that. Sounds like fun.'

'They sing like angels,' said Nita.

'You ought to hear them,' said Rocco. Cass shot him a look. He beamed back at her.

Mike was an architect, and apparently yes, he was an angel too, because her mother had said so. He'd drawn up the plans for their kitchen and now he'd come up with some sort of fancy notion for the roof, which included taking most of it off and turning part of it into a sun terrace.

'You're having a terrace?' asked Cass, as she shovelled more of the baked fish onto her plate.

Rocco nodded. 'Uh-huh – your mother reckons if they're right about global warming that our flat roof is going to be like St Tropez, so while we've got the whole thing stripped back to bare bones, why not? Who wants this last bit of fish?'

Mouth full, Mike waved it onto his plate. 'Yes please, god, that's really fabulous . . .'

'Worth getting up at seven for?' asked Rocco in passing. Mike, quite reasonably, looked mystified.

'It's a close call,' said Cass. 'Did you get to the airport on time?'

Rocco pushed the bowl of vegetables in her direction. 'Certainly did. Your mum was going to pick them up, but you know what her driving is like.' He tipped his hand sharply left and right.

Nita made as if to hit him with the spoon.

'Oh, come on, Nita. Last time we went to Stansted you reversed over some poor bugger's hand luggage and then drove off with both back doors open,' said Rocco, topping up Cass's wine glass.

At which point Nita hit him with the spoon. 'You are such a liar. Here baby, take the last of the potatoes . . .'

Supper at their house contained more nurturing in one evening than most women got in a lifetime.

'And be fair,' continued Nita. 'Rocco's enough to drive Francis of Assisi to drink. Nag, nag, nag, look out for this, did you see that, mind that cyclist. Don't drive in the middle of the road . . . He would drive anyone loco. Talking of which, Rocco tells me that you and the All Stars are off on tour?'

'Um,' said Cass, through a mouthful of sauce, 'A fortnight today. You are coming to the concert, aren't you? Rocco – you did tell her, didn't you?'

The pair of them nodded. 'As if we'd miss it,' said Rocco. Cass couldn't work out quite just how much of that was sarcasm. 'We can get you a ticket if you want to come along too, Mike, can't we Cass?' continued Rocco.

Cass glared at him – not that Rocco noticed.

'That sounds great. Where are you going on tour?' Mike asked.

'Cyprus. Seven days of singing with our lot and about twenty-five other choirs. It's their first a cappella festival. I know it sounds nuts but it'll be great. We've got some

43

workshops and rehearsals together, a few performances and lot of sun, sea, singing and . . .'

All three of them looked expectantly in her direction, waiting for the pay-off line. Cass reddened and held up her hands. 'It's a competition – the winning choir gets a trip to the States. We're going to be singing in a Roman amphitheatre.'

'Really – well, sounds like fun,' said Mike, politely.

'Sounds way, way too Butlins to me. So what's happening to the pooch, the puss and the old hacienda while you're away?' Rocco asked casually.

'Kennels, cattery and most probably closing down for a few days. The boys are both at Uni at the moment – not that I'd ask them to come home and house-sit. They'd eat me out of house and home and leave the place wrecked. And Jacko's busy – that's a local guy who helps me out in the shop,' she added for Mike's benefit. 'Besides, I need a break, and business is usually slow at this time of the year anyway. People will ring if they want anything special.'

She and Mike had already had the, *So you're an architect, how very interesting* conversation, followed by the *Rocco tells me you're an interior designer section,* to which Cass had added the *actually these days I mostly restore and sell old furniture* speech, so at least he was up to speed with her professional life.

'And people will come back. I'll put a sign in the window.'

'How very twenty-first century . . .' said Rocco, steepling his fingers. 'We've been discussing this, haven't we Nita? How about if we stepped into the breach for you?'

'What do you mean? I wasn't aware there was any breach?' Cass said suspiciously.

44

'Y'know, pick up the pinny, mind the fort,' said Rocco.

'Do you mean run the shop?'

Her mother and Rocco did some very slick synchronised nodding.

Cass stared at the pair of them. '*Because?*'

'Actually, it would just be me during the day,' said her mother apologetically. 'Well, most days, and I couldn't promise it would be every day, but we can look after the animals, can't we Rocco? I've always wanted a cat. And Buster loves us.'

'And while we're at it, we wondered if we could maybe borrow your house as well.'

'*Because?*'

'Well, because first of all we can keep an eye on the place,' said Nita. 'I mean, you always have nice things there. V*ery nice* things, according to Rocco.'

Cass held tight to Rocco's shifting gaze. He reddened.

Mike meanwhile looked backwards and forwards, as if he'd got good seats at centre court.

'And this whole thing about having the roof off. I mean, we all know it's going to be great when it's done, French windows coming off the sitting room onto a roof terrace – great views. Mike's done an amazing job with the plans, haven't you Mike? I did tell you that we've got to have the roof off, didn't I?' Rocco said after a few seconds.

'I think you may have mentioned it.'

'Well, they're going to take the old chimney stack down at the same time, and our builder has got a gap in his schedule and he said if we can stand the noise and the chaos he'll come and do the roof before the bad weather sets in. I said to your mother that we should have had it done before we had the kitchen, really . . .'

45

'I didn't know how bad it was, did I? I mean I had no idea – really. I'm not a builder . . .'

Before they started a full-scale spat, Cass said, 'Which would be in a couple of weeks' time, would it? The roof coming off?'

Rocco, cornered, nodded. Mike was about to say something but Cass cut across him. 'Which would make me being away convenient,' she suggested.

'The thing is Cass, we're prepared to work round you, aren't we, Rocco?' said Nita, shovelling the last of the sautéed potatoes onto her plate.

'They're taking the roof off, not taking the house down,' said Cass.

'You know how much I hate noise,' said her mother.

'And dust,' said Rocco. 'I mean, can you imagine what it's going to be like? Kango drills, brick rubble, hairy-arsed builders lolling on around sacks of cement reading the *Sun*. And you know your mum works from home. The studio is going to be knee deep in rubble.'

'We were planning to just sheet everything down and move into a hotel or something.'

Rocco nodded in agreement. 'That's right, and we've booked industrial cleaners for when they've finished.'

Mike had the good sense to say nothing.

Cass shook her head. 'You'll need to get industrial cleaners in *before* you move into my place.'

'That's not true, sweetie,' said her mum. 'Your place is really lovely – so cosy. Rocco was telling me about the choir trip and said you were going to be away for the week. And we just thought—'

'We wouldn't be any trouble,' said Rocco.

'We thought we'd be doing you a favour.'

Cass looked from one to the other. 'I should have known that there's no such thing as a free lunch. This is a done deal, isn't it? The pair of you have set me up.'

'No, no of course not,' Rocco said. 'As if – think of it more as a happy coincidence, providence smiling on us all. Your mother has always fancied running a shop. What do you reckon then, sound like a good idea?'

'I mean tell us honestly, what do you think?' said Nita.

'That my place is small and full of animals. And my shop is smaller and full of tut?'

'Uh-huh, well we already know that. We've been round to your place before.' Nita turned her attention to Mike. 'It's the most amazing place. A real Aladdin's cave. You should go some time.'

'Yes, but not to stay in,' said Cass. 'And not to have to deal with the vagaries of the plumbing or root through the fridge or see what I've got hidden at the back of the airing cupboard.'

'Oh come on. You're just being paranoid,' said her mother.

'And, besides, you could probably fit the whole of my house in your kitchen,' protested Cass.

'You can, we've already measured,' said Nita. 'But the good news is it's not going to come as a surprise. And we love Buster and Mungo.'

'And this way your shop stays open, and we get to stay sane, pootle through your warehouse and cherry-pick your stock,' said Rocco.

Her mother got to her feet. 'Take no notice of him, Cass. I promise you it'll be fine. You can have a great, stress-free break and we get a dust-and jackhammer-free week. Now I've made the most fabulous pudding

47

– strawberry shortcake. Would you like some pudding, Mike?'

He nodded. 'Sounds great.'

Cass laughed. 'Be very careful with these two, they lull you into a false sense of security with food and then bam – they'll be moving in.'

Rocco handed her a clean side plate. 'We'll take that as a yes then, shall we?'

Did they really think she was going to be thrown off track by dessert? 'What about if your roof's not done by the time I get back from Cyprus?'

'They've promised it will be, but if it isn't then we'll just move into a hotel for a day or two,' said her mother.

Cass stared at the two of them, busy planning and plotting, and smiled. 'And you'll keep the shop open?'

'Oh god, yes,' said Rocco, waving the words away. 'You know that your mum has always wanted to dabble in dealing and rag rolling. And I'll be in and out, keeping the home fires burning, you'll hardly know that we've been there – and besides places get damp when you don't keep them aired. Especially this time of the year . . .'

'And burgled,' said her mother, sliding a huge plate of strawberry shortcake cut into thick wedges on the table between them. 'Let's not forget burgled.'

Mike picked up a cake slice. 'Shall I be mother?'

Which was one amongst the many thoughts in Cass's head as they waited for Ms Soprano to check the lyrics of a song they'd sung for the best part of three years and to pitch a note that she had hit every week since.

Since having supper at her mother's, Mike had rung and left a message on Cass's machine and she was weighing up whether or not to ring him back, even if he wasn't her type. Which threw up the question: what *was* her type, and was it a type she wanted to hang on to?

Fiona meanwhile, moved in a little closer and said in a whisper, 'So, can I buy you a drink – just a quickie? On the way home? Just to say thank you?'

Cass stared at her. 'Thank me? There's really nothing to thank me for, Fee. And besides, I've got way too much to organise, you know, what with going away and the animals and the shop and . . .' Which was the excuse she planned to use on Mike, too, if he rang again. Cass looked away, deliberately leaving the sentence hanging in the air between them.

Undeterred, Fiona moved closer still. 'Me too, but this won't take long, really. I just wanted to talk to you about the other night.'

Which was exactly what Cass was afraid of. Somewhere in the back of her head she thought she could hear a cage door creaking open on rusty hinges, making Hammer House of Horror sound effects. This wasn't going to end well unless she made a concerted effort to keep her mouth shut. So, instead of words, Cass settled for a grunt.

'The thing is,' Fiona said. 'This is hard for me to say really, but you know what I'm like – a bit of a control freak.' She pulled a comedy face and then paused, apparently expecting Cass to correct her, but when nothing came, continued, 'What I wanted to say was that I'm sorry about the other night, and that you were right. Totally. So thank you for that.' She held up her hands in a gesture of surrender. Pax.

Cass stared at her. 'Sorry?' she said, struggling to keep her expression neutral.

'The other night. Thank you. You were right about Andy and me, and the whole stalking thing. He's been really stressed at work and things haven't been right for – well, months really – and then I read in the paper that they'd been making staff cuts at his place and you know what men can be like – bottling things up, not talking about what's really bugging them. And the move's been stressful. I mean, he grew up near Cambridge, so we both know the area but it was still a big change. Anyway, I'm certain that's what has been making him twitchy and a bit pre-occupied, the not-knowing if he's going to be one of the ones for the chop. He says his job's safe, but you never really know, do you? – and I can't have helped, being off with him, putting two and two together and coming up with . . .' She laughed nervously. 'Well, you know what I came up with. Andy and I talked about it on Sunday, when we'd got some quality time together.

I said, "Andy, I know there's something wrong, I want us to talk about it, and I know what it is." Cass, he went all pale – and I said, "It's all right, Andy – it's been all over the papers – it's all the job cuts, isn't it? Why didn't you say something?" And although he didn't really say very much about it, I could tell he was relieved.'

'I bet he was,' Cass said, before she could stop herself.

'And the upshot of it is that everything is fine,' said Fiona, ignoring her.

Cass stared at her. 'Fine?'

'Uh-huh. Absolutely. I told him about what we'd talked about. You and me. Not all of it, obviously, I didn't want him thinking he was living with a maniac,' she laughed. 'So I just explained that I'd needed someone to talk to and that you told me straight out that I should be talking to him, not to you. Anyway – we talked for a bit; well, I talked and he listened. Andy's always been a good listener and –' Fiona smiled – 'and I've persuaded him to come to Cyprus with us, with the choir. Isn't that great? I thought it would be a bit of a second honeymoon.' Fiona reddened. 'Not that we had a first one, I mean we're not married, but you know what I mean. I've already asked Alan and he said it will be okay. We'll just get a room to ourselves. I mean it's two to a room, I had been thinking that maybe you and I could share – but anyway, Andy's coming and he's going to roadie for us.'

'We're an a cappella choir, Fee, all we've got is us and our voices and a crate of brown ale for Alf.'

Fiona giggled. 'I know, but I thought it was just what we needed. We could do with a change of pace. We've been talking about a baby – well, at least I have. I mean, if I don't do it soon – tick-tick-tick.' She tipped her head from one side to the other, miming a biological clock.

If only Fiona's timing had been that accurate during the introduction to the last number, they'd have it done and dusted by now, and they wouldn't be having this conversation, thought Cass ruefully, trying very hard not to meet Fiona's eye.

'It's all right for you, you've already done the whole parenthood thing,' Fiona said, managing to make having children sound like a package holiday to Greece. 'How old is Joe now?'

'Twenty-one.'

'And Danny?'

'Twenty.'

Cass could almost see Fiona's brain doing the maths. 'I was nineteen when I had Joe.'

Fiona smiled. 'See, I wish I'd started young, got it all out of the way, but better late than never – how're they doing?'

'Fine,' Cass began, relieved that across the room Alan was busy tapping the music stand to attract their attention. 'Busy doing all the things kids do at Uni.'

'Studying hard?'

Cass smiled; she was thinking more along the lines of getting drunk, running up a huge debt and staying out late, but didn't say so.

'It must be lovely for you,' said Fiona. 'Seeing them grow up – I was saying to Andy I'd like two, although I'd really like one of each.'

'Anyone here want to sing or shall we just carry on chatting?' Alan said, his voice cutting through the din like a band saw. 'I'd like to remind you all that I get paid whether you sing or not and that the meter is running.'

'So all's well that ends well,' said Fiona brightly to Cass, turning her attention back to Alan.

'Sorry?' said Cass.

'Me and Andy. *All's well that ends well.* You stopped me from making a total fool of myself.'

'After four then,' said Alan, raising his hands to bring them in again.

Cass stared at Fiona; she couldn't help thinking that maybe she should say something after all. Although Cass had a feeling that, whichever way she played it, this wasn't going to end well. Which led Cass on to thinking about what it was she did know for certain, which wasn't much, and from there to Fiona having a baby and from there on to how very complicated life could become without you trying.

52

'Are you with us?'

'What?' Cass looked up and realised to her horror that the whole choir had stopping singing and turned to look at her. She reddened furiously. 'Sorry, is there a problem?' she blustered.

Alan smiled. 'That rather depends on how you feel about modern jazz,' he said.

Cass sensed this wasn't going to end at all well either. 'I was singing, wasn't I?' she asked.

'Oh yes. You most certainly were,' said Alan. There was a pantomime pause. 'Unfortunately you weren't singing the same song as the rest of us.'

Cass stared at him. 'Really?' She said incredulously. 'Are you sure?'

Beside her, Welsh Alf and the rest of the lads nodded earnestly. Embarrassed didn't anywhere near cover what she felt.

Cass's feelings of preoccupation stayed with her all the way home. And her thoughts were certainly not just about Fiona and Andy. The to-do list in her head was steadily growing longer and longer. Usually they went to the pub after rehearsals, so it would be after closing time when she wandered back home and there would be other people around coming back after a night out, but heading straight back after choir the streets seemed almost deserted. It was cold, the wind busily scouring rubbish up out of the gutters for dramatic effect, and under every streetlight lay a pool of film-noir lamplight, not that Cass noticed. The dog and cat were upset she had arrived back early having planned a night of chase, chew and snore, but she didn't notice that either and headed up to bed for an early night.

Trouble was that the night seemed never-ending and full of dreaming and waking and thinking and dreaming some more. Cass's dreams were long and complex, full of Fiona and Andy and the girl in the market, and some kind of giant fish – possibly beginning with H – flapping about on a roof terrace, along with angels and singing and unseen tensions and hurrying, and hiding and a sense of impending doom; by the time the morning came, Cass was completely exhausted and relieved to get up.

Chapter Four

Rolling out of bed, Cass pulled on jeans and a sweater, deciding what she needed was a walk with Buster to clear her head before opening the shop.

Outside, the new day was grey and heavy as an army blanket, but unseasonably warm, so that as Cass walked down High Lane to the river it felt almost clammy.

It was ten by the time Cass opened the shop up, the new day still so overcast that she needed to put all the lights on to shake off the gloom. It didn't help her mood at all. In the workshop she pulled the dustsheet off the armchair she'd been working on the day before, and took stock of what still needed doing. Cass bought most of her furniture and bric-a-brac in from car boots and at auction, giving things a new lease of life. Sometimes she painted them, other pieces were re-upholstered or just plain old-fashioned restored, giving chairs and tables, beds and bookcases, sofas and sideboards a quirky, idiosyncratic, more contemporary twist, so that everyone from designers through to arty first-time furniture buyers came along to the shop to see what she currently had in stock.

The armchair Cass was working was stripped back to the frame and looked like something you'd find in a skip, although with a bit of TLC it would be just the kind of thing people would want in their home, a handsome feature in heavy corn-coloured linen that just screamed style and luxury.

While she sorted out her tools, Buster settled himself into his basket under the bench and turned his concentration to sleeping, while Mungo the cat curled up on the discarded dustsheet. Hanging on the wall behind the bench in the workshop was a calendar on which Cass had been marking off the days to the All Stars' concert and tour with big red crosses.

Cass was really looking forward to a little late season sun. There would be dinner and dancing and warm nights sipping cocktails out on the terrace, and the thought of a week of beach life and sunshine lifted her spirits no end. She picked up a little tacking hammer and surveyed the frame of the chair, mentally busy thumbing her way through her wardrobe while her hands worked.

It didn't look as if she was going to be rushed off her feet, and so Cass pinned up the set list for the concert and started to work her way down through the songs. Buster and the cat studiously ignored her.

Cass liked to practise a little every day even when they didn't have a concert. When she was alone she'd put a CD of the choir's current repertoire into her player – Alan recorded all the parts – so Cass sang along as she tapped away at the chair, sang while she replaced the beading, stained and bees-waxed a little mahogany sideboard in the main shop, and sang while she put the undercoat on a little chiffonier that she planned to distress, although Cass had stopped herself humming the tunes under her breath in the street and when there were punters in the shop, because she was conscious that it disturbed people – and there was that whole mad-old-biddy, slippery-slope thing that she sometimes felt herself sitting at the top of.

Cass was halfway through the first set and well into the second verse of *Moondance* when the shop bell rang.

Buster opened an eye but didn't bother barking or moving.

'Some guard dog you turned out to be,' Cass murmured as she got to her feet. Putting down her hammer, Cass went into the shop, dropping a handful of brass tacks into the pocket of the big canvas apron she was wearing.

'Hello?' called a male voice rather tentatively from the front of the shop.

Cass looked at the man for a second, struggling to place his face.

'Mike,' he said warmly, heading towards her extending his hand. 'We met the other night at your mother's house? Mike? I'm the architect?'

Cass reddened, embarrassed. 'God of course, I'm so sorry,' she said hastily. 'I was miles away – working . . .' She didn't mention the singing, as she indicated the back of the shop with a nod of her head and the last of the tacks cupped in the palm of her hand in case he might need some sort of visual aid. 'I wasn't expecting to see you here,' she said although, even as she said it, Cass realised it sounded more like, *I wasn't expecting to see you again.*

'Right,' said Mike. 'I did ring. I was going to ring again but I didn't want you to think I was stalking you.' He tried out a laugh.

And then there was a silence while Cass tried to work out if Mike had dropped by to see her, which was flattering, or whether he was curious about the shop, or had been prompted by Rocco and her mother. It felt awkward, and Cass was just wondering what she should say next when Mike said, 'Actually, I'm looking for a dresser and your mum said this was a good place to start. You've got some lovely stuff in here – apparently.' His gaze roamed around the shop's interior. 'She's right, it is an Aladdin's cave.'

'You could say that. Sorry I didn't return your call.' Cass rummaged through various excuses that would be mutually painless. 'I've been up to my eyes with the concert and the trip.'

Mike nodded.

'I've got a couple of dressers in at the moment, one's out the back in the store, that's quite nice, small, pine, probably turn of the last century, classic two-drawer two-cupboard. Or I've got a really lovely early Victorian one if you've got the room. It's Irish, very rustic and huge.' She guided him back into the shop, where one wall was dominated by a dresser that was nearly eight feet long and almost as tall, currently decked out with various bits of blue and white china.

'Wow, that is amazing,' said Mike appreciatively, running his hands over the deep wooden dresser top that was cut from one great plank of timber. The front edge was uneven where it followed the profile of the tree, and the wood itself had aged down to a rich, dark ginger; it showed signs of a combination of long use and great care.

'It's one of a kind.'

Mike nodded and stood back to take it in. 'Nice . . .'

'But a little too big for what you had in mind?' suggested Cass.

'No, actually not at all,' he said, still looking it over. 'I've just finished converting an old chapel in Steepleton and it would look great in there. I've got a really nice kitchen – I'm like your mother, I love to cook.' As he bent down to open the row of doors he revealed a neatly combed-over bald patch, confirming her suspicions that he was nothing like her mother. 'Actually, it would be perfect. Assuming we could come to an agreement about price.'

Cass watched him thoughtfully as he worked his hand and eye over the old wood. The dresser was one of those things she loved but hadn't been able to shift. Handmade by an unknown craftsman, it was beautiful if somewhat quirky, with oversized half-moon metal handles and shelves with fronts that followed the shape of the tree the plank was cut from rather than being squared off. Mike picked up the price tag, a little white parcel label tucked discreetly through one of the handles.

'Will you take an offer?'

Cass considered it for a moment.

'What I mean is, is this your best price?'

'It is if you want me to arrange to have it delivered, it is. It weighs a ton,' Cass said.

Mike hesitated, but if he was expecting Cass to waiver he'd picked the wrong bunny. 'Fair enough. Would you mind if I measured it up?' he asked, pulling a tape and pad out of the pocket of his Barbour.

'Be my guest,' said Cass. 'Is there anything else I can interest you in?'

Mike set the tape out along the top of the dresser and Cass instinctively caught hold of the dumb end. 'How about lunch?' he said, as he jotted the numbers down.

'Oh very smooth,' she said.

Mike's eyes were alight with mischief. 'I like to think so – I really enjoyed supper with Rocco and your mother the other night, but it would be nice to talk to you without the dynamic duo filling in the blanks.'

'And hogging the limelight?'

'Exactly,' said Mike.

'So, looking at my dresser was just a cunning ploy to ask me out?'

'No, I really do want one and Rocco was right, this would be perfect in the new kitchen. It's one of the nicest ones I've seen in a while. Presumably it comes to pieces?'

'Uh-huh – the shelves slide out and the top lifts off the base, which divides into two, the bun feet unscrew and finally the fretwork trim and finial top lifts off – mind you, it's still not exactly a flat-pack.'

'Will you hold it for me while I just double check that it will fit?'

Cass nodded. 'Consider it done.'

'When could you arrange to have it delivered?'

'Probably by the end of this week – as long as we're talking cash.'

Mike nodded. 'Okay. And how about to lunch?'

Cass smiled; the bottom line was that Mike still wasn't her type. 'It's a nice offer, but I don't close at lunchtime. And I'm hardly dressed for eating out . . .' She glanced down at the work shirt and jeans she was wearing under her apron.

'It is short notice,' said Mike shifting his weight from foot to foot.

Cass suspected he was about to add, *Maybe another time then* or, *Ah well, never mind, worth a shot,* or maybe even suggest they made it dinner instead in which case she had

60

better come up with a good excuse quickly, when he said, 'Actually, I don't mind what you're wearing. I was thinking maybe just grabbing soup and a sandwich. Local greasy spoon.'

'You really know how to impress a girl,' said Cass wryly.

Mike laughed. 'I thought I'd aim low and see what kind of reception I got, bearing in mind you didn't ring me back.'

Cass winced. Although Mike hadn't been the only customer she'd had in during the morning, there weren't that many people about and lunchtime rushes were rare as hen's teeth except in midsummer. She glanced back at the workshop; there was nothing in there that wouldn't keep. Right on cue her stomach rumbled. He grinned.

'Okay, but I can't be too long.'

His expression brightened. 'Great, where do you suggest? I don't know the area very well.'

'How do you feel about wholefood?'

Cass could see Mike trying hard but he couldn't quite hold back the grimace. 'Fine,' he managed. 'Are we talking lentils here?'

'Not necessarily. My friend runs a really good cafe just across the road. They do some fantastic food and all of it is sickeningly healthy.'

'Okay, sounds like a plan,' said Mike. 'Although I should warn you I don't do tofu.'

'Me neither. I'll need to lock up,' said Cass, heading back towards the workshop. Buster looked up at her as she picked up her handbag from under the bench and brushed the dust off. 'I'm expecting you to keep an eye on the place,' she murmured, bending down and scratching him behind the ears.

A few seconds later Cass followed Mike out into the street and pulled the shop door to behind her.

'So,' he said, as they fell into step. 'How's the singing going?'

'Are you sure you want to know?' She looked him up and down; it was no good. Something about Mike irritated her, which was never a good sign. How was it her mum had ended up with Rocco while she attracted men like Mike?

He smiled. 'Uh-huh – your mother and Rocco tell me that you're brilliant.'

Maybe it was because he was acting as if they already knew each other, maybe it was the way he appeared to be fiddling with something in his jacket pocket, maybe it was the sniffing.

'My feeling is that they're probably biased,' said Cass, as they headed across the green towards the cafe on the corner.

'Great shop. I'd really like to take a good look round sometime.'

'Thank you,' she said. 'Feel free.'

'How long have you lived here?'

'About twelve years.'

He glanced back over his shoulder. 'Good spot.'

And he was too cheery.

'I think so.'

'Cool,' said Mike, which didn't deserve comment.

Cass's shop was long and narrow, a sitting-room's width with a big bow window at the front, overlooking High Lane and a triangle of grass across the lane, which was set with mature limes, some remnant from a more rural age that had got trapped between the river and the rest of the town.

'There are some really interesting little shops around here.'

'It's kind of grown over the last few years. It used to be quite rundown when we first moved here, but quaint, and so the property was a reasonable price. Being close to the river is quite a draw – gradually lots of old hippies and craftsmen have moved in. Summer it's really busy. People come down at the weekends to walk along the river, walk with their kids, paddle. That's how we first found it – on Sunday the place is full of visitors trying to force-feed a dozen of the fattest ducks you've ever seen; they waddle up from the river en masse, and there's a swan who is way too fat to break a sweat, let alone anyone's arm.'

Mike laughed.

'Oh, and then we have this guy who shows up on a tricycle, wearing a boater. He parks up under the trees over there and sells old-fashioned ice cream from a cold box on the front.'

'Great place for weekend mooching.'

'Fortunately for me. I get a lot of passing trade.'

'So how did you end up selling furniture?'

'Long story. I've always had an eye for a bargain and been a bit arty. I used to have a market stall when the boys were little, buying things in, restoring them, painting them up . . .'

They fell into step. High Lane had quickly become a little community in its own right. On the corner closest to town was Lucy, who designed and made silver jewellery, while in the shop alongside her a guy called Shaun made shoes and could mend anything made of leather known to man, and then further along Nick and Susie ran the wholefood cafe and shop, that by some fluke of geography had a river view and a wide front garden that they had transformed with climbers and geraniums and bright umbrellas into a little oasis of calm. There was a gallery at the far end of the green in the old granary that fronted the river, and next door to that was a clothes shop and a flower shop. Tucked in between them all were little cottages that had been snapped up by people looking for homes that had more to them than housing estate chic. Cass loved it all.

The cafe was half full when they arrived and Cass, having said her hellos, was shown to a table overlooking the garden.

'What made you move here?' Mike asked as he glanced down the menu.

'It's a lovely place to live and I really wanted a business I could run from home – when the boys were little it was important.' She paused. 'Did Rocco tell you about Neil?'

He nodded, then said, 'They didn't say much.'

'Well, after we lost Neil I felt we needed to have a home and job that held us all together and this place seemed like it. The kids were almost nine and ten when we moved in. Lost always strikes me as such an odd euphemism for someone dying. It makes me sound as if I was careless and a bit feckless – anyway, it was a difficult time for everyone. He was only thirty-eight.'

'I'm sorry.'

Cass smiled. 'Thank you. It's a long time ago now but I still miss him and it's odd because it's one of those things a lot of people can't handle. They can manage divorce, single parents, being abandoned, leaving – all sorts of things – but they can't handle dying . . .' Cass laughed and took a handful of roasted seeds from the little pot in the middle of the table, waving the words away.

'If you could give us another minute or two,' said Mike as the waitress made her way to their table, notepad in hand.

Cass glanced down at the menu. What she didn't tell Mike was that even now she loved Neil more than she knew how to say and missed him every day, and that – without meaning to – she compared every man she had met since against him; and there had been no one who even came close. She understood that memory played tricks with your mind and that, by dying, Neil often appeared as she wanted him to be rather than how he was – but she still missed his voice and the smell of him and the way he made her feel better, and his laugh and . . .

And although Cass hadn't planned it that way, and despite several boyfriends, it was hard for someone to walk in the shadow of the dead, someone who never grew old, who never got fat, never farted, whose life was sealed in the vaults of memory and as a result could never go on to shag her best friend or leave her stranded in the rain or ring up to argue about child support or who should have the house.

'See anything you fancy?' Cass asked. When she looked up to see how Mike was doing with the menu, she caught him staring at her, which made her redden at the un-intentional play on words.

'I'd like the cauliflower, mushroom and aubergine satay with wild rice,' said Mike to the waitress.

'And I'll have the roast autumn vegetables with cashew couscous. And a glass of apple juice,' Cass said.

The girl scribbled the order down and Mike handed the menus back. 'And just a glass of tap water,' he said.

'So,' he continued as the waitress retreated. 'Maybe I should tell you all about me and my life.' He made it sound like a treat.

Maybe lunch hadn't been such a good idea after all.

'Didn't we do this at Rocco's?' asked Cass, lightly.

'Not without your mum and Rocco filling in the blanks, remember?'

Cass decided not to say anything, but it was all right because Mike was way ahead of her. Where she'd taken two minutes to give him a précis of her life, from his body language he had obviously got lunch booked for a full-scale rundown of life on planet Mike. Although at least it meant she didn't have to say anything, Cass thought as she shook out her napkin.

'Okay well, I'm divorced, I've got a son and daughter, *Robert* and *Charlotte*, they're eighteen and sixteen and they live with their mother in *Carlisle*. I moved down here about three years ago to set up in business with *Charles*, a friend of mine.'

The way Mike emphasised the names as he talked made Cass wonder if there was going to be a test afterwards.

'I do some private work – Rocco's roof, for example, and bigger corporate things with Charles.'

'Your partner,' Cass chipped in.

'Yes, although that's purely in the business sense, you understand,' Mike said. And then he smiled to make sure he still had her full attention.

Obviously this was a speech Mike had prepared earlier. Cass settled down to listen. While they ate, Mike talked about his divorce and doing up the derelict chapel and plans he had for the garden, where he'd been on holiday and where he'd like to go, how he liked to work out and play golf and play squash and then, while Cass ordered

66

coffee, Mike talked about good food and girlfriends and by that time it was almost two o'clock and Cass had barely said a word and Mike was still in full flow. Another ten minutes and she suspected her ears would start to bleed.

Cass glanced up at the clock. 'Much as I'm enjoying your company Mike,' Cass said, wondering if he did irony, 'I really need to be getting back to work.'

'Me too.' Mike nodded. 'Oh, is that the time, gosh it's gone so quickly. Time flies when you're enjoying yourself. Well, it's been lovely.' And then he added, 'I was wondering if maybe I could see you again some time? I mean, we seem to be getting along nicely.'

Cass smiled noncommittally. How did you say to someone politely that you would rather push needles in your eyes?

'Maybe we could have dinner after the concert?'

Maybe Mike was just nervous – maybe he would be all right once she got to know him. Cass picked up her bag. And maybe Elvis would bring the bill. Who was she trying to kid? Mike was good looking and nicely dressed but he was also boring and totally self-obsessed.

Meanwhile the girl, who bore no resemblance to the King, set the bill down on the table between them.

Mike picked it up and before Cass could speak, cast his eye over it, saying, 'Not bad. What shall we do, shall we just pay half each? You don't get neighbourly discount by any chance, do you?' As he spoke, he took a purse from his jacket pocket and started sorting through it for what she had a horrible suspicion would probably be the exact money. If Cass had been harbouring any doubts at all about Mike, the purse and the half-each shot was enough to make her mind up.

'No,' she said before picking up her bag. Cass glanced at the bill and dropped her half plus a generous tip onto the side plate. 'I really have got to be getting back. Thanks . . .'

As she made her way to the door, Cass was conscious of Mike following close behind, hurrying to catch up like an anxious terrier.

While they had been in the cafe, the day had started to soften into a misty gold autumn afternoon. Despite being barely two o'clock, the daylight was already beginning to fade and the lamps lit in the shop window, protection against the gold grey gloom, welcomed her home – as comforting as any lighthouse.

High Lane had always been one of those good memory places where she and Neil had brought the kids when they were little, walking down the hill first with buggies and later holding their small sticky hands in summer and winter, in shorts and in duffel coats, down to the river and the cafe and the ducks, and then later to lunch on a friend's narrow boat or walk along the tow path. It had seemed some sort of omen when the shop had come up for sale in the weeks after Neil died.

It had been one of those places that they'd said if they had the money, the chance, the freedom to buy there, then they might just do it. And then there it was and Cass discovered, thanks to Neil's insurance money, that she did have the chance.

She'd found it so hard being in their old house without Neil, and although friends and family said the feelings would pass and that she should wait before making any big decisions, she'd known they were wrong. All she could see were the kitchen units Neil had put in, the bathroom with the wonky tiles that they'd re-tiled one Christmas when pissed and the garden they'd built and it didn't bring her comfort, just a constant aching nagging reminder that she had lost her best friend and the person who loved her most in the world.

And so one sunny autumnal afternoon, not unlike this one, she walked down to the shop, looked in through the windows, hands cupped around her face so she could see inside, and knew without a shadow of a doubt Neil would want her to have it. It felt like his final gift to her.

Mike didn't stand a cat's chance in hell against memories that powerful. 'Thanks,' Cass said as they got to the shop door, realising that she had barely said a word to him on the way home, lost in her own memories. Thanks for what was less clear.

'My pleasure,' Mike said. 'You know that Nita and Rocco have saved me a ticket for the concert tonight? I just wanted to check that you don't mind? When you didn't call back . . .'

Cass tacked on a polite smile. 'I'm very busy,' she said. 'Now I've really got to go.' She turned the keys over in her closed fingers.

'Okay, well in that case I'll see you later then,' Mike said brightly, and with that he leaned in a little closer and, catching hold of her shoulders, kissed her on the cheek before she had a chance to pull away. 'I'll ring and let you know about the dresser . . .'

'Right,' she said between gritted teeth, and then he turned and headed off down the lane towards town. Cass watched his progress for a second or two and then wiped her cheek. She really needed to have a word with Nita and Rocco about their choice of men. A purse, for god's sake . . .

Humming along to 'Another One Bites the Dust', Cass unlocked the shop door and went inside. Buster padded out of the workshop to check up on her, sniffing to see if lunch had stretched to a doggie bag.

Inside the shop was pleasantly warm after the nip of autumn outside. Cass stood in the doorway, slipped off her coat and took a look around. The soft lighting made the shop look inviting and slightly mysterious, the deep patina on the old wood and heavy lamps adding a glow, a promise of treasures hidden inside.

The whole place smelt of lavender and beeswax polish and she hoped was tempting enough to encourage would be buyers to linger, to savour, to buy. There were lamps and bowls and objets d'art on the side tables, shelves and floor, but not so much that people felt overwhelmed, or so cluttered that special things got lost in the melee.

Beyond the window display there were armchairs and a sofa, two Windsor chairs and a deep-buttoned brown leather chaise. Folded into a big basket on one of the dining tables was a pile of household linen, another basket on a little cabinet had paperweights in it and another held old keys.

There was a linen press of snow-white sheets and pillow cases, a period tailor's dummy dressed in a black felt coat and cloche, and behind that a cabinet from a milliner's shop, filled with dress jewellery, watches and tie pins. In a bowl by the door to the workshop were antique buttons, some still on their original cards, along with hair slides and combs, brass doorknobs and more keys, and beside that a letter rack in which were a collection of Victorian cards.

Cass spent a lot of time making sure things were shown off to their best advantage. It was almost as big a labour of love as re-upholstering, restoring or re-finishing the furniture in the first place. She trailed her fingers through the basket of buttons. Once customers had found the shop they tended to come back again and again.

Pleased with the way things looked, Cass picked up her apron and headed into the workshop, letting Buster out into the yard en route.

The shop and cottage spread untidily over three floors, with a little workshop and storeroom at the back of the shop and beyond that a small courtyard garden. On the first floor were the kitchen, sitting room and two bedrooms, with a bathroom tucked between them, French windows opening from the kitchen out onto a tiny roof garden that extended out over the workshop. Up under the eaves on the floor above were two long attic bedrooms with dormer windows and a shared bathroom, overlooking the pan-tiled roofs of the hippies across the way. Cass rented the attic rooms out to foreign-language students during the summer to help make ends meet.

Over the years, Cass had built a reputation for dealing in interesting things at good prices and was happy to customise, re-cover, re-stain or even rebuild to order, so that there were several interior designers who used her regularly. Which meant, between selling furniture, collectables, rugs and curtains, some nice dress jewellery, and re-upholstering for herself and customers, as well as renting rooms to students, and doing odd design jobs for Rocco, life was usually very full and just about paid for itself. Although some days she thought it would be brilliant to have a man in her life to share things with, Cass didn't feel she needed a relationship to make her whole.

She settled down to work and by half-past five had

almost finished the work on the armchair, sold a nice gilt mirror and an occasional table, one of the Windsor chairs, a set of cuff links and silver picture frame. Not great, but not bad at all for a slow day. And, as the afternoon crept past, Cass started to think more and more about the evening's concert. As the clock crept closer to five, Cass was beginning to get twitchy, feeling as if time was ticking by faster – she needed to shower, iron her frock, walk the dog, feed him and the cat . . . the jobs started to stack up in her head, all clamouring for attention.

Just as she was locking up, humming through the opening bars of a medley of Gershwin numbers, someone rang the shop doorbell. When Cass ignored that, they banged on the shop window. Hard.

She considered her options; the window display was good but not that good. Who was so desperate for a bentwood rocker and three table lamps that they couldn't wait until tomorrow? The workshop and most of the shop, where the back stairs led up into the cottage, were in almost complete darkness now the lights were off. Cass edged forward round a particularly pretty rosewood screen and peered out from the shadows into the lane.

Outside, her mother and Rocco were standing back to back under the streetlight. Her mother was wearing a black full-length fun fur coat and a leopard-print hat. They had their mobiles out and were busy tapping in numbers, like busy bookends. An instant later the shop phone rang, followed a nanosecond later by the house phone; three rings later and her mobile rang. They were obviously desperate. Cass watched as they waited and then peered up at the first-floor window of her sitting room, which looked out over the green.

'Cass, Cass are you in there?' shouted Rocco.

'For goodness' sake, don't do that, it's really common shouting in the street,' growled her mother. Behind her, Cass could hear Buster shuffling around trying to make up his mind whether it was worth his while breaking out his famous big bad bark.

'Oh right,' said Rocco. 'So have you got a better idea; I mean, where is she? It's barely knocking-off time. What are we going to do if she's not in?'

'Cass!' yelled Nita. 'Where are you, darling?'

Under cover of darkness, Cass crept up through the shop and opened the front door, surprising the pair of them. 'What do you want?' she said.

They looked a little sheepish. 'Oh there you are, we were worried about you,' said her mother. 'You're okay?'

'Cock-a-hoop. What are you doing out here?'

'Bit snappy today, aren't we? I thought we'd just drop by.'

'Did you ring Mike? He was really keen, you know,' said Nita.

Cass lifted an eyebrow; if their Discovery was parked any closer to the shop doorway it would be a ram-raid.

'No, I didn't ring him. I've told you before that I can make my own terrible mistakes without any help from you two.'

'He said he thought you were really interesting,' said Rocco.

Cass stared him down. 'So is the mould on whatever it is in the back of my fridge, but I wouldn't want to wake up next to it. Now – what are you both doing here?'

'Oh come on, he seems nice,' said her mother. 'And very nicely turned out.'

'Okay, I went out to lunch with him today and before

you ask I have no plans to do it again – now what do you want?'

'Really,' continued Nita. 'Why not? We thought you two had hit it off.'

'He has a purse . . .'

'Ah,' said her mother.

'He asked me out to lunch and assumed that going halves was okay.'

'Ah.'

'Not that I mind going Dutch. Not that I'm against sharing, but he counted out the exact money – to the last penny. You have to admit that is tight.'

Her mother looked suitably shocked. 'My god, I'd got no idea. Mind you, that explains why he is so good at bringing things in on budget.' She paused. 'Aren't you going to invite us in?'

Cass looked at the pile of boxes in the back of their 4x4. 'Probably not.'

Rocco's mind was still elsewhere. 'Did we ever introduce you to Dirk?' he said. 'I mean, there's got to be someone.'

Nita elbowed him. 'Not now, sweetie – look, Cass, darling, we thought we'd just bring a few things round now so's there's not a last-minute panic. Just sort out where stuff's going. Get the grand tour before you leave. Get the feel of the place . . .' As she spoke Nita's eyes were moving round the interior of the shop, as if she couldn't quite make up her mind what to do or say next. 'You can show us what's what, explain how the cooker works and the animals – walks and that kind of stuff. And the shop lights.'

'Mum, we've got ages yet.' Cass stared at them, saw the expression of panic in Rocco's eyes, and then the penny

74

dropped. 'No – this is outrageous. The builders are coming in early, aren't they?' asked Cass.

Nowhere to run, nowhere to hide, Cass's mum held her hands up in a gesture of surrender. 'They said they had a cancellation – they're starting first thing,' she said.

'And you want to move in early?'

Living above the shop had always made commuting easy and getting away tough. People – friends, family, customers – in the know would often linger, hoping to be asked round to supper, or would pop by on a weekend to borrow an emergency bed or a dining table and a few spare chairs. Several times over the years, as she'd struggled out the door on the heavy end of something, Cass wondered whether it would have been more lucrative just to set up a furniture lending library. And of course when it came to getting away from the shop she couldn't swing the excuse that she was just leaving for her journey home.

At least tonight her mother had the decency to look sheepish.

'No,' Cass said. 'This isn't on. You're not due to move in till the end of the week. I've got stuff to do – things to bleach. And I'm knackered – this is the last thing I need. I've got loads to do and I've got the concert tonight.'

Cass had been planning on giving them the attic rooms, which she had intended to do over with her best white cotton bed linen, a brass bed and a set of ruby red full-length velvet curtains she'd given a customer first refusal on once the holiday was over, along with a nice original 1920s throw and matching bolster – keeping the door firmly shut until they arrived, so that no one furry or smelly would be tempted to sleep in their bed before the weekend.

She thought they could use the other room in the attic

as a makeshift office and studio, but she needed to take up a table and various bits and bobs to aid the transformation. And before they arrived Cass had got Buster booked in for a bath, planned to groom the cat, de-flea the pair of them and then spray the whole house with industrial-strength air freshener. She'd already been through the storeroom and earmarked a couple of things to bring in to beautify their ad-hoc flatlet. What Cass did not have were contingency plans for them showing up early.

Meanwhile Rocco was back outside the shop, busy shuffling boxes out of the Discovery and onto the pavement.

'I haven't got the attic ready yet. It's still set up for students.'

'Oh, don't worry,' said Nita. 'We can have the room next to yours – it'll be easier and there are less stairs.'

'And what exactly is all this?' asked Cass, staring in horror at the growing pile.

'You don't mind, do you? They're valuables, sweetie, books and tapes and precious, precious treasures that wouldn't stand the dust or the rubble or the clearing up afterwards.'

'How much more is there?' Cass asked, as Rocco dragged a tea chest out of the back of the Discovery.

'Not that much more.'

Cass held her ground until her mother weakened. 'About another two loads,' she said after a moment or two's pause.

'No!' said Cass, standing firm in the doorway as Rocco headed towards her with an armload of things from the über pile. 'Look, it's one thing borrowing my house, but quite another to take it over entirely. If you want to store this stuff we'll take it down to the warehouse and put it in there.'

Nita didn't look convinced. 'But it's very precious. I thought we could stack it in our room.'

'I've got to get ready for the concert tonight.'

'Well, we won't stop you. Besides, surely it's more like a dress rehearsal tonight?' said Nita. 'Isn't it? You know, for Cyprus?'

'Seven for seven thirty,' snipped Rocco accusingly, tapping his watch. 'That's what it says on the tickets.'

'Not if you're in the bloody choir, it doesn't. I've got to be there by six fifteen and it's nearly twenty to now. I need to shower and – and what the hell is that?' she said incredulously as Rocco struggled in with what looked like a badly wrapped corpse.

'The bust and lower torso of Lady Hamilton. Your mum bought her for me for my fiftieth. Very rare and we love her, don't we Nita? We usually keep her in our bedroom.'

Cass sighed. It was pointless to argue. 'Knock yourself out,' she said, handing them the shop keys and turning back towards the stairs. 'I have to get ready. Just make sure you set the alarm and don't let the dog out . . .'

'Off you go then, we'll be fine,' Rocco called after her. 'We can take this stuff upstairs by ourselves. And then we can go back for another load later.'

'You know where the spare room is,' said Cass. 'But it's your own fault that it's not all spruced and fluffed and full of crisp white linen.'

'Oh it's alright,' said her mother over one shoulder as she lifted a tiny vanity case out of the back of the Land Rover. 'We've brought our own.'

What could she say to that? With a sigh, Cass headed upstairs to get ready. The dog followed her.

Chapter Five

When, a little while later, Cass padded into the kitchen fresh out of the shower, wrapped up in a robe and towelling her hair dry, Rocco – apparently on standby – handed her a mug of freshly brewed coffee.

'We promise we won't get in the way,' he said in a conciliatory voice. 'And I'm really grateful to you for letting us stay. You know your mum's not good with chaos.'

Cass lifted an eyebrow. 'Then you might be in for a surprise. Chaos follows me around like a stray cat.'

He pulled a face.

'Rocco, all joking aside . . . you're very welcome to stay, I've already said that, but I'm going to need some space over the next few days. I've got loads to do before I go out tonight, let alone go to Cyprus. I need to track down the iron, grab something to eat, glam up, lock up, walk the dog. I haven't got time at the moment to be all polite and hostess-y . . .'

But Rocco was a step ahead. 'Don't worry about us. Your mum brought some home-made butternut squash soup and rolls, enough for all of us if you're hungry – oh, and the boys rang while you were in the shower. Danny wanted to wish you good luck, and Joe said is there any possibility you could see your way clear to lending him fifty pounds? Nita said she would send him a cheque.'

'For goodness' sake. Where is she?'

'She's taken the dog out for a wee and I'm just giving the cat a tin of tuna.'

Cass peered out from under the towel. The kitchen was tidy, there was a bowl of roses on the windowsill and someone presumably had packed the dishwasher – unless the dirty dishes had been spirited away by magic.

'This isn't quite what I had in mind when I said space,' said Cass.

There was an elegant, unfamiliar cafetière on the kitchen table, alongside three white bone-china mugs, a tin of posh biscuits and a can of John West's finest that Cass had planned to stir into a pasta salad on a day when she couldn't be bothered to cook. Mungo, the cat, was on the floor, sitting by a large empty pie dish, licking the last remnants of fish off his lips.

'That's lovely, Rocco, and I'm a very patient woman, but I need to get organised.'

'Well, haven't we been saying that for years?' said Rocco brightly. 'We're only too happy to help while we're here. Me and your mum were just talking – how about we set up a lunch date with Dirk when you get back? He's Swedish, I think, or maybe it's Finnish . . . ?'

'Rocco, I mean I need to get organised *now*, this minute, I'm running late. I need to do my hair, paint my face and iron my – oh my god, what's happened to my frock?'

Cass looked around in horror; it had been hanging on the doorframe between the kitchen and the hall.

'Don't panic, your mum put it in your room in case we knocked it off when we were bringing the boxes in. Oh, and she whipped the iron over it and spot-cleaned whatever that was on the front.' He pulled a face. 'I'm not going to ask.'

Cass peered at him. 'How can you two have done all this?' she said, lifting a hand to encompass the kitchen. 'I couldn't have been in the shower more than ten minutes.'

Rocco shrugged. 'It's a gift.'

'So what we're saying here is that really I've got no room to complain?'

'No, not really, we know we're in the way and we're trying to be good – oh and I've just put the soup on.'

Cass smiled and held up her hands, aping surrender. 'Okay, pax. How are you with eyeliner?'

Rocco grinned. 'Did I ever tell you I was a New Romantic?'

Shaking her head, Cass made her way into her bedroom, the dress – a deep purple brocade number with a landslide of matching beads over the shoulders and bodice – had all the understated charm of a Gothic funeral chapel. It was boned and laced, and no matter how much makeup she slapped on with it, Cass always looked thin, pale and interesting. Despite the added pallor, it gave you cheekbones to die for. It was currently hanging on the wardrobe door in her bedroom and certainly looked as if it had had a bit of a once-over.

All the women in the choir regularly scoured local charity shops, eBay, auctions, and the attic in an attempt to out-glitz each other, and this particular dress was a real contender, with a flattering cut and acres of heavy purple silk that Welsh Alf referred to as Cass's Ribena look.

A feathered headpiece, black boa and black evening gloves completed the ensemble. It was a look that took a bit of time to get together; the trouble was that tonight time was one of the things that Cass didn't have in excess. It was nearly quarter past by the time she'd pulled on fishnets, a pair of boots and added enough eyeliner and lipstick to balance the whole look – without any help from Rocco – and hurried out into the kitchen.

'You really ought to eat something before you go,' said Nita, as Cass grabbed her dog-walking coat from the back of the kitchen door. As she pulled it on over the evening dress, her mother's expression changed. 'Oh please Cass, please tell me you're not going out in *that*?' she said incredulously. 'It looks like something slept in it.'

'Or possibly on it,' added Rocco

Cass glared at him. Rocco was sitting at the kitchen table stroking the cat, which – ever the opportunist – was curled up in his lap, purring like a circular saw. Her mother meanwhile was feeding the dog with what looked remarkably like fresh steak.

'I'll be fine. And there's a buffet afterwards, so I'll grab something to eat then,' said Cass. 'And this coat is really warm. It looks so cold and miserable out there. It's not the weather for some slinky little number.'

'I wasn't saying it was, but that . . .' Nita eyed her up and down thoughtfully. 'Actually, you look as if you've just stepped out of a film.'

'Keira Knightley?' suggested Cass hopefully, looking around for her handbag.

'No, who was the fat one on *The Poseidon Adventure*, Rocco? The one who got drowned? You look as if you've been rescued from a cruise liner and wrapped in an army blanket.'

'Well, thanks for that,' said Cass, adding a knitted scarf.

81

'Now presumably you're going to tell me I look like Paddington?'

'Not in that hat,' Rocco chipped in.

'Right. If you've finished insulting me, I'm off.'

'I thought you were going to drive,' said Nita.

'By the time I've got the car out of the garage and faffed about de-misting it, gone round the one-way system and then found somewhere to park, it'll be as quick to walk – besides, it'll be good for me.'

Her mother pulled a face. 'All the more reason for you to go in the car, if you ask me. Do you want Rocco to take you?'

Cass shook her head and pulled on a pair of gloves.

'Take something with you. I could whip you up a cheese roll if you like.'

'Mum, please – I'm late now.'

'At least take this banana,' said Nita, getting to her feet and pulling one out of a bowl of fruit that had mysteriously appeared on the kitchen dresser. Cass mumbled her thanks and got out quickly before anyone asked if she had done her homework.

Out in High Lane it was dark and damp and there was a real bite in the air. Winter was on its way. Head down, Cass hurried up the hill into town, resisting the temptation to run. One thing was for certain, she'd never be able to sing if she arrived doubled over and panting.

It was already dark and the streets were almost deserted, the little market town centre quiet, caught in the lull between the shops shutting up and pub life beginning. Collar turned up, Cass scurried down past the church and out through the precinct onto the market square, empty now except for a few boys hanging around under a streetlamp, smoking and laughing, and the last of the shoppers tailing off home. As she hurried on past Sam's Place – lamps lit against the darkness but otherwise empty – Cass couldn't help glancing through the windows to see if Andy and the girl, by some alchemy, were still trapped inside.

The Corn Exchange stood on the far side of the market square, testament to an age when it was okay to punch above your weight and boast to the world just how great you were. The building was like a Jack Russell, small but noisy. Although it was far from huge, it still boasted a nice line in Doric columns supporting a huge ornate portico, the relief above set with reclining Greek gods and a balcony. Beneath that was a flight of broad stone steps leading up to the two main double doors, currently closed to keep out hoi polloi.

Struggling to catch her breath, Cass hurried round the back, down a narrow alley, to the stage doors. Like a lot of things in life, once you got behind the ornate façade, the rest was a disappointment, the bulk of the hall was plain, utilitarian and built from red brick.

Backstage the choir were still busy practising their grand entrance into the auditorium – the good news being that, although there was lot of milling about, the choir hadn't actually started their run-through yet. At the front of the stage, resplendent in tails, Alan was encouraging everyone to queue nicely with strictly no gouging, no fistfights and no biting. The grand plan was for people to filter in from both sides of the stage, in their sections, the whole thing looking as effortless, composed and well choreographed as something from *Strictly Come Dancing*.

Tension was beginning to build backstage, and there was a real hum of anticipation as people made final checks through personal lists and last-minute details. Some of the singers were humming tunes from the set list, while others fluffed and straightened their clothing. Alan – who was taking deep, cleansing, calming breaths – rallied the music stands, while everyone else fiddled with glasses, bow ties, hair and gloves.

In the wings the sopranos, gathering like moths under a bare bulb slung from the lighting rig, had broken out a rash of mirrored compacts to check their lipstick and do a little nose-powdering. Passing them hastily, Cass went up the stairs to the green room, taking the steps two at a time, pulling off her coat as she went. She bobbed down to take a look into the mirror above the makeup benches and teased her hair into some kind of order. The feathers on her hat had suffered a bit on the mad dash to the hall, and she was a little flushed and wild eyed, but other than that didn't look so bad. Another quick tinker with her hair, a quick whip round with the lippie, and Cass was off down the steps to join everyone else. And not before time, as the first group of singers was busy making its way into position ahead of her.

On the far side, from behind the tabs of the stage, Fiona waved to her. 'I was going to give you a ring; I was worried you might not make it. I've saved you a place,' she said in a loud whisper.

'Thanks,' said Cass, still breathless, easing into the space between Fiona and Welsh Alf. Alf nodded a welcome. He had some announcing to do and was preoccupied with the task, running his finger down the super-sized print on his prompt sheet whilst silently mouthing the words. He was dressed in a beautifully cut dinner suit, a rotating red-sequined bow tie and matching red cummerbund –

which fortunately didn't rotate, while alongside him Fiona was a vision in a sage-green ball gown, with matching evening gloves and an old gold little confection of a hat with a matching veil and sequins. It looked good alongside Cass's purple number as they made their way down onto the stage.

'Nice dress,' said Cass out of the corner of her mouth, as they moved into position. 'EBay?'

Fiona looked affronted. 'God, no, you've got no idea where those things have been. No, I got it from Bella.'

Ahead of them, Alan was opening the music up and settling himself into position.

'The place in Cambridge?'

Fiona nodded.

'It's new?' said Cass, as Alan lifted his baton to bring them all to attention.

'Of course it's new; Natasha always finds me something lovely.'

Cass stared at her. 'Natasha?'

'She owns the shop; I buy a lot of things from her. They do a lot of very nice labels. I mean, we're going on tour – I wanted a few special bits and pieces to go with.'

There wasn't a lot to say really. The whole point of the choir's evening dress theme was that it was ironic and that – especially if you asked the staff to keep an eye out for you – you could pick up a ridiculously OTT evening dress in almost every charity shop in England for under twenty quid, because a lot of women felt they could only wear them once or twice.

'It's an investment,' said Fiona, tucking her slinky old gold clutch bag up under her arm. 'And Andy loves it. It's such a great shape.'

Cass's dress had cost ten quid from Barnardo's, new with labels still in it. The hat had been a pound out of a bargain basket in Mind, although to be fair Fiona wasn't alone in her fears about origins. Cass had sprayed the hat with flea spray before wearing it, just in case.

On stage, resplendent in tails, stiff collar and monocle, Alan called for quiet. There was a lot of nervous giggling and hand-rubbing and a low hum of nerves as they got ready for the first number. Cass felt a flutter of excitement and then everyone started to focus. Within a few seconds the slight hum of conversation faded and died.

The house lights went down, and very slowly the curtains opened to reveal rakes of tiered seating. And then the curtains stopped moving and for an instant there was complete and total silence.

Outside, in the darkness of the town hall car park, Amelia shifted position, before repositioning the rug up over her legs and then checking the time. It was coming up for a quarter to seven.

She'd seen the ad in the local paper for the All Stars' concert and had no doubt that Fiona would be there. She'd rung the town hall to see when the choir was expected. 'Any time between six and six thirty,' said the girl on the front desk. 'Mind you, if you're with the choir and want parking you'll need to be here early. It fills up really quickly when there's something on. If you're singing, come to the front desk, we'll validate your parking . . .'

'Thanks,' said Amelia.

And so here she was, in the shadows, settled down in the single row of parking bays that ran diagonally along one of the back walls and which gave her a panoramic view out over the rest of the car park.

She wanted to see Fiona.

Amelia gnawed away at a troublesome little tag of skin close by her thumbnail. She had hoped that Andy would drop Fiona off by the stage doors, but so far he was a no-show, so unless they were running very late – and from what she had heard about Fiona that sounded unlikely – they had probably already arrived and Fiona was inside by now, which was annoying.

Amelia tore the top off a Snickers bar and took a bite. So far she had seen a broad selection of humanity ambling in – fat women and thin men, thin women and balding men, and tall women who were around 40 and a lot who were well over – and none of them was Fiona. Amelia had naively assumed that by some alchemy of association she would be able to tell whether Andy had told Fiona about her and about the baby.

The heater in her car had packed up and she was cold. Amelia had been cradling the mobile phone in her lap for the best part of half an hour and her fingers were numb. As the moments ticked away toward seven, she flicked down through the menu: the numbers for home, the numbers for work. She hesitated for a few seconds over each of them, trying to guess who the person listed might be: mother, or a brother, or someone at work. Her eyes scanned down, absorbing each name in turn, the light from the display giving her pale skin a peculiar hue so she almost looked as if she was under water. Finally when she got to a name she did recognise, Amelia pressed call.

* * *

In the hall, Alan raised his baton. Cass was aware of everyone watching him for the count, heard a collective in-breath, and then from beside her Cass heard the faint sound of a mobile ringing and then the panic and flurry of Fiona as she desperately tried to find it in her clutch bag and silence it. It got louder as she dragged it out.

'Oh god, I'm so sorry,' she spluttered as the components of the melody started to splinter and fall apart around her. 'It's Andy's phone,' she said in a loud stage whisper. 'I've got to take it, he lost it a few days ago and – oh bugger,' and then she scuttled offstage with the phone pressed tightly to her ear.

A few seconds later Fiona reappeared, still murmuring apologies, making a great show of switching it off. 'Sorry, sorry,' she said, holding it above her head. 'It was important, sorry about that – off now.'

'Anyone else got their bloody phone on?' growled Alan.

After running through a couple more numbers and practising the opening bars and the closing notes for a few of the other songs, Alan gave them ten minutes to go to the loo, have a fag, and repair hair and lipstick as necessary before the performance. It gave Cass time to break out the banana from her evening bag.

'Sorry about the phone,' said Fiona, as they all headed up to the dressing room. Cass shrugged, just relieved that it hadn't been hers that had rung. The pair of them slid onto one of the benches, side by side in front of a mirror.

'Don't apologise to me. Although it's not like you to leave it on,' said Cass, peering into the mirror to give her hat a few last-minute adjustments in between mouthfuls of banana.

'I know, but I got this text message this afternoon. Did

88

I tell you Andy lost his phone; last week, I think it was? Anyway he's been so lucky – it was really expensive: someone texted me today to say that they'd found it and they'd ring back at about half six. That was her ringing to arrange for us to meet up. I suppose I ought to have put it on vibrate really – I was going to give her our address and suggest that she post it on, but it's a lot to ask and she could be anyone. That's what she said, "You don't want to do that. I could be anybody." So then she suggested she drop it off somewhere, and did I ever come in to town, so she could give it to me in person? Wasn't that nice of her? Andy thought it was gone for good. You see, whatever you read in the papers, there are honest people out there.'

Fiona pulled out her lipstick and, leaning forward to check her reflection, did a little bit of a repair job before pressing her lips together. 'The other good thing is that when we got talking she said she was in town tonight and offered to drop it off in the interval. How lucky is that?'

Someone somewhere rang a bell.

'Five minutes,' called Welsh Alf, who was standing outside on the fire escape. 'Anyone got a mint? Only if my missus finds out I'm still smoking she'll half me,' he said, stubbing out his fag on the sole of one of his patent dancing pumps before climbing back inside.

Waiting in the wings with the rest of choir, Cass glanced around. There was a glitter of sequins and glint of jewellery as everyone waited; there was a bubbling, expectant silence bursting with anticipation. This was it. This was the moment they had been waiting for. The All Stars had spent weeks and weeks getting to this point, rehearsing, going over numbers until they were as tight, as perfect as they could be. Behind her, Welsh Alf took a few deep breaths and shimmied his shoulders to try and ease the tension.

Out beyond the heavy curtains in the auditorium, Cass could hear the audience coughing and shuffling and making their way into their seats. Not long now. Not long . . .

Feeling a flutter of excitement, Cass shifted her weight and straightened her dress, stretching up to relax her back and neck; as she did, she caught a glimpse of a little video screen mounted on the wall in amongst the ropes and rigging behind the stage hands. She smiled to herself as she made sense of the images: somehow Rocco and her mum had managed to blag themselves front-row seats. Her heart sank as she spotted Mike sitting alongside them.

The seat thing was a real gift – Rocco always managed to look as though he was *someone*; as a consequence he was the one that was always upgraded on aeroplanes, the one who was shown to the best tables in restaurants, the one who was taken to the head of the queue in clubs. And so tonight, there he was, seated alongside the mayor and someone else from the council wearing a lot of chains and badges, two men in painfully smart suits and an elderly woman in a hat. Wherever Rocco was, he had the gift of making it look as if he belonged there.

Presently he was chatting away to a woman in a natty suit while Nita and Mike were amusing themselves reading through the programme.

The image on the security screen wasn't that great – it was grey and grainy and rolled between shots – but nevertheless Cass could pick out several faces of the choir's nearest and dearest, stalwarts to a man or woman, who supported the All Stars wherever they went. Alan's wife, Glenda, referred to by one and all as Mrs Alan, Welsh Alf's missus, Ron's wife and kids, the sopranos' other halves, children and mothers, family friends, and Fiona's partner Andy sitting on the end of the row . . .

'Two minutes,' Alan's voice was no more than a whisper. 'Let's start to make a move, shall we folks? And remember no talking, keep it nice and quiet. And can everyone make sure that their phones are switched off . . .' He eyed Fiona, who had the good grace to redden.

The front ranks started to shuffle slowly forward, followed by the altos and the tenors.

'Come on, that's us,' said Fiona, as Welsh Alf made a move, but Cass's attention was still firmly fixed on the little screen set amongst the ropes and pulleys. At the back of the hall, just in the shadows under the balcony, in an area just grainy enough so that she couldn't be a hundred per cent sure of what she'd seen, stood the blonde girl from the market. The girl was looking straight up at the stage, arms wrapped around her midsection, her elfin face pale in the darkness. Cass stared, trying to be sure.

An instant later the house lights went down and the girl's face was lost in the darkness. Finding herself the last one in the wings, Cass hurried to catch up with the rest of the pack. A few seconds later the curtains slowly opened and Alan stepped forward to welcome everyone to the concert, stage lights bouncing off his monocle, and then he turned back to the choir and paused, smiling, waiting for the audience to settle before tapping his baton and raising his hands.

'After three,' Alan murmured. 'One two three,' and as the words faded, their first number, a Maori greeting song, began rolling out over the heads of the audience, mellow and soft and as inviting as a warm blanket. Despite her best efforts to resist, Cass felt her gaze drawn back to where she had last seen the blonde girl. And then the harmonies kicked in one after the other, tumbling notes from soprano down to the deep basses, and the sound was almost three-dimensional, and for an instant Cass fell silent and let the sound wash over her, a lump forming in her throat.

They sounded beautiful, and as the choir gained confidence and began to settle down, the sound rolled out into the auditorium like a golden wave. As it did, Cass's focus shifted away from the audience to concentrate instead on holding the tune and the lyrics and all the things that they had practised since the beginning of term.

In reality they had rehearsed it so many times that the song, the words, the tune, every part was almost instinctive, almost as if it was a part of her, the sensation, the elation of the melody filling her up like champagne bubbles. Cass smiled as the notes soared and the harmonies twisted around each other. Along with the people in the choir, and learning the tunes and the sense of being part of something, this sense of elation when it finally all came together was one of the main reasons that she loved to sing. The choir, in good voice, sang as one.

When Cass glanced down into the audience, the whole of the front row, including the mayor, Rocco, her mum and Mike seemed completely enrapt by the music, which was exactly the way it should be. As the first number faded, there was a great thunder of applause that rolled up towards the stage, and Cass couldn't help but smile.

The first half of the concert seemed to fly by in an instant, moving through a whole range of great songs sandwiched between bursts of genuinely appreciative applause. Maori and African folk songs, Gregorian chants, Gershwin classics, finger-snapping doo-wop hits, and Gospel songs flowed by. Cass caught Rocco's eye as the choir dropped seamlessly into a medley of Bob Dylan numbers, four parts wound tightly around the melody and the harmony and the beautiful, poetic lyrics. It felt as if she was flying.

He grinned up at her, eyes alight, and mouthed the word *Fantastic*. Cass grinned back at him. Sitting alongside him, Mike was smiling too, and for a moment Cass felt a white-hot flicker of regret. What a shame she didn't fancy him. While she was having such a brilliant time, it would be nice to have someone down there who she loved and who was on her side, cheering her on, besides Rocco and her mum. Neil would have been really proud of her, she thought sadly. There were so many things that she wished he could share. Just to see the boys growing, life changing, the seasons turning. Tears welled up in her eyes. The music faded. For an instant Cass felt lonely and then the feeling was gone. Into the stunning silence that followed, the applause exploded.

A moment or two later the curtains closed. It was like a spell breaking; the concentration and the focus vanished in an instant and people began to jiggle and jiffle around, and then break ranks and head back towards the dressing room.

'Well done everybody, not bad, not bad,' said Alan, beaming from ear to ear. 'Now, go grab yourselves a glass of wine and get back here. And remember, alcohol in moderation is wonderful for the vocal cords. No ifs, no buts, no excuses . . .'

They didn't need a second invitation. Cass made her way round the back behind the tabs and through a fire exit, and then headed down the steps into the hall, where audience, family and friends were waiting.

Rocco was still in the front row, standing now to welcome her. 'Best one yet,' he said, hugging her and giving her a kiss. 'I was just saying to Her Maj the mayor here that we've been rooting for you since day one. Haven't we, Nita?'

Alongside him, her mum and the mayor smiled indulgently at Rocco and then the mayor held out her hand. 'Fabulous performance, my dear,' she said, in a voice that wasn't a stone's throw from the queen in terms of pitch and intonation. 'My husband and I do so enjoy choral performances, don't we, Cyril?' she continued. 'We've been so privileged during our year in office to see some magnificent things.'

Talking of which, Cyril, the mayor's consort, was busy buying raffle tickets from the choir's secret weapon, Debbie – who was Alan the conductor's sixteen-year-old niece, and her school friend, Lou, who between them were an artful mixture of winsome, giggly and knowing St Trinian's lookalikes. Unsurprisingly, they sold raffle tickets like hot cakes.

Cass smiled and the girls did one of those little girlie finger-only waves, while relieving the mayor's husband of another fiver.

'Come along Cyril, we really should mingle, dear,' said the mayor, her smile as narrow as knicker elastic.

The auditorium was hot and airless and they were all corralled in the front row, the mayor, the posse of men with chains, Cass, Rocco and Nita. At the back of the pack,

Mike was trying to make himself heard or seen or noticed. Finally he mimed knocking back a drink.

Everyone, including Cass, nodded.

'Red or white?' he mouthed.

'Red,' she said, and then to her mum. 'Amazing how a complimentary glass of wine can rouse a man.'

Nita lifted an eyebrow. 'I told you he's a nice guy.'

'I prefer mine without purses.'

'You can be so picky sometimes,' her mum said, eyes alight with mischief.

'How about we head that-a-way instead?' Rocco said, indicating the open doors at the back of the hall. At the far end of the row a couple of minders plunged into the scrum to rescue the mayoral party and guide them through the melee, which luckily Mike disappeared into.

'Some people are just amazing,' said Cass, watching him vanish in amongst the sea of heads. 'He'll probably be round the back blagging the mayoral champagne.'

Nita laughed. 'Don't be so cruel.'

Cass was too polite to elbow her way through the crowd, so she fell into step alongside Rocco and her mum. Slowly they shuffled out into the foyer and the bar and Cass waved and said hello to the people she knew as they went. It was slow progress.

Beyond the entrance foyer, the front doors to the town hall were open, fresh air wafting in. Mike came over carrying a fistful of glasses.

'There you are. That was rather good,' he said, offering up a glass in her direction.

'I'm glad you're enjoying it, and slightly worried that you sound so surprised . . .'

'Actually, I meant getting out of the hall with the mayor

95

– nothing like grabbing your chance. I gave her one of my cards; I mean, networking is what it's all about these days – but yes, you were wonderful. Amateur choirs – didn't know what to expect really, if I'm honest. What have you got in store for us in the second half?'

Something about his tone was really infuriating. 'More of the same,' said Cass.

He smiled. 'Good-oh, so how do you feel about us going on for supper or something afterwards?'

Cass hesitated. 'Well actually I'm . . .' She was what? Her mind raced. 'I've got a lot to do.' It sounded exactly like the out-and-out lie that it was.

'What a shame. Another time maybe?'

'I'm not so sure that's a good idea,' she said lightly. 'I'm really busy at the moment.' *Why didn't he just take the hint and shut up,* screamed a little voice at the back of her head.

Unfortunately Mike was unstoppable. 'Playing hard to get, are we?' he purred.

Cass fixed on a smile, trying hard not to be rude – although she had a sneaking suspicion that unless Mike got the message soon she wouldn't have a lot of choice.

It would be a lie to say that the conversation flowed between them, because it didn't. Instead it was punctu-ated with silences and inane comments and a growing sense of doom. Friends breezed by and said their hellos and were introduced and moved on. Rocco and Nita had holed up with someone from the college that Rocco used to work with, leaving Cass to flounder.

'I enjoyed the Bob Dylan stuff,' Mike said.

Cass nodded: talking to him was like pulling teeth. 'Good. There's more in the second half.'

'Great.'

Why was it that the whole dating lark was always so awkward? Cass knew without a shadow of a doubt that she didn't fancy Mike, but couldn't quite bring herself to say so or to abandon him, while silently berating herself for being so bloody polite.

She was relieved when Fiona came over. 'Have you seen Andy?' she asked, peering out over the crush in the bar. 'He's got to be here somewhere.'

'He was in the audience when we were singing.'

'I know. I just wondered where he'd got to. I said I'd meet him in here. By the door.' Fiona, up on tiptoe, craned left and right, trying to pick Andy out amongst the crowd. Currently most of them were still moving forwards towards the bar to be served. 'I was going to get a drink and then go and pick up the phone. The girl I was telling you about is here somewhere. She said she'd try and pop by if she could.' As she spoke, Fiona craned again, looking around at the sea of faces, a movement so compelling that Cass couldn't help but do the same.

'This is just so bloody annoying. I told Andy I'd meet him in here,' Fiona carried on, glancing at her watch. 'Look, I won't be long, if he comes back in the meanwhile, can you tell him to get me a white wine and that I've gone to get his bloody phone.'

Cass nodded, but there was something niggling away at the back of her head. 'How are you going to recognise the girl, Fee?' she called after her.

'She said she was wearing a pale brown coat, kind of gingery. And that she's blonde and quite small,' said Fiona, pushing her way back through the press of people. 'I mean, how hard can it be? I'll just look for someone waving a phone in the air . . .'

Cass felt a cold finger track down her spine. 'Excuse me,' she said to Mike and the others, handing Rocco her glass. 'I won't be a minute.'

'Was it something I said?' Mike said, obviously meaning it as a joke. Cass was tempted to say yes, but instead shook her head and called after Fiona, 'Wait, I'll come with you – Fee . . .' But Fiona had already disappeared into the crowd milling around them in the crush bar.

'Excuse me, excuse me,' said Cass, trying to ease and elbow her way between the punters. It was amazing just how determined people could be to close ranks when there was a glass of lukewarm chardonnay and a plate of mushroom vol-au-vents on offer. Cass wasn't sure which way to go: did she head out into the market square, search the foyer, or head backstage? Would it be better to go outside or stay by the bar? She couldn't remember where Fiona said she was going to meet the girl with the phone. In the end, Cass decided to start outside and work her way back through the crowd; surely Fiona couldn't have gone far.

Heading for a fire exit, Cass emerged into the cold night air halfway along the service road that led from the market square around to the back of the car park. Just outside the doors a little posse of smokers was huddled together under a streetlight. Cass's eyes took a second or two to adjust to the gloom. She looked left and right and, not seeing either Andy or Fiona on the road to the car park, headed back towards the lights and front of the Corn Exchange where other people were gathering. The façade of the building was wider than the building itself, so that there was a small hidden area, maybe six foot deep, in a pocket of shadow immediately behind the façade on either side; on this side it was where they stored the bins.

As she walked towards them, Cass spotted Andy in the shadows in animated conversation with someone. An instant later, she saw who he was talking to. His companion was small and blonde and wearing the same coat and scarf combination that she had been wearing last time Cass saw her. Instinctively Cass slowed down, trying very hard not to stare, trying to look casual, as if she was just out for a breath of air between halves. They were talking. Cass slowed some more.

'What on earth are you doing here?' Andy was saying. He sounded agitated and upset.

'I needed to see you,' the girl said.

'Oh for god's sake, Amelia, please stop doing this. This is ridiculous,' he snapped, and as he spoke the girl pulled away from him.

'For you maybe,' she wailed as Andy tried to grab her arm, but she was too quick for him and, slippery as an eel, she scurried off towards the people at the front of the hall and the brighter lights. 'What am I supposed to do?' she shouted back at him.

And, for an instant, as the girl hurried away, Andy looked up and caught Cass's eyes, just like before in the market place. In that instant there was a peculiar flash of recognition, and then his attention turned back to the girl.

'Come back,' Andy called after her. The girl turned – for an instant she looked back at him – and then she was gone, vanishing in amongst the concertgoers.

Cass felt her chest tighten. There was no mistaking her; she was the girl from Sam's place, the girl on the market square. The girl Andy had met before. Cass couldn't stop and stare and so carried on walking. Moments later she rounded the corner and saw Fiona standing on the top of the steps, under the portico, surveying the crowd, her gaze moving randomly over the faces, trying to pick out the face of someone she didn't know.

As Fiona looked over towards Cass and waved, the girl was already hurrying up the steps towards her, holding a slim shiny black phone in front of her in the same way people produce a police badge in the movies.

Cass followed closely behind, trying to catch her up.

As the girl drew level, Fiona looked at her, her expression reflecting the question not yet voiced.

Cass, hurrying as fast as she could, joined them seconds later as Fiona said, 'Hello,' to the girl. 'Are you looking for me?'

'That rather depends,' said the girl, sounding bright and sunny and warm. Cass wondered if Fiona would pick up on how false she sounded – but apparently not.

'Are you the person who's lost a phone? I spoke to you earlier . . .'

'Yes, yes I am,' said Fiona. 'Thank you. It's my husband's, well my partner's,' Fiona laughed, rambling. She was holding out her hand. 'You know what I mean, I hate the word partner . . .' She glanced across at Cass. 'Andy's phone,' she said triumphantly. 'Great isn't it, Cass? I mean, I thought it was gone for good. This girl found it . . .'

The girl turned to clock Cass. 'Is this your friend?'

Fiona nodded. 'Yes, we were at school together.' And then an odd thing happened. The girl extended her hand to Cass. 'Pleased to meet you,' she said, all smiles.

Cass was at a loss as to what to say, but good manners prevailed. 'Hi,' she said, 'pleased to meet you too.'

Satisfied, the girl turned her attention back to Fiona. 'I knew it was you.'

'You did?' Fiona looked puzzled. 'How did you know?'

'There's a photo of you on the phone.' The girl made a show of flicking through the phone's menu. 'I was just looking to see whose it was. Eventually I just phoned "Home",' she giggled.

'Well, I'm just glad you found it. I bought it for Andy, my partner, it was a present. For his birthday . . .'

'Really?' said the girl. 'Well, in that case, I'm extra-glad that I found it.' She turned the slim shiny black and silver phone over thoughtfully in her fingers, although she made no attempt to hand it over; instead she lingered and smiled and toyed with the phone as if she was waiting for something. Seconds passed.

Cass watched Fiona, who was growing increasingly uncomfortable, until eventually something clicked and she said, 'Oh god, I'm so sorry – of course there is a reward. Obviously – you must think I'm crazy – sorry.' And with that she opened her bag and began to fiddle around inside, finally pulling out a twenty-pound note. 'There and, as I said, we're very grateful. Thank you.'

The girl smiled. 'Thanks, that's very kind of you.'

Cass could see Andy hurrying up the steps towards them. She couldn't help wondering what had kept him.

'I can't tell you how grateful I am. Oh, I'm so sorry, I didn't get your name?' said Fiona.

'Amelia,' said the girl. All smiles, still holding the phone loosely between her thumb and forefinger.

Andy was there now; he made a show of stepping up to stand alongside Fiona. His expression was totally impassive but Cass was close enough to see the whites of his eyes and for the first time she really understood what was meant by car-crash TV. There was no way she could walk or look away. Andy meanwhile looked Amelia up and down as if she was an unexploded bomb.

'Hi,' he said, directing his attention towards Fiona. 'So there you are, I couldn't find you.' He sounded defensive. 'Great first half. So what's going on?'

Amelia turned towards him, refusing to be ignored or overlooked. 'Hello,' she said. 'You must be the partner. Nice to meet you. Nice phone . . .'

His gaze didn't falter. 'That's right. How can we help you?' There was a heavy emphasis on '*we*'.

'Amelia found your phone,' said Fiona, apparently unaware of any tension between them. 'I mean how lucky is that?' She turned back to the girl. 'Where did you say you found it?'

Amelia smiled, all the while her gazed fixed firmly on Andy. She glanced over her shoulder towards Sam's Place – Cass found herself holding her breath.

'Over there,' she said, pointing across the market square to nowhere in particular.

Fiona nodded. 'Right, well, that's fabulous. What an amazing stroke of luck . . .'

Cass waited, watching the expression on Fiona's face as Cass mentally moved on to the other questions that just had to be pressing, things like: *when* did the girl find the phone, and where was it *exactly* that she had picked it up, and why she hadn't made contact earlier? Hadn't Fiona said the phone had been gone a week? But before Fiona could say anything else, Andy held out his hand in a no-nonsense gesture.

'Yes, a real stroke of luck, fabulous. Thank you, I'll take that, shall I?' he said. His tone was cold, matter of fact and far from grateful.

There was a moment of stillness. Amelia looked from face to face and then very slowly handed Andy the phone. 'Actually, I'd better be going. It's been really nice to meet you both,' she said. And then she turned and was gone, away into the crowd.

'Well, wasn't that lucky?' said Fiona brightly. 'Really restores your faith in human nature, doesn't it?'

What planet was Fiona on? Cass glanced at Andy; she very much doubted that those were the thoughts running through his head. He slipped the phone into his jacket pocket.

'Oh no,' said Fiona, glancing down at her watch. 'Come on, we haven't got long. Oh sorry – how rude. Cass, you've met Andy, haven't you?'

Andy looked at her and then held out a hand. 'I don't think we've been formally introduced. Nice to meet you,' he said.

And then there was a pause. Cass wondered if he was hoping that she wouldn't mention seeing him with Amelia. Were his eyes imploring her to keep schtum, or maybe she was imagining it – maybe he hadn't seen her in the alley at all.

'Andy,' Cass said, and he nodded, the smile he gave her slightly undermined by the little tic under one eye.

'I really enjoyed the first half,' he said. 'The choir seem to be getting better and better every time I see them.'

Cass nodded, wondering if he was just being polite.

Beside them Fiona laughed. 'God, the man can be such a creep. Aren't you going to say how nice her dress looks? Or her hat? Come on, Andy, – I need a drink . . .'

'You've found him then,' said Rocco, by way of greeting as they made their way back into the bar.

103

'We'd almost given up hope, hadn't we Nita?' said Mike. 'And we've barely had a chance to speak, really, have we, Cass?'

'I'm so sorry, that is so my fault,' said Fiona, offering Mike her hand. 'My name's Fiona. I'm Cass's friend.'

'Mike,' he said lifting her hand and pressing it to his lips. 'You look stunning.' Fiona giggled, and then did a funny little pleased-with-herself shimmy and, having purred her thanks, went on to tell him all about the phone.

'So not quite Mr Right, then, ay?' said Rocco, sotto voce, as Cass took a glass from a passing tray.

'Hardly,' she murmured.

'Have you tried telling him you're not interested?'

Cass laughed. 'He won't take the hint,' she said. 'Mind you, by the look of it he's already moved on. If he gets much closer to Fiona he'll be in that dress.'

On the other side of the group, Fiona was still going on about the girl and the phone, honesty in Britain today and god knows what else. Mike appeared to be lapping up every word.

'He's a good man.'

'Rocco, there is a huge difference between being good with roofs and being good with women.'

Rocco laughed, and grabbed a glass from a passing waiter for Nita, while Cass stood back and took it all in, aware that Andy was very subtly trying to attract her attention.

'I mean, it was such a decent thing to do. Don't you think?' Fiona was saying. 'Obviously I gave her a little some-thing as a reward. A thank you from me and Andy . . .'

'Presumably you'd cancelled the contract, reported it missing?' asked Mike, conversationally. 'The companies are usually quite good with all that – I'd got my new phone within 24 hours; it didn't cost me a penny.'

'Andy handled all that, didn't you, darling?'

Andy nodded, although from his expression Cass had a feeling he had no idea what Fiona was saying, his attention apparently elsewhere, eyes moving across first her face and then the faces of the rest of the audience.

Mike meanwhile launched into a conversation about phones and phone companies, free upgrades and who offered what, which Fiona was only too happy to join in.

'Can I have a word with you?' asked Andy in an undertone as he leant forward to slip an empty glass onto a table behind her.

Cass hesitated – a word with Andy really was the last thing she wanted. But before she had time to reply Fiona said, 'We need to get back. I can't see any of the rest of the choir. I think everyone must have already gone . . .'

Cass glanced around the bar; Fiona was right. Unnoticed, the place had begun to empty out. Cass was torn between relief and panic.

'Break a leg,' said Nita, catching hold of Cass's hands, pulling her close so that she could hug her. 'So that's Andy, is it?' she hissed when her mouth was level with Cass's ear. Cass felt her heart sink. She'd completely forgotten that she'd spent half of Saturday night telling them all about Fiona's invitation to stalk him. 'Can't see what all the fuss is about myself. I mean, he's not exactly Brad Pitt, is he?' said Nita.

Cass glanced over her shoulder. Her mother was being unkind. Andy had a kind of lived-in, whipped-puppy-dog face and big brown eyes that made him look soulful and deep.

Mike meanwhile was still holding her glass of wine and waiting for Cass to say something. 'Sorry,' was the only thing that came to mind. 'I've got to go,' she said. Hardly scintillating conversation.

'It's fine,' he said. 'Looking forward to the second half – go get 'em. I mean I understand . . .'

Cass looked at him, irritated. For heaven's sake, what was there to understand?

He smiled. 'Anyway, fingers crossed, I hope the second half goes as well as the first.'

Fiona, who was almost out of the door, suddenly swung round. 'Oh Mike, you are coming to the party afterwards, aren't you?'

Cass stared at her, willing her to shut up.

'I didn't know there was a party, Cass didn't mention it,' he said, brightening up and smiling at Cass, whose immediate reaction was to hold up her hands in protest.

'I didn't mention it because I wasn't planning to stay for more than ten minutes and then I want to head straight home,' she said. 'I've got people staying.'

'We're not people,' protested Rocco, 'We're your parents – well, at least one of us is, I'm more of a hanger-on.'

'Why don't you invite them along as well, then?' said Fiona.

'Yes,' said Rocco, 'why didn't you invite us along as well?'

'Because I didn't think you were going to have moved in yet. I haven't put your name down on the guest list. My plan was to go home, watch TV, drink hot chocolate and . . .' And what? She looked from face to face. 'I've still got to pack for Cyprus.'

'Oh come on Cass, don't be such an old fart – it's going to be great. Everyone's going,' said Fiona.

'I know. I met Alan's wife in Tesco's buying the Twiglets earlier in the week,' growled Cass. The last thing she wanted was to be caught in a room with Andy who wanted a word and Fiona who wanted a baby and Mike who wanted to take a shot at happy-ever-after, though possibly by the way he was eyeing Fiona up, not with Cass.

From somewhere close by came the sound of the five-minute bell.

'And then maybe we could all go on somewhere later?' suggested Fiona. 'Anyway, we can sort that out afterwards. See you.' She did a little fingertip wave towards Andy, Nick, Rocco and Mike, and then caught hold of Cass's arm and headed out into the press of people.

'So that's the new man, is it?' Fiona said as they made their way round the back towards the stage.

Cass looked at her in surprise. 'No. He's the architect Rocco and my mum have hired to draw up the plans for the work on their house.'

'That's not what he told me. He told me you went out to lunch with him, *à deux*. You're a dark horse, Cass. I don't know how you do it. You have all the luck. Why didn't you say something before?'

Cass stared at her in amazement. 'What? What's to say? That my mother fitted me up with an unsuitable bloke – again. I mean, how sad it is when your parents try to find you a man?'

But Fiona ignored her. 'The other night, when I was round at yours, you didn't say anything about him.'

'That's because there wasn't anything to say.'

Fiona giggled. 'I wouldn't say that. Like I said, I don't know how you do it. He's gorgeous.'

Cass shook her head; Fiona was obviously a lousy judge

of character. Ahead of them, gathered in the wings, the rest of the choir were all ready and raring to go on. Cass slid into position alongside Alf and a few seconds later fell into step as everyone headed onto the stage, keen for the second half to kick off.

'I must look a complete wreck. I didn't even get the chance to do my hair or lipstick or anything,' whispered Fiona, pulling and patting her perfectly coiffured bob as they took their positions.

Cass glanced around the auditorium as Alan lifted his hands. Down at the front Rocco, her mother and Mike were back there amongst the dignitaries, whilst Andy was sitting at the far end of one of the rows around halfway back. As she caught Mike's eye, he smiled and waved, although she would have sworn blind that an instant before he had been eyeing Fiona up. As her concentration settled back on him, he winked. It was not a good look. The way he screwed his face up made it look like Mike had got some sort of nasty facial tic.

Chapter Six

'Ladies and gentlemen, sopranos, altos, tenors, groupies, hangers-on and general riff-raff, I'd like you all to raise your glasses and toast our musical director, Alan, without whom this would have been bloody nigh-on impossible. I give you Alan . . .'

Welsh Alf had wholeheartedly embraced his role as master of ceremonies.

The function room in the town hall was on the first floor, with ornate double doors at either end that on one side opened out onto a balcony overlooking the main auditorium, and on the other led out onto a balcony overlooking the market square. Perfect for Eva Perón moments, thought Cass, sipping a glass of lukewarm cava.

The main entrance, at the head of a broad flight of stairs, was flanked by an array of plump, slightly grubby cherubs climbing the supporting door columns. It was an impressive room, with heavily gilded plasterwork ceilings, chandeliers and acres of oak panelling. It was also, when you looked closer, a little tired and, when the heating was on, smelt of cats' wee.

Tonight the smell was masked by a miasma of perfume,

aftershave and garlic dip, and was heaving with the choir and their friends and family. There was a real buzz of delight as everyone basked in the glory of how well the concert had gone, along with the added excitement of the forthcoming trip to Cyprus.

Alf lifted his glass.

'Alan,' murmured the assembled crowd in four-part harmony.

'So let's eat, drink and be merry,' continued Alf.

'For soon we fly,' added Cass in an undertone.

Rocco laughed.

At one end of the room, the caretaker had set out a couple of trestle tables that were currently buckling under the weight of a pot-luck buffet organised by the choir and its supporters. Nita needn't have worried about Cass starving: the choir buffets were legendary.

Before Fiona had invited Cass's mum, Rocco and Mike to join them, Cass had planned to grab a bite and run, but that option didn't seem very likely now. When Cass had headed upstairs with Rocco, Nita and Mike in tow, Fiona had headed off to the ladies the minute the final bows had been taken.

While Welsh Alf presided over the event, a couple of the others were dishing out more wine and cava, which Rocco had made a beeline for.

'Cass, that was so good – the choir sounded great,' said Nita, balancing her plate and glass like a seasoned professional.

'Thank you,' said Cass. 'And thanks for fussing over me.'

Nita smiled. 'I'm your mum, it's my job. Besides, that dress looks so much better once I'd run the iron over it.

And I promise we'll be good while we're staying at yours. I did tell Rocco that we really ought to ring before we turned up.'

'Then why didn't you?'

'Because Rocco said you'd lock up the shop and hide out the back,' said her mother, deadpan.

Cass snorted. 'He's got a point. I don't mind you being there, it's just that I was banking on you showing up just before I left. I feel guilty that the place isn't tidy.'

Nita waved the words away. 'Who cares about how tidy it is?'

Cass laughed. 'You do . . .'

At which point Rocco appeared carrying four more glasses. 'What, no Mike?' he asked, looking around.

'He was here a minute ago.' Cass glanced over her shoulder. He had certainly come upstairs with them and she could have sworn he was there for the loyal toast. 'I thought he was with you. Probably getting a head start on the buffet.'

'And there was me thinking maybe you two had sneaked off somewhere,' said Rocco, conspiratorially. 'Overcome by lust—'

'Rocco, I don't fancy him, is that clear?' Cass snapped with exasperation.

'Women always say that, but they come round.'

Cass stared at him. 'What women?'

'Meg Ryan, Julia Roberts, your mother – it's how all good romances start.'

'Oh please. He has a purse—'

'So did Robin of Sherwood.'

'He's not Kevin Costner . . .'

'Thank god – I didn't mean him, who's that one off the

telly? The one with the little beard,' Rocco asked, turning to Nita for help.

'Mike's not my type.'

'Yes, but he seems quite keen,' said Nita.

'I don't care how keen Mike is. I don't fancy him – at all – not if he was the last man on—' She saw the expression on Rocco's face and froze. 'He's behind me, isn't he?' Cass took a breath. 'Rocco—'

'Halloo,' said Mike from behind them, voice cutting through the conversation like a razor. He was carrying a couple of glasses of tepid chardonnay. Behind him was Fiona. In the ten minutes or so between the last curtain call and everyone else heading upstairs for the bun fight, she had managed to do her hair, change into a black mini-dress and killer heels and apply enough lipstick and perfume to ensure Chanel never went out of business.

'So this is where you all are, is it? And you started without me? Shame on you. That my wine?' she asked Mike as she slid one of the glasses from between his fingers. 'You don't mind, do you, darling?' she said to Cass.

'Not at all, help yourself,' said Cass in amazement, unsure whether Fiona was talking about the wine or Mike. Standing alongside her, Mike practically had his tongue hanging out.

Given carte blanche, Fiona took a long pull on the wine and then shivered. 'God, that's so just much better,' she said, running her fingers through artfully tousled hair. 'I really needed that. And it's nice to get out of that dress, I could barely breathe. It's incredibly well boned . . .' She wriggled suggestively.

'It's not the only one. It looked absolutely fabulous,'

purred Mike. Cass glanced across at him, wondering if that was a fleck of drool on his chin.

'Really?' said Fiona. 'Thank you, that's such a nice thing to say. I really wasn't sure about the colour . . .'

'Oh no, it was great,' said Mike. 'Perfect. Really suited your skin tone.'

Cass stared at him in amazement. Okay, so she didn't fancy him, but lusting after your friend – right there in front of you – just wasn't cricket.

As if reading her mind, Rocco leaned in closer. 'Maybe he's trying to make you jealous?' he said in an undertone. She was too polite to punch him.

'Well, the good news is that it isn't working,' she said, and took another pull from her wine glass.

Cass had seen this saccharine side of Fiona before, at school when they'd been caught on their way back from the pub at lunchtime, aged 16, and then later at Fee's mum's house when Fiona had been trying to persuade everyone it was all a complete misunderstanding. She'd batted those eyelashes and pulled that face and said that they'd just been out for a walk, going to the post office, visiting the poor, tending to the sick – when in hot water any lie would do – and for some ungodly reason, it had worked. Fiona had had the whole guileless ingénue thing off pat then, and apparently all these years on she'd still got it. Andy meanwhile was heading their way with a huge plate of finger food and a couple of glasses.

'Hi honey,' he said, offering Fiona a glass of wine.

'Too slow,' she said icily, holding the one that Mike had given her aloft.

Andy looked slightly uncomfortable before setting his

offering down on a side table. 'Sorry about that, took me a little while,' he said trying out a smile. 'I got held up.'

'Some things never change, do they Andy?' Fiona said with a thin smile and then, lifting her glass, she continued, 'Anyway let's have another toast, shall we? Here's to the tour and friends old and new.'

As she spoke she looked pointedly at Mike. Rocco and Nita had downed the wine in one, before taking the glass from the side table that Andy had brought over.

'I was thinking that maybe we could go on somewhere afterwards, Andy, what do you think?' Fiona said.

'Sure,' said Mike a little too eagerly. 'Where had you got in mind?'

'How about Sam's Place, over the road?' Fiona said. 'Apparently it's really good.'

'Sounds like fun,' Mike said.

'Fee, it's Tuesday,' Andy said. 'It's going to be dead as a doornail over there this early in the week – that's if it's even open.'

'Well, I'd like to go,' said Fiona. 'And Mike would like to go, wouldn't you, Mike?'

Which really set the tone for the rest of the evening; conversation was oddly and horribly uncomfortable. Andy was twitchy, Mike was flirting for England and Fiona was annoyed with one and all over the other. She was also downing white wine like it was going out of style.

Eventually Cass headed off to the loo, followed a few seconds later by Fiona.

'Yum yum,' said Fiona, smacking her lips together as she redid her lipstick. 'Turning out to be a good evening. Don't you think?'

'Not really. What are you doing, Fee?' said Cass, watching her primp and preen.

'What do you mean, *what am I doing*? I'm just kicking back and enjoying myself – letting my hair down a bit. I need it after the couple of weeks I've had. For god's sake, Cass. You're always such a stick in the mud. We're not sixteen any more – I don't need a mother.'

'That isn't exactly what I meant.'

'What do you mean then?' said Fiona.

'You've spent most of the evening flirting with my date.'

Fiona aped non-comprehension, and then laughed. 'What? Oh don't be ridiculous.' Cass stared her down until Fiona giggled. 'Oh, lighten up for goodness' sake.'

'He's my date.'

Fiona waved the words away. 'This is just like when you had a crush on Jamie Boyd.'

'What?'

'Jamie Boyd, tall, kind of spiky hair,' Fiona mimed him as she spoke.

'I remember who he was, I'm just amazed that you do. And it wasn't a crush. He asked me out when we were in sixth form.'

'Uh-huh, and then you got really upset when I went to the pictures with him.'

'No Fee, I was upset because you didn't tell me he wanted to meet *me* at the pictures. I was upset because you turned up instead, and I was *really* upset when I turned up and caught you with your tongue halfway down his throat . . .'

Fiona laughed. 'That wasn't what happened at all, you see that's exactly what I'm saying – you're imagining things and this is no different. You said yourself you're not that

115

interested in Mike, and my flirting with him is only a bit of fun. He knows that I'm not serious—'

'What about Andy?'

'What *about* Andy?'

'Well, don't you think it's a bit – bit . . .'

'A bit what?'

'Well, rude, insensitive? You said yourself that things haven't been that great between the two of you recently.'

Fiona pulled out a compact and patted away the non-existent shine on her nose. 'Which is all his fault, and besides, I told you, we've sorted all that out now. I've told him that he needs to buck his ideas up. We all have pressure at work. Cass, you have to understand Andy can be so selfish, it'll do him good to know that he's not the only fish in the sea.' Fiona pressed her lips together and took a long hard look at her reflection. 'He takes me for granted.'

That wasn't how it seemed to Cass, but she knew better than to try and work out what was going on inside Fiona's head.

Fiona leaned in closer to the mirror to add a little lip gloss. 'Anyway, you don't really mind, do you? I didn't think you were that keen on Mike . . .'

What could Cass say? 'Actually, you're right. I'm not . . . Knock yourself out.' Which on reflection was probably not the wisest thing she had ever said.

Chapter Seven

'Oh, don't be such a stick in the mud, Cass. Come on, come and have a drink with us – just one little drink,' cajoled Fiona. 'God, it's still early yet. And you're not driving – c'mon.'

It was around ten thirty and the post-concert guests were thinning down to the hard core.

'We've already had this conversation,' said Cass. 'I'm going home. I'm knackered.'

'We won't be that late, I promise. I really fancy a bit of a bop . . .' Fiona wriggled provocatively, and then waved a perfectly manicured hand around the room in a great show of inclusion. 'And everyone else is coming. It'll be fun.'

Which was a little bit of an exaggeration; from where Cass was standing it looked like everyone else was going home. A posse of sopranos was busily clearing away the last of the food, while another two choir members were collecting glasses on trays. Die-hards from the choir committee were packing the spare bottles of wine back into boxes and the mayoral party had long since left. Lots of the choir had already slipped away home and Cass was keen to join them.

So far she had managed to neatly avoid being alone with Andy, and Mike had kept Fiona busy. It wasn't the easiest party she had ever been to, although Rocco was good value, as always, and kept everyone amused with outrageous stories about the great and good that he had done design work for over the years; all this with Cass's mum looking on and shaking her head indulgently. Rocco was in the middle of one story when Fiona issued her invitation to Sam's Place.

'I mean, seeing her on the TV,' he was saying. 'You'd think butter wouldn't melt but my god, she was such a pain. She'd bought this stately home. Anyway in the ensuite off her bedroom we'd installed and taken out three bathrooms before we finally came up with a shade of pink that she liked – and then she said, "I want birds, what are those ones called that stand on one leg? Oh and you know, I hate all that oak panelling in the bedroom, is there anything I could have that is less oppressive? I was thinking we could have something kinda sparkly?" She didn't care what happened to the panelling or that it was all original Jacobean or that most people would pawn their kidneys for something so, so grand . . .'

'So?' said Mike.

'So I sold it on,' said Rocco, wryly. 'And then we slapped up this amazing Perspex walling full of pink glitter—'

'He brought me a piece home,' said Nita. 'It looked amazing.'

'Like a glittery ice lolly, with added flamingos, very Barbie does Las Vegas when it was all finished,' said Rocco. 'Bedroom and bathroom. It looked kind of retro-kitsh when we'd got it done, although Ms Lolly-pop wouldn't know irony if it upped and bit her teensy-tiny little arse.'

118

Around them, people were beginning to stack tables and put away the chairs.

'So, what do you say guys?' said Fiona, bored. 'One for the road at Sam's Place?'

'Oh all right. Why not?' said Nita, who was also several glasses of chardonnay into the evening. She turned to Rocco, 'Fancy going on somewhere?'

Rocco nodded. 'If you want to.'

Fiona looked pointedly at Cass, who felt obliged to answer. 'Thanks but no thanks. I'm going to finish this and then head home.' She lifted half a glass of chardonnay.

'Oh come, Cass. Half an hour,' implored Mike. 'It's only across the road.' Cass took a long hard look at him. Her guess was that he was more interested in spinning out the evening with Fiona than having her company.

'I know where it is, Mike, but I can't go in looking like this. I look like Mortitia and I've got work tomorrow,' said Cass. 'Besides, I'm saving myself for Cyprus.'

'It's not a case of can't, it's won't – and we've all got work tomorrow,' said Fiona, in a high-pitched, whiny little-girl voice. 'Just one more drink. What do you say?'

She looked across at Rocco, Nita, Mike and Andy, appealing for support. Fiona had knocked back an awful lot of wine since they'd got upstairs and from what Cass could see had barely touched the plate of food that Andy had brought over.

After a few awkward seconds, Cass picked up her bag and jacket and said, 'See you later.'

'In the review they said they're trying to attract a better class of clientele. Older – you know,' said Fiona defensively.

Rocco grinned. 'Sounds like our sort of place. We won't be late.'

Nita glanced at Cass. 'Cross my heart,' she said with a grin.

Cass shook her head, while in her imagination she could already hear the pair of them staggering in, in the wee small hours, her mum trying to take off her shoes while doing that whole, *Sssssssh, there are people asleep* thing while the dog went ballistic and Rocco fell up the stairs giggling like a lunatic. She'd been there before and – knowing her luck – they would think it was a great idea to invite the world and his wife back for coffee, or in this case probably Fiona and Andy and Mike.

'You've got a key, haven't you?' said Nita, trying to be helpful.

Cass laughed. 'It's my house, Mum – remember?'

'So Sam's Place it is, then,' said Fiona triumphantly.

Cass held up her hands in surrender. 'I'll see you later.'

But before she could get away, Andy said, 'Actually Fee, I know you want to go but I think that maybe we should be heading home too. I've got to be up early tomorrow.'

Fiona rounded on him. 'What? Where have you been for the last ten minutes? We've just said we're going . . .' She paused, waiting for Andy to reply and, when he didn't, continued, 'Oh right, well in that case we'd better be going home then, hadn't we?' her voice heavy with sarcasm. There was a nasty, spiteful little pause. 'For god's sake, Andy, you're so boring. Why won't you take me to Sam's Place?'

Andy stared at her, totally wrong-footed. 'What? It's got nothing to do with Sam's Place. It's just that it's getting late and you're—'

'I'm what?' growled Fiona.

Cass glanced at Rocco, who lifted his eyebrows, while

Mike seemed to be enjoying the growing tension between them. Cass was pleased she was on her way home. Andy, meanwhile, tried hard to sound conciliatory. 'Fee, you haven't had anything to eat and you're drunk – and I'm tired. I've got to be up at six. Come on, let's go home, honey . . . We can go another time.'

'I don't want to go home. Why don't you want me to go? Just tell me, why don't you?' Fiona repeated belligerently.

Andy looked totally bemused. 'It isn't that I don't want you to go, Fee. I said that I'd take you some time.'

'Oh yes, right. Some time? Some time never,' spat Fiona. 'I want to go now,' she said, stamping her foot.

Cass realised that Fiona was a lot drunker than she had first appeared and was getting more and more upset.

Andy caught hold of her hand. 'Fee, please . . .'

'How about we just pop over there for half an hour?' said Mike in what Cass suspected had little to do with compromise and more to do with keeping Fiona on side. 'Grab a beer. It's practically on the way home. Come on – I mean, it's only across the road,' Mike repeated.

'Thanks, but I think Fiona's had enough to drink already,' said Andy, still holding her arm. Fiona's expression was murderous.

'Count me out,' said Cass, finally making the move to go. 'See you later,' she said, briefly kissing Rocco and her mum. 'And thank you for coming.'

'Don't I get a kiss too?' said Mike, all smiles and smarm. Realistically the answer was no, but the atmosphere was tense enough and so Cass brushed her lips briefly against his cheek.

'Maybe I could phone you some time?' he said in an undertone.

Cass shook her head. 'Thanks, but I don't think so,' she said, and moved away before Mike could say anything else. When it came to persistence, Mike was way up there with fungal infections and dandruff.

'Night,' she said to Andy, and then to Fiona, and with that turned to leave, every instinct telling her that things were going to turn nasty before too long. Just as she got to the top of the steps she felt a hand on her arm. She just hoped that it wasn't Mike.

'Will you be all right walking back on your own?' asked Andy. 'Would you like me to get you a cab?'

Cass looked up at him. 'No, I'll be fine, but thanks for asking – you should go and keep an eye on Fiona.'

He hesitated, glancing back into the room. 'She's not normally like this. I don't know what's got into her.'

Cass raised an eyebrow. 'I'd have said a lot of cheap chardonnay.'

Andy laughed and then looked uncomfortable. 'That girl tonight, I know you saw us in the car park.'

Cass held up her hands in surrender. 'Andy, it's none of my business.'

'It's not what it looked like. Fiona trusts you. She told me that she'd talked to you about us . . .'

Cass sighed; she didn't like to tell Andy that Fiona didn't want to talk so much as engage her as a spy. On the far side of the room, Fiona had one arm draped around Mike's shoulders, but that didn't stop her from staring over at Cass and Andy with an expression like thunder.

'Andy, I don't know what's going on between you two and I don't want to. I told Fee if you two were having problems then it was you she should be talking to, not me.' She smiled wryly, 'I've got enough stuff of my own to sort out. Night, night . . .'

Andy half turned and then turned back as a thought struck him. 'About Mike – he was your date tonight, wasn't he?'

'In a manner of speaking, I suppose he was, but . . .' Cass, running out of words, pulled a face and laughed, 'Not much of a date.'

Andy nodded and smiled. 'You'll be all right?'

Cass nodded and headed downstairs without looking back.

Cass was woken in the wee small hours by burglars, or maybe it was an earthquake or possibly the end of the world. The dog barked and then barked some more, there was banging and crashing and then giggling and then Nita said, 'Sssssssssssssh, be quiet. I'll just take my shoes off; take your shoes off Rocco; there's people asleep.' All this in a voice loud enough to wake the dead. About thirty seconds before Rocco fell up the stairs.

Burying her head under the pillow, Cass just hoped that they hadn't invited Fiona and Andy and Mike back for coffee.

Chapter Eight

'So,' said her mum, looking down at the tick list she was holding in her hand. It was Saturday morning, a few days later, the day of the flight. Outside it was cold and dark and Cass was almost ready to leave.

The past few days had been something of a trial; it had been a long time since Cass had lived with anyone, let alone her mother. It might have been different if Nita and Rocco had seen themselves as guests, but they didn't, and so all the boundaries were blurred.

In less than a week Nita, without really trying, had slipped in under the domestic radar and appointed herself Queen of Bleach. While Cass was at work she had de-cluttered the cupboards, restocked the fridge, organised the kitchen drawers, sorted out the airing cupboard and not only emptied the dirty laundry basket right down to the bottom – past the Indian skirt that needed hand washing and wringing into creases, the white silk blouse that took two hours to iron and the red hippie top, the colour of which ran like buggery – but had also ironed everything and put a few stray buttons back on as well.

Cass knew that she ought to feel grateful and knew that her mum was only trying to be kind and helpful, except that seeing all those clothes hanging neatly in her wardrobe felt more like criticism than help.

In lots of other ways it was like having the boys back at home. Nita and Rocco were constantly on the phone; they stayed up half the night talking rubbish and watching weird things on TV and they drank like fish.

Nita liked to sing in the bath, with the door open, and Rocco walked around the place with the phone tucked under his chin, dressed in an unnervingly short bathrobe. Their friends rang them all hours of the night and day and three afternoons on the trot Cass had come upstairs from work to find strange people sitting at the kitchen table drinking tea and eating biscuits. Nita left her makeup all over the bathroom and filled up the bin with enough tissues and cotton wool to perform open-heart surgery on half of East Anglia. Worse still, Rocco often crept up behind Nita and made her squeal with an unnerving combination of surprise and delight. Cass didn't want to know exactly how that worked.

And the two them were noisy and giggled and had private jokes, and left the lights on, and Cass found herself going around switching things off behind them and asking them to turn their music down, and wondering who exactly was the grown-up here.

Midweek she had found the pair of them out on the terrace, with someone called Bas, all wrapped up against the cold, all looking sheepish.

'Are you smoking out here?' Cass had demanded, hands on hips, as Nita giggled and flapped the smoke away. Cass couldn't help but notice that her mother was holding her breath.

'No,' Rocco said, offering Cass the roll-up. 'It's just a bit of grass, that's all. We gave up smoking cigarettes years ago, didn't we, Bas?'

Cass held up her hand to decline the tab end now being proffered by Bas. What exactly was the protocol with parents and drugs?

'You're buying grass?' she said incredulously, staring pointedly at Nita.

'Oh good god no,' said Rocco, looking all self-righteous and slightly offended. 'No, of course not, your mum's been growing it on the windowsill.'

What could you say? 'Would anyone like a cup of tea?' asked Cass

And between getting stoned and goosing her mother, Rocco walked the dog, mended the loo seat, sorted out the dripping tap in the kitchen and re-siliconed the shower tray, all without being asked, which instead of making Cass feel grateful made her realise just how much she missed having a real man about the place and just how easy it would be to be envious that her mother had.

And however old you are, listening to your mother having sex is never easy. Hearing your mother have *really good* sex was far, far worse.

So by Saturday morning Cass was happy to be leaving, even if it was way too early to think straight.

By some dark alchemy, Nita looked fabulous. Hair brushed, eyes bright, all wrapped up in a pale blue robe that did something impressive to her complexion, she bore more than a passing resemblance to Helen Mirren. Cass, by contrast, felt like shit and suspected she looked worse.

'Passport, travel sickness pills, something to read on the flight – do you want to borrow anything of mine? I've got as much chick lit as a girl could ever need.'

Nita carried on reading down the list while Cass raised an eyebrow; she was standing in the kitchen of the flat, suitcase at her feet, waiting for Rocco to come round with the car to take her to the pick-up, despite her insistence that she could just as easily call a cab.

'Okay,' Nita was saying. 'I've ironed your clothes and I've popped a couple of packets of biscuits in your bag in case you get a bit peckish – I mean, you never know what you're going to get at a hotel. Oh, and there's some mints, and multi-vitamins – have you packed a warm coat?'

As well as the ironing and the odd jobs, the kitchen was spotless, there were fruit, roses and a crisp white table-cloth on the table. The whole place smelt of fresh coffee and new bread, courtesy of some swish steaming whizz-bang machinery that had been brought in by Nita and Rocco after they swore blind that they couldn't live without it. Cass looked round and sighed, missing her homely mess while taking the list from her mum's outstretched fingers.

It was written in block capitals – presumably, Cass thought, in case she wasn't bright enough to deal with anything else. She noticed that on the bottom her mum had also written down a list of emergency numbers, including her own home number. It was the early hours of the morning, far too early to argue about how old Cass was and how she was quite capable of sorting her own life out thank you very much, and outside it was pitch black and cold as ice.

'There are some custard creams and some shortbread – I mean, you might get peckish, I know I always do, and you can't always get room service.'

Cass glanced at her watch. The choir were travelling by coach down to Gatwick to catch an early flight to Paphos, four hours away by plane, and two hours ahead of the UK time-wise. Come mid-afternoon, Cass was planning to be holed up in a little cafe somewhere, sipping iced coffee and watching the world go by. She could hardly wait, England at half past three on a drizzly autumn morning was hardly the most inviting place in the world.

The All Stars' first choral get-together in Paphos wasn't until dinner time that evening, and so there would be time for her to have a little scout around town and explore before the thing kicked off. She'd never been to Cyprus before.

Alan had managed to get them a good deal, so they were travelling on a scheduled flight and booked as a party into a hotel with a sea view, slap-bang in the centre of the main harbour area. Cass glanced at her watch again.

'Camera?' asked her mother, pulling Cass back into the moment. 'Now don't forget to ring when you get to the hotel. And make sure you keep your passport safe, don't talk to strangers, and you need to check if you can drink the water.' Nita paused and then, lowering her voice, continued, 'Have you got condoms?'

'For goodness sake, Mum,' Cass gasped, feeling her colour rise. 'Do you mind?'

'Well, I'm just saying,' said Nita defensively. 'I mean, you never know, better to be prepared. You never know when you might want to—'

'Mum, that's enough, thank you,' said Cass, jumping into void.

Beside her, Buster whined miserably; he wasn't a dog who appreciated late nights and early mornings or lectures on health and safety.

'I was only saying,' repeated Nita.

Cass sighed. 'I know.' She leant forward to scratch Buster behind the ears. 'I'm going to miss you,' she said.

Nita reached out to give Cass a hug. 'I know darling, but we'll be fine here, don't you worry.'

'I didn't mean you,' Cass said with a grin.

Nita laughed. 'Everything is going to be okay; Rocco's ordered in a lorry-load of tuna for the cat and has promised His Nibs here lots of long healthy walks. While you're away I thought I'd have a little go at those windows, and have another tidy of your airing cupboard.'

'There's really no need.'

Nita clapped her hands. 'But there's just so much junk in there, I don't know how you can find anything.'

Cass bit her tongue. There was only so much she could cope with at this time of the morning and a row over what constituted junk did not qualify.

Cass hadn't heard a word from Fiona since the concert, although Mike had rung up to ask if she'd like to go out for supper and – in passing – asked whether she happened to have Fiona's number. Fortunately Rocco took the call and, after much waving and gesticulating on Cass's part, he had steered the conversation towards beams and roof timber and the joys of their new roof and terrace, and any chance of dinner or chasing Fiona appeared to have been lost in a wealth of design and building trivia.

Outside, below them in the street, Rocco pipped the horn.

'You don't mind if I say bye-bye up here, do you honey? Only I hate long farewells,' Nita said.

Cass kissed her on both cheeks. 'It's fine by me. See you soon.'

'I love you,' said Nita.

'I love you too,' said Cass, meaning every word.

'I hope you have a lovely time,' her mother called down the stairs. 'And don't forget to—'

But Cass had already closed the door.

The good news was that she was one of the last to board the bus, and so Cass had to sit a couple of seats back behind the driver, well away from Fiona and Andy, although she did manage a friendly wave. When they got to Gatwick, Cass kept out of the way. The natural order of things was that usually the basses hung out together so, if she didn't want to get stuck sitting with Fiona and Andy on the plane, she had to make plans now.

'Hi Alf, how's it going?' she said, slipping into the check-in queue between Welsh Alf and Ray. Behind them Norman and his flower-arranging wife were deep in conversation about who had got the passports; she had come along for the flora and fauna, apparently.

'To be perfectly honest, I'm not that keen on flying,' Alf said, as Norman and his wife started unpacking her handbag.

He did look a little peaky. Cass smiled. 'Have you taken anything?'

'M' missus bought me some tablets, but it says on the packet I can't drink with them and to be honest I'd rather have a couple of stiff scotches – calms me nerves a lot better than those things. And Ray's never flown before, have you Ray?'

Cass glanced at Ray, who looked even paler than Alf. 'You'll be fine,' said Cass. 'Stick with me. I've flown lots of time, piece of cake.' Out of the corner of her eye she could see Norman being frisked by his wife for their passports.

Cass's hotel room had a balcony with a view facing west out over the bay in Paphos. The sounds of the Mediterranean lapping against the shore were as slow and rhythmic as a sleeping breath and the sun felt warm on her body. Cass tipped her face up towards the late afternoon sky and smiled.

She was sitting outside with a long cool drink, had her shoes off and feet up, catching the first welcome rays of the holiday. It was pleasantly warm – in the low twenties – and afternoon sunlight, already touched with the first gold of evening, picked out the ripples on the ocean like shimmering threads. Oh yes, this was the life – this was just what she needed.

On the balconies below her, Cass could hear voices as people made plans, changed outfits and negotiated who was going to have which bed – while Norman's wife wanted to know what he'd done with the camera. Cass meanwhile had time to just take in the view and let the stress of the last few days ebb away.

It had been a long flight sandwiched between Welsh Alf and Ray. They had watched anxiously all the way through the safety demo, paled to the colour of skimmed milk during take-off and passed the four-hour flight reading and re-reading the what-to-do in-the-case-of-an emergency card.

First mention of the Channel and Alf had insisted on getting the life jacket out from under his seat and sitting with it on his lap until the stewardess had told him that nobody was having any breakfast till he put it away, at which point Cass had ordered them both a double vodka.

Arriving in Paphos, the pair of them had swaggered down the steps of the plane like World War Two fighter pilots. 'Piece of cake,' Alf said as he helped Cass with her bag. 'Almost wish I'd brought the missus now.'

By some amazing, unbelievable and joyous stroke of luck they were among the last to find a cab at the airport and the last to arrive at the hotel. As she got to the desk, Cass was met by Alan and one of the hotel managers.

While Alf and Ray took their key and headed up in the lift, Alan called her over to one side. 'Cass,' said Alan. 'I'm sorry about this – but you're the odd woman out in the party.'

Cass laughed. 'I would have said there were a lot odder women than me on this trip.'

Alan looked slightly embarrassed, as Mrs Alan, sitting in reception, looked on. 'It's entirely my fault,' he said. 'There were a couple of last-minute changes in the numbers and – the thing is, apparently there has been some kind of mix-up; everyone else has already got their keys but unfortunately they haven't actually got another room free on the same floor as the rest of us. We're one person over – Geno here . . .' He indicated a tall guy with huge brown eyes, shoulders that would block doors and thick black hair combed back off a face that Cass suspected was probably much sought after – along with the rest of him. 'And I wondered if you would mind having a room on a different floor? I mean, it's only a floor's difference, and you wouldn't have to share – if I was on my own I'd take it myself but with my good lady being here . . .' His voice trailed away, explanation unnecessary. Mrs Alan didn't look the accommodating kind.

For a woman of such considerable bulk, Mrs Alan had very little in the sense of humour department. What she did have were thin lips and a tight perm and was holding her handbag like it might make a break for freedom at any minute.

Cass's thoughts of 'room over the kitchen with a view of the bins' probably showed on her face, and she hesitated just long enough for Geno, the under-manager, to explain in faultless English that it was entirely his mistake, hand on his heart, and that there was an insufficient number of the basic twin rooms. He went on to say that he was personally desolate, not to mention responsible, and was so sad, so very very sad about spoiling her holiday – and wondered if she would accept not only his personal and heartfelt apologies, but also an upgrade to a superior double room on the top floor.

He smiled, quite obviously waiting to see how he'd done so far. Geno was probably in his early thirties, was cocky and charming and one hundred per cent pure trouble. Cass couldn't help smiling.

'It sounds fine,' Cass began.

But apparently this was not what Alan was expecting either and, hearing the word superior, leapt into the breach. After all, he was in charge and if Cass was concerned about being on her own then maybe he and Mrs Alan should take the other room after all.

But Geno was unstoppable. He would carry Cass's bags himself, oh yes he would, and by the way his name was Geno and he wasn't married and he was free most afternoons. And he had worked in London, which was why his English was so good and had anyone ever told her that she had the most beautiful eyes? Cass smiled to herself as he promised to show her just how lovely the island was . . .

Which was why Cass was here on the balcony of the Centrale, with her complimentary slippers, the keys to the minibar, and a gift-wrapped fruit basket, reading through the week's itinerary, cradling a long gin and tonic while the people on the floor below were fighting over who should have the mint on the pillow.

According to the brochure, everyone was going to meet up at seven in the foyer, before walking along the seafront to one of the huge international beachside hotels, the Athena Grande, to join a first-night, welcome-to-Cyprus dinner with the rest of the choirs.

They were also going to be introduced to El Gran Coro del Corazón – the Big Heart Choir – who were sharing their hotel and had also flown in for the festival. Over the following days all the choirs would meet up at the various hotels to rehearse together for a joint concert on Saturday evening, being staged at Kourion, one of the most impressive archaeological sites on the whole island, where there was a huge Roman theatre, set high up in the hills, with spectacular views out over the bay. It was a real treasure and a great honour for the choirs to have permission from the Department of Antiquities to sing there.

There would be daily trips out and a concert by participating choirs every evening at the ancient amphitheatre close to the Roman ruins in Paphos Harbour, performances that would be judged by an international panel of judges, who would then decide which choir would fly, all expenses paid, to America to take part in a US a cappella choir competition the following year.

Cass was just mulling over the details of the itinerary

when there was a knock at the door. She was tempted to ignore it, but whoever it was knocked again and then again, louder now.

'Coming,' Cass said finally. Maybe it was Geno coming to see how she'd settled in. Or Alan coming to offer to change rooms. She opened the door.

Andy was standing out in the hallway, looking sheepish. 'Hi,' he said, looking left and right. 'Do you mind if I come in?'

Cass stared at him and then past him. 'Where's Fiona?'

He didn't answer; instead he said, 'I was going to ring you after the concert, to apologise and to have a chat. There's not many people I can talk to really. I'd like to explain about the other night . . .'

'Look, I already said there's nothing to explain, really – it's none of my business. Where is Fiona?'

'Having a siesta. She hates flying. The tablets she takes make her sleepy. She'll be out for ages yet. Do you mind if I come in? I won't be long – just five minutes.'

Cass hesitated and then, finally, when it was obvious that he wasn't going to go, waved Andy inside. 'Five minutes,' she said.

He looked round. 'Nice room. Ours isn't as plush as this.'

'There was a mix-up with the numbers. They were a room short . . .'

'And you got this?'

'They upgraded me.'

'Nice.' He made a show of looking round some more, not that there was an awful lot to see.

There was an awkward pause. Cass felt uncomfortable. Did she invite Andy to sit down? There was only one chair

135

and Cass wasn't sure she wanted to sit on the bed. Did she suggest he sit on the bed or did they both stand? What was the etiquette for confession? They could hardly go out on the terrace, because by some trick of acoustics you could hear every word from the balconies around, and she didn't plan to offer him a drink because she didn't want him to stay that long.

'Shall I get a chair in off the terrace?' he suggested.

'Great idea,' said Cass with relief.

It took some manoeuvring to get the chair in, and although the room – according to Andy – was much larger than the one he and Fiona had, it wasn't big by any standards. The catches on the French windows and the wooden slatted shutters were stiff and unwieldy and they had to move things to get the other chair in and then shut the doors up, so Andy's five minutes were up by the time he had sorted out the seating – and without the sea breeze the room was hot and heavy and horribly claustrophobic, which meant fiddling with the air conditioning, and all the time the minutes ticked by and Cass felt more and more uncomfortable. Something about sharing a secret with Andy made her nervous. God only knew what Fiona would think if she found them together.

'So,' said Andy, finally seated. 'It's a job to know where to start really.'

'Five minutes,' said Cass gently. 'I've already said I don't think this is really my business.'

Andy was tall and broad shouldered with a good face, crisscrossed by laughter lines; sitting in the space in front of the window, he dominated the room. He was also obviously genuinely upset.

'I wouldn't have come up here, but I don't know who else

to talk to. I met up with Amelia – that's her name – about six months ago. It was amazing – completely unexpected, totally out of the blue. Things have been tricky between Fee and me for a while. I'm not justifying lying to her, I just didn't want to hurt her.' Andy paused, looking at her as if gauging Cass's reaction. Cass didn't say a word. So, Fiona had been right about Andy all along.

Andy reddened. 'Okay – from outside it looks like I'm taking the easy way out by not saying anything,' he said, holding his hands up in surrender. 'Fiona can be a difficult person to deal with when she's upset. As I said, things hadn't been going well between us for a while now. We'd been trying to work things out. We'd considered counselling and stuff. We were going to have a trial separation . . . Anyway, to cut a long story short, I was in the process of moving out when I met Amelia. Meeting her just blew me away. It changed the way I looked at everything – changed the way I felt about myself, about my entire life.'

Cass looked at him; wasn't that what every man who ever had an affair said? Every man who lied and cheated on his wife or girlfriend?

'I think I've heard enough,' said Cass, getting to her feet.

'No please,' he said. 'You have to believe me; I've been trying to find a way to tell Fiona but I can't.' He sighed, wringing his hands. 'Did you know she wants a baby? And Amelia isn't easy either. She keeps telling me that I should tell Fiona about her and then the other night—'

'You thought that she might.'

'I don't know. . . . I didn't know what she was planning to do – she can be unpredictable. I'd more or less guessed that she'd picked my phone up but when I saw her there with Fiona . . .' He ran his fingers through his hair. 'It's all such a fucking mess. I told Amelia that I was going to try and talk to you about it.'

Cass stared at him. 'Me? Why me?'

'Because you're the only one who knows about her and Fiona.'

Cass wasn't sure what to say – *was she supposed to be flattered?*

'In some ways I wish I'd never met Amelia, or at least met her later when I'd sorted all this out – but that isn't how life works, is it?'

He paused, as if waiting for Cass to say something, and when she didn't said, 'Then a couple of weeks ago, Amelia told me that she's pregnant.'

Cass stared at him in a mixture of amazement and shock. 'Oh sweet Jesus,' she said before she could stop herself.

At which point there was another knock at the door. Cass ignored it annoyed that her peaceful idyll was rapidly turning into Piccadilly Circus.

'You can't carry on like this. Fee is bound to find out about Amelia. It won't be me who tells her, but trust me, somebody will. And when she finds out, how is she going to feel when she discovers Amelia's pregnant? You've got to talk to her—'

The knocking got louder.

'Cass, Cass are you in there?' said a familiar voice from outside the door. 'It's me, Fiona.' As if there had been any doubt.

Cass froze.

Andy looked as if he might have a heart attack. 'She'll go ballistic if she finds me in here,' he hissed.

Cass stared at him. 'What?'

'She thinks that I fancy you.'

Cass groaned. 'Oh for god's sake, that's all we need.' As if life wasn't complicated enough.

'What did you say?' shouted Fiona.

'I said *I won't be a minute,*' called Cass, while Andy looked frantically around the room.

'Don't tell me you're planning to hide in the wardrobe?' groaned Cass.

'I've got to hide somewhere.' He pulled open the French windows and headed out onto the balcony. 'There's something else you need to know. About Amelia—'

'No, no,' said Cass, holding her hands up to her ears. 'I don't want to hear anything else about Amelia.'

Cass could hear Fiona out on the landing, getting increasingly annoyed. Hurriedly she bundled Andy out on to the balcony, and an instant later had closed the doors and pulled the curtains and shutters behind him.

Cass bounded across the bed and opened the door, planning to head Fiona off into the hallway, but Fiona had other ideas and pushed the door wide open before Cass could do anything to stop her.

Fiona raised her eyebrows. 'Well, well, well. All alone, are we?' she said, making a great show of looking round the room.

Cass made every effort not to look guilty.

'Curtains drawn in the middle of the day – and oh my god, just look at the state of the bed. You're a dark horse, Cass . . .'

Cass glanced over her shoulder; the bed was a mess from where she had clambered over it in an effort to get to the door before Fiona knocked it down.

Fiona picked up a pillow and dropped it back onto the bed. 'I was talking to Alan in reception; he told me you were up here and had really hit it off with one of the managers.' As she spoke, Fiona started exploring, opening the bathroom door and peering inside, looking through the wardrobe – whilst all the while Cass's heart galloped away nineteen to the dozen.

'Nice room,' she said reflectively. 'Maybe Andy and I should get an upgrade too – what's the view like?'

Cass gasped and made a lunge for the terrace doors, although it was more of an instinctive reaction than a plan.

Fiona grinned triumphantly. 'Oh, so this is where you've been hiding him, is it – let's have a little look, shall we?'

Cass made a vain attempt to step between Fiona and the doors but it was like trying to stop a freight train. Fiona threw aside the curtains and doors and opened up the heavy shutters. 'Here I come, ready or not,' she said, still giggling.

'Don't,' Cass protested. 'Please, it's not what you think.' But it was too late; Fiona was already through the doors and out on the balcony. Cass closed her eyes and sank on to the bed, waiting for the screams of indignation and the scene that was just bound to follow. There was a hush. Cass took a deep breath; it was coming any second now.

'Oh,' was all Fiona said.

'Oh?' said Cass, slowly opening one eye.

'Well I thought you'd got someone out here,' Fiona said, looking left and right. She sounded deeply disappointed. 'Alan said he thought you'd got a man up here.'

Cass stood up and went out to join her. She took a long hard look around the balcony, which was around six feet wide and maybe twelve feet long. Fiona was right; against all the odds it was empty. Cass wasn't sure whether to be relieved or panic-stricken. They were three floors up.

She looked over the handrail. Below them was another floor and below that the roof of the restaurant – a drop of maybe fifteen or twenty feet. Not an impossible jump, but not likely unless Andy was prepared to risk a broken neck rather than face Fiona's wrath. Cass glanced upwards – there was another balcony above, sheltering the terrace, so that didn't seem very likely either. Then, just as Fiona – looking decidedly crestfallen at not having caught Cass *in flagrante delicto* – was heading back inside, Cass saw a tuft of something wedged in the long wooden palings that made up the dividers between the balconies. There was one on either side of her balcony. They were around eight feet tall and topped with a row of sharp spikes on a curved bar, obviously meant as a deterrent to balcony hopping by the drunk and foolhardy. The terrace next door seemed a lot smaller than hers, but there was a chair pushed up against one of the panels and a little tuft of fabric on the top. It was pale blue and looked uncannily like the colour of Andy's cotton shirt.

Nervously Cass followed Fiona inside.

'So what were you doing with the curtains shut? It's beautiful outside,' said Fiona, waving a hand out towards the terrace.

'Headache,' said Cass quickly. 'Flying. It always gives me a headache.'

'Really,' said Fiona, not looking at all convinced. 'And that's why you've got the doors closed as well presumably?'

Cass nodded. After all, why should she lie when Fiona could make up her own answers?

Fiona laughed conspiratorially and tapped the side of her nose. 'Well, you know what – I don't believe you, Cass. I heard a man's voice when I got out of the lift and I'd swear blind that it was coming from this room. I don't know where you've hidden him but good on y'girl! To be honest I wouldn't mind a bit of full-on lust in my life at the moment.' As Fiona spoke she flicked the crumpled sheets aside, presumably checking to see if Cass had hidden a man under the divan. 'Andy is being such a pain in the arse. We haven't had sex for months, he's barely speaking to me at the moment, and then when I woke up he'd buggered off somewhere. This was supposed to be a second honeymoon . . .' She laughed. 'Not that we've had a first one yet, but you know what I mean. Anyway, I'm going to go down to the bar, see if he's there – do you fancy a drink?'

Cass shook her head. There was no way she wanted to go anywhere with Fiona, least of all anywhere she might run into Andy. Cass realised as she showed Fiona out into the hallway that she hadn't really had time to think about what he had told her. Fiona was going to be devastated as well as livid when she found out.

Watching Fiona vanish into the lift, Cass turned to go back inside, and then noticed that the door next to hers – the one she assumed Andy had climbed over the balcony to get to – didn't actually have a number and appeared to be some sort of housekeeping or service room at the end of the corridor. The corridor then turned a right angle onto another broad landing, with bedrooms running off it. Keeping an eye on the lift just in case Fiona reappeared, Cass tried the door handle. It was locked.

'Andy?' she hissed, lips pressed close to the wood. 'Andy,

are you in there?' There was no sound from inside, so she knocked, wondering if perhaps he was hurt. After all, the partition between the balconies was topped by spikes; anything could have happened.

'Andy?' she said, louder this time, and knocked harder, feeling a flutter of panic. God, how would she explain it if he was injured? 'Andy, are you all right? Are you in there?' Cass paused for a few seconds, listening intently and at the same time wondering how it was exactly that inside half an hour she had gone from not knowing what the hell was going on to being a co-conspirator?

'Can I help you?' said a heavily accented female voice from behind her.

Cass, still holding the doorknob, swung round and came face to face with a young woman dressed in a blue overall, hair tightly pulled back into a ponytail; she was carrying a bundle of clean towels.

'I think my friend might be in here,' Cass said, pointing to the door.

The young woman looked puzzled. 'It's no possible,' she said in passable English. 'This is towels and sheets for this rooms. Not people.' She held out the bundle of clean linen to make her point.

Cass nodded. 'I know, but have you got a key?'

The girl looked confused. 'You want me to open it?'

Cass nodded again.

The girl shrugged and then pulled a long chain out of her overall pocket, on the end of which was a huge bunch of keys, and unlocked the door. She pushed it open and stood to one side so that Cass could look. The cupboard was quite narrow and lined along both sides with slatted wooden shelves, each of them neatly stacked with towels and sheets. At one end was a small window around a foot square. It was closed.

'No people,' the girl said.

Cass had to agree with her. No people.

So where the hell was Andy? Cass thanked the girl, who pulled the kind of face that implied it was nothing in the great scheme of things, then she locked up and headed down the other corridor, leaving Cass alone outside the cupboard door wondering what had happened to him.

Maybe Andy was more agile than he looked and had gone up and over the roof; maybe he had dropped like a cat onto the flat roof of the restaurant below, climbed down the rough stone wall and was even now sipping a margarita in the bar.

Cass was torn – did she carry on looking, did she assume it was all okay, go back to her room and do nothing? Where the hell was he?

'Psssssst.' It looked as if she might have the answer.

Cass looked back along the corridor towards her room; Andy was peering round the door of the room on the far side of hers. To her surprise, Cass felt nothing but relief.

'Where did you go?' she said.

'Over the partition onto the balcony next door—'

'Yes, but what about the chair, and the fluff?'

Andy looked at her as if she was crazy.

'Oh never mind,' Cass said. 'I thought you'd gone this way,' she pointed towards the linen store.

'No. I managed to get over the other side, and someone had left the shutters undone. Thank god there was nobody in the room.' He smiled. 'Thanks.'

Cass stared at him. 'Thanks?'

'For listening, and for not saying anything to Fiona. I didn't mean to put you on the spot. Look, I better be going . . .' He pointed to the stairwell.

And then he was gone and Cass realised that there were lots of things that she wanted to say to him.

Back in her room, Cass phoned home; apparently back at the shop everyone was okay, it was still raining, and her mother was cooking some sort of Cypriot meat and vine-leaf thing to celebrate Cass's holiday in the Med.

'It feels a bit like we're on holiday too,' said Nita as she arranged the vine-leaf wrapped bundles in a oven-proof dish. She and Rocco were in the kitchen; they had a bottle of wine open. They were already on their second glass.

'Shame about the weather in that case. You reckon we can get a refund?' said Rocco.

'How about we have a party or something?' said Nita, ignoring him.

'Are you serious?'

'It would be fun; it'll take your mind off the rain. And besides, isn't having a party what you do when the grown-ups are away?'

'In case it escaped your notice, we *are* the grown-ups, remember?' said Rocco.

'Oh phooey – you might be. There's that fabulous refectory table downstairs in the shop – maybe we could have people round for dinner? Actually, we could have the party down there. It's the perfect party pad.'

'I'm not sure Cass would like it,' said Rocco.

Nita waved the words away. 'Oh come on, she wouldn't know . . .'

Rocco raised his eyebrows. 'Isn't that what all teenagers say as soon as the grown-ups are away?'

Nita pulled a face. 'You're no fun.'

Rocco drained his glass. 'I think you'll find I am – how long have we got till the leaves are done?'

Nita giggled. 'About half an hour.'

'Plenty of time,' Rocco purred as he pulled her closer.

Chapter Nine

'So I would like to welcome you all to Cyprus, most especially to our host hotel the Athena Grande and to the very first Cyprus international a cappella choir festival. Tonight eat, drink and be merry, for tomorrow we sing. Ladies and gentlemen – I'd like to propose a toast: to the *choir*!'

There was a great cheer as the assembled company lifted their glasses and responded, 'The choir.'

Cass, Fiona, Andy and the others were sitting in the huge dining room of the Athena Grande at a mass of circular tables set with flowers, wine glasses and candles. On a dais, at a long table, the various choral leaders and musical directors sat with their wives and partners, looking down onto a room packed to the gunnels with choirs of every description from gospel through hot rock to majestically Bulgarian.

As the master of ceremonies and chief festival organiser, Perry Hulme – a small, enthusiastic American who was apparently something big in the USA–European A Cappella Alliance, an organisation he managed to make sound like the musical equivalent of NATO – sat down, there was thunderous applause and cheering.

To make things more interesting, the choirs had been split up and seated at various tables around the room, which was how it was that Cass found herself sitting between Estonian Bekya, a very dour, gaunt-looking man, thin as string with hair the colour of rank butter, and George, a great big jolly Father Christmas-lookalike who had flown in from Vermont 'along with my good lady Kathleen, a most talented soprano and my daughter Eleanor-Jean who sings tenor', and who laughed a lot.

As the formalities concluded, a great posse of waiters and waitresses descended on the tables with trays and started serving up the first course in what Bekya explained, in halting English, was a selection of traditional Cyprian meze – a seemingly endless stream of little dishes made up of olives, village salad, local fish, warm bread, halloumi cheese, fresh vegetables and grilled local meat – followed by fresh island-grown fruits cut into slices, all prepared in a variety of ways and served in terracotta bowls.

'It is traditional locally to serve seven courses,' Bekya said sagely, tearing off a piece of bread from a warm loaf drizzled with what turned out to be olive oil and lemon juice. 'I read it in a guidebook. Would you like me to name them for you?'

Cass stared at him. 'Are you serious?'

Bekya nodded. 'Oh yes – their advice would be don't rush to eat everything. Savour the tastes and, even though the bread seems very nice, unless of course you are looking to rapidly gain weight, to just take a very little. See . . .' He tore off a piece as an example. It was huge.

As Cass raised her eyebrows, deadpan Bekya continued, 'I personally am hoping to gain around a stone while I'm here. My new girlfriend, she hates skinny men.'

After the first three courses – one of bread and olives, taramasalata and hummus, another of little bowls of salad, the next of zucchini cut into batons and fried in the crispest and lightest of batters, George leaned over and said in a stage whisper, 'You think they're gonna be serving any real food?'

'What kind of thing had you got in mind?' asked Cass, as George nervously eyed the dishes being delivered to the table.

'Maybe a twelve-inch Americana and some loaded potato skins, or a T-bone and a side of cheesy fries – I mean, they have that most places.'

Bekya pushed one of the newly arrived dishes closer. 'Why don't you try some of this?'

George pulled a face.

'It's very good,' Bekya continued, tipping back his head to down an anchovy like an eager seal.

George's face was a picture,

Bekya handed him a plate of deep-fried calamari.

The waitress, taking his expression of horror for enthusiasm, set a heaped bowl of squid stuffed with rice, peppers and onion down alongside it. It was more than George could cope with – he beckoned her closer. 'Scuse me, miss. Could you maybe fix me a burger and fries?'

Bekya leaned in to join the conversation. 'Proper food,' he added with a wink. The girl smiled and headed back towards the kitchen.

George was really missing a trick, as the squid was fabulous. In fact all the food looked and tasted superb and, washed down with local wine, Cass couldn't think of a better way to kick off the festival. Bekya was right; it wasn't a meal that could be rushed, and, more than that, it really was the perfect way to break the ice.

The waiters and waitresses patiently explained what each of the dishes were – the stuffed squid, the chargrilled aubergine slices served with lemon juice, the anchovies, the little balls of minced lamb, the huge succulent prawns sautéed in butter and garlic; it seemed to go on and on. Around the table the diners dipped and sipped while everyone compared notes and chatted about the food. Across the table opposite Cass sat a rather timid tenor from the All Stars who, far from home, and several glasses into the local plonk, was flirting outrageously with a lady from Ireland on one side and a Cypriot girl on the other. He grinned when he noticed Cass looking at him, and lifted his glass in salute – he was obviously having a whale of a time.

Cass rapidly realised that appearances could be deceptive. Sitting alongside her, Bekya, was a scream, with a wickedly dry sense of humour, while George who, after having eaten his way through a couple of burgers and a plate full of fries, explained that he was on a mission from God and had long ago welcomed Jesus into his poor sinful life, was – well, just plain evangelical. He believed amongst many other things that drinking alcohol was a sin, as was the consumption of anything that 'struck the senses as strange and unnatural'. God alone knew how he felt about fornicating tenors but Cass felt – from the laughter and double entendres raging on the far side of the table amongst the gigglesome threesome – that they would all find out by the end of the evening.

Choirs, sober or half cut, were in it for the singing as well as the social life, so by the time the fruit and coffee were served, songs were breaking out like bush fires all over the dining room. Cass caught snatches of local songs, pops songs, three- and four-part harmonies, barbershop, folk songs and international classics.

Bekya, well into his cups, turned to Cass. In his thick

Eastern European accent he drawled, 'So, Cassandra, do you know the song "My Way"?'

Cass laughed. 'Is there anyone who doesn't know it?'

'It is my favourite song,' said Bekya. 'I have tried to persuade my choir to sing it, it is a beautiful song, it comes from the heart.' And with that he got to his feet, took a deep breath and broke into the opening lines.

To Cass's left, Evangelical George pulled a face, obviously a little unsure as to whether letting a Commie loose on an Ole Blue Eyes classic came under the heading of sin or was something that struck the senses as strange and unnatural.

'I've got one for you,' said the Irish girl, sitting next to the All Stars tenor on the far side of the table. '"Galway Girl"? It's one of the songs we've been working on in the choir, but sure the chorus is simple enough. You'll pick it up in a jiffy . . .'

Which, despite all manner of language barriers, they did. From there they ran roughshod over Elvis, African chants, the Beatles and something obscure that involved lots of droning over three notes from Bekya.

Several choruses, a coffee and a couple of liqueurs later, Cass headed – a little unsteadily – off into the maze of corridors behind the main dining room to find the toilets, and repair the havoc that almost three hours of solid eating, drinking and having fun had wreaked.

Music really was an international language. People were singing together in the hallways, creating unlikely quartets in the foyer, and Cass suspected she could hear at least one intrepid soloist from behind the closed doors of the men's toilet.

Outside in the hallway, Welsh Alf was busy checking his rockabilly quiff in a large mirror, while alongside him

Ray was sorting out his jacket and cuffs. There was more than a whiff of aftershave in the air.

'Don't you two look the cat's pyjamas?' said Cass with a grin as she made her way towards them. 'Having a good time?'

'Oh yes. Great night, great night,' said Alf, all smiles, eyes bright with drink. 'I was worried that it was all going to be – well you know – a bit stuffy, to be honest, specially with it being a competition and all that, but it looks like it's going to be a real good laugh, doesn't it? I almost wish I'd brought the missus along now.'

Cass smiled.

'So how's it going?' asked someone from behind her. Cass swung round and came face to face with Andy.

She smiled politely. 'We were just saying it's going a lot better than we thought it would. How about you?'

He smiled. 'It almost makes me wish I could sing. We've got some really interesting people on our table. Fiona wasn't awfully keen on us being separated so I had a quick word with Alan and he said we could sit together.'

At which point Fiona came out of the loo, still pressing her lips together after what was presumably a lipstick repair job.

'Oh there you are,' she said to Andy. 'I thought maybe you'd disappeared again . . .' Then, catching sight of Cass, she painted on a tight little smile. 'Well, there you are too. There's a coincidence. How's it going?'

'Great!' said Alf brightly, before Cass could reply. 'Food's good, isn't it? I was just saying I almost wish I'd brought the wife now . . .'

But Cass sensed that Fiona wasn't at all interested in Alf or his domestic arrangements.

'I think we'd better be getting back to our table,' Fiona said. There was just the merest hint of an edge in her tone. Holding Cass's gaze, Fiona slipped a proprietorial arm through Andy's. 'Did Cass tell you that she's pulled?' she asked.

'What?' said Cass in amazement.

'Really? Well bugger me, girl, you're a dark horse,' said Alf, grinning broadly. 'Who's the lucky fella? Anyone we know?'

'Oh come on, don't be so coy, Cass. I mean, we're all adults here,' said Fiona slyly, and then turned her attention back to Andy, Alf and Ray. 'Alan told me that Cass has got herself sorted out with a toy boy. In the hotel not more than ten minutes and she's got her hands on one of the managers.' Fiona grinned at Cass. 'Alan pointed him out tonight in reception. Nice work if you can get it, sweetie.'

In spite of herself, Cass felt her colour rising as Alf turned and smiled at her. 'Atta girl!' he said. 'Nothing like a little bit of holiday romance. But you want to be careful, you know what these foreign blokes are like – all smarm and charm, good-looking lady-killers – don't you let him break your heart.'

'Oh pul'ease,' Cass protested. 'The man showed me to my room.'

'Says you,' said Fiona. 'Nothing better than a little sun, sea and sex to put a bit of a twinkle in your eye . . .' At which point she made a great show of curling her leg around Andy and draping an arm across his shoulders. 'Which is just what we've got planned, isn't it, sweetie?'

Cass dropped her gaze, willing Fiona to shut up while Fiona finished off the manoeuvre by grabbing Andy by the chin and sticking her tongue halfway down his throat. While it had to be said that Andy didn't exactly fight her off, from the look of surprise in his eyes it was the last thing he was expecting.

'Did Andy tell you that we've arranged to upgrade too?' continued Fiona as she broke away. 'The room we were in was just so pokey – so there'll be a spare room on the floor with the rest of the choir now if you wanted to move back down.'

Cass managed a smile. 'I'm fine where I am, thanks. Excuse me . . .' and with that hurried into the loo, grateful to be away. Inside there was a queue. Some of the queue were singing. Cass took a look in the mirror; the combination of a four-hour flight and the afternoon's adventures with Andy, along with a huge meal and way too much wine were beginning to take their toll – and it wasn't the kind of thing that could be cured with a bit of lippie. Maybe it was time to head back to the hotel.

Inside the main hall, someone had broken out a balalaika and was plucking out a Greek folk dance, while someone else was heading back in with a guitar and god-alone-knew what else in a couple of instrument cases.

Cass stepped out onto the hotel steps for a breath of air.

Outside, despite the fact they could smoke in the hotel, Welsh Alf had made his way out into the moonlight, and he and a gang of fellow nicotine addicts were all busy enjoying a cigarette under the stars. The night was still warm, a stark contrast to the weather they had so recently left behind in England.

Cass pulled her jacket up around her shoulders as the breeze rolled in across the sea, prickling across her skin like the breath of a lover. The random thought made her feel lonely, and all at once she felt tired and much in need of her bed.

'You're not off are you, pet?' asked Alf. 'It's only just warming up in there. Morris has gone back to the hotel to pick up his harmonica and the little foreign lass who was on my table has asked the manager if we can borrow their piano.' He grinned. 'Or are you off to meet His Nibs? On a promise, are you?'

Cass smiled. 'You don't want to believe everything Fiona tells you.'

Standing in the shadows under a palm tree, Alf was reduced to a moonlit silhouette and a little single red-hot eye that glowed all the brighter as he took another long pull. 'Then why don't you come back in with the rest of us?' he asked. 'Don't let her faze you.'

Cass smiled. 'I'm fine Alf, and not at all fazed.'

She glanced back into the foyer and beyond that through folding doors into the hall, now heaving with people dancing. Realistically there was no way anyone would miss her if she left.

Someone else opened the door to join the smokers, and from inside came the sounds of a party in full voice. Cass headed off through the gardens and then down along the promenade towards their hotel. It seemed a world away from home. The lampposts were strung with fairy lights, their tiny twinkling beams reflected in the sea and, even though it was low season, most of the restaurants and bars were open and busy, music rolling out of them like an invitation, while others were alive with conversation and laughter.

For a moment or two it made Cass long to share it with someone. Nita and Rocco were right, it was too soon to settle for singledom. Unexpectedly she felt a great wave of sadness for loves lost, and from knowing that the only way she would find what she wanted from life or from

155

love was to risk everything all over again. It never really got any easier, unless of course you risked less, and shared less – but then, what was the point of that?

At times like this, Cass missed Neil more than it was possible to put into words; grief rolled through her like a dull cold ache, bringing tears unbidden to her eyes. Cass forced herself to smile and looked skywards. 'This is all your fault, you know,' she murmured. 'If you hadn't decided to bugger off and leave me here on my own, it would have been all right. You'd have loved it here. Great beer, weird people – we could have had such a lovely time.' A single tear rolled down her face. 'I miss you . . .'

Cass headed up the broad steps to the reception area of their hotel, feeling subdued and sad.

The Centrale was much smaller than the Athena Grande, probably less than a quarter of the size, but was homely and welcoming. Its stone walls and terraces, set with comfortable furniture and urns of plants and flowers, gave it real character. The façade around the ground floor made it look more like a local house than a hotel.

Small by resort standards, the hotel was set in a pretty pedestrianised area in its own small gardens, with a pool and a bar that opened up onto it. Around the pool and grounds were citrus trees and elegant evergreens, set alongside tubs of flowers, bougainvillaea, and hibiscus that clambered up over a large loggia and terrace. The main entrance was softly lit; tinted green-glass doors opened silently as Cass headed towards them.

There were a handful of residents in the foyer, mostly couples, reading or sharing a glass of wine or deep in conversation, sitting in easy chairs or on sofas gathered around low tables, sipping after-dinner cocktails and coffee. There was music playing. In the stone fireplace, someone had lit candles. It was a place where people lingered and relaxed rather than hurried through, using the space more like a sitting room than a thoroughfare.

Cass stood for a few seconds, taking in the view of the gardens beyond the reception area, enjoying the way the light played and reflected on the silky still waters of the pool, catching the heady scent of jasmine as it crept in through the open doors that led out to the poolside terrace. It was the most perfect evening.

'Hello, so have you had a good time tonight?' said a male voice behind her.

Cass, unsure whether the comment was being made to her, turned round to see Geno was standing behind the bar. Dressed in a black shirt with sleeves rolled back to his elbows, which was tucked into denim jeans, he was no less gorgeous than when she had seen him earlier in the day. If anything, out of his suit, he was even better looking.

And even more dangerous. Cass smiled. *Down girl*, she murmured, as her libido kicked in. Realistically, Geno was not the answer, she thought as he made his way over to her. Easy on the eye, though.

'It's been good,' said Cass, still smiling. 'Long day though. I'm tired. How about you?'

He grinned. 'Me too. Would you maybe like to join me for a nightcap? I'm off duty now.' Geno, not waiting for a reply, took down a glass from the shelves. 'So what would you like to drink?'

Cass surveyed the bottles thoughtfully.

Meanwhile Geno leaned a little closer. 'We could go dancing later if you like. You like to dance?'

Cass, who was thinking that dancing would probably

finish her off, hesitated just long enough for his grin to broaden.

'No strings,' he said, holding his hands up in surrender.

At which point another Greek boy in his early twenties, in a suit and obviously still on duty, walked past the end of the bar with a tray of empty glasses. 'And if you believe that, you'll believe anything,' he said in perfect English.

Geno groaned.

Cass laughed.

The young man slid the tray onto the counter top and held out his hand. 'Hi, I'm Nick – presumably you've already been introduced to Geno, my evil twin,' he said with a grin. 'His reputation is almost as big as his ego. Just watch him . . .'

Alongside her, Geno rolled his eyes. 'Take no notice, actually he is my cousin but he's only a puppy – he's just jealous,' he said.

Cass laughed as Nick winked and headed off towards the kitchen.

'So, what will you have?' Geno asked, trying to get his seduction back on track.

'Something light.'

'How about you try something local?' suggested Geno. 'We make a real good orange liqueur on the island. It's very nice with soda or lemonade.' As he spoke he took a bottle down off the shelf and showed it to her. 'You like to try?' he purred.

Cass nodded and Geno poured a measure out over half a glass of ice, topping it up with lemonade before opening a beer for himself.

'You know you are very beautiful. Don't take any notice of Nick – he's here on a working holiday. He likes to make fun – you know, to tease, to play – he's just a boy you know, not a man like me.' He paused and then said, 'How about we go out onto the terrace?'

'Don't the management mind you drinking with the guests?' asked Cass.

'No, it's fine,' he said, guiding her outside and pulling a chair up for her at one of the poolside tables.

'My uncle Alex, he owns the hotel. The whole of our family, we have all worked here at some time or other: me, my brothers and cousins, Nick . . .' He smiled again. 'Greek families, what can you say?—Have you been here before?'

'To Cyprus? No, this is my first time.'

While they made conversation, around them guests drifted upstairs and away to bed, leaving just a few die-hards by the bar. Cass stretched; it was almost time for her to call it a night.

'You know you are very beautiful,' Geno purred again.

Cass laughed. *Ten out of ten for persistence,* she thought. 'And you are a terrible flirt.'

His eyes lit up with mischief. 'You can't hold that against me. Would you like me to top up your drink?'

Cass looked at her glass; she had barely been aware of drinking it. 'Why not?' she said.

He smiled. 'My thoughts exactly. Same again?'

Meanwhile, down at the Athena Grande, an impromptu variety show had broken out in the dining room, with an ad hoc band, dancers, singers, jugglers, and goodness knows what else waiting in the wings. At this particular moment, an enthusiastic and appreciative audience was cheering a couple of belly dancers on.

Fiona was talking to a couple of altos from the All Stars

at their table, and they had been joined by another soprano and a couple of tenors.

Stuck on the fringes of the conversation, Andy could feel the mobile phone in his jacket pocket. He'd set it to vibrate and it was buzzing like an angry insect in his pocket. Fiona glanced across at him, almost as if she guessed. 'Are you all right?' she asked.

Andy smiled. 'Just tired. I was just going to go and get a breath of fresh air. Anyone else want another drink?'

'Oh, yes please,' said one of the altos, pulling her handbag up onto her knees. 'If you're going to the bar, I'll have a white wine, please.'

'It's fine,' said Andy, waving away her offer of payment. He caught the eye of one of the other women who had dragged a chair up next to Fiona. 'What would you like?'

'A Bacardi and coke.' A few minutes later, Andy headed off towards the main bar, armed with a list.

His phone had to have rung at least half a dozen times in the last fifteen minutes. The bar was packed to the gunnels with revellers. Gamely Andy joined the press of bodies, pulling out his phone. And as he did it rang again in his hand. It was Amelia.

After Amelia had turned up at the concert, he'd gone through the numbers on his phone with a fine-tooth comb just in case she had messed around with it – and sure enough, she'd added her name and phone number in the directory so that it would come up in the caller display whenever she rang.

He'd erased it out so that now just the number flashed up, but Andy knew the number off by heart. It was tempting to let it go to voice mail, but experience told him that she would just keep on ringing and ringing until he answered, and how long would it be before his phone was lying around and Fiona picked it up? 'Hi Amelia,' he said, pressing the phone tight to his ear so that he could hear her over the hullabaloo of the bar.

'Where are you?' she asked petulantly. 'I've been ringing you for hours – where have you been?'

'I'm away for a few days – we discussed this. Are you okay?'

'Where are you?'

'I'm in Cyprus.'

'What do you mean, is it on business?'

'No, I'm—'

'Oh no, don't tell me, you're with Fiona, aren't you?' Amelia snapped, cutting him short and rolling the name around in her mouth like it was a bad taste.

'Yes you knew that,' he said, talking too loudly, finger in his ear. *This whole thing was a mess.*

'Sounds like you're at a party.'

'Amelia, I can't talk for long. What's the matter?'

'They've thrown me out.'

'What?'

'They've thrown me out,' she said, more emphatically this time.

'Who's thrown you out?'

'You know I was sharing this place with Dougie and Bo?'

'Uh-huh,' he said noncommittally. Andy had no real idea who she was talking about or really where she was living. In the months since they'd first met, Amelia had been vague about her living arrangements and never invited him to go back to where she was staying and so, after a while, Andy had stopped asking; it didn't pay to upset her. So instead he picked her up in the car, met her

161

in pubs and clubs and out-of-the-way places where Fiona wouldn't see them.

'Well, they want the room back and so that's me . . . out. What am I going to do now, Andy? I've got nowhere else to go . . .' She left the question hanging.

'Won't they let you stay until you find somewhere else?' Andy said, easing his way in to the queue behind a Pavarotti-sized man and a woman who was so thin you could have grown beans up her, phone still pressed to his ear.

'God, you don't know them. I mean, they are just so arsy, and Dougie is being so unreasonable. I mean I've told him at least ten times that I'll pay him something towards the bills when I get some money, and okay, so maybe I didn't put the stuff back that I'd had out of the fridge, but Christ, he can be so unreasonable. I mean, okay so yes, I *have* been paid but I need that money. I told him. I've got things to buy – things for the baby.' She lingered over the word *baby*, her trump card, her lever, but Andy wasn't falling for it. So far she had already borrowed five hundred pounds off him and he'd had no sign that any of it was coming back.

'The baby doesn't need anything yet.'

'But I do,' snapped Amelia. 'I need to eat.'

'Of course you do, but you're still working, aren't you?'

'I know, but I lost my purse and Billy, the guy there – at work – said that he wouldn't sub me any more of my wages. I mean how unfair is that? I've earned it. I mean, it's my money – and I had to walk in to work because I hadn't got the bus fare. The guy can just be such an arsehole.'

Talking to Amelia was like walking through a room full of flypapers. One step and you were stuck on something, peel that away and before you knew it you were stuck on something else.

'I'm always having to sort stuff out for him, and okay, so he did say I wasn't to go on the Internet while I was at work but for fuck's sake, I mean what century is this guy living in? Ten minutes on Facebook, that's all it was, and when I said that, he starts going on and on about me being late every day. Which is his fault because he wouldn't give me the money I'm due, for my bus fare. So I said I know my rights, you sack me and I'm going to take you to a tribunal. I've seen him looking up my skirt. And I'm pregnant. . . . And he said I might as well get my things and go home then and that he'd see me in court. Bastard.'

'Whoa,' said Andy, leaping in to the void. 'So are you telling me you've been sacked and you're getting thrown out of your digs?'

'It isn't my fault,' she said.

Andy sighed. It never was. Nothing, none of it was ever Amelia's fault. Ever. Like the baby; she'd told Andy it was an accident, she'd got no idea how she'd ended up pregnant, she'd been on the pill and the baby was a mistake, that she hadn't meant it to happen, but that wasn't how it felt to Andy. Life on planet Amelia was always a train-wreck.

'Anything important?' said a voice behind him.

Andy turned round. Fiona looked at him expectantly. 'Hi,' he said, and then shook his head, covering the mouth-piece to answer her and miming as much as speaking. 'No, no – it's fine.' Then, 'Look, I'm sorry,' he said into the phone, 'I'll give you a ring when I get back. Okay?'

'What?' screamed Amelia indignantly. 'No, it's not okay, Andy. You can't, you—' but even as she was shrieking furiously, Andy was pressing the red button to end the call and scurrying round inside his head to come up with an answer to Fiona's next question.

Which was, 'And who is so important that you've got to ring them while we're away on holiday?'

'Actually they rang me.'

Fiona lifted her eyebrows.

'It's some guy wanting to see if I wanted to go to his leaving do on Friday.'

'And you said . . . ?' asked Fiona.

'He was out of luck.' Andy indicated the crush of people around the bar, 'Sorry it's taken so long but the queue is so slow.'

Fiona nodded. 'Maybe you should be a bit pushier. Who was it who rang you from work?' She said it casually. In all fairness, Andy couldn't blame her for being suspicious. Trouble was, the longer this went on, the more trapped he felt by both of them. He hated lying to her. Maybe Cass was right, maybe he should just tell Fiona, get it over and done with. After all, when it came right down to telling her, there wasn't a good time.

Fiona was watching his face, waiting for a reply.

'Maybe we could find another bar,' Andy said. 'I'm sure they can't have only one in a hotel this size.'

Fiona glanced round the room. 'You're probably right. Maybe we could ask someone. So *who* was it who rang you?'

'Mitch,' he said, the lie tripping off his tongue.

'Mitch,' Fiona repeated, as if filing the name away for future reference.

'Uh-huh,' said Andy, rifling through his pockets to check he had his wallet. 'I think you probably met him at last year's Christmas Party, kind of chunky with curly hair? Works in sales? Ex-rugby player?'

'Right,' she said. Ahead of them the queue had finally begun to move. He could see Fiona considering, sifting through the photo album of her memory for Mitch. The only good thing from Andy's point of view was that it wasn't a complete lie. Mitch *was* leaving, like dozens of others he'd been made redundant as part of the company restructuring, so if Fiona rang – and the way things were going it was more than possible – then Mitch would have already left by the time they got home. Andy also knew for a fact that Mitch had been planning a leaving party, he just hadn't been invited; but no one else would know that.

Fiona nodded, although he guessed she wasn't altogether convinced. Andy shuffled forwards – the problem was that the more he lied, the harder it was to find a way to tell Fiona the truth. One lie had seeded a forest of others.

Cass was right; they should talk. Andy looked across at Fiona. He knew how much Fiona wanted a baby. How would she feel once she knew he already had one?

'Penny for them?' she said, retouching her lipstick and pressing her lips together to blot them.

'Sorry?'

'You know, for your thoughts. What are you thinking? Penny for your thoughts.' She paused, waiting for a reply. 'Oh come on, Andy – keep up. We *are* having a severe sense-of-humour failure, aren't we?' she said, dripping sarcasm. 'This is supposed to be a romantic get-away and you're walking around with a face like a wet weekend.'

She was right of course. 'Sorry,' Andy said, even though it sounded lame.

Fiona's shoulders dropped miserably. 'Oh, for god's sake, Andy. Look, I know things at work aren't going well and it must be hard for you, but let's just enjoy ourselves while we can, shall we? It'll all still be waiting for you when you get back. Won't it?'

Andy nodded. He already knew that. Amelia certainly wasn't going to go away. Maybe now was the moment to tell Fiona. Just come out with it, get it over and done with, deal with the fallout. Hadn't Fiona just said she wanted to know what was on his mind?

Andy took a deep breath, steeling himself for what was to follow. 'Fee, there are things we really need to talk about,' he began. 'I know this may not be the ideal time but I—'

Fiona held up her hand to quieten him. 'Not now.'

'What do you mean, not now? You just said—' he began.

'I know what I said,' said Fiona, cutting him short. 'But when I said "penny for them", what I was hoping was that you might say something romantic – something lovely. Something, *anything*. For god's sake, Andy, we're on holiday. You always ruin everything.'

He stared at her, but had no idea how to reply.

Fiona sighed. 'I was really hoping that we could – you know – just relax and chill out, rekindle a bit of romance. I thought you might even have something to ask me, you know . . .'

Andy waited, not daring to second-guess what *you know* might mean.

Fiona continued, 'I know you've said that you haven't really planned on a family, but in some ways this would

166

be the ideal time to start one, wouldn't it? We've got time off together, away, there's no pressure.' Her voice was conniving, wheedling.

No pressure? Andy stared at her, was she mad? They had discussed it before, for hours, for days, weeks – he didn't want a baby. He loved kids but being a dad had never been up there on his must-do list, even though now he was having to revise it. More to the point, although Andy couldn't bring himself to say it so brutally, Andy didn't want a baby with Fiona.

Fiona, meanwhile, was in full flow. 'I really think that a baby is just what we need. It would give us both something to look forward to, to focus on, Andy, to plan for – to take your mind off work. I think it would be good for us. Tell you what, to be honest I don't really want another drink. How about we go back to the hotel? I don't know about you, but I'm exhausted.' She smiled slyly and winked.

Andy felt his heart lurch. There was no mistaking what was on Fiona's mind. She caught hold of his hand. 'Wouldn't it be romantic to make our first baby while we're here – on holiday? We'd always remember it.' She giggled and pressed herself against him. 'We could call him Cyprus,' she purred. 'You know, like Brooklyn Beckham. It's the kind of name that would work even if it was a little girl, like Paris Hilton. Cyprus Phillips-Sharpe has got a really nice ring to it. I was thinking we'd be hyphenated.'

Andy could think of a lot of things he'd rather be.

Chapter Ten

Cass was comfortably settled into one of the chairs by the pool at Centrale. She and Geno were amongst the last half-dozen people sitting out on the terrace. Cradling her second or third drink, she had spent the best part of an hour listening to Geno telling her just how lovely she was and how he would like to show her the island. He really, really would. Trouble was, the day was catching up with her and Cass could feel her eyelids fluttering, her head nodding forward.

'You look ready for bed,' he purred. 'Or I'm boring you maybe?'

Cass snapped to. 'Sorry, no no, not at all – it's just been a really long day. I think I should go up to my room.'

'You maybe want me to show you up there?' he said in a low voice. 'A beautiful woman like you really shouldn't be going to bed alone.'

Cass stared at him, struggling to suppress a laugh – it was obvious that although he said it in a light, joking way, he meant every word. When it came to lechery, Geno was quite unstoppable.

'No, thanks for the offer,' she said, 'but I can probably find it on my own, thank you, and thanks for the drink . . .'

'Well, well, well, what have we got here?' said a voice from across the hotel foyer. Cass turned to watch Fiona and Andy making their way across the terrace towards them, catching the look of surprise on Andy's face as he clocked Geno sitting opposite her.

'Well, hello there,' said Fiona, grinning. 'I wondered where you'd got to.'

Geno – ever attentive – got up and pulled out the chair for Fiona.

'Have you had a good evening? Would you like a drink?' he asked pleasantly.

Fiona tipped her head from side to side in a show of weighing up the options. 'Well, I'm not sure. I mean, I wouldn't like to interrupt anything,' she purred. 'Maybe you two love birds want to be alone?'

'I can assure you you're not interrupting anything,' said Cass. 'I was just going up to bed.'

'Really?' said Fiona, as she sat down in the proffered chair, eyes alight with mischief. 'In that case, maybe I should save you from yourself – I'll have a white wine.'

Cass picked up her handbag. 'Let me get these Geno.'

Smiling, he waved Cass's offer away. 'No, really it's my pleasure. So you would like . . . ?' He hesitated over what to call Fiona.

'Fiona,' Fiona said, 'and this is my partner, Andy. We'll have a white wine and a beer, won't we?'

Andy nodded. As Geno headed for the bar, Fiona leaned closer. 'Yum, yum, very nice. No flies on you, are there? Are you sure that we're not interrupting anything?'

'No, I was just about to go upstairs on my own. He's really not my type.'

Fiona pulled a face. 'Really? What a waste – if he was mine I wouldn't waste time talking.'

'The guy's a professional lech,' protested Cass.

'And your problem with that is *what* exactly?' laughed Fiona, watching Geno's progress to the bar. 'My god, he has got the cutest bum.'

Andy looked uncomfortable.

Cass reddened. 'Please Fee, behave yourself – even if *he's* like that, I'm most definitely not.'

Fiona winked. 'That's not what I heard. I saw the state of your bedroom this afternoon – remember?'

The next fifteen minutes or so were the most uncomfortable Cass had had in a long time. Fiona, glass in hand, managed to make everything she said sound salacious and came out with more double entendres than Graham Norton. She was tipsy, flirtatious and seemingly unstoppable. And Geno matched her word for word.

It was obvious from the first couple of remarks that Fiona assumed Cass was planning to take Geno upstairs as soon as their backs were turned, and that she had already spent the afternoon in bed with him. In the end, Cass stopped protesting because it was painfully obvious that she was just adding fuel to the fire. Five minutes in to the conversation, and it was also obvious that Geno was in his element. Andy's contribution, which was to suggest that it was high time they all went to bed, brought on hoots of laughter and a suggestive wink from Fiona.

'Don't you think maybe you've had enough?' suggested Andy when Fiona asked Geno to get another round in.

'We're on holiday, Andy,' Fiona protested. 'God, you can be such a killjoy,' she said, waving Geno away to refill all their glasses.

As soon as Geno was on his feet, Cass made her escape, thanking Geno for his company and bidding them all good night before hurrying upstairs, glad to finally be on her own.

'Come on, come back,' called Fiona. 'Don't be a party pooper.'

Cass waved the words away. 'Good night. See you tomorrow.' She smiled at Geno who shrugged, *what can you do?* Cass didn't wait to find out and, instead, headed for the stairs and the sanctity of her room.

Her room on the third floor was lamplit and someone had been up and turned down the bed. With its balcony and view out over the bay, her room was the perfect antidote to the crazy goings-on downstairs.

Through the open window Cass could hear the sea rolling up onto the shore. She slipped off her shoes and padded out onto the balcony, settling down to watch the night sky.

Cass had been looking forward to the All Stars' trip to Cyprus for weeks, but she could see that without some careful manoeuvring it was going to be spoilt by Fiona's mood and the tension between her and Andy.

From somewhere inside the room, Cass could hear her mobile ringing and decided to ignore it. Realistically there was nothing that couldn't wait until morning. Probably . . . was there?

Her brain clicked a notch; unless of course it was Rocco or Nita. Maybe there was a leak in the plumbing, maybe they couldn't find the stop-cock, maybe the cat had got run over, or the dog had chewed through a live cable. Cass closed her eyes, trying to shut out the cacophony of possible disasters, knowing full well that she wouldn't be able to rest now until she knew who was calling and why.

It was Rocco. She picked it up half a ring before voice mail kicked in.

'Hi sweetie,' he said. She could hear music in the background and voices and raucous laughter. 'I know it's late but I thought I'd give you a ring – you in bed?'

'No, I'm fine. What's that noise?'

He laughed. 'What noise?'

'The music.'

'Oh that. Me and your mum decided to invite a few friends back; we didn't think you'd mind. Bas and Mike and Louise – you remember Bas—'

There was a loud crash and an explosion of drunken laughter that cut him short before he could finish the sentence.

'What the hell was that?' said Cass.

'Oh nothing – it's fine: is that jet lag or early onset middle age? Stop fretting. Nothing is the matter. I thought we'd give you a ring, you know what your mum's like. We hadn't heard anything from you and we wanted to make sure you'd landed safely and were okay.'

'Everything is fine. When did you decide to throw a party?'

'It's not really a party, Cass, it's just a spur-of-the-moment thing – we asked Lucy from across the green and the people from next door in case it gets a bit loud.'

'Loud,' snapped Cass. 'What do you mean loud, Rocco? If I'd wanted my house wrecked I'd have asked the boys to come home for the week.'

'Don't be silly,' said Rocco. 'Nothing's going to get wrecked. Do you want to speak to your mother?'

And with that he was gone, leaving Cass with a soundtrack of laughter and chatting and some hardcore Hendrix, before Nita grabbed the receiver. 'Hi darling – how was the flight?' she said, giggly with high-pitched good humour.

'It was fine, are you stoned?' asked Cass accusingly. There was silence. 'Rocco told me that you're having a party . . .'

'I know. Well we are, and we're having a lovely time, you never told me your neighbours were so lovely – hi Peter, Harry, nice to see you – yes, just go on through, drinks in the kitchen.'

'Mum?' said Cass.

'Yes darling, we just wanted to let you know everything is just dandy here. We're fine, the animals are happy and we sold that Chesterfield you were moaning we would never shift.'

'For . . . ?'

'For the asking price plus delivery,' said her mum blithely.

Cass was actually going to say, *For god's sake, Mum*, but the sentiment was lost in a hoot of laughter coming from the receiver. Seems as if they had got the phone on loudspeaker. 'And the man said he'll be coming back to look at a desk. The roll-top?'

'Fabulous.' Cass sighed. 'And nothing's flooded or on fire?'

Her mother laughed. 'Not yet,' and then she added, 'Only joking, no of course not, everything is just fine. We've just got a few friends round – oh, and we had someone ring up about a room.'

'A room?'

'Uh-huh, she went on and on – said she needed to sort out somewhere to stay. A student?'

'For next summer?'

'Oh I don't know – it all sounded a bit vague.'

'It's probably the agency. If she rings back, I'm taking bookings – the rates are on a sheet by the phone in the workshop.'

'Oh okay,' said Nita, although she sounded distracted. 'Oh and then there was something about a job? In the shop?'

'I put a card in the newsagent's on Miller Street.'

'Right, well someone rang about that but I told her you were away at the moment in Cyprus.' Cass could hear some sort of mumbling and guffawing then Nita said, 'Look, I've really got to go, darling, Rupert's just shown up with Sonia and . . . No, don't worry,' she called to someone else, and then to Cass, 'It'll be all right. I'll get some carpet cleaner tomorrow – as long as you're all right, that's the main thing.' And with that Nita hung up – leaving Cass holding the phone, all alone in the silent room.

Chapter Eleven

The following morning, Cass was feeling a little delicate, not helped by the bright sunshine pouring into the hall where they were rehearsing. It was like something out of *Star Wars*, white and hot, searing into the retinas of the terminally hung over and the still three-parts pie-eyed. Outside the sky was agonisingly blue.

The All Stars were working with another choir, which meant that Fiona was standing a couple of rows back and Cass, picking her way through a flurry of notes, wondered about the etiquette of wearing sunglasses in doors – after all, it worked for Bono. Her head ached, her feet ached and her eyes felt as if someone had taken them out and sandpapered them.

And, despite everyone's best efforts, no one seemed quite able to get the hang of the tune that Varnia, a very nice, very patient woman from the Baltic, and leader of one of the other choirs, was going through, part by part, note by note, over and over again. Varnia appeared to be dressed in hippy assault gear, consisting of open-toed sandals, faded desert combat trousers and a turquoise kaftan. Her spiky blonde hair was wound up in a piece of camouflage netting hung with seashells, feathers and seed pods and she wore enough beads, bangles and earrings to set up a one-woman jewellery business – none of which was helping anyone's headache.

Around half ten she clapped her hands, ignoring the winces of pain and said, 'So, people, I think perhaps we should maybe take a little break for coffee. We all had a long day yesterday, and I think perhaps everyone is a little bit tired. Why don't you take it outside on the terrace? Grab a few lungfuls of fresh air and maybe rehydrate a little? We've had bottled water put out for you in the foyer – I'm sure it'll help.' It was a tactful approach.

Mornings had been allocated for singing – there were rehearsals and lots of optional workshops – and the afternoons were set aside for sightseeing. Cass had re-read the itinerary over breakfast rather than make conversation; not that many people had made it down, and those who had all looked a little peaky.

Cass picked up her bag and headed outside. Pegged to a notice board in the foyer were lists for people to sign up for day trips. In the quiet space away from the rest of the crew, Cass scanned down the lists and considered her options. There was lots of history and culture on offer. Would it be better to hide in her room and risk Fiona – or Andy, come to that – tracking her down, or should she go on one of the trips and risk them coming along? Fiona didn't strike Cass as a coach-trip girl, but you never could tell. So, ruins or island geology, flora and fauna? It was a tough call.

Meanwhile Nancy and Val, two beautifully preserved sopranos from the All Stars sashayed over, bearing cups and saucers, handbags over their arm in a manner that reminded Cass of the Queen on a state visit.

Apparently they were rehearsing in a room on the floor above with Oscar, another guest musical director who came from Spain and was a real sweetheart. 'He is such a flirt,' said Nancy with a girlish giggle. 'We've been in stitches all morning, haven't we Val? And you should see the way he moves.' She nodded towards the boards. 'See anything you fancy?'

And when Cass wasn't quick to reply continued, 'We're going to do the village tour this afternoon, aren't we, Val?'

'And the winery,' added Val, with a grin. 'Apparently the local wine is superb.'

'What about you?' said Nancy, tapping the board with one perfectly manicured nail.

Cass looked at the two of them, a vision in tailored pastels, and hesitated. The pair of them were great company but she certainly wasn't ready for the afternoon tea and comfy sandals brigade yet. Nancy tapped the board again. 'It says there's not a lot of walking.'

Was that meant to encourage her? Cass took another look at the list. Amongst other things was a guided walk of the mosaics on the outskirts of Kato Paphos, and other historical sites, including a tour of the Tomb of the Kings, which was apparently a city of the dead – Cass sighed; she knew how that felt. 'I think I'm probably going to do this one.'

The women nodded in unison. 'As long as you're doing something. Be a shame to come all this way and then spend the whole time tucked up by the pool with a book and a Bacardi Breezer,' they said, before heading back upstairs to the arms of Oscar.

Cass was just about to head back to Varnia's group,

when Nick appeared from the managers' office. He smiled. Cass found herself smiling too.

'So, you managed to get away from Geno's clutches last night?' he said, grinning.

Cass stared at him. 'How do you know?'

'He came to bed moaning about how he thought he was losing his touch.'

Cass laughed.

Nick glanced at the boards. 'You're thinking about going out on one of the trips?'

'Yes and no. I'm not sure which to go on – and if I want to go out this afternoon I'm supposed to sign up before twelve.' She moved closer and took a long hard look at the places on offer. 'Anything you'd recommend?'

Nick glanced down the list. 'The mosaics are pretty impressive,' he said.

'Oh, okay – and local too?'

He nodded. 'Actually, yes – they're about ten minutes' walk away – if you like I could maybe show you. I'm off this afternoon, if you fancy it . . .'

Cass smiled, searching around for an excuse. 'It's very kind.'

He grinned. 'Don't worry, I'm no Geno. It will do me good to get out. If I'm around here the staff just keep asking me questions and ringing my room . . .'

'Isn't that what managers are for?'

He nodded. 'Uh-huh, but not ones on their afternoon off. And besides, I'm only over here for a few months, part tourist, part wage slave, so I'm trying to see something of the island besides the Centrale. Getting away isn't always easy—'

'You mean I'd be a good excuse?'

He grinned. 'You could say that. It's hard to get away without one.'

'You live in?' Cass asked. The question was out before she realised how it sounded.

'Uh-huh, part of the time – I'm sharing a villa, but when we're on call the staff have rooms on the top floor, above yours. Anyway, if you're interested we could walk down after lunch, if you like.'

Cass hesitated long enough for Nick to grin. 'Don't tell me, your mother told you never to go off with strange men.'

Cass laughed. 'Actually you're right, she did, although she didn't take her own advice. You should see my stepfather.'

Nick smiled. 'Okay, well in that case I'd suggest this one.' He pointed to one of the sheets of paper. 'Kourion – after all, you are going to sing there. It is very impressive and they take you to other historic sites, to a castle and—'

Cass stopped him mid-sentence. 'Actually you know – I think I'd prefer to go to the mosaics . . . One thing I want to make clear, though. I'm really not looking for a holiday romance.'

Sometimes it paid to trust your instincts.

By way of a reply Nick grinned. 'That's good. Me neither.'

'Because I'm old enough to be your mother?' teased Cass.

He pulled a face. 'No – that wasn't what I was going to say at all. Age is no measure of anything. You're a very beautiful woman.'

Cass laughed aloud. Even if neither Nick nor Geno were her type, there was nothing quite like a bit of attention from a couple of good-looking guys to boost your ego – at the very least they didn't have a purse, she thought, wryly.

Nick giggled. It was such a warm, disconcerting sound. 'I picked that line up from Geno.'

'I'd let him have it back if I were you.'

'Actually I'm engaged, so I'm off the menu. How about we meet up at around three o'clock outside the hotel?'

Cass nodded, 'Three o'clock then?'

'Great – look, I have to go.' He smiled. 'See you later.'

Cass was just helping herself to a bottle of water to take back into the hall, when two things happened. First of all, Fiona appeared at the top of the steps that led down into the dining room, and secondly Cass's mobile rang. She hadn't realised that it was on, and so the ring tone took her by complete surprise. She was just relieved it hadn't gone off during the workshop.

'So, one not enough for you?' said Fiona, watching Nick heading off towards the office.

'No, I mean – it's not like that.'

'Really? So nothing going on between you and lover boy then?' said Fiona, as she picked up a bottle of water. 'Geno's gorgeous. To be honest, Cass, I don't know how you do it. I really wish someone was chasing me at the moment. Andy is being really odd.' She glanced around the almost empty dining room. 'Heaven only knows where he's got to. He told me he was going to explore the old town this morning. Me, I'd have preferred an extra couple of hours in bed.' She looked at her watch and then tapped the face with one perfectly manicured nail. 'We should be getting back to rehearsals.'

Cass meanwhile, was busy trying to dig the phone out of her bag.

'Oh I'd leave it,' said Fiona dismissively. 'If it's import-ant they're bound to ring you back or leave a message.

I mean, we're on holiday for goodness' sake. You can't do anything about it, even if it is important. I was saying the same thing to Andy. He's had god knows how many phone calls from work since we got here. What is he expected to do? Fly back? No respect for other people's privacy, some people.'

The phone stopped ringing just as Cass got to it. The missed call log said it was Rocco. Cass hesitated; she wasn't sure she wanted an update on the state of the carpet.

At which point Varnia came out and clapped her hands. 'Come along,' she said cheerfully. 'We have got a lot to get through before lunch.'

Making a mental note to call Rocco back later, Cass switched off her phone, tucked it back into her bag and headed back into the function room.

'So,' said Nita, showing the girl up to the top floor. 'This is the room. Lovely views. And then there's a shared bathroom this side.' She sighed and closed her eyes for a few seconds. Not that it helped. 'You'll have to excuse me, I'm feeling a bit delicate today. We had a late night last night.'

The girl smiled. 'It's really nice. The room.'

Nita nodded. 'It is, isn't it? So . . .'

The girl's smile broadened, 'So when can I pick up the key?'

As instructed, Nita had read the notes on the wall by the phone. 'I just need to take some details. If you'd like to come downstairs we can fill in the forms. What did you say your name was again?'

'Amelia,' said the girl, glancing out of the bedroom window at the green beyond. 'Amelia Cummins.'

* * *

Down by the harbour, Andy was sitting under an awning drinking good coffee and watching the world go by. On one of the jetties a large sailing ship dipped and tugged, testing its moorings; behind it a row of luxury cruisers moved gently on the swell, while in the shipping lane a whole flotilla of smaller boats came and went about their business – fishermen taking out anglers, a dive boat heading out to deeper water, full of people slick as seals in their borrowed wetsuits. In the water lapping the harbour wall, fish gathered in glittering schools waiting to be fed by the tourists, and on a sheltered breakwater, two pelicans basked in the morning sun.

It was comfortably warm, a light breeze rippling the shallow water up along the shoreline; the sun was so bright that the sea was almost impossible to look at without sunglasses.

Andy stretched, enjoying the warm breeze on his skin and the anonymous bustle of the people around him. This was the most relaxed he had felt for weeks. His phone was switched off, Fiona was safely tucked away in her singing workshop and there was no call on his time until 1.00, when they were meeting for lunch at the hotel. 'Meet up with everyone' was what Fiona had said, but that wasn't what she meant. What she actually wanted was for Andy to report back.

During the morning, Andy had explored the yellow stone castle that protected the harbour entrance – according to the guidebook there had been a castle on the current site, built and rebuilt since the Byzantines constructed the original.

Later in the day, Andy planned to wander around the wealth of mosaics and Roman villas that spread out in a huge historical excavation site beyond the harbour – although if Fiona had her way she would probably want him to join her in spending the afternoon by the pool while she read and topped up her tan.

Andy paused, aware of just how bitter he sounded. When the hell had that happened? And how? This wasn't the kind of man he was. And this certainly wasn't at all how he'd imagined his life turning out. At what point had he turned from man to henpecked mouse? And was that a mixed metaphor?

The arrival of the waitress offering to top up his coffee took Andy's mind off metaphors, mixed or otherwise. She was in her late teens, slim and blonde, with liquid brown eyes and a smile that lit up her whole face – and his too, come to that. She held out the coffee pot in his direction and he nodded and she carried on smiling as she filled the cup to the brim.

'You're having a nice time in Cyprus?' she said. Her accent was thick, but her voice and manner were charming.

He nodded. 'Very nice, thank you.'

She smiled again. 'I 'em practise my English,' she said, eyes alight with mischief. 'You don't mind?'

'No, not at all, where are you from?'

'Latvia.' The word rolled around her mouth like a marble. 'I have been here nearly six month . . .'

'Really?' He didn't know anything about Latvia but she smiled anyway.

'So you are here on holiday?' she asked, and then, before he could reply, she spotted another table looking for service. 'I am very sorry, but I have to go now,' and, still smiling, went over to take their order.

Andy sighed. How the hell had life got so bad that

making an impression on an eighteen year old was the high spot of his day? He had ended up in a situation that in no way resembled anything that he would have chosen. He wasn't weak. Or maybe he was? Andy watched the fishermen casting off the promenade, while his mind turned the same thoughts over and over.

The harbour was a lovely place; Andy was on holiday but he was unhappy: unhappy with his job, unhappy with his life and, most of all, the women in it. Cass had been right. Why couldn't he just come clean, spit it out about Amelia, whether Fiona wanted to hear it or not? It was so easy to say and so hard to do. He was being cowardly, something he despised.

Wasn't he denying her the chance to find the things that she wanted in life? Wasn't he being cruel and selfish hanging on to her when really he should take the pain and let her go? And it would be painful. Oh by god, it would be painful.

Fiona could be dark and hurtful when she was cornered, or angry or just pissed off – at the moment, she had every right to be all of those things. He was keeping so much from her, but if he opened up where did he begin? Did he just say it was over? Did he explain?

Hadn't he hoped when he first met Amelia that somehow she might offer him a ticket out? Hadn't he hoped that Fiona would find out by osmosis and dump him? Hadn't he hoped that somewhere in amongst the chaos there was a new life for him?

He and Amelia had had their first real get-together in the restaurant of a smart but impersonal businessman's hotel out on the bypass. He had been nervous, wondering if after all the talk she would turn up – the people in reception had given them sideways glances as she'd kissed him in the foyer, caught hold of his arm.

'I didn't know if you might chicken out,' were her first words. 'I've been really looking forward to seeing you . . .' and then she had slipped her arm through his and he knew then he was lost.

There had been all kinds of knowing looks from the waiters as they'd settled down at a table to talk. Amelia was very physical and emotional and Andy had reddened as one of the guys grinned at him. He wondered what the hell he would have said if Fiona had shown up at that moment.

Amelia was beautiful and young and manipulative and he had no idea how to handle her.

Across the harbour, a boat coming in to dock suddenly revved and then cut its engine, the sound knocking him out of his reverie. Andy took a mouthful of his coffee which had gone almost cold.

In idle moments he couldn't stop his thoughts returning again and again to Amelia, and what he should do about her and the baby. She was lovely, elfin-like, funny, quirky – such great company at first that he hadn't seen just how damaged, how manipulative or how strange she could be. That compelling child-like quality was both a charm and a curse – and now she was pregnant. God, it was all such a bloody mess . . .

'Excuse me,' said a soft female voice. 'You want that I should bring you the lunch menu?'

Andy looked up at the waitress. 'Sorry?' he said, refocusing on those big soft brown eyes.

She smiled. 'Now it is lunch time,' she said, pointing to her watch. 'Maybe perhaps you want something to eat?

A little fish – the fish is very good.' Andy watched her finding the words. She had a nice mouth. And then he had a flutter of panic.

'What's the time?'

The girl pulled a face, so he pointed to her watch again. 'The time?'

Comprehension dawned and she turned the face towards him. It was 12.35 and time he was gone. 'No food, thank you, I've got to be going,' he said, and picked up the little curled paper bills that she had so carefully tucked into a circular pot on the centre of the table, listing the coffee and cake he had already had.

'Can I pay you?'

She smiled again. 'Of course.'

He pulled out a couple of notes and handed them to her. She made as if to go back inside to get the change, but he shook his head. 'It's okay, keep it.' She smiled again, wider this time, and wished him a happy day. Andy decided not to disillusion her.

'What? What do you mean she's moved in?' said Cass incredulously. It was lunchtime and people were queuing to make their way around the buffet, which dominated one side of the dining room. Cass, halfway back in the queue and famished, had, up until two minutes earlier, had her eyes fixed on a large slice of quiche and a big bowl of salad. She was trying to keep her voice down.

'But we thought you said it was all right,' said Rocco, sounding bemused; thirty seconds earlier he'd rung to let Cass know that someone had arrived, loved her new room and was settling in nicely. 'Would you like to talk to your mother?'

'I can't believe you've let my spare room to a complete stranger – just like that.'

'But she said you knew,' protested Rocco. There was a pause. Cass didn't know what to say.

'And that you'd spoken. She did – really,' said Rocco. 'Your mum said something about someone coming through an agency.'

'Just let me talk to Mum.' Drunken Chinese whispers.

'Excuse me,' said the woman behind Cass. 'Can I get to the coleslaw?'

'Yes of course, I'm sorry,' said Cass, shuffling to one side as the woman elbowed her way into the gap, then watched as she piled her plate up with salad and ham and new bread. Cass was busy being the woman she hated, the woman who talked on the phone in public places, excluding the real live people around them, and at the same time slightly annoyed that the real live people were there at all – all this and now she had a lodger.

Meanwhile Rocco had handed the phone over to her mum. 'Hello darling – how are you?'

Cass couldn't bring herself to say anything nice, so Nita continued, 'Rocco went out with Buster first thing this morning while I was getting ready to go down to open the shop; anyway, the doorbell rang round the back of the cottage and I thought he'd left his key behind – and there she was on the doorstep.'

'I said you could take bookings, not take someone in.'

There was a deep silence. 'I thought you said the agency would send someone . . .'

'I said they might ring to organise for next year.'

'Well, anyway, she seems very nice. Her name is Amelia – she said that she knew you. I think she came here to

187

have a little chat – anyway, then she said that you knew who she was, that you'd talked to whatever his name is about her, and then she said she hadn't got anywhere else to go. I thought you must have known all about it.'

Cass felt her heart lurch. 'What?'

'Amelia, she said that you knew – oh, the name is on the tip of my tongue. Who is the man you're supposed to be stalking?'

'Andy,' said Cass, stunned.

'That's it – Andy.'

'And so you rented her my spare room?' said Cass, incredulous.

'Well, not exactly. I mean not straight away, no – I invited her in and offered her a cup of tea first.'

'Oh well, that's good,' growled Cass, her mind racing. 'I wouldn't want you to forget your manners.'

'Is there a problem?' said Nita.

Cass didn't know where to begin. 'Well yes – Amelia isn't a student, she is Andy's pregnant oddball girlfriend.'

There was an odd silence.

'Ah,' said her mother after a few seconds.

'Ah doesn't halfway cover it, Mum. I've got no idea what she's doing there . . .'

'I'm sorry, Cass,' said Nita, sounding increasingly anxious. 'I mean, she seemed so plausible – and she said she knew you and she looked really poorly. And then she told me that the people she had been living with had thrown her out – and I suppose I put two and two together and . . .'

'It's all right, Mum, it isn't your fault. Well, not entirely.'

'It's bitterly cold here today, and it looked like rain – I couldn't just leave her out on the streets.'

Cass sighed, torn between shock and disbelief. 'Mum, this isn't your fault – well it is, but it isn't . . . What I mean is, this isn't our problem. I'm not sure what's going on but this girl is nothing to do with me and I don't want her staying in my house. Can you get her on the phone, please?'

'Well I would, but she said she was going up to her room for a little lie-down.'

'It's not her room and I don't care whether she's in labour. Please, Mum, just get her on the phone,' said Cass.

Another woman next to her in the queue was manoeuvring around her as if Cass might lash out at any second. She smiled an apology; the woman dropped her gaze and scurried past.

'I'll go up and talk to her,' said Nita. 'She's such a little lost soul – I mean, couldn't she just stay till you get back?'

Cass sighed. 'No, no she couldn't,' she said between gritted teeth. 'Now if you could just get her on the phone then I'll try and sort this out.'

'But I'm in the shop at the moment, I can't leave,' said her mum and then added in a whisper, 'there's a woman in who wants to buy the green chaise. I'll put you back on to Rocco.'

Andy walked briskly along the harbour-side walk, not wanting to be late for lunch with Fiona. He hurried down past the shops and little cafes, back towards their hotel. The smell of garlic in the air piqued his appetite.

He checked his watch as he headed into the foyer of the Centrale; it was twenty to one-ish, which would give him enough time to grab a beer and a glass of wine and find a table out on the terrace before Fiona showed up.

Just as Andy was giving one of the bar staff his order, he spotted Cass hurrying towards him and smiled. 'Hi,' he began, not that she looked as if she was in the mood for small talk.

'I need to talk to you,' Cass said. She wasn't smiling.

'About last night,' Andy began. 'I'm really sorry, we didn't mean to interrupt—'

'I don't want to talk about last night,' snapped Cass. As she spoke, Cass pulled a mobile phone out of her pocket and waved it in his direction. 'I want you to ring Amelia now and tell her to get out of my house.'

'What?' said Andy.

'You heard me,' said Cass in a stage whisper. 'I want her out of my house.'

People in the foyer were starting to stare. 'I don't know what you're talking about,' he said.

'*What* did you say to her?' continued Cass.

Andy's eyes narrowed as he re-ran what Cass had said to ensure he had heard it correctly. 'I'm not with you,' he said. 'What did I say to who?'

'It's not rocket science. Amelia showed up at my shop this morning and managed to persuade my mother who is looking after it to let her in – to let her stay. *In my spare room.*'

'I don't understand.'

'*You* don't understand,' growled Cass, moving in closer. 'How the hell do you think I feel?'

Andy stared at Cass. 'I don't understand how she found you and why she thought you'd take her in.'

'Neither do I – but, according to my stepfather, she said that you had told her that I'd been talking to you and Fiona – *and that I had understood, and that I was kind and a good listener and had been really helpful.'* Cass's voice boiled with barely contained fury.

'Ah, yes,' spluttered Andy. 'Well I did say something like that.'

'And Amelia obviously presumed that if I was prepared to help you and Fiona, that she was included in the deal as well.'

Andy was struggling to keep up. 'How did she find out where you lived?'

Cass stared at him. 'How the bloody hell would I know, Andy? I have got no idea – what did you tell her?'

Andy paused, re-running the recent conversations he'd had with Amelia. 'I'm not sure really. I told her you'd talked to Fiona, and that you were the woman at the concert – and . .'

God, it was all coming back to him now. He'd been trying to make conversation that didn't involve Fiona or pregnancy, or homelessness or abandonment and all those demons that chased her. It had all seemed harmless at the time: Andy had told her that Cass ran an antique shop in town, that she was decent and kind and level-headed and had talked to Fiona, and Amelia after about five minutes of what was basically just chitchit, had sounded calmer and less upset. It hadn't occurred to him in a month of Sundays that Amelia would track Cass down.

'It was just conversation,' he said. 'I mean, I didn't think she would do anything – I mean not turn up.'

Cass sighed. 'Well she did.'

'I don't understand, why did they give her the room?'

'Because they're kind and gullible and I rent rooms out to students in the summer and when she showed up – well, there was some kind of misunderstanding and, to cut a long story, your precious Amelia just moseyed on in.'

'No . . .' Andy began.

'Oh yes,' said Cass.

'So there you are, Andy,' snapped Fiona. 'I've been looking for you all over the place.' She looked at Cass and smiled thinly. 'Sorry, was I interrupting something?'

Cass took a deep breath; Fiona's smile was glacial. Andy looked like a rabbit caught in the headlamps.

Cass hesitated; what the hell was she going to say? 'No, I was just –' she paused, reaching around inside her head for something plausible – 'Just asking if I'd seen you,' Andy finished, and glanced down at his watch. 'I was just saying I'd arranged to meet you at one – and it's barely five to. Oh, and I've ordered you a glass of wine. Would you like one, Cass?'

'We said half twelve,' said Fiona.

He frowned. 'Did we?'

Fiona pulled a face and then forced a laugh. 'I wish you'd listen to what I say, Andy. I've been looking all over the hotel for you. Did you know your phone is switched off?' Not waiting for a reply she continued, 'Anyway, I don't know about you but I'm absolutely famished. And I was thinking that maybe we could take a little nap after lunch.' She winked, and then turned her attention to Cass. 'Sorry, so Andy said you were looking for me – did you want something?'

Cass shook her head, not trusting herself to speak.

'Oh okay,' said Fiona, not sounding at all convinced. 'Have you signed up for any of the little excursions?'

'No, I was going to go out but something's come up.' She fixed Andy with a furious stare.

Fiona laughed and cut her short. 'Oh yes, I remember, I saw him this morning . . . all right for some,' she said and then turned her attention back to Andy. 'Right – so . . .'

'So,' said Andy, 'in that case how about we grab some lunch? It looks good.'

Fiona hesitated, sharp eyes moving along the snaking queue for the buffet tables. 'How about you go and get us some food, sweetie. I'd like a quick word with Cass.'

Cass felt her heart do an odd little double flutter. 'I don't . . .' she began.

'Oh, Andy can get us all something, can't you?'

Andy nodded, but Cass fleetingly saw a look of panic cross his face.

'Come on,' said Fiona briskly. 'You and I need to talk.' And with that, she stalked out onto the terrace.

Cass glanced at Andy and then said in a low whisper, 'You have to sort this out. You have to ring Amelia. I want her out of my house.'

He nodded, although Cass wasn't altogether convinced. Turning, she followed Fiona out onto the terrace, wondering what exactly was going to happen next. Was there going to be a big scene? Cass could feel a twenty-four-carat gold headache coming on. She slipped into a seat at the table Fiona had chosen and waited.

Fiona meanwhile began to pace, rubbing her hands, biting her lip.

'Fee—' Cass began, but as she spoke, Fiona rounded on her. 'Cass, I want you to tell me exactly what the hell is going on?' she said in a miserable voice.

Cass took a deep breath, steeling herself for the fallout, but Fiona hadn't finished.

'Are you deliberately rubbing it in? All that dirty flirty stuff with half the staff. I mean, you're old enough to be that boy's mother . . .'

Cass felt her mouth drop open in total amazement. This really wasn't the conversation she had imagined having. 'What?'

'Oh come off it,' snapped Fiona furiously. 'You heard me, you and your bloody toy boys. You know how bad things are between me and Andy at the moment, and there's you rubbing it in. That guy last night and then that boy this morning. What are you trying to prove? I mean, I'm as broadminded as the next person but – what will people think? This a choir trip, not an eighteen to thirties holiday.'

Cass was thunderstruck; everything was always about Fiona. Finally, when she spoke, Cass struggled to keep her tone even. 'Fiona, it's not like that at all, trust me. For god's sake, Geno's a lech and Nick's just being friendly. He's the same age as my boys—'

'Really? Well in that case why are you chasing him?' Fiona pulled a face and then, to Cass's horror, she saw Fiona's eyes filled with tears. 'Why you – why have *you* got him?'

'I haven't. I'm not doing anything with anyone.'

Fiona stared at her and then mumbled, 'Oh god . . .' But before Cass could say anything, Fiona sniffed, a great big tear rolling down her cheek.

'I've had enough of this. I'm sorry, Cass. You must think I'm such a bitch,' she said, and then, slipping into the seat opposite Cass, pulled a tissue out of her bag. 'I can't go on like this. Things aren't working out. I'm fed up with Andy, with my whole life. He is so bloody awful at the moment. I mean, I'm trying my best with all this job thing but for god's sake we're on holiday and he is being such a miserable git.' She sniffed, struggling to smile. 'Geno asked me out just now – he said that I looked sad . . . How come a complete stranger can see it when my boyfriend can't?'

'Because – because he's a lech, Fee. He's fishing.'

'Oh that's right, what are you saying? That I can't get a man?'

'No, of course not,' Cass stared at her. 'Tell me that you're not going, Fee. You're not are you?'

Fiona nodded. 'I might. It would serve Andy right . . .'

'You're joking,' said Cass.

'No, I'm not, he takes me for granted. I'd give my eye-teeth for a bloody good seeing-to and somebody who pays me a bit of attention. I know that Andy is a bit apprehensive about the whole fatherhood thing, but the way we're going there isn't a hope in hell of me ever getting pregnant. I can't remember the last time we . . .' She paused, wiping her nose vigorously. 'Well, you know. I don't think he really wants a baby.' She blew her nose. 'I know that's what he said, but I thought that I could talk him round; I'm beginning to think that he really means it.'

Cass stared at her. What the hell did she say now?

Fiona sighed and pulling out another tissue, wiped her eyes. 'God, I must look such a mess. I put Andy being funny down to stress at first, but it's driving me mad. I just want to be with a man who wants me, someone who makes me feel beautiful, Cass. I mean, it doesn't seem that much to ask, does it? There is this guy at work – you mustn't say anything to Andy – but he keeps flirting and asking me out and saying how good I look and how he likes my perfume and my clothes; then the other night at the concert, Mike – that guy who you're dating. I mean, how do you do it? He was so nice and he rang me the next day to ask if I could do lunch some time. And then he texted me and said if I was worried about that maybe we should cut the lunch and just head straight off to bed . . .' Fiona giggled and then wiped away a stray tear. 'I couldn't work out whether he was joking or not, but I'm so tempted.'

Cass still didn't know what to say. 'He's got a purse,' was all she could manage.

Fiona pulled a face. 'What?'

'Mike. He's not worth it, he's got this purse – it's not sexy.'

Fiona snorted. 'Neither is living your life with Andy, I can tell you – I'm so fed up with him. What do you think I should do?'

'Do?' said Cass.

'Yes *do*,' snapped Fiona.

What Cass really wanted her to do was go away so she could have some lunch in peace. The last thing she wanted was to be privy to any more of Fiona's confidences – or Andy's come to that.

'I think that you should talk to Andy,' she said.

'You keep saying that, but he won't talk to me.'

Cass sighed. 'Okay, just don't rush into something that you might regret. You're worth more than that, take your time,' said Cass. She paused, waiting for Fiona to say something.

'That guy Geno – seriously, I think he is really nice,' purred Fiona.

Cass stared at her in amazement. 'What?'

'Geno, the manager – he is really cute.'

Cass sighed; there was no helping some people. 'And slimy,' she said. 'Let's not forget slimy.'

'I thought he was charming. So, are you going out with him this afternoon?' asked Fiona, pulling out her compact to repair the damage.

'No, I *was* going out with Nick – but, like I said, I've got things to do.'

'Well in that case maybe I should go?'

Cass stared at her. 'What – with Geno? You're not serious?'

Fiona smiled slyly. 'I might be. He said he was off and that he'd really like to show me the sights sometime. I could do with a little attention, a bit of TLC.'

At which point Andy showed up with a tray full of food. 'Here we are. I hope I've got enough – I just got a little bit of everything,' he said, resting the tray on the edge of the table. Cass murmured her thanks, taking the knife and fork Andy handed her.

'What are your plans for this afternoon?' asked Fiona, helping herself to a bowl of salad.

'Me? I haven't really got any. I thought you said you wanted a nap,' Andy said, as he started to decant the bread and drinks and a pile of napkins.

'I do, but if you fancied going out on one of the trips, then don't let me stop you. After all, it's your holiday too,' Fiona said. 'I wouldn't mind. Really – it would do you good to have some time to yourself, some time to unwind.'

Cass stared in amazement; Fiona really was a piece of work. Cass decided she had had quite enough and held up her hands. 'Actually, if you'll excuse me,' she said. 'It's too hot for me out here. I'm going to go back inside.'

Fiona shook out her napkin and spread it over her lap, and as she did so she gave Cass a theatrical pantomime wink. 'Fair enough. I like the heat, me. God this looks lovely,' she said, turning her attention to her plate. 'I'm absolutely famished. Bon appétit.' And with that Fiona skewered a large juicy prawn and waved a fork in Cass's direction by way of a goodbye.

As soon as Cass had gone, Fiona slumped down in the chair. 'I'm totally exhausted, Andy,' she said. 'It's been a really tiring morning.'

Andy meanwhile was considering her offer. 'Actually, I'd quite like to go and see the mosaics – there is this amazing archaeological site down by the harbour.'

Fiona smiled. 'Well why don't you go there, then, and I'll stay here and have a little siesta?'

'If you're sure,' he said.

'Oh, I'm absolutely certain,' said Fiona, skewering another prawn.

Chapter Twelve

Cass made her way back into the cool shade of the dining room and picked up another tray. At this rate it would be dinner time before she got anything to eat. The queue had thinned now down to the elderly, the picky and the people scuttling round busily helping themselves to seconds. Welsh Alf was amongst them.

'Lovely grub,' he said, shovelling a huge pile of potato salad onto his plate.

Cass smiled as she picked up a pair of tongs. 'So people keep telling me. I just want to get some and then eat it in peace.'

Welsh Alf nodded. 'Fair enough – you want to try the quiche – my missus would kill to make pastry like that.'

Geno, who was standing at the reception desk, caught her eye and waved a hand in greeting as Cass took a plate. When she smiled in return he left his work and came over. 'You have a nice morning with the singing?' he said, handing her a knife and fork from the bundles on the tables.

'Perfect, thank you.'

'Good, and have you got everything you want?' he asked, indicating the buffet.

Cass nodded. 'Yes, lovely – it looks lovely.'

'Very nice,' interjected Alf. 'Very nice indeed. I was just saying to Cass you've done us proud, it's a lovely spread.'

Geno smiled, moving in closer, while Cass waited for Alf to move on to the cold meats and cheeses. He grinned. 'You maybe want to see the sites? I'm off duty at two. I thought maybe we could go for a little drive . . .' He must have seen something in her face, because he continued. 'No strings, cross my heart. I have the perfect spot all picked out – you want me to show you on the map?' he indicated that she should follow him back to reception.

Cass smiled as she worked her way round the different bowls and platters. 'No, thank you.'

'You don't know what you missed,' he purred.

'I think I can probably guess,' Cass laughed, and with that she said her goodbyes and headed over to an empty table in a quiet corner of the dining room to finally have her lunch, relieved not to have to make small talk.

Amelia wasn't answering her phone. Andy punched the number in again and got the same infuriating message, 'Your call is being directed to the voice mail for this number. To leave a message, please press one. To re-record . . .' Andy snapped the phone shut. He'd already left a message. '*Amelia, can you ring me, this is ridiculous – where are you? We need to talk.*'

Probably not the most encouraging message he had ever left for anyone, but he wanted to find out what the hell she thought she was playing at. He didn't need to record it again. Andy glanced at his watch. It was nearly half past two and there were little groups of choir members gathering in the foyer waiting to go out on the various trips.

He recognised lots of the faces from the flight and the dinner the night before, all ready with bags and cameras and hats. He considered his options.

Fiona had gone upstairs straight after lunch with strict instructions that she didn't want to be disturbed. Once she had eaten lunch she'd really seemed to flag.

'I think I might be getting a migraine,' she'd said, closing her eyes and leaning forward to rest her forehead delicately against her fingertips. 'It's probably the flight catching up with me.'

Andy had to admit she did look a bit pale. 'Is there anything I can get you?' he'd asked.

'No, no it's all right. I've got some painkillers up in the room – I think just a couple of hours' sleep, maybe three, should do the trick.' She screwed up her eyes and winced. 'Is there anything you want to get out of the room? Only it would be great if I could just sleep, Andy – you know, not be disturbed.'

Andy smiled and nodded sympathetically. 'Are you sure?' There was nothing he'd like better than to be somewhere else for three hours, but he wasn't a complete bastard, he hated to leave her when she felt unwell.

'Really,' she said. 'I just need some sleep.'

'Okay, well in that case I'll come up with you and grab my camera and stuff.'

Fiona nodded. 'Okay,' she said. 'I might just nip and get some bottled water from the bar first.'

'I'll get it for you . . .'

Fiona shook her head. 'No, no really, Andy, I'm fine. I'm better left alone really – please.' And with that she was up and away and Andy was heading upstairs with a disproportionate sense of relief that was almost equal to his sense of guilt. This had to stop – something really had to give. They couldn't carry on like this.

Which was why he had rung Amelia before heading off to the mosaics. As he walked down towards the harbour, Andy rang again. 'Your call is being directed to the voice mail for this number. To leave a message, please press one. To re-record . . .'

Cass meanwhile had got herself a long cold drink and gone upstairs to her room. Once she was settled out on the balcony, she dialled the shop.

Her mother picked up on the third ring, the height of efficiency. 'Hello, Cass's Emporium, can I help you?'

'It's me.'

'Well, I didn't know that, did I?'

'You make it sound like a brothel.'

Her mother giggled. 'Did I ever tell you about the time your father and I went to Amster—'

'Yes you did, and no, I don't really want to hear about it again. How's things?'

'Not bad – quite quiet.'

'I meant about Amelia.'

There was a little silence and then Nita said, 'I know – the thing is, it was an accident. I'm really sorry Cass . . . I went up to talk to her earlier and she is in a terrible state. No job, nowhere to go and this chap – what's his name?'

'Andy.'

'Well, he seems to have more or less washed his hands of her. You know that she's pregnant? Not a great state of affairs really.'

'Mum, darling, this is not my problem, or yours – presumably she's got friends and her own mum.'

202

'Well, that's just the thing, apparently they've had a falling out as well and she doesn't want to go back there either.'

'This isn't our problem Mum, and Andy can't just abandon her . . .'

'She said that she didn't want to talk about it.'

Cass sighed; she could see her plans for a restful afternoon rapidly fading into oblivion. 'Let me talk to her.'

'Well, like I said, she's in her room at the moment as far as I know.'

'My room . . .'

'What dear?'

'It's my room, my house and I want her out.'

'Seems a little harsh.'

Cass rolled her eyes and looked heavenwards. 'Mum, just go and knock on her door and say that there is a phone call for her.'

There was a pause. 'I don't think she'll fall for that, Cass, how would anyone know that she was here? And besides, I can't really leave the shop . . .'

'Mum, I'm not trying to trick her, I just need to talk to her. Just drop the latch on the shop door and take the phone up into the flat.'

She heard her mother sigh heavily. Cass waited; she could imagine every step, through the shop, up the stairs, the knocking at the door.

'Hello dear, are you in there?' she heard Nita say.

There was a muffled sound.

'Amelia – it's the phone for you. No – no it's not Andy.'

Cass sighed; this was crazy. After a few moments she heard a door being unlocked and then heard her mother say. 'It's my daughter Cass – she'd like to have a quick word with you.'

And then there was the scuffle of the handset being passed over and finally Cass heard the soft anxious breathing of her unwanted lodger. The one thing Cass hadn't really worked out was what she planned to say. There was a long silence.

'You can't stay in my house, Amelia,' said Cass as calmly as she could. 'I understand that you're in a bit of a muddle at the moment, but you can't stay there. Do you understand?'

'Andy told me that you talked to him and to Fiona,' Amelia said. She sounded fragile and vulnerable and terribly young. 'I didn't know where else to go. And then your mum showed me the room . . .'

Cass sighed. 'Amelia, you can't stay in my house.'

'But—'

'But nothing,' said Cass, gently but firmly. 'It's not up for negotiation. I have to go.'

'I've got nowhere else to go . . .'

'That isn't my problem.'

'Andy said—'

'I don't care what Andy said, Amelia. Ring him and talk to him – maybe he can help you.'

'You are just *so* unreasonable.'

Cass almost laughed.

'He said that you were easy to talk to . . .'

'I am, but my mum shouldn't have let you in. Now get your things together and go home. And if you don't leave, then I'm going to have to call the police.'

There was a short silence and then Amelia said, 'My mum threw me out.'

'I'm not surprised. Ring her, apologise . . .'

There was another much longer pause and then Amelia said, 'Do you think that'll work?'

Cass thought for a moment. 'I'd give it a shot. It always worked for me. Now why don't you go and pack—'

'You don't get it do you? I haven't got anywhere to go.' She paused and then said, 'I'll tell Fiona. I'll ring her now and tell her that you knew all about me. You and Andy and about the baby and everything, I will . . .'

Cass sensed that it was meant to be a trump card, and remembered back when her boys used to have temper tantrums. She seemed to remember when Danny hit the terrible twos he regularly held his breath until he went blue. The best strategy had been to ignore him and call his bluff.

'Good idea,' Cass said calmly. 'I won't be blackmailed. Presumably you've got her number?'

'What . . . ?' spluttered Amelia.

'When you took Andy's phone, presumably you took Fiona's number down as well. Ring her. I think it's a great idea. It's time all this was out in the open,' said Cass, without a shred of emotion.

'You don't think I'll do it, do you?'

'To be honest, I don't really care,' said Cass. 'Now please give the phone back to my mother.'

'Do you think she'll go?' said Nita, obviously on her way back downstairs if the lumping and bumping was anything to go by. 'She's in a bit of a state. 'I'm quite worried about her.'

'Mum, she is whiny and difficult and she isn't ours to worry about,' said Cass.

'I know dear, I know. I recognise all those qualities.'

'You're not saying I was like that are you?' said Cass indignantly.

'No, of course not,' said her mother, 'but I was.'

Cass laughed. 'Don't be silly . . .'

'No it's true. I was horrible until I was about thirty.' Nita laughed, a warm, sexy rasp. 'Some people would say I still am. Ask Rocco. The thing is, it was all your father's fault. Because he was so much older than me he was very indulgent and I took full advantage. It's one of the great joys of having an older man, or come to that a much younger one; they are just so indulgent.'

'You mean like Andy?'

'I'll talk to her.'

'Mum, please don't get involved. She is not a stray that needs taking in. If she's not gone by the morning you should ring the police.' As she spoke, Cass made her way out onto the balcony and wedged the phone between her chin and her shoulder as she tried to get the top off a bottle of juice.

'That's not very charitable,' said Nita. 'And besides, it's too late darling. After all, I feel that it's my fault she is here in the first place and I think she'll talk to me, she doesn't see me as a threat.'

Cass laughed. 'Well in that case she is a fool.'

'How cruel.'

'Which reminds me, how is Rocco?'

'He's not cruel, at least not to me – he's fine, he's out at the moment walking that dog of yours. Do you have an idea how much rump steak that creature can eat?'

At which point there was a knock on the door. It took Cass a second or two to realise that it was someone knocking on her door.

'Mum I've got to go—'

'About Amelia . . .'

But Cass had already opened the door.

'Hi,' said Nick. 'I was waiting downstairs.'

Cass stared at him. In the fuss over Amelia, she had totally forgotten that she'd promised to meet him. He was dressed in cream chinos, a white tee-shirt, and a tan. He smiled, looking nervous, shifting his weight from foot to foot. 'I wondered if you'd maybe changed your mind.'

Cass hesitated; there was nothing she could do about Amelia – or anything else come to that – and so she grinned and said, 'No – no, I just got waylaid. I'll be five minutes – ten at most.'

He looked relieved. 'Great. I'll be waiting downstairs for you then.'

Cass nodded. 'Won't be long,' she said.

'He sounds nice, going anywhere nice, are we?' asked Nita at the other end of the phone. Cass shook her head and laughed.

Upstairs, on the bed tucked up under the eaves of Cass's cottage, Amelia sat cradling her mobile phone in her lap, wondering what to do next. Maybe she should ring Fiona, maybe she should – it would serve them all right. She waited for a few more minutes to see if Cass's mum was planning to knock on the door again, maybe give her another lecture. And when none came, she pressed 141 to withhold her number and then dialled Fiona's mobile number from memory. It rang twice; Amelia wasn't altogether sure what she planned to say, if anything. It was good just maybe to know that she could tell Fiona if she wanted to, but she was cheated because after two rings a recorded message said, 'Your call is being directed to the voice mail for this number. To leave a message, please press one. To re-record your message please press two.' For a moment Amelia was angry, and then she felt relieved.

Andy was down amongst the mosaics, camera in hand, exploring the villa of Dionysus. The sun was warm on his back and, if it hadn't been for the women in his life, then he would have been having a wonderful time.

Nick insisted on paying for Cass to get into seeing the mosaics down by the harbour. As they walked, along winding gravel paths, between stands of twisted conifers, Cass said she thought the place was beautiful, and Nick smiled, and murmured his thanks, apparently taking the compliment personally before speaking. 'For the British the whole of Cyprus is a good mixture of familiar and foreign. People come back again and again. For me I was born here and then grew up mostly in England. My mother is Cypriot –'

And as they walked, and worked their way through the guidebook, he asked her about her job, the shop, her pets, her whole life, and then told her about college and what had brought him to Cyprus, about his family and his fiancée, the hotel and working for his uncle, while guiding her along the paths towards the remains of the villas. It felt a little like going on a hike with one of her kids' friends. Cass sighed and began to feel the tension ease out of her shoulders.

Many of the mosaics, things of great beauty that would be under glass and untouchable in the UK, were open to the elements; only the most complex and complete were protected under cover of wooden villas. There were no gift shops or restaurants, or handrails, and only the scantest pieces of information – and, thought Cass as she scrambled up over a great heap of rubble to look at another mosaic, a healthy disregard for health and safety.

'Here,' said Nick, pulling a bottle of water out of his rucksack as they reached the top. 'Would you like one of these? I brought a couple.'

'Oh, yes please,' she said, taking it from him. 'I'm amazed no one's opened a cafe round here.'

Nick nodded. 'Uh-huh. Maybe I'll finish my business course and come and set one up.'

Cass laughed as she took a long hard pull on the water. 'You'd make a fortune,' she said.

Andy shouldered his rucksack and then pressed redial on his mobile. Amelia's phone was still switched off which, if he was honest, was a relief. Back at the hotel Fiona was asleep and all was well with the world. Overhead the sky was a clear, matchless blue.

He glanced at his watch. He'd been gone for nearly an hour and was relishing the peace and quiet. Ahead of him a party of oriental tourists, noisy as a gaggle of geese, giggled and jostled into position on one of the walkways that surrounded some of the most striking mosaics, posing for a group photo.

Andy hesitated as people tried to set up the camera to take time-delayed shots. There was much laughter and wailing as they scurried backwards and forwards – until in a combination of words and mime Andy asked, 'Would you like me to take it?' He pressed an imaginary button down with as much finesse and skill as he could muster.

The party leader, a tiny Chinese girl with a huge smile and a terrible haircut, nodded and bowed then said, 'Very nice,' and indicated the group before handing him the camera.

That isn't what Andy would have said, but he took the photo anyway, which was when he saw Cass and one of the guys from the hotel heading out towards one of the main mosaics, deep in conversation. He hung back with the Chinese tourists and watched them walk by, not altogether sure why he was hiding.

Cass and the young man were chatting as they walked, and the boy handed a bottle of water to Cass, and she said something that made him laugh. Andy realised that he was envious – the thought surprised him.

It was around five when Cass and Nick walked back to the hotel. He'd got to get back on duty for six.

'I've had a lovely afternoon,' Cass said as they got to the main doors.

'Me too,' he said, and then very gently he leant forward and kissed her on the cheek. It was totally unexpected and made Cass redden.

'Maybe we could do it again before you go back. Go somewhere else – there's some amazing places . . .'

Cass, nonplussed, nodded. 'I'd like that.'

'See you later,' he said with a grin and jogged off towards the back of the hotel.

Cass smiled as she went upstairs. He'd been easy company and she'd had a great afternoon, even though it was hot and her feet ached – and if she was honest he'd kissed her cheek with the same passion as you'd kiss a maiden aunt.

Cass glanced out of the window and decided she might follow Fiona's example. A little siesta before dinner was just what the doctor ordered. Before she slipped off her clothes and slipped under a single sheet, Cass took a glance at the itinerary – there was an option to have an early dinner, followed by a concert by two choirs at the amphitheatre in Paphos. Tickets were available on the gate; audience members were advised to bring a cushion. Cass set the alarm on her mobile for six thirty, lay back amongst a bow wave of pillows and, closing her eyes, was asleep in seconds.

At around half past five Andy wandered back to the hotel. It had been a good afternoon. He'd explored the mosaics, taken dozens of photos and then, on the advice of a plump, red-faced Irish woman, had grabbed a taxi and gone up to take a look around the Tombs of the Kings, a stunning necropolis about two miles north of the harbour.

Sitting on a boulder under the late afternoon sun, watching the lizards scuttle, Andy had texted Amelia. To his surprise she had texted him right back, saying that she had already talked to Cass and that she would ring him when she got a chance.

Tired but happy would best describe his state of mind as he headed back to the hotel. The foyer at the Centrale was cool and dark and deserted apart from a receptionist tucked up behind her desk with a phone pressed to her ear, so Andy headed upstairs to his room. Ignoring the lift, he took the stairs two at a time.

While out exploring the ruins he'd been thinking. He'd have a word with Cass, and decided that he and Fiona would just enjoy the next few days. He'd no great desire to ruin either Fiona's trip, the choirs', or his own, and then as soon as they got back to the UK he'd tell Fiona about Amelia – all about Amelia. Then, when the firestorm had passed, he would tell Fee that it was over; obviously Amelia and the baby changed things. Obviously. Although he couldn't imagine for a moment that he'd be saying any of this uninterrupted. Was he being a coward to put it off? Then again, what difference would a few more days make?

One thing was very certain, repeated the voice in his head – they couldn't just carry on living like they were. The voice had transformed during the course of the afternoon from a strong manly tone to – as he got closer and closer to the door of their room – a high-pitched squeak. And all that bollocks about how it was better to hurt Fiona a little now rather than lead her on and hurt her a lot more later sounded like complete drivel now. Never mind how much he would have to hurt Fiona, it worried him considerably more just how much she was going to hurt him – and not just emotionally.

Up on their floor, Andy tapped tentatively on the door of the room and waited. 'Hi – it's me. I'm back,' he said. After a few seconds, when there was no reply, he tapped a little louder. When there was still no reply, he slid the key-card through the lock. The little light flashed from red to green and as he pushed the door it swung open. Inside, the room was in total darkness. The light from the open door barely seemed to even prick the gloom. It was deadly quiet, uncomfortably hot and still.

'Fee?' he called in a soft whisper. 'Are you all right? Did you have a nice sleep?' There was no reply. He was relieved the door hadn't closed as it offered the only light.

'Fee?' Andy felt a sudden flutter of panic. It wasn't like

her not to wake up. Fiona wasn't usually a heavy sleeper, normally at home she was wide-awake the minute he opened the bedroom door. He fumbled for the light switch but, unable to find it, made his way across the room towards the French windows, planning to open the heavy curtains.

Anxious and in a hurry, Andy had forgotten that there was a coffee table standing between the chair and a dressing table at the far end of the room and – not seeing it in the darkness – walked straight into it, banging his shins and then, losing his balance and falling over the top of it, he knocked off the complimentary fruit basket, the slippers and a jug full of flowers as he did so. There was a crack and crash of something hitting the floor.

Mid-flight, and scrabbling around for a handhold to stop him falling flat on his face, Andy managed to grab the flex of the TV, which tipped forward, teetered for a second and then crashed down through the coffee table in a terrifying explosion of glass and bamboo. As he finally fell towards the floor, Andy found the curtains, grabbed a handful, and with one last lunge managed to pull them clean off the wall. The room was instantly flooded with light and from somewhere close by Andy could hear his mobile ringing.

'Bloody hell – what on earth are you doing in here?' said a familiar voice from behind him.

From amongst a sea of glass, water, flowers and over-ripe kiwis Andy, scrambling to his feet, looked back towards the door. Cass was standing in the doorway holding a little floral dressing gown tight around her. 'I was next door, you woke me up. Jesus look at the mess . . .'

In the alcove by the window the bed was empty.

'I couldn't find Fiona,' he said lamely. 'I mean, I thought she was in here. She said she was getting a migraine. She said she was coming upstairs for a sleep.'

Andy looked back at the bed, just in case by some trick of the light he had missed her.

Cass meanwhile tucked her hair back behind her ears and fastened the tie on her robe, looking around as she did so. 'Well, it doesn't look like she's here, Andy. And that looks like it might need stitches.'

Andy pulled a face, not at all sure what Cass was talking about, and then he looked down at his hand. There was blood dripping across his palm and trickling down his wrist, where he had crashed through the table.

'Oh bugger,' he said, picking up a bundle of serviettes from the fruit basket.

Cass took a towel out of the bathroom. 'Sit down and let me have a look at that,' she said. He did as he was told, while she examined the damage. 'You know, we're a community choir not a rock band,' Cass said as she dabbed at the cut.

He pulled a face. 'I'm not with you.'

'God, you're slow on the uptake – we don't trash hotel rooms.'

There was little pause and then Andy laughed and realised as he did that living with Fiona had made him wary, afraid to see the joke. And then he laughed some more.

Cass stared at him. 'It wasn't that funny. Here, let me take a look at your other hand.'

Andy giggled some more.

'Actually, I don't think the cuts are that bad, they're not

214

deep. I've got a first-aid kit in my room. I'll go and get it, get some plasters and some antiseptic. Have you got any aftersun?'

'What?'

'You've really caught the sun.' She reached out towards him and then stopped. 'Sorry – your nose is really pink.'

'Oh right. I went to see the mosaics this afternoon.'

'Really? Me too.'

Andy decided not to let her know that he'd seen her there. 'Fabulous, aren't they, did you get up to see the Tombs of the Kings?'

'No, but the person I went with said they were worth a look.' Then Cass stopped and there was a funny little pause. Self-consciously Cass said, 'Anyway let me go and get my first-aid kit.'

He didn't want her to go.

'I need to talk to you,' he said.

'Well, looky here at you two all cosied up – how very domestic,' said Fiona, sashaying into the room, with a bag slung casually over one shoulder. 'Finding you with my man is getting to be something of a habit,' she said to Cass, and then looking around she said, 'What the hell happened? Oh my god, we haven't been burgled, have we?'

Fiona was immaculately made up, wearing a navy and white polka dot sundress, oversized sunglasses and killer wedges. Andy took another long look; she looked great, certainly much brighter than she had earlier in the afternoon.

'You're feeling better?' he asked.

'I'm fine,' she said, dismissively. 'What exactly is going on?'

Andy waved a hand to encompass the chaos. 'It was an accident, I didn't mean to . . . I couldn't find you – I fell over in the dark.'

'Have you never heard of electric lights?' said Fiona, her tone condescending and cool.

'I didn't want to disturb you . . .'

'Well luckily you didn't. Mind you, if I'd been asleep I'd have been lucky to get out without being brained by something. What the hell is all this stuff anyway?'

'I thought you were in here asleep. I've only just got back,' said Andy, on the defensive. 'I thought I'd surprise you . . .'

'Well I wasn't here,' said Fiona, somewhat unnecessarily. 'I got up about half an hour ago. I felt so much better. I thought I'd nip downstairs and get some air. You'd better ring down to reception and see if they can get someone up here to clean all this mess up. Oh my god, there's broken glass *everywhere* . . . !'

Andy looked at Cass and then said, 'I woke Cass up – all the noise – and I've cut my hand . . .'

'Why are we not surprised? Oh Andy, the carpet is soaked. Here, give me the phone and I'll ring housekeeping – sit still, I don't want to get blood on my shoes.'

Cass meanwhile hung back, listening to their conversation. Something didn't ring true about what Fiona was saying. For a start, you didn't have to be a genius to see that nobody had slept in the bed for ten minutes, let alone two hours, and also, even in this light, Cass could see the sunburn on Fiona's shoulders, nose and back. She hadn't been asleep all afternoon, she'd been out somewhere – and Cass had a horrible feeling she knew who she'd been with.

Fiona had picked up the room phone and was about

to tap in a number when Andy's mobile, on the floor by the bed, rang. Before anyone else had a chance to move, Fiona swept down and picked it up.

'Hello,' she said.

And then there was a pause. Andy and Cass stared at one another in mute horror.

'Who is this?' And then there was another pause. Cass held her breath.

'What did you say?' said Fiona. This time the pause seemed to go on forever.

And then Fiona nodded and handed the phone to Andy. 'It's some telesales thing. They want to know if you're happy with your car insurance. How the hell did these people get hold of your number? Tell them you're on bloody holiday.'

Cass let out a silent sigh of relief and, as she caught Andy's eye, realised that he was doing exactly the same thing. Meanwhile Fiona was on the phone to reception, schmoozing the housekeeper.

Cass gratefully backed out and headed off to her room, while Andy, sitting on the edge of the bed, pressed the serviettes to his cut hand. Around him the room looked as if it had been hit by a hurricane.

The first concert at the amphitheatre in Paphos was by two choirs from Estonia and Spain. The sun had set by the time Cass and the others set off from the hotel for the walk to the concert and, although it was still warm, the night air had a chilly edge that tugged and nipped at their hair and hems. Cass was wearing a jacket and had brought a pashmina along too, as well as the recommended cushion.

She made a point of avoiding Fiona and Andy.

The procession down through the harbour and in through the gates of the Roman site had a real carnival atmosphere to it. People in evening dress carried lanterns and blankets and hampers of food. Others walked arm in arm. Cass found Welsh Alf and Ray in the melee and got herself into the space between them for the walk.

The broad pathway from the museum gates to the amphitheatre itself was lined with little lamps – candles set in jars – that led off into the warm blue velvet darkness.

About half a mile away, between the cypress trees and the rolling scrub, and cut into the natural rock, the semi-circle of tiered seating – more strictly called an odeon rather than an amphitheatre, according to Cass's guide-book – was sheltered from the sea breeze by the surrounding hill that backed onto cliffs.

Cass crested the hill and in the distance she could see the Roman theatre lit with a subtle mix of flaming torches, candles and carefully placed spotlights. Here and there were braziers sending sparks up into the night sky. It looked fabulous.

Cass fell into step between her fellow basses, and listened to their stories about the day they'd had and the things they'd seen and was happy to sit between them on one of the tiers of the ancient theatre to wait for the concert to begin.

'I brought a tartan rug if you get a bit chilly,' said Ray as they settled in. Locals with baskets and trays plied their wares up and down the stone steps, selling programmes, hot roasted nuts rolled in honey and served in waxed paper cones, little dishes filled with sliced fruits, cold drinks and local delicacies folded into pitta bread or threaded on long thin wooden skewers. It looked, and smelled, wonderful, and Cass couldn't help thinking that this must have been exactly what the place had been like in its heyday.

'You missed a trick today, we went to a Cypriot delight factory – lots of free samples,' said Alf joyfully. 'I bought some to take home for the missus and some for tonight.' He started to rootle around in a bag at his feet.

As he did, Cass glanced around her at the other faces picked out in torchlight. Andy and Fiona were a few seats along and, to her surprise, Andy was looking in her direction. Caught completely unawares she found herself staring back. An instant later Fiona glanced up, waved and then got to her feet and came over.

'I wondered where you'd got to. I have to tell you – I have had *the* most amazing afternoon,' she squealed, ignoring Alf and Ron and squeezing herself unceremoniously in next to Cass. 'You wouldn't believe it . . .'

'Oh, whereabouts did you go?' asked Alf conversationally, holding out a box of Cypriot delight towards her. 'We went to the sweet factory. They're very keen to point out that this side of the border it's called Cypriot delight and not Turkish and it was very interesting how they made it, wasn't it, Ray? Here why don't you try a piece? It's lovely.' He shook the box at her. 'So, pet, where did you say you went?'

Cass shot Fiona a warning look. Fiona responded by winking. 'Where *didn't* I go?' she purred.

Below them, in the front of the broad semi-circle of stone that made up the stage, the choirs were starting to assemble. 'Oh bugger, I'd better get back,' Fiona said. 'I'll tell you about it later . . .'

Cass rather hoped that she wouldn't, but without another word Fiona wriggled her way back out and made her way through the other seated people back to her seat.

'Fiona seems a lot happier today,' said Alf, rattling the box of sweets in her direction. 'Amazing what a bit of sun can do for you.'

Cass took a piece of delight, said thanks and kept her thoughts regarding Fiona to herself.

Meanwhile, the first choir were being given their opening notes, and Cass's attention shifted from Fiona and Andy to the evening's entertainment. All the women had their hair up and were dressed in gold floor-length dresses, the men in open-neck pirate-style shirts with matching gold cummerbands. They looked fantastic. She could see Bekya, who had shared her table the night before, standing in amongst the tenors, and waved. He couldn't see her but it didn't matter. It was nice to recognise a face amongst the many.

The conductor, a tall slender woman dressed in a claret velvet evening gown, raised her hands, and the first notes rang out around the ancient auditorium, filling it with sound. The acoustics were amazing and the pure beauty of the Eastern European harmony brought tears to Cass's eyes. She would have come to Cyprus for that moment alone.

Alongside her Alf sighed, 'Bloody hell, they're good aren't they?'

They sang like angels for an hour and with every new song, every solo, every extraordinary, unlikely Baltic harmony, Cass couldn't think of a place she would rather be than under a canopy of stars, out in the warm Cyprus night. When the final bow came and the audience started to applaud, it filled the night air like a volley of rifle shots, echoing again and again around the ancient stones.

As it died the master of ceremonies and chief organiser of the event, Perry Hulme, walked across to the front of the audience, his progress tracked across the arc by spotlight.

'Ladies and Gentlemen,' he said, lifting his arms in a gesture of thanks, 'I'm sure we all want to thank Nadia's fabulous choir for their efforts this evening. After the interval, España's famous Big Heart community singers will continue with their own particular brand of magic. I think while I'm up here we should also thank the Department of Antiquities for letting us use this extraordinary space and to those volunteers who have spent the last few days setting up all the things that have gone to making this place so special. And also to thank our judging panel for their efforts this evening.' He indicated a row of worthies at the front, all in full evening dress and none of whom Cass recognised.

There was a great crackle of applause. 'So, a twenty-minute recess – there are plenty of refreshments available and then we continue in the second half with the songs from the Spanish heartland.'

Already traders were congregating by the foot of the terraces, eager to work their way up and down the aisles. Cass stretched. 'Would either of you like coffee? It smells great – or how about a glass of wine?'

'I'll have a coffee, how about you, Ray?' said Alf, dipping into his pocket. Cass waved his money away.

'It's fine. I'll be back in a couple of minutes, just keep my seat warm.' She got up and eased her way past the rest of the audience on her tier, then made her way down the steps to the floor of the amphitheatre, where people were queuing for everything from wine straight from the cask through to CDs of the Estonian choir.

Finding the queue for coffee, Cass settled down to wait behind two or three of the others from her choir and a mass of other singers and locals. There was a real buzz of excitement in the crowd. Cass smiled as Alan, their musical director, eased past to join the queue for wine.

'Just getting the good lady a little vino. Great audience, eh? Be fantastic to sing for this lot.'

Cass nodded. 'It's an amazing place. Great acoustics.'

'Oh there you are. Hi Alan,' said Fiona, easing in along-side them. She was glowing. 'Andy's just going to get us some wine.' She looked left and right, as if checking they couldn't be overheard. 'I was really tempted to cry off and have an evening back at the hotel.'

Cass fixed on a smile, but didn't ask why, instead finding herself at the head of the queue asking the nice young woman for three white coffees. Making her apologies, she headed back to the stands where Alf had once again broken out the Cypriot delight.

As soon as the concert was over Cass, not wanting to hear any more of Fiona's little weighted asides, slipped away to the hotel.

Avoiding Fiona at the concert set a pattern – over the next couple of days after breakfast the choir sang new songs with other groups and took part in various work-shops that ranged from barbershop harmonies to African drumming. They would then rehearse their own concert material for half an hour or so before lunch.

As soon as the choirs broke up for the afternoon's R&R, Cass would hurry upstairs, grab a book and her bag and camera, and head up into the old town, a taxi-ride away from the more touristy port area, or walk down to the harbour, or sometimes just lock the door and sit, quiet and unavailable on her balcony, ignoring all knocks, calls or phones, basically doing anything to avoid Fiona and Andy. A couple of times Nick had offered to come sightseeing with her, and both times, keen for peace and quiet, she'd declined.

To be fair, Fiona didn't seek her out; she seemed to have something else on her mind, and although she could probably guess what it was, Cass decided not to enquire. No news really was good news.

Cass phoned home, but got Rocco, who said that her mother had the matter in hand – which could mean anything, and she decided she didn't want to go into details. Nor did Cass want to listen to Andy's angst or excuses, so running and hiding were really the best options left to her. Not that it was a trial – Cyprus was beautiful. So far, although she had seen Fiona and Andy, Cass had managed to avoid being alone with either of them, and was really enjoying exploring Paphos under her own steam. So one morning after breakfast when she spotted Geno behind the reception desk, it took her two seconds to clock him and even less to smile politely and make her way over to the notice board advertising the bus trips. Maybe it was time to branch out and see a few more of the sites that the island had to offer. On the far side of the foyer, Nick was talking to one of the guests and raised a hand in greeting.

'We're just trying to make up our minds which one to go on this afternoon,' said Nancy, one of the pastel sopranos loitering alongside the list. She pointed to a poster. 'Have you been on any of them so far?'

Cass shook her head.

'Oh, but you should. While you're here. Shame not to, really. We did this one yesterday.' She tapped one perfectly painted fingernail on a picture of a hilltop village. 'It was right up in the mountains. Stunning views.'

'And fantastic food,' added Val, a vision in peach, as she pulled a pen out of her handbag. 'So what shall we sign you up for, Cass? Historical or cultural?'

Cass laughed, 'What do you recommend?'

'Oh, or there's shopping,' said Nancy helpfully, pointing to one of the lists. 'The week's going so fast, isn't it? We were only saying this morning – anyway, we're thinking of going on the shopping trip just before we go back and buying all our Christmas presents. They do fabulous shoes here, and jewellery.'

Val lifted one perfectly plucked eyebrow. 'Oh yes, and who are you buying those for then?' The two of them giggled furiously.

'Maybe the historical tour?' said Cass.

'Good choice, castles, ruins – and they stop for tea too,' said Nancy, leaning forward to add Cass's name and their own to the list. 'And don't forget the winery.'

When Cass looked up, Geno was standing on the other side of the board looking at her. 'You are signing up for one of the tours?'

Cass nodded. 'Seems a shame not to.'

'You know, if you want to explore, then I'd be happy to show you the sights.'

'Thanks,' said Cass frostily. 'But I'm all booked up, thanks.

'I can always make time to show a pretty woman around. I have had my hands full the last couple of days and today also, but tomorrow – how about we go tomorrow?'

224

Cass pulled a face; maybe he had misunderstood, maybe she had. 'I thought you were busy with my friend,' she said, pointedly.

This time it was Geno who grimaced. 'Your friend?'

Cass said nothing and then after a few seconds Geno grinned. '*Your friend*? Ah yes, but it's not like we're married – and she tells me she is busy tomorrow. I could show you some of the sights . . .'

'Thanks but no thanks.' Geno leaned a little closer, all smiles. 'I thought you were avoiding me.'

Cass, trying to think of something that would shut him up, hesitated just long enough for Geno's smile to broaden. 'So, that's a yes then, is it? When can you come?'

The two sopranos giggled. 'Well not today, chuck, we've just all signed up to go look at some castles,' said Nancy, tapping her pen against the names on the board.

'And we're stopping off at the winery,' said the second. 'Again.'

He smiled. 'Well, I hope you have a wonderful time ladies, we have some very beautiful places in Cyprus.' And then, turning his attention back to Cass he said, 'So, tomorrow then?'

Cass was about to reply when Nick appeared. 'I'm afraid she's already booked,' he said with a wink.

Cass could have kissed him.

Geno hesitated and Cass, leaping into the void said, 'That's right . . .'

Geno shrugged. 'Ah well – your loss. I hope you have a good time,' and with that he was gone.

Cass smiled at Nick. 'Thank you.'

Nick grinned. 'My pleasure. . I keep planning to have a

word with my uncle but the truth is some women come here looking for a bit of holiday fun.'

'And Geno is only too happy to oblige?'

Nick nodded and then added, 'So would you really like to come out with me tomorrow?'

Cass stared at him. 'You were serious?'

His grin widened. 'I'm not Geno. Don't worry . . .'

At which point Fiona sashayed past, Andy a step or two behind her.

'Don't disappoint the boy,' Fiona said with a sly grin. 'Nothing like a little holiday romance.' Behind her, it was obvious that Andy hadn't caught what was being said or the subtext.

Cass nodded absently. Nick grinned. 'Three o'clock tomorrow then? If I pick you up at the front?'

Cass smiled. 'Okay.'

He nodded. 'I'll look forward to it.'

The two sopranos watched him make his way back to reception. 'Very nice,' purred Val appreciatively.

Nancy slapped her arm. 'You behave yourself,' she said with a grin. And then to Cass said, 'Coach leaves at two. Would you like us to save you a seat?'

Which was how Cass found herself in a tour party made up from the different choirs, being shown around a series of castles, villas and Roman ruins – one thing you could say about Cyprus was that it wasn't short on history.

It was a great afternoon.

The coach had picked the singers up from their different hotels after lunch, and now set them down in reverse order – the Centrale was the first and the last stop, so Cass found herself amongst the last half-dozen day trippers as they pulled up outside the main doors and clambered down the steps of the coach. Against all the odds she had had a really good time, with the prospect of a shower, supper and another concert to follow. Cass smiled; the All Stars' concert was scheduled for the following evening, so tonight she planned to just enjoy the food and the music.

Tired but feeling good, Cass strolled through the lobby with a handful of postcards she planned to post in reception – one for Rocco and her mum, one each for her sons – and a huge appetite.

Behind the desk, Nick lifted a hand in welcome. Cass did the same and was about to head up into the dining room when she heard the tap-tap-tap of high heels crossing the marble floor. She didn't bother looking back until she heard Fiona call her name.

'Cass, Cass – wait up, wait for me.'

Cass groaned and, pretending not to hear, headed out towards the terrace.

'Cass, stop. I've been waiting for you. I need to have a quick word with you. I thought we were friends. Are you deliberately avoiding me?'

Cass turned as Fiona hurried across the foyer towards her. She looked fabulous, in a blue silk halter-neck dress, her hair twisted up into a knot. She had caught the sun on her shoulders and cheeks, but none of this disguised the fact that she didn't look at all happy.

'No, of course I'm not avoiding you,' Cass lied. 'And anyway, I thought you were otherwise engaged.'

Fiona grinned. 'You can talk. Anyway, I'm really glad I've caught you,' she hissed, threading an arm through Cass's and falling into step alongside her.

'Because . . . ?'

'Because I need you to cover for me,' she said, pulling

227

Cass conspiratorially close. 'You know how bad things have been and how bloody boring things are – well, they're not so boring now.' She giggled. 'For the last couple of afternoons I've managed to persuade Andy that I've needed a little nap and so he's been out exploring, but today – well, he suggested that we hire a car and go up into the badlands, but then after we saw you this morning I told him that you'd invited me on a coach trip and that I'd said yes – you and me, and that you were putting our names down. He was pleased.'

Cass stared at her. 'Pleased?' she repeated.

'Yes, very pleased. That I was getting out and about without him. Seeing something of the island. I told him I was humouring you and that I would go out with him for a quick trip tomorrow.'

'What?' said Cass.

'I think he was a bit worried in case we'd fallen out, you know – friends and all that, and then there was all the kerfuffle about Andy not being able to find me the other day and you being in our room – in that robe. You have to admit, Cass, it didn't leave much to the imagination. The trouble is, you know what I'm like, I just said the first thing that came into my head. Attack is the best form of defence and all that. After you left he said, "Where have you been?" and I said, "Never mind about where I've been, what were you doing with my best friend in our room?" I didn't mean anything by it but he got upset. I mean, I know he isn't likely to fancy *you*. You're so – well, you know what I'm saying here. You're lovely but you know, ordinary, down to earth. You know . . .' She did a big pantomime shrug.

Cass shook her head in amazement.

'What I'm trying to say is that he's just pleased that you and I have made up. I told him that you'd booked it as a way of making amends.'

'I did?' Cass had stopped in her tracks, feeling a great flood of outrage. 'Amends, what the hell for? And *ordinary*, what exactly is that supposed to mean?'

Fiona looked surprised that Cass had reacted badly, 'I meant that as a compliment; what I mean is that you're not high maintenance. Anyway, all you have to do is tell Andy I've been with you all afternoon. Knowing him he probably won't ask or say anything anyway.'

Cass lifted her eyebrows. 'Fiona, this isn't right . . .'

'Oh, don't be so naive,' Fiona said, taking her lipstick and a compact out to start work on her makeup. 'I took a leaf out of your book, that's all. I've been adding a little bit of spice to my life, and it's doing me the world of good. Geno is gorgeous – and he's got this fabulous little villa just out of town towards Limassol. Although, actually I think he's just borrowed it – but it's got a pool and everything. Not that we've had that much chance to use it,' she added slyly.

Cass stared at her and shook her head. This was crazy. Between them, Andy and Fiona had put Cass in an impossible position, and turned her holiday into a complete nightmare

From behind them came the electronic ping as the lift reached its floor and the doors opened. Several people got out, Andy amongst them. He was dressed casually in a tee-shirt with jeans under a linen jacket, and Cass couldn't help but notice that he was busy tucking his mobile into his pocket as he made his way over to them. These two just had too much going on – too many secrets and too much to hide.

'I've really got to go,' Cass said to Fiona, slipping out from her grasp. 'I need to have a shower and get ready for dinner.'

'No, please wait,' said Fiona, catching hold of her arm. 'Just say hello to Andy. Please . . .'

Cass glanced around; it was too late to go anywhere anyway. Andy was hurrying towards them, smiling warmly, which made her feel deeply uncomfortable.

'Hi, had a good time, did you?' He sounded way too bright and bouncy.

'Oh yes, we certainly did,' said Fiona. 'We had a fab time, didn't we, Cass?' And as she spoke she grabbed the handful of postcards out of Cass's hand and started flicking through them before choosing one at random and handing it towards Andy. 'We had a really good day – these are fab, Cass.' She glanced up at Andy. 'My camera packed up for some reason. I was going to ask you to take a look at it. It might be the batteries. Which was your favourite place?' she said, rounding on Cass, winking so furiously that it looked as though she had a nervous tic. Behind them, other people were coming in.

One of the other women who had shared Cass's coach said, 'Nice afternoon?'

'Yes, it was, wasn't it?' said Fiona brightly, ignoring the woman's slightly bemused reaction. Cass gathered her postcards back into a heap.

'Right,' said Andy. 'Well, I'm glad you had a good time. Would either of you like a drink before we eat?'

Cass shook her head. 'No thanks, actually I'm really not that hungry,' she lied, and with that turned and headed back upstairs, deciding that she'd grab a sand-wich or a quick snack in one of the cafes on the walk down to the theatre rather than sit in the dining room with those two.

As she climbed the stairs, Cass pulled out her phone and rang home, hoping that, there at least, things had been sorted out. Even if they hadn't, she wanted to hear the voice of someone who was on her side, someone who loved her, no matter what.

'Mum?'

'Hi honey, it's so nice to hear from you. How's it going? How's the weather?'

'It's lovely.' Cass looked out at the ocean, sun sinking slowly in the west, and sighed. 'Actually the whole trip is a game of two halves.'

Her mother laughed 'Well, all's well here. Oh, and Rocco sold the chaise yesterday – that regency striped one – for cash, for the asking price. I don't think we are ever going to hear the last of it. And Buster and the cat are just fine. Rocco's walked the dog miles. And we've fixed that dodgy light in the workshop . . .'

The trivia soothed her. She told Nita about Cyprus, Nita told her about how the days had gone, but finally they had to get around to Amelia. 'Mum . . .' Cass didn't need to continue with the rest of the sentence. They both recognised something in her tone.

'Darling, I promise she will be gone by the time you get back. We've rung round all sorts of places to try and find her somewhere. She is—'

'Not our responsibility.'

'No, I do know that, but she is also a poor damaged lost little soul.'

'And still not our responsibility.'

'No one else seems to care about her. I suggested she

231

rang her mum but Amelia said she won't have her back. And before you say anything else, I know, I know – don't worry. You enjoy your holiday; it'll all be just fine.'

Cass smiled. 'You always say that, Mum.'

'And I'm always right. Now, tell me what else is happening.'

Cass paused for a moment, wondering where exactly she should start, but ended up giving a blow-by-blow description of the trip she'd taken, what the island and the hotel were like – and, after fifteen minutes of gossip and laughter, she hung up with a strange sense of relief. Apparently the stain had come off the carpet as well, which Nita was proud of.

Cass was just about to pick up her bag and jacket when there was a tap-tap-tap at the door. She opened it to find Andy standing in the doorway.

Cass groaned. 'Whatever you've come to say, I don't want to hear it.'

'I haven't seen you around,' he said.

'Deliberately,' said Cass, blocking the doorway. 'I've been keeping out of your way. Have you spoken to Amelia?'

'Yes, albeit briefly – but I think we're getting it sorted out. It's hard for her. She blames me,' he said, moving uneasily from foot to foot.

'Hardly surprising, is it? I mean, it is *your* responsibility – you can't just abandon her.' And then she stopped, sick and tired of all the games the pair of them were playing, and angry at being put upon. 'Andy, actually, please go away. I've had enough. I'm supposed to be on holiday. I've been looking forward to coming here for months. None of what's going on between you and Fee is my fault and none of it is anything to do with me. You understand?

I don't want to be privy to any more of your family's little dark secrets. Leave me out of this. Out of all of it . . .'

Andy pulled a face. 'All of what?'

Exasperated, Cass said, 'You have to talk to Fiona – you have to tell her soon.'

There was a moment of silence and then, from somewhere behind him, Fiona said, quietly, 'What is it you have to tell me, Andy?'

Cass groaned and felt her heart sink while Andy's colour drained away to nothing. He swung round. 'Are you following me?'

Fiona pulled a face. 'Why? Should I be?'

Andy turned back to Cass. 'I just told her I was nipping upstairs to get my wallet.'

Cass shook her head in frustration. 'Right and why tell the truth when a lie is so much better,' she snapped.

'And presumably while you were up here you thought you'd check up on little Miss Squeaky Clean, did you?' barked Fiona. 'I suppose this answers my question really.' She swung round to look at Cass, her face cold and angry and full of hurt. 'So this was why you were so rude to me downstairs?'

'What do you mean, rude?' said Cass in amazement. 'I wasn't rude to you. I lied for you.'

Andy was about to say something but he was way too slow.

'You've been seeing Andy behind my back, haven't you?' Fiona growled. 'While I've been having my afternoon nap.' And then she swung back to confront Andy. 'You see – I knew there was something going on all along, I knew you were lying to me, Andy,' she said, poking him with an angry finger. 'All this time.' And then she swung back, as if she didn't want to let either of them off the hook. 'And what sort of friend are you, Cass? I mean, she's so bloody *ordinary*, Andy.' Fiona spat it out as if it was the ultimate insult. 'How could you, she is so, so—' Fiona's voice was rapidly rising to a bellow.

'Ordinary is nice once in a while,' snapped Andy. 'And so is kind, and warm, and she listens to me.'

Cass was horrified. 'No, I don't,' she protested. 'Leave me out of this.'

'Oh really,' said Fiona, ignoring Cass and hitting her stride. 'So you're saying you *are* seeing her, are you? How long has this been going on? I thought you were my friend,' roared Fiona. 'Was it you that he's been seeing all this time? Was it you? You know you played me for a complete fool – and to think that I asked you for your help. You two must have been laughing your bloody socks off at me – you bastards!'

Cass backed away, worried what Fiona would do next, all the while looking at Andy, willing him to say something, but instead he looked totally shocked and mystified by Fiona's outburst.

'For god's sake, Andy, do something, tell her the truth,' Cass finally begged, in desperation. How thick could one man be?

Andy shook his head. 'Fiona doesn't want to hear the truth – surely you've realised that by now? She only hears what she wants to hear. She doesn't listen to anything I say – doesn't matter what it is. I tell her that I don't want a baby and she just assumes that I'm making it up.'

'Oh that's low, how dare you?' snarled Fiona, but Andy carried on, apparently oblivious. 'I've tried talking to her about what's going on for weeks now, but every time I've got anywhere near the subject she's shut me out. I tell her that I'm unhappy and that we need to talk and she doesn't want to listen, Cass. She doesn't want to understand.'

Cass stared at him in disbelief, willing him to untangle the knot he was tying.

'And I suppose that's where you come in, is it?' snapped Fiona to Cass.

'Fee, this is not what you think,' protested Cass lamely. '*Andy, for fuck's sake, just tell her.*'

Fiona swung round to Andy. 'Yes Andy, just tell me. Tell me,' she shrieked.

Cass stood waiting for Andy to say something – seconds ticked by. 'Please Andy,' said Cass, feeling exhausted. 'Please explain to Fee what's going on.'

Andy took a deep breath as if to compose himself, and when he spoke it was in a cool, even gentle voice. 'Fiona, there is something I really have to tell you—'

Fiona made as if to say something, but Andy held up a hand to silence her. 'Please,' he said. 'Just listen for a few minutes.'

Indignantly she pressed her lips together in a thin pleat of fury, crossing her arms across her chest.

'Fiona,' he continued in the same low, even voice, 'You have to believe me. This has got nothing to do with Cass. The only thing she's ever done has been to try and help. And listen.'

Fiona's expression hardened, but Andy shook his head and something about his manner kept her quiet. 'This isn't about Cass, this is about you and me.'

Cass stared at him, willing him to clear the air, willing him to get to the point, but apparently now that he finally had Fiona's attention, he had no intention of being rushed.

'Fee, I've been unhappy with the way things have been between us for a long time. You know that. I wasn't going to talk about this until we got back home because I didn't want to spoil the holiday, but you won't let go, will you? And there's no good time to tell you this. Fiona, it's over.'

There was a long, dark, dangerous pause, the shock registering on Fiona's face. Then she said, 'What?' her voice cold as ice. 'What do you mean it's *over*?'

'I don't want to be with you any more,' he said. His tone was flat, matter of fact.

Cass closed her eyes. She hadn't been sure which part of the story Andy had intended to start with, but it sure as hell wasn't this one.

'Please Andy tell her why,' she said. 'Please tell her . . .'

Fiona swung round to face Cass. Her face was red with fury, eyes brimming with tears. 'Oh, don't worry, I can guess why. Well, I hope the pair of you are fucking happy. You're ruined my holiday, you've ruined my life – you bitch.'

Cass reeled as Fiona drew back her hand and slapped her hard across the face, tears filled her eyes and she gasped as Andy leapt forward to protect her.

Fiona, meanwhile, stormed inside their bedroom and slammed the door shut behind her. An instant later Cass heard banging and cupboards being flung open in what she assumed was a frenzy of packing.

Andy was still standing with his mouth open. 'I'm so sorry,' he said, putting his arm around her. 'Are you all right?'

'Of course I'm not all right. Why the hell didn't you tell her about Amelia?' said Cass, still stunned, rubbing her cheek. It was hot and red and stinging.

'I didn't get a chance,' he said. 'It'll be all right. I'm sure she'll calm down.'

Cass stared at him and shook her head. Talk about a natural-born optimist. He obviously didn't know Fiona at all. 'Calm down? You have got to be joking,' she said. 'She hit me.'

Before Andy could say anything else, the door to the room next door was flung open and Fiona started throwing Andy's clothes out onto the landing, followed by his shoes, books, toiletries – a bottle of shampoo bounced across the carpet, the cap popping off before emptying itself all over the far wall in an explosion of blue-green gel.

Andy started to gather things up. 'Or perhaps not,' he muttered as he scooped up a dressing gown and his swimming trunks.

Chapter Thirteen

Cass, still reeling from Fiona's accusations and the slap, decided that whatever was going to happen next she didn't want to be any part of it, so she picked up her things and, headed down the stairs and into town, leaving Andy still gathering up his possessions.

On the corner, a stone's throw from the harbour, Cass found a quiet little bistro and went inside. As it was early, the place was almost empty. Cass was shown to a table and pulled out her book, trying hard to ignore her shaking hands and the way her heart was thumping. She couldn't remember anyone ever hitting her before. She'd been so stunned that the emotional sting of it and Fiona's accusations were only now beginning to sink in. She got the waiter to bring her a drink and made the effort to calm down, watching the sea, and the people walking down towards the harbour. However, the peace didn't last long. She'd barely had a chance to glance through the menu when Andy appeared at the window and waved to her.

Cass decided to ignore him. A waiter approached and asked if she would like another drink at about the same time as Andy came over.

'Cass, we need to talk.'

She looked up at him. 'Oh no we don't. Go away. I want to eat in peace and I don't want another scene.'

'I promise you there won't be – I'm sorry. I had no idea she'd react like that.'

'She thinks we're having an affair.'

He reddened. 'I don't know where she got that from. She doesn't really think that. I'm sure when she calms down she'll be so sorry.'

Cass leant forward, 'Andy, are you totally stupid? Yes, she does.'

'No, she doesn't, she thinks—'

'Andy, this is not a pantomime. She thinks I'm having an affair with you. And before that she just thought you were having an affair.'

He looked puzzled, and started fiddling with the cutlery as if letting the words sink in. 'Really? Why on earth did she think that?'

'Because of all the bloody creeping about you've been doing over the last few weeks – presumably since you first met Amelia. She came round to see me to ask if I would spy on you.'

Andy paled. 'Really? When?' he said. 'Come on. You're joking?'

Cass shook her head. 'Why the hell would I do that? You know when she told you that we'd had a talk?'

He nodded.

'Fiona came round one evening and asked if I'd spy on you. She brought a wig . . .'

Andy stared at her.

'You were acting suspiciously and she wanted to know what was going on. You must have just started seeing Amelia.'

He sighed and then shook his head. 'But I'm not like that.'

Cass stared at him in amazement. 'But you *are*, Andy. Fiona was right about you.'

'But she isn't, I've been trying to find a way to tell her. I've spent the last few months trying to work out how Amelia and now the baby can fit into my life. I've never been in the right relationship at the right time to have a family before and then suddenly I find out I'm a father—'

'And now you've abandoned Amelia too.'

'I haven't – it's complicated. I did say that whether she wanted the baby or not, I would try and help her financially.'

'You're all heart,' said Cass grimly.

'This isn't my responsibility Cass.'

Cass stared at him in horror. 'You really are a complete bastard. She's your girlfriend, she's pregnant – how can you possibly say she's not your responsibility?'

Now it was Andy's turn to stare. 'What – who is?'

'Amelia, your girlfriend,' snapped Cass.

Andy's face was a picture of confusion. 'She's not my girlfriend,' he protested.

'Well, whatever she is,' said Cass angrily.

'No, no, what I mean is Amelia's *not* my girlfriend. Amelia is my daughter.'

Cass felt her jaw drop. 'Your daughter?' she murmured. 'But I thought . . .' Cass struggled to catch her breath, trying to get her head around what that meant. 'You mean the baby's not yours?'

He shook his head. 'No, of course it's not. I've spent weeks trying to work out how to tell Fiona about Amelia and get it all out in the open – I mean, how hard can it be?

240

"*Fiona I want to tell you about my daughter, her name's Amelia – she's twenty and I didn't know she existed until a couple of months ago when she rang me out of the blue and said, 'Hi, my name is Amelia and you used to know my mum when you were at Uni.' 'I'd really like you to meet her.'*"

'Why didn't you just tell her?'

Andy sighed. 'You want the truth? I don't think there is any way that Fiona could understood what Amelia showing up means – or what a shock it was to find out about her. Maybe I should have given her the chance, but my every instinct is that Fee wouldn't have understood, and she certainly wouldn't be happy. Instead I think she would be hurt and jealous, anxious and angry and threat-ened. I couldn't deal with those things on top of having to cope with Amelia.'

'She thought you were having an affair.'

'She ought to know me better than that.'

'You can hardly blame her. You started getting a lot of text messages, emails – she thought you were behaving oddly, and then she found a piece of paper with a time and place on it.'

Andy pulled a face. 'Really?'

Cass nodded. 'That was when I said that she needed to talk to you about what was going on, and that me sneaking about wasn't going to sort anything out.'

'God,' Andy said, running his fingers back through his hair, 'I'm really sorry – I'd got no idea. Do you know what it said on the piece of paper?'

'Sam's Place, eight o'clock,' said Cass, the message still as clear in her mind as when Fiona had first told her, even though it all seemed a long time ago now.

Somewhere, behind Andy's eyes, Cass could see

comprehension dawning. 'Sam's Place,' he said, almost to himself.

'The place you wouldn't take her to,' said Cass.

Andy looked up in surprise. 'You're not serious, are you?' he asked.

'Maybe I'm not, but Fiona was. She thought you wouldn't take her there because that was where you were meeting your other woman.'

'Oh god,' he said. 'It wasn't anything – why didn't she say something? It's complete madness. Basically, the only reason I didn't want to go was because it looked like one of those something-and-nothing places, you know, food's expensive and bad, with designer beer and overpriced coffee. I'm also not twenty-five any more.'

'You don't have to explain it to me. She thought you wouldn't take her because you were seeing someone there.'

'At Sam's Place?'

Cass nodded. 'And that was where I first saw you with Amelia.'

She could see Andy staring at her, saw him about to protest and then saw him catching up. 'That's right, you're right. At eight o'clock in the morning in the market square – she was on her way to work, she asked me to meet her. It was bitterly cold, we had a coffee.'

'And I was there buying fish. I saw you by accident.'

'Really? That's amazing. Did you tell Fiona that you'd seen me?'

Cass shook her head, thinking about how much she had agonised over her decision to say nothing. 'No, I didn't – I mean, what was there to tell? Amelia could have been anyone. Andy, this is madness. If you want Fiona back why don't you just tell her about Amelia and be

242

done with it? Things can't be any worse than they are now, surely?'

Andy sighed. 'I was going to just now, but something keeps holding me back. It's almost like I don't want her to know. And to be honest, I don't want her back.' He sighed, suddenly looking tired and lost and at the end of his tether. 'We'd already got to the end of "us" before we moved down to Norfolk, but I was thinking maybe this was the change we needed. Fiona's brilliant in so many ways, and I do love her. I suppose we both knew this was the last-ditch attempt to make it come right. But after the first couple of months I think we both realised that nothing had changed. Fiona makes everything into a drama, and the bottom line is that everything is always all about her. This thing with Amelia is hard enough to deal with—'

'Because she makes everything into a drama?' Cass said.

He laughed. 'My track record with women doesn't look that great, does it?'

And against all the odds Cass felt sorry for him. 'So, what are you going to do now?'

'Well I think I've already done it. I promise that as soon as I get home I'll sort Amelia out and get her out of your house.' The waiter handed each of them a menu. 'You hungry?' Andy asked, glancing down the list of dishes.

'Actually,' said Cass, 'I'm ravenous – but I need to eat and then get to tonight's concert on time.'

'Okay fine, well in that case, let's order.' He glanced up at the waiter. 'What's good and quick?'

The man smiled and took them on a guided tour of the evening's specials. Once they'd made their choices, Cass settled back and let him order the wine.

'And you'll definitely sort things out with Amelia?' Cass said as the waiter brought them their food.

'I've arranged to have lunch with her as soon as we get back – although the way today went, that may be sooner than I'd expected. My plan had been to get home, talk to Fiona, tell her about Amelia and, if things had gone well, arrange for them to meet.'

'Over lunch?' said Cass in surprise.

'No – no, that would all have got way too messy,' he said, mopping up the sauce from the seared prawns that they were busy working their way through. 'I have this amazing capacity for getting myself involved with complex women.'

'I think you'd find women a lot less trouble if you told them the truth from the start,' said Cass.

'You think I'm a coward.'

'No, not really a coward, just stupid – you need to make a better fist of living your life.'

He nodded. 'You're right.' The wine waiter offered him the bottle, label first. 'It's fine,' he said, waving the man to pour it. 'Fiona has been really down, tired. She's been sleeping every afternoon since we got here – except on the trip she went on with you today. I've tried to give her some space.'

Cass, avoiding his eyes, picked up her glass and took a sip. These two still had far too many secrets. Did she say something, did she keep quiet? When she looked up, Cass was surprised to find Andy looking at her. 'What,' she said, trying to make light of it, 'have I got something pink and prawny stuck in my teeth?'

'No, no you haven't,' he sighed. 'I was just thinking that this is nuts. You've ended up in deep shit for being a good

244

friend – you've got my girlfriend on your case, my daughter in your house. Would you like to punch me now or later?'

In spite of herself, Cass laughed. 'I don't want to punch you at all, Andy. All I want is to get my home back, my life back and to have a great time while we're here. I've been looking forward to this trip for months.' She sighed, 'Look, I've really got to go. I've got tickets for the concert this evening.

'Me too – look, let's finish this and I'll walk you down there.'

Cass looked at him. 'I don't think that's a very good idea, do you?' Smiling she got to her feet and opened her bag.

But Andy shook his head. 'This one's on me,' he said, and with that Cass finished her glass of wine, got up and headed down towards the amphitheatre, joining a steady stream of people on their way to see the evening's perform-ance, pulling her jacket around her shoulders as she went.

Ahead of her she could see Alan and his wife, little gaggles of other choir members amongst the general public and other choirs. So far every evening the tiers had seemed full of people. She sighed. It was such a shame that the thing with Fiona and Andy was being played out now. Deep in thought, she didn't notice Bekya falling into step alongside her.

'You look a little bleak,' he said.

Cass laughed, this from a man who looked as if he would be perfectly at home in a crypt. 'I was wondering if you might like to get under a blanket with me and my girlfriend Alya.'

Skipping along beside him, struggling to keep up with his daddy-long-leg strides was a diminutive blonde. She smiled as Cass met her eye, and held out a hand. 'Good evening. Bekya has told me about you – he was telling me you were a lady bass; I was expecting someone altogether hairier. With more – you know.' She waved a hand in the general direction of Cass's chest.

Cass laughed. 'Well in that case I'm sorry to disappoint you. I really enjoyed your concert the other night – it was brilliant.'

'Of course, why wouldn't it be?' Bekya said with a sly grin. 'Of course the regular beatings help. We are hoping we're going to win the competition and infiltrate the decadent Yankee heartland. Actually, I'm glad we spotted you. You remember our American friend? George?'

'How could I ever forget?'

'Well, he and his good lady wife and his beloved daughter have been our constant companions since we met at dinner the other night.' There was a heavy dollop of sarcasm in his tone.

Alya pulled a face. 'I think they believe they are rescuing us from some terrible hellish Estonian nightmare. They gave me a leaflet asking if I was ready to welcome Jesus into my life. And over breakfast he took me on one side and said if we ever needed sanctuary . . .' Alya rolled her eyes heavenwards. 'And then they asked if we were cohabiting – well, at least he did. He was keen to hear any details.'

Bekya nodded. 'And then his wife, she said, "Now now, George, you know that the good lord says don't judge lest you be judged".'

'Which would have been just fine if he hadn't spent all day yesterday on the terrace staring at my . . .' Alya waved towards her cleavage, which it had to be said was fairly impressive, even from where Cass was standing.

'You can hardly blame him. It's a lovely view,' said Bekya with a shrug.

At which point Alya slapped him. Hard.

'See what I mean about the beatings?' he said miserably. 'Anyway, if you would like to share our blanket you would be very welcome.'

Cass smiled. 'Sounds like a great idea.'

A second or two later they were joined by Alf and a handful of altos. She had no doubt that there was going to be some sort of fallout from the run-in she had had with Fiona, although she no idea what or when it was going to happen – in the meantime Cass was relieved to find herself in such convivial company.

Bekya and Alya, and their easy good humour, were an instant hit with Alf and Ray and the altos, and several of Bekya's friends came over to mingle before the performance kicked off, so when the lights finally dimmed, Cass had no idea whether Andy or Fiona were in the theatre or not. The evening's choirs were an ex-pat group who had helped set up the festival, and did a whole series of 1950s and 60s numbers, which were toe-tappingly good; after the intermission they were followed by a black gospel choir who – had there been a roof on the theatre – would have raised it.

'Would you like to join us for a drink back at the hotel?' suggested Alya to Cass as the final bows were taken and people around them started to get to their feet. 'We are having a little party. The hotel manager comes from the same town as our choir.' As she spoke she waved a hand to extend the invitation to Alf and the rest of the gang. 'All of you. It will be fun. Much dancing and singing.'

'And drinking,' added Bekya helpfully.

Cass nodded. 'Why not?' and joined the throng of singers heading back to the Athena Grande, where it seemed the Estonians were already famous and, as far as management were concerned, the contest's natural winners.

There was food laid out for them, along with enough wine and vodka to float a battleship. Cass danced, sang and generally made merry. Whatever was waiting for her back at the hotel could keep.

At around midnight Alf came over to say his good nights. He caught hold of her hands and gave her a kiss, one on each cheek – apparently all this continental living was rubbing off on him. 'See you in the morning, pet. I'm going to have an early night – I want to be fresh for our concert tomorrow. And I've got my announcing to run through.' He grinned and then patted his jowls with the back of his hand. 'I need my beauty sleep – unlike some people,' he said. 'And besides, I promised I'd give the missus a ring tonight and it wouldn't do to sound as if I was having too good a time, would it? You'll be all right walking back on your own?'

Cass nodded, and wished him good night before being swept out onto the dance floor by Bekya.

As the number finished and he escorted her back to the bar, Alya came over. 'Your name *is* Cass, isn't it?' she asked, looking terribly serious, an expression that didn't sit well on her tiny elfin features.

Cass nodded, wondering what was going to come next. One run-in with a jealous girlfriend was more than enough for one night. 'Why?' she asked cautiously.

Alya pointed over towards the double doors. 'Because there was a man looking for you a little while ago, he said it was urgent. He was over there.'

248

Cass's mind did a quick recce of possible reasons that someone might be looking for her, starting with Alf having a rethink and feeling anxious about her walking home on her own, and ending up with mangled children, an electro-cuted mother and Buster on the railway line – there was a downside to having an overactive imagination. She ended up with the most likely: Andy.

'What did he look like?'

Alya considered for a second. 'Not bad – nice,' she said. 'With dark hair and good eyes.'

Sounded even more like Andy. 'Did he say what it was about?'

Alya shook her head. 'No, he said it was –' she pulled a face as if trying to find the right words – 'just for you – not to tell anyone else.'

Like that helped. Cass looked around the hall trying to pluck a face out of the crowd, and then, from amongst the dancers where she had been standing, she saw the face she had been looking for.

Andy . . . Cass sighed. Who else would it be? As their eyes met, he hurried over to her, pushing his way through the crowd.

'Cass, I'm so glad I've found you. Is Fiona with you?'

Cass stared at him. 'Do you really think that's likely?'

'Have you seen her?'

'Since she called me a bitch and slapped my face, no,' said Cass. 'Why?'

Andy looked around anxiously. 'She's gone – she's not in the hotel. She's not in the bar or on the terrace; I've looked everywhere. I'm really worried about her. After I spoke to you I went back to the room to see how she was. She seemed to have calmed down a lot. She'd been crying and – then she said she'd be okay, and that she just needed a bit of time to herself and she'd see me at the concert. After she went, I tidied up and then went down to the theatre. She showed up late and she was kind of odd – not that it's that surprising really. But anyway, during the interval she said she didn't feel very well and wanted to go back to the hotel.

I offered to go with her, walk her back – but she didn't want me to, she said there was no point and that she'd be fine. I took her to where the path joins the harbour road. Anyway, I went back there straight after the show. And she'd gone . . .'

Andy had obviously been trying to order the events in his head, replaying them to get the order set, to try and work out what had happened and when.

Cass stared at him; it all sounded horribly like an alibi. Andy, meanwhile, had a glazed expression, as if he couldn't quite believe what was happening.

'I'm sure she'll be fine, Andy. Did she take anything?'

There was a flash of panic on Andy's face. 'What do you mean, like pills or something?' he asked, sounding even more anxious. 'Oh my god, it never occurred to me – I never thought to check. We've only got things like paracetamol, diacalm, some antihistamines—'

'No, not pills, I meant a jacket, money – her passport?'

'Bloody hell, I didn't check that either.' He paused. 'Actually wait. Wait – let me think. I know that she had a jacket with her and she's got her bag, so I presume she's got money and her wallet. Our passports are in the safe in our room. Maybe I should go and check to see if they're still there?'

'Gently Andy,' said Cass, touching his arm, trying to

quell his panic. 'She's probably just gone for a walk. I'm sure she's just fine. There's no reason to think she's . . .' Cass couldn't bring herself to say the word that had popped unbidden into her head.

'In trouble?' suggested Andy. 'She wouldn't do anything silly – she wouldn't – Christ . . .' He stopped, obviously unable to say the words.

'No,' Cass said in a soothing voice.

'I know she was upset about what I'd said, but it was more than that – she sounded kind of strange.'

'In what way?' asked Cass.

'It's hard to put my finger on . . .'

'Try,' said Cass.

He took a deep breath and then said very slowly, 'I know this sounds crazy but it was almost as if – it was like she was relieved.'

Of all the emotional strangeness Andy might have come up with, relief had been nowhere on Cass's radar. 'Relieved,' Cass repeated.

Andy nodded. 'That's right. I know it sounds strange, but it was like she was glad that she'd caught me out. Even if it wasn't true. Glad that I'd told her it was over. And now I'm worried that she might have done something . . .' This time he left the implication hanging and his tone darkened. This time Cass had no trouble filling the gap.

'Are you saying that you think Fiona might be a danger to herself?' Even as she was saying it, Cass knew from experience that when the chips were down Fiona was far more likely to be a danger to other people, in an emotionally destructive rather than lone-gunman-on-the-roof way.

'I don't know – god, this is such a mess. What if – she's, you know – done something silly?'

Cass touched Andy's arm. 'Before we go there, let's go back to the hotel – she's probably up in her room by now. It's been a rough time for everyone.'

Andy nodded. 'And it's all my fault,' he said.

Cass was about to say something to console him, but stopped herself – when you came right down to it, Andy was right, most of it *was* his fault.

'Come on,' said Cass, 'let's go back.'

They hurried down the esplanade, Andy talking all the way, going over and over what he'd said and what she'd said, the words passing like rosary beads worked from hand to hand. Cass said nothing; after all, what was there to say?

Upstairs Andy unlocked their room and then for some reason stood aside so that Cass could look inside first; one thing was for certain, Fiona wasn't there.

The windows onto the terrace were open, the bedside lamps lit and there were clothes strewn all over the bed, others in a large blue suitcase balanced on the coffee table, some on the floor, still more in a pile on one of the chairs.

'God, have you been burgled?' said Cass, trying to make some sense of it.

Andy looked uncertain. 'What?'

'Was it like this before you left?'

Andy hesitated. 'Like what?'

Cass picked a shoe up from the dressing table. Its other half was on a chair by the bed. Alongside it was a blouse and a sock and a pile of carrier bags. 'All this mess.'

Andy nodded and then nodded again, as if he was catching up. 'Sorry – yes. It always looks like this. Fiona's not very tidy.'

It was an understatement; the room looked as if they

252

had been running an upmarket jumble sale. 'So you're saying that your life is always this untidy?'

He nodded again. 'I'm a bit tidier,' he offered.

Cass dropped the shoe back where she'd found it. 'Looking at this lot, how the hell are we going to work out if she's taken anything with her?'

Andy looked blank.

'Can you just check to see if Fee's taken her passport?'

Andy opened the safe; her passport was still there, along with his. He couldn't be sure whether she had taken any cash because he wasn't sure how much they had had to begin with, although he was certain if Fiona had her wallet then she had her bank cards with her.

None of this was helping find Fiona, although Cass's instinct was to leave things a while and see if she turned up. Fiona didn't really strike Cass as the suicidal type.

'Tell you what,' said Cass, after a few fruitless minutes spent staring at what looked like a scrimmage in a designer clearance sale. 'Let's go downstairs and take another look round the hotel. Someone is bound to have seen her.'

Andy didn't look so convinced. He dropped the dress he had been holding onto the bed. It was the petrol blue silk halter-neck that Fiona had been wearing a day or so earlier, and something about it and the whisper of Fiona's perfume played on Cass's mind. Andy's anxiety had clouded her judgement. Cass had a damned good idea who Fiona was with, if not where. It was just a case of finding her.

Downstairs, Fiona wasn't in the bar, nor was she in the TV lounge or out on the terrace. She wasn't by the pool or out in the gardens. No one had seen her in the bar next door or in the little coffee shop that backed onto it.

Andy, driven by guilt, was getting more and more frantic with every passing minute. 'Maybe we should just ring the police. It's getting late – anything could have happened to her. I don't understand why she hasn't come back. I shouldn't have said anything . . .'

Getting away from the melodramatic, Cass didn't like to point out that Cyprus was one of those places where you felt safe walking at night, that there were at least two or three night clubs within walking distance and the bars were still open on the main strip as well as in all the hotels. There were a lot of other places to look before they started getting the police on the case. Not that any of this was helping Andy. You didn't have to be a mind-reader to see how guilty he felt. She stared at him. Maybe she *was* taking it too lightly – maybe Andy was right to be worried.

They were just walking back across the foyer to reception; Andy planned to go and take one more look in the bar.

Cass was beginning to think maybe it would be simpler if they did ring the police – certainly it would make Andy feel better and make him feel as if they were doing something – when she spotted the boards set up with the list for the trips, and something clicked.

People were still coming in from their evening out, people from the choirs, and other guests, most heading either towards the bar or to the stairs or lifts taking them up to bed. Cass, meanwhile, hurried across to the reception desk. The girl, a smoky-eyed brunette, smiled at her. 'Good evening, may I help you?'

Cass nodded. 'I wonder, could you tell me if Geno is on duty this evening?'

The girl's warm but professional veneer didn't shift for

an instant. 'I'm not sure, madam, let me ring through. Who should I say is calling?'

Cass gave her name and the girl called someone and – still holding Cass's gaze – said something in Greek and then nodded. 'He is on later, but Nick is here – he will be out to see you in a moment, if you would just like to take a seat.' She indicated the chairs and sofa arranged around a traditional Greek fireplace on the far side of the foyer.

A few seconds later, Nick came out of the office looking gorgeous in his crisp dark suit; he smiled when he saw her. 'Hi, you must be psychic. I'm just about to go off duty. Would you like to join me for a drink?'

Cass, smiling, shook her head. 'Nice idea but no, I've got a bit of problem. I'm looking for my friend . . .' she paused. 'You remember – Fiona? I think she's been seeing Geno . . .'

Nick nodded. 'I know who you mean. I haven't seen her this evening but I've been on duty – is there a problem?'

'I don't know, I don't think so, but I really need to find her. Do you know where Geno is? I think she may be with him. My friend said that he has a villa near here?'

Nick nodded. 'That's right, three of us rent one a little further down the coast – but there's no need to go all that way. Geno's on call tonight. He should be taking over from me. He'll be staying here tonight, in the staff flat.'

'So he's here now?' said Cass.

Nick laughed. 'Well in theory he should be, but so far I haven't seen him – mind you, that doesn't mean he's not about.' He glanced at his watch. 'He's like a bad penny. I'm expecting him any time at all. His car is in the car park – knowing him he's having a quick drink somewhere else or with someone else.' He grinned. 'The man is a dog—' And then he realised what he'd said and reddened. 'I mean—'

Cass stopped him. 'I know just what you mean and it's fine. I just need to find Fiona and make sure that she's okay. If he turns up, can you tell him I'd really like a word with him?'

He smiled. 'Sure thing. Are you sure you won't join me for a drink?'

'No, but thanks – I need to find my friend.'

Cass turned away to consider her next move. She could see Andy in the bar talking to some of the other singers from the choir – he seemed to be in deep conversation, and one of the women was pointing back out towards the harbour. Cass decided that what she planned to do next was probably best done alone. She turned and hurried back upstairs, up past the floor booked for the choir, up onto the one above where she and Andy and Fiona had rooms, and then, pushing open the heavy fire doors at the far end of the hallway, up the final flight onto the top floor that Nick had told her earlier in the week was used for staff accommodation.

The plush veneer of the public rooms ceased as soon as she turned the corner into the final stairwell – gone were the thick red and blue heavily patterned carpet, the half-height panelling and butter-coloured walls, to be replaced by utilitarian white emulsion and bare concrete treads. On the half landing stood a cluster of chairs, with an ashtray balanced between them on an upturned crate. The long corridor beyond the fire door, although clean, was lit by a series of bare bulbs hanging from the ceiling. There was a sense of the top floor being off limits to paying guests, the air warm and clammy, smelling of cleaning fluid and stale water mixed with tobacco smoke and after-shave. Halfway down, by the lift doors, there were service carts stocked and ready for the next day, along with buckets and mops and trays piled high with little cartons of milk, sugar, tea and coffee. Several of the doors had signs on them. Some Cass could understand, while others were written in Greek, tacked on with tape or pins.

Beyond the service area and the trolleys, the corridor changed character again, becoming more domestic, like the corridor of student flats or cheap bedsits. Here and there people had hung posters and pictures on the walls, and pinned postcards to the doorframes. Some doors had names on, and from behind some Cass could hear the low burble of music or TV, from another the soft resonant burr of snoring.

Cass wasn't sure what exactly she was looking for, and with each step was getting slightly more concerned about someone finding her there – and then, just as she thought that she'd got it wrong, Cass heard a voice and stopped mid-stride. It was a voice she would have recognised anywhere. It was Fiona and she was laughing – more accurately she was giggling, softly.

Somewhere close by, Fiona was having a fine time. It certainly didn't sound like she had any current plans to top herself. Cass stood very still, thinking about what she should do next, when she heard someone coming and swung round, trying to come up with an excuse. Except she didn't need one, because it was Andy.

'There you are,' he said. 'I wondered where you'd got to. I followed you upstairs – the fire doors hadn't quite shut. What . . .'

But before he could finish, from somewhere close by

came the sounds of Fiona giggling again, except that this time the sound was throatier and dirtier and ended in what was unmistakeably a low earthy groan. And then, just in case there were any lingering doubts about what was going on behind the closed door of the room, Fiona moaned, 'Oh yes, yes – yes – oh my god yes . . .', words that were accompanied by the sounds of bedsprings working furiously and a mind-blowing groan.

There was a horrible silence. Andy looked at Cass, Cass looked at Andy, and watched as every last shred of colour drained from his face. 'How long have you known about this?' he whispered.

Cass shook her head. 'Oh right, so this is my fault too, is it? she hissed.

For a second it looked as if Andy was going to burst into the room; Cass held her breath and then he swung back and walked away. 'How could you—?' he began, but Cass silenced him with a look.

'Don't you dare try and foist the blame for this onto me,' she said. 'You brought it on yourself – you're all secrets, the pair of you . . .'

'But you knew she was seeing someone else,' he persisted.

Cass shook her head, although what she really wanted to do was to punch him. 'Not for certain.'

'Why didn't you tell me?' he said, his voice tight and painful.

'Andy, don't – this is so rich – you're the one who didn't tell Fee about Amelia; you're the one who told Fiona it was over between you. You're the one who said that you didn't want to be with her.'

'But—'

'But bloody nothing,' Cass snapped angrily. 'You said

yourself your relationship has been going downhill. What did you want? Fiona to go limping off, licking her wounds?' Cass shook her head, furious with herself for arguing Fiona's corner.

Andy's expression hardened but Cass wasn't impressed. 'Don't look at me like that, I'm not the one creeping around trying to make sure my girlfriend doesn't know what's going on in the rest of my life . . .' She stopped. This was pointless and hurtful and getting them nowhere. 'Look, none of what's going on between you two at the moment is pretty, Andy. And, as for what Fiona has been up to, bottom line is – I didn't know for certain and I wasn't going to ask.'

'Well you don't have to be a rocket scientist to work out what was going on in there,' growled Andy, flicking his head back towards the doorway they had moved away from. 'And there was me thinking she might have topped herself. Bloody hell – I'm such an idiot.' He rubbed his hands up over his face and through his hair, as if wiping away the residue of his anxiety. 'She didn't go on that trip with you either, did she?'

Cass looked at him, wondering for the briefest of instants whether there was any point in sustaining the deception. 'No, she didn't – the pair of you put me in an impossible situation.'

Andy nodded. 'You're right. I'm sorry,' he said. 'Maybe when all this is over I could buy you a drink.'

Cass looked at him, bemused. 'Andy, that is such a stupid thing to say.'

He laughed. 'Don't worry – forget I said it.'

'So what are you going to do now?'

Andy looked into thin air, as if considering his options,

and then very slowly he turned and headed back down the corridor towards the room currently being occupied by his girlfriend and A.N. Other.

Cass was about to ask him whether or not he thought it was a good idea, and that maybe it would be better to wait until Fiona came out and talk it through, when Andy kicked the door in.

The door must have been on some kind of bolt or Yale because at first it didn't open so much as bulge and buckle and bend, and so Andy kicked it harder and this time it splintered and then gave way, revealing a large messy bed-sitting room lit by a couple of lamps, with two beds pushed together in the middle of the room.

Cass hadn't meant to follow Andy and hadn't meant to look.

Inside, Fiona was scrabbling across the room, pulling the sheet with her to cover her naked body, while on the bed Geno, trousers round his ankles, was making an effort to pull them back up – which, given the current state of play, was proving a little tricky.

It seemed as if breaking the door down had drained Andy dry – he stood in the centre of the room, unmoving, arms hanging by his side, broken and breathing hard. 'I thought you were dead,' he said.

'I might as well have been for all you care,' snapped Fiona, trying hard to pull her clothes on whilst still covering herself with the sheet. 'What the hell do you think you're doing bursting in here?' she snarled indignantly. 'And what is *she* doing here?'

'She was helping me look for you. We've been worried.'

'Oh *we* have, have *we*?' hissed Fiona, her tone dripping venom.

Cass shook her head. 'I'm off, I don't need this,' she said to Andy and then added, 'Why don't you just tell her the fucking truth?'

She didn't bother to hang around for his reply. At the very least Fiona was safe.

'Wait, wait for me,' said Geno, pulling on a shirt and picking up a suit jacket. 'I can explain . . .'

Cass didn't wait; instead she pulled the wrecked door shut and headed back to her room. Leaving the lights off, she locked the door behind her, slipped off her clothes and fell into bed, drifting off to sleep to the soothing sound of the sea through the open French windows.

Chapter Fourteen

The choir were supposed to assemble the following morning in the function room for a run-through of the set for the evening's concert. Alan had added 'Prompt ten thirty start' to the itinerary in red felt-tip, lest anyone decided to linger over breakfast.

Cass had been up early, eaten breakfast before eight, gone for a walk down by the sea and decided it was time that she pulled out of the game Fiona and Andy were busy playing. She tried ringing home but no one was picking up and so at twenty-five past ten she headed to the hall to meet up with the rest of the gang.

There was a buzz of expectation and anticipation inside the room: tonight's concert really was what everyone had come for.

Alan, resplendent in an unnaturally Hawaiian shirt and crisp white chinos, cheeks and bald patch already pink from the sun, made his way into the centre of the loose horseshoe that the group had formed and took his spot, centre front.

Basses to his far right, tenors and altos right and left of centre, sopranos to his left. Once in position, his eyes moved slowly across the groups; body language calling them silently to order. The conversation in the hall faded from a babble to a murmur to a complete silence.

Cass looked around. There was no sign of Fiona.

'Right,' said Alan. 'Well, this is it folks – let's do a quick warm-up to get those voices going and then we'll do a run-through of starts and finishes. Nothing too strenuous – we'll save our voices for tonight; just relax and have fun. The judges are looking for style, substance and pure old-fashioned enjoyment and we've got plenty of that. So we'll start with some humming to get those vocal choirs warmed through . . .'

They worked for around an hour before Alan dismissed them. 'This evening we'll be going on in the second half – so we've got the first two tiers on the bottom right hand, behind the judges reserved for us, and we'll want to meet up in the hall here about seven thirty for a little warm-up and then walk down so we're all there at the start of the interval in the marquee by the stage entrance. Any questions?'

'Where's Fiona?' asked Ray in the little babble of noise that followed. Cass shrugged.

'I don't know . . .' Cass began.

'It's all right; I saw her last night,' said Alf knowledgeably. 'She didn't feel very cracky. Apparently, she was going to take something and go to bed. Mind you, as I said to her, to be honest, as long as she's there tonight, she's probably just as well in bed.'

The two men nodded sagely. Cass decided to keep her thoughts to herself.

'And we're off on a trip today,' said Alf. 'Mrs Alan arranged it.'

Ray nodded. 'Something cultural apparently.'

He made it sound like a trip to the dentist. 'We're doing her a favour,' said Alf. 'They weren't going to run it if they didn't get above a certain number. She asked us specially.'

Cass smiled, glad that Mrs Alan hadn't invited her, and followed everyone out into the foyer for coffee. Nick waved to her from behind the front desk and Cass smiled at him. It pulled him away from what he was doing and over to have a chat.

He nodded towards the hall. 'It sounds great.'

'Well, we'll see tonight.'

'You still on for this afternoon?'

Before Cass could reply he continued, 'I've been thinking,' said Nick. 'Maybe I could get off early and we could go somewhere and have lunch instead of waiting till three.'

'I'm grateful that you rescued me from Geno yesterday, but you don't have to take me out.'

Nick grinned. 'Don't get cold feet. It'll be great to have a drive up into the hills.'

Cass paused; at least if she was off somewhere with Nick then there was no way that she would run into either Fiona or Andy. 'You know, you're right – what time?'

'What time does your rehearsal finish?' he asked.

'We've just finished . . .'

He nodded. 'Okay well, in that case, how about I pick you up at the front in about half an hour?'

'I thought you said you weren't free till lunch time?'

Nick grinned. 'I had to cover for Geno last night – I reckon he owes me one. God alone knows where he got to. It was almost two before he finally showed up.'

Cass decided to keep mum.

'So half an hour then?' he said.

Cass nodded.

'Do you swim?'

'Yes . . .'

'In that case bring a swimsuit. I know this great spot if you fancy a swim.'

Across the foyer, Val and Nancy, carrying coffee cups, wandered past on their way out to the terrace and smiled knowingly. 'Nice work if you can get it,' said one in an undertone.

Cass laughed and then headed back upstairs to get ready.

When she came down again, Nick was waiting for her in the foyer. He was chatting to one of the receptionists, and dressed in faded jeans and a cheesecloth granddad shirt, unbuttoned just low enough to emphasise his broad suntanned chest, with its sprinkling of dark hair.

He smiled and raised a hand in greeting as she walked towards him. Cass smiled back, wondering if she might need to stop to wipe the drool off her chin. He was beautiful – around six foot tall – and with his black hair and equally dark humorous eyes he looked good enough to eat. Just a shame he wasn't about twenty years older and not engaged, thought Cass wryly.

'All set?' he asked, taking her beach bag.

She nodded, and with that he settled his hand in the small of her back and guided her out towards the front steps.

'You sure you got everything?'

Cass laughed. 'You sound like my mother.' As she spoke, Cass looked across to the foyer. Andy was sitting at one of the tables cradling a drink. Neither said a word, although for a few seconds their eyes met; something about Andy's expression made her falter, but she made herself turn away.

'Okay?' asked Nick as they stepped outside.

Cass nodded, making an effort to regain her composure. 'Fine, now tell me again what the plan is?' she asked as he opened the door of the Jeep, which was parked up under the shade of the trees that ringed the hotel gardens.

'Lunch first at this little taverna up in the mountains – it's run by friends of my family, they've owned it for years. It's very simple but they are great people, and then I thought we could go for a walk on the beach and a swim. There is this amazing place, it's a real wilderness; you'll love it, on one of the beaches up there the turtles come to lay their eggs.'

'Sounds fantastic – but I can't be late back. It's the concert tonight.'

He grinned. 'I know. I've already bought my ticket. Five be okay?'

Cass nodded and without a backward glance climbed into the Jeep. As they pulled away, Nick got a folded sheet of paper out of the glove compartment. 'I have a map if you'd like to see where we're going.'

And so they headed out of Kato Paphos, out past the roadside cafes with the broad sandy verges and bars and the shops selling ice cream and buckets and spades, out along the coast road towards the Akamas peninsula. Although it was late in the year the breeze was warm, and the scent of the trees and the sea and the wild thyme rolled in through the open windows of the Jeep.

It wasn't long before they turned off the main road and headed out along a broad dirt track between rocky crags, rolling forest and deep gorges, where the azure blue sea was framed by great stands of tough evergreens, junipers and twisted wind-bent conifers.

Nick, chatting away as the scenery unfurled like a bright ribbon, was good company, and in between stunning views and amazing scenery, Cass told him all about Fiona and Andy and Amelia, and found out about his family and working in Cyprus and the plans and dreams he had and about Geno's reputation – although Cass, seeing the way the receptionist had looked at Nick as they left, suspected that he might not be alone in having one.

By the time they stopped at a little hillside farm outside Polis for lunch, Cass was happy, relaxed and starving. The taverna was just a single room with a covered terrace, set so that the prevailing wind blew through to cool the air. One corner inside was separated off from the assortment of tables and chairs by a high stone bar, and behind it Maria, the owner, talked and laughed and sang whilst cooking. She kept the doors open as she cooked, framing a view to die for out over the steep rolling hillsides, the breeze now carrying the tantalising smell of garlic and meat, slow-cooked in an outdoor, wood-fuelled oven. Maria's husband and children joined them for lunch, along with all manner of uncles and cousins. Nick guided her through the dishes Maria had prepared, picking out the tastiest morsels. Although this might well have been one of the simplest meals that Cass had eaten while she was on Cyprus, it was by far and away the best.

After lunch, amid much hugging and encouragement to return, Nick helped Cass into the Jeep and they headed even further off the beaten track, out through the forests and miles and miles of unspoilt countryside, till finally they reached a sheltered bay, where Nick pulled up under the heavy canopy of conifers.

'We have to walk from here,' Nick said, indicating a

steep path down to a neat horseshoe of pristine sand sheltered by stands of broken rock.

'It's beautiful,' said Cass, though the words sounded inadequate.

He nodded. 'First time I came here I couldn't believe there were places like this left in the world. Lots of local people hope that this will become a national park, although it is hard to stop the slow creep of hotels and resorts – tourist are a great cash crop,' he said with a grin, helping her out of the Jeep. It was the first time they had touched and it gave Cass an odd sensation as his fingers closed around hers.

As they headed between the trees to the path, Nick moved a little closer and pointed down the coast. 'Further around the peninsula, green turtles come every summer to lay their eggs on the beach; it is totally unspoilt here – few people bother to come out this far,' he said, and then catching hold of her hand made a show of guiding her down the steep, uneven path.

There was no doubt about it, Cass thought as she picked her way between the boulders, Nick was gorgeous – but she didn't feel the need for the attention or the buzz a little bit of guilt-free lust might bring. She wondered whether that was what he was expecting. The idea that her libido might have curled up and died was worrying.

They made their way down towards the beach; it was steep, with loose shale in places that made it slippery. As they got almost to the bottom, Nick turned and helped her over a tumble of rocks, catching hold of her waist as he gently lifted her down onto the sand – and for a moment, just a moment, Cass thought that he might kiss her. The idea made the heat rush to her cheeks.

It was obvious that he felt the little frisson too.

'I think we maybe need to sort a few things out,' Cass said.

He coloured. 'I'm sorry – you think that maybe I am going to try and seduce you?' he asked. His tone was gentle and enquiring. 'Is that what you are expecting?'

It was almost as if he was reading her thoughts. 'It had crossed my mind,' she said, her eyes not leaving his.

He nodded. 'Mine too. Is that what you came out with me today for – you know, like your friend, Fiona. I mean, she is . . .' He pulled a face and his expression said it all.

Cass sighed. 'No. I'm sorry and I hope you don't think I've led you on, but I'm not like Fiona, Nick. Not at all. I'm having a great afternoon and you're gorgeous, but if you're expecting a roll in the sand,' she glanced down at the beach, soft and secluded as a feather bed, 'then you're out of luck. Please don't be offended, but it's not the kind of person I am. Would you prefer to go back to the hotel? I mean, I would understand.'

Far from looking offended, he looked relieved. 'No, no I'm having a great time. You're a very attractive woman and I'm a red-blooded man – but it's not what I had planned either. I'm not like Geno. I thought it would be nice to take a drive out with you. You're good company and great to be with – I'm really enjoying showing you some of the sights. It's funny people assume because of what I do, you know, working in the hotel and all that, with all the tourists and the girls, that I am some sort of a stud, you know?'

He grinned and blushed. 'They think I am always getting the guests into bed, collecting notches on my bed post – but actually I leave that to Geno.' He laughed. 'My fiancée in England, Beth – she's lovely, and once I've got my masters degree and have got myself set up either here or in the UK, we're going to get married, have a family.'

Cass smiled; any sense of awkwardness evaporated and she let him lead her down onto the sand, him chattering about his fiancée and working together in the hotel trade.

Finally they got to an outcrop, a pleat of rocks that ran out into the sea forming a natural jetty and ideal place to sunbathe, where Nick suggested they go in if she wanted to swim.

Cass found a sheltered spot to change and then walked slowly into the sea, letting her body ease slowly into the clear water. A few feet away from her, Nick slipped beneath the surface and glided out into the sheltered waters. Cass, still standing, watched the way his broad shoulders and muscular arms propelled his body through the water, and grinned to herself. Just her luck to pick the only faithful hunk on Cyprus – but even if he was off limits, there really was no harm in window-shopping. Who wouldn't want to watch his pert bum as he flipped over in the water and swam back towards her?

As he broke the surface, Nick was grinning, 'Come on,' he said, running his fingers back through his hair, now sleek and dark as a seal's pelt. 'The water is fabulous.'

He was right. Cass went deeper, letting the water take her weight. It was warmer than she had expected, but still made her tingle and shiver as she slid down beneath the wind-rippled surface, sighing as she dipped down into the water, covering her shoulders and head.

Swimming out a little way from the shore, Cass rolled over onto her back and stared up into the clear cloudless sky, watching sea birds wheel and turn on the thermals above them. The only sounds around her were the sigh of the water as it broke onto the beach, the wind overhead and the lap-lap-lap of the foam against the rocks, a counterpoint to the splash and hiss of Nick making his way through the clear water.

Cass closed her eyes for a second, relishing the sensation of the water cradling her, the sun on her face and the soft caress of the breeze over her face, chest and belly. It was as close to perfect as life could get.

'Is that your phone?' asked Geno.

Cass, cradled in the total calmness of the soft rocking water, blinked, trying to make sense of what he'd said. 'What?' she asked, rolling over.

Geno nodded back towards the shore. 'Your phone, it's ringing.'

Cass felt as if she had been robbed of her sense of peace and calm, and waited for a few seconds to see if it would stop. It did, and then no more than a minute later started to ring again. Cass, annoyed at being disturbed, headed back inshore, wading through the water, limbs as heavy as lead after the weightlessness of the sea, wondering who it might be. Fiona? Andy? Someone from the phone company offering her a free upgrade? Or double-glazing. She pulled a towel out of her bag, dried her hands and then pulled out the phone. It said 'shop' in the caller display, which meant it was either Rocco or her mother, or possibly Amelia finally agreeing to have a proper conversation with her.

'Hello?' said Cass.

'Oh hello, darling it's me,' said her mum. 'You rang?'

'Yesterday. I wanted to see how things were . . .'

'You mean you don't trust us with the shop and the animals?'

'Or renting rooms out.'

'Ouch,' said Nita.

'What's happening with Amelia?'

'Well . . .'

There was a little pause that Cass didn't like the sound of at all. 'Well what?'

'Well, I can't throw her out on her ear.'

'Mum, we've talked about this, you can. She is there under false pretences.'

'Ummmm.'

'What is that supposed to mean?'

'She seems to have fallen out with her whole family, although to be honest I can understand why.'

'What's that supposed to mean?' asked Cass, with a growing sense of apprehension.

'Well, she's just like every other young person living at home; she doesn't clear up, she doesn't wash up, she leaves the bath—'

'Mum, Mum wait, hold up. She isn't at home, she's in my home and she should be pulling her weight – what the hell am I saying? – she shouldn't be there at all. Is she there now, can I speak to her?'

'No, she's out at the moment, that was what I wanted to talk to you about really.'

'Mum, why don't you get Rocco to go upstairs and collect all her things and put them outside?'

'Oh no, we couldn't do that – no, what I wanted to say was . . . It's a bit tricky really.'

Cass pulled the towel up around her shoulders – the calm and tranquillity of her day at the beach rapidly being replaced by an impotent rage. 'Just tell me.'

'Well . . .'

Cass waited. It must be bad; her mother wasn't normally known for her reticence.

'You remember Mike . . . ?'

'The one with the purse.'

'Well . . .'

'Oh for god's sake, Mum. What?'

'He's been taking Amelia out.'

'What?'

'It's all a bit odd. Amelia isn't terribly easy to talk to. I'm sure it's probably her hormones – anyway, Mike turned up here on – on – I can't remember whether it was Monday . . .' There was another frustrating pause. 'Or maybe it was Tuesday.'

'Mum, the day really doesn't matter.'

'No, maybe not. Anyway, he said he loved the dresser he'd bought and had come to look and see if there was anything else. Anyway, I needed some bits and bobs from town and had asked Amelia if she was going out if she'd get them. She wasn't terribly keen – and then Mike . . . well, to cut a long story short, Mike offered Amelia a lift into town.'

'You should have put her stuff on the doorstep.'

There was a deadly silence.

'They were gone most of the afternoon.'

'Oh, come off it, Mike is . . .' Cass was going to say 'old enough to be Amelia's father', but something stopped her dead in her tracks. Amelia was young and beautiful and terribly needy, and Cass had no doubt she was cute as a button as far as most men were concerned.

'She came back all giggly and – well, you don't need to be a rocket scientist to work out what's going on there. He picked her up again this morning. I mean, it's not

273

right,' her mother was saying in a forced whisper as if the world and his wife were listening. 'I mean he's old enough to be her father. And I don't like to speak ill of people, but Amelia's a bit of a handful – I'm certain she's leading him on. Mike was telling her all about that house he's been doing up. . . . I'm mean, I'm not old fashioned, Cass, and I'm as broad-minded as the next woman – the thing is she's very manipulative and I'm worried that she'll end up moving in with him.'

'Yes . . .'

'Well, he's not very suitable,' Nita said. 'Don't get me wrong, he's a great architect.' Cass could hear her mum running out of steam. 'I feel such a fool for letting her in in the first place,' she said. 'All this is my fault.'

Cass could hear the hurt in her mum's voice and eased up. 'No it's not – Mike is a big boy and I'm sure he can take care of himself,' said Cass gently. 'And what he gets up to with Amelia is none of our business.'

'That's not how it feels,' said Nita glumly.

'Don't let it get you down. We'll sort it out – I promise.'

'What if she moves in with him?'

Cass laughed. 'Well at least she'll be out of my hair.'

Nita sniffed. 'That's not very kind,' she said darkly.

'I know – I love you.'

'And I love you too, darling.'

Cass looked back into the bay where Nick was watching her intently. 'All right?' he mouthed.

Cass nodded. 'Fine,' she said. 'Look, Mum, I've got to go – I was just having a swim.'

'Sounds like fun, see you soon. When's the big concert?'

'Tonight.'

'Break a leg.'

274

Cass laughed. Given the way life was currently going, there was every chance it might be a prophecy rather than a good-luck wish.

Cass said her goodbyes and hung up. As Cass turned, Nick was behind her holding a towel. 'You okay?'

Cass nodded. 'Uh-huh.'

'How about one more swim and then we head back?' he said.

'Sounds like a plan.'

It was getting late by the time they pulled up in front of the Centrale. Nick helped her out and then handed her her bag. 'Thank you, I've had a great time,' Cass said.

'Me too,' Nick smiled and reddened slightly.

'Maybe, when you're back in the UK, I could return the compliment – you could bring Beth down with you.'

'She'd like that. She worries about me working over here on my own.' He laughed. 'I can't think why. Anyway, I have to go – I need to see where Geno has got to,' and with that he caught hold of her hands and, pulling her close, kissed her fleetingly on the cheek.

'See you tonight,' Nick called back over one shoulder as he made his way towards the office.

Which was when Cass noticed Andy standing by reception holding a brochure, which was when she heard herself saying, 'Thanks for a lovely time.'

Which was when Nick turned round to blow her a kiss and purred, 'The pleasure was all mine.' Which was when Cass found herself blushing, furiously.

For a moment Andy opened his mouth as if he might say something and then, crestfallen and changing his mind, turned and headed back towards the lift. Cass watched him go.

As Cass was about to head upstairs, Alan hurried over looking as pink and sweaty as he had earlier. 'Oh Cass – thank goodness – I need your help. They're drunk,' he said anxiously, catching hold of her arm and dragging her across the foyer. 'All of them. What are we going to do?'

Cass stared at him, wondering who had died and left her in charge.

'Who is drunk?' she said, sensing she was about to open a can of worms.

'What do you mean, *who is drunk?*'

It seemed a perfectly reasonable question.

'The bloody bass section,' he snapped. 'And my wife.'

'What *all* of them?' said Cass, incredulous.

'Well, other than you and presumably Fiona. It was my wife's idea; she thought it would keep them out of trouble. She caught them in the bar yesterday lunch time playing down-in-one with a bottle of tequila and two off-duty holiday reps and decided that – rather than risk a replay today – they should all go on this tour with her this afternoon. Anyway, apparently the coach stopped somewhere on the way home and the driver suggested they try this local punch. She says she thinks someone must have spiked it. God knows what was in it. Come on – hurry . . .'

Outside by the pool, Alf and the rest of the lads were just finishing a chorus of 'Nelly Dean', while Alan's good lady wife joined in with the descant. It was the first time Cass had ever seen her smile.

'Oh for god's sake. We need to get them inside and get some water and coffee down them,' said Alan to Cass. 'Can you go and spread the word, see if we can get some of the others to give us a hand? I'm just bloody grateful that we're not on until the second half.'

But the word had already spread. A handful of sopranos and a gaggle of altos appeared on the terrace to help minister to the drunk and terminally merry. After a few minutes, Alan suggested everyone split into pairs and take one of the offending basses upstairs to their rooms instead of making a public spectacle of themselves in front of the other guests. Which was how it was that Cass found herself in a lift with her arm around a very cheery Alf, with an alto called Helen clutching his other side.

Apparently Helen used to be a nurse, she informed Cass as the doors of the lift hissed shut. Cass wasn't sure whether this meant Helen was able to cope with whatever life threw at her, or was just able to hold her drink. Whichever it was, she didn't look amused, although Cass was grateful she was there as Helen was able to throw Alf around like a sack of carrots.

'Did anyone ever tell you that you're a lovely woman?' Alf said, to no one in particular. Alongside her, Helen groaned and hoisted him up a little higher.

'You know, I only had a couple,' Alf protested, 'and I've got announcing to do and I think I've lost m'notes. God only knows what was in that punch. It must ha' been that we'd not eaten. I mean, did you see the state of Mrs Alan?' he giggled. 'Pished as fart. I got on the bus behind her, my god that woman is a size – arse swaying around like a hippo on heat. Big mistake wearing those shorts . . .'

Neither woman said a word as they part guided, part carried, part dragged Alf out of the lift and onto the landing.

'Have you got your key?' asked Cass as they got to the door of his room. Alf made a great show of patting his pockets and rifling through his trousers till Cass spotted it tucked into the hankie pocket of his blazer.

Helen leant Alf up against the wall while Cass unlocked the door.

'We really need to get him in the shower,' said Helen, kicking the door closed behind them. 'Lukewarm shower, lots of hot sweet tea and plenty of water.'

'I don't take sugar,' complained Alf.

Neither of them took any notice of him. 'I'll make the tea and there's water in the minibar,' Cass said. As she picked up the kettle to fill it, Alf fell onto the bed.

'I'll put the shower on,' said Helen. 'You get him undressed.'

'Me? I thought you were going to do it,' said Cass. 'You were the nurse.'

Cass looked at Alf who had an expression on his face that suggested he thought all his Christmases had come at once. 'Don't fight, girls, plenty of me to go around,' he said. 'Oh actually I feel a bit poorly.' He pressed his fingers to damp slack lips. 'I feel a little bit sick.'

'We can't put him in the shower, in the state he's in he might drown.'

On the bed, Alf was struggling to unbutton his shirt. His belly was the colour of old suet.

'Wouldn't be much of a loss as far as I can see.' Helen looked at Cass and pulled a face. 'I'm not staying.'

'You can't leave me, you said downstairs that you used to be a nurse . . .'

Helen sniffed. 'I said I'd help get him up to his room, and besides I was a midwife, he's got nothing there that I'm used to tackling. We need a man.'

'Oh please – look, hang on here for a few minutes, I'll see if I can get someone to help.'

Without waiting for an answer, Cass headed out into

the corridor which, sod's law being what it was, was deserted. Cass thought for a few seconds – she needed someone she could rely on, someone who hadn't just gone back on duty – someone who owed her. Big time. Cass hurried upstairs onto the next floor and made for Andy's room. Whatever was going on between Fiona and Andy, this was an emergency.

Andy was sitting all alone out on the balcony watching the sun slowly sinking over the sea, but his thoughts were elsewhere. Fiona was right about one thing, he hadn't been there for her for months, not since Amelia had rung him the first time. There are days that change a life and that had been one of them.

All those months ago, when he got off the phone and Fiona had come in from shopping, there had been a moment when he could have said something, could have told her, but he didn't. It would be so hard to live with the consequences and the repercussions and so he had said nothing.

If Fiona had known about Amelia, then as far as she was concerned he would have had no excuses to deny her a baby – after all, she would reason, he already had one, so why couldn't she have one too? In Fee's eyes, Amelia would be a bargaining chip, not a person, not someone who needed to be understood or made a place for in their lives. And it would be painful. Oh by god, it would be painful.

Fiona could be so cruel when she was cornered or angry or just pissed off, and she had every right to be all of those things, but he didn't want that to happen while he tried to sort out the situation with Amelia. He had been keeping so much from Fee, but if he had once opened up, where would he start?

And then of course there was Amelia. '*My mum's told me so much about you*,' she had said when they'd first met. Which was funny, because Andy had only the vaguest recollection of Amelia's mother's name, and couldn't for the life of him conjure up a face to go with it.

The closest he could get to her was a group of friends sitting in the Botanic Gardens in Cambridge, pleasantly stoned and giggling. There had been two or three girls in long summer dresses, boys with long hair, latter-day hippies and new romantics caught up in the fusion of youth and fashion statement. They had had beer and someone had ordered pizza. Andy could remember lying on his back, hands behind his head, looking up at the azure blue sky and feeling as if life couldn't get any better than this. And maybe he had been right, he thought ruefully; maybe that had been the zenith, and everything else since then had been a long slow decline. God help him if that were true.

'*I've brought some photos to show you of when I was little*,' Amelia had said, pulling a box out of her handbag. They'd met in the restaurant of a smart but impersonal businessmen's hotel out on the bypass.

'*Mum's told me all about you.*' Had Amelia said that when she was sorting through the photos? Or was it when they spoke on the phone? The photos were in a little wooden box with a hinged lid and, as she sorted through them, all Andy could think was *when* had they conceived her, him and this woman whose name he barely knew and whose face he couldn't remember? And what had there been to tell about him back then? What had there been to say about him?

Working it out, he must have been about twenty-one when Amelia was conceived. When he was twenty-one he'd been cocksure – not bad looking, although he could only really remember what he looked like when Amelia handed him a Polaroid of himself and a gang of other lads sitting in a punt on the Cam, but there was nothing about him that, in Andy's opinion, was at all memorable.

For an instant when he looked at the picture, fading and with the plastic film rolling up at the edges, he could hear the other guys laughing, he could smell the stale water of the Cam and the beer on their breath, the intoxicating heat of summer at its height.

His eyes moved from face to face; on one side of him there was Finn and then Jack, Colin and another boy at the back with short cropped curly hair, whose name slipped through Andy's mind like small change through a grating. Finn, who had long wavy hair and was wearing a paisley waistcoat, had a girl under each arm, one blonde, one brunette, both laughing, both looking up at him. Andy had no idea whether either of them were Amelia's mother and couldn't bring himself to ask.

Andy had taken one final look at the picture and then handed it back to Amelia, who had tucked it back in amongst her other treasures, this sacred relic of her past. For a fleeting moment he wondered if in her handbag there was a scrapbook that went with the photos, full of used bus tickets and failed condoms, a curled toothbrush and maybe a lock of hair, all stuck down with discoloured Sellotape.

Andy closed his eyes, trying to imagine what it was that her mother could possibly have told Amelia. He wished now he'd taken a longer look at the photo, spent more time studying the faces. Was it that day, the day when they had hired a punt and filled it up with cider and beer and the girls had said they should take food, and the boy whose name he couldn't remember had fallen in, was it that day when they had made Amelia?

Did he and Amelia's mother do it in the dark, on the riverbank on a rug under the spread of a willow tree, some drunken giggling fumbling screwing overheard by friends trying to do the same. Or was it in the morning? Had she stayed over after a party and he found her in his bed at the little bedsit in the drab draughty house he shared a couple of streets up from the station? And how was it he couldn't remember? Surely something so momentous should have been seared onto his brain forever?

And then Amelia had pulled out another pile of Polaroids and Andy didn't want to see any more of the pictures of when he was twenty-one, when he had been shallow and idealistic and arrogant, with long legs and long hair, and would have said anything to get laid . . .

How was it he couldn't remember Amelia's mother? Had they dated? He didn't know anything about her other than the name Amelia had given him.

'*Liz, Liz Cummins*?' She had said it smiling, first of all as a question, and then a statement. 'Liz Cummins.' Because in Amelia's head there was no way her mother would be anything other than important to him. And Andy had nodded and smiled and he repeated it over and over in his head, trying to find a face that went with the name.

And then his smile was easier, thinking that maybe he had seen her a few times, remembered taking her to a barbeque – or was that Liz Turner? The images were vague and broken like old film clips and, try as he might, even when he looked at Amelia's distinctive pretty features, he couldn't conjure her mother from the bones that surely were half his and half Liz's.

There were girls he remembered: Carol Hunt, Gill Bunting, who he had dated for the best part of what, two years? Vanessa Jones – God he would have sold his soul to have gone out with Nessa Jones.

And that of course was the rub; there were people who he had secretly loved, people in life that he had loved who had only barely been aware of him, those who he had pined for, but never asked out, or who had been going out with someone else, a best friend – or who were just well and truly taken. Nessa had been one of them; she'd been going out with Finn – in fact was still married to Finn, as far as Andy knew.

Was Liz one of those, someone who he hadn't really been aware of, someone who had held a candle for him, someone who had finally got her hands on him and had him and, satisfied with one bite of the longed-for, dreamed-of cherry, had moved on. The idea made him smile; he was arrogant, but not that arrogant. Even from where he was standing now, Andy could see that back then he hadn't been everyone's idea of a catch.

In the last few weeks his thoughts had returned again and again to Amelia and the realisation that, while he'd been working at his first job, while he had been dating and getting drunk, and getting dumped by Gill and nursing a broken heart, moving house, buying cars, going on holiday, looking for love, that all that time somewhere his daughter was being born, learning to walk and talk and growing up, and that he hadn't seen any of it.

And when finally Amelia had handed him a photo of

her mother, Liz and a tiny baby, Andy had struggled to recognise her. In some ways he wished he could, it would make this moment sweet and special and make all those things that she had told Amelia about him true.

Liz Cummins was small and blonde with pale blue eyes and a soft hormonal smile. She was peering down at the baby cradled in the crook of her arm, protective and yet at the same time incredibly vulnerable and fragile and, as he looked at the two of them, his eyes had filled up with tears.

Tears of relief, at finally seeing her; tears of regret for all the years he hadn't known about Amelia, and tears of self-pity. Where had all the time gone since he had been twenty-one and so very full of himself, so very, very sure?

Amelia had handed him another picture. This time Liz was sitting on a low wall; she was barefoot, leaning forward, tucking a strand of hair back behind her ear, and the baby was held tight against her chest with the other arm. She was laughing at whoever was holding the camera. The baby was smiling too.

Andy closed his eyes. The terrible thing was that – even seeing the photo – he just didn't remember her, although now at least he knew what Liz looked like. Had they dated? Maybe it had been a few months in the spring and early summer before he met Gill, when the Cam was full of punts and couples and people having fun. He stared at the face, wondering if Liz had been fun; she wasn't the one he had taken to the barbeque, and Andy was sad about that because that had been a great night and he and whoever it was had had a brilliant time and tumbled into some sort of hayloft at the bottom of the garden, dragging off each other's clothes, mouths locked together, high on lust and cider and youth, and he wished it had been then that he had made Amelia.

And this time, sitting on the balcony overlooking Paphos harbour, he didn't hold back the tears as they rolled one by one down his cheeks. God he was such a bloody fool.

Cass hurried up to Andy's room and hammered on the door. 'Andy, are you in there?'

There was silence, Cass knocked again. 'Andy? Andy, I need your help.'

After a moment or two the door flew open. Andy was dressed in jeans and a tee-shirt; close up he looked as if he might have been crying. 'What? Come to tell me all about the double date you've been on with what's-his-face and Fiona and that under-manager, have you?'

Cass raised her eyebrows. 'What?'

'Oh come off it, she's buggered off somewhere again and I saw you with lover boy.'

Cass shook her head. 'Andy, I haven't seen Fiona since last night, and what I get up to in my spare time has nothing to do with you.'

He raised his hands in surrender. 'Sorry, you're right – you must think I am such an arsehole. Apologies – it's not been a good day. On top of everything else, despite spending most of the day in reception on the phone, I can't get a flight home . . .'

'I'm sorry, but I really need your help, Andy – Alf is pissed and we've got to be warmed up, ready and on stage in . . .' Cass looked at her watch; it was nearly six. 'Shit, look, can you come with me, we need to try and get Alf in some sort of order.'

'How come he got drunk? I thought this was the All Stars' big moment.'

'It's not just him. Look, I'll explain on the way down there. We have to try and get him sobered up and I've got to get changed and . . .' He was standing in the doorway watching her. 'What are you waiting for, Andy?'

To her amazement he grinned. 'God, it's going to be so quiet when we get home,' he said.

Cass raised her eyebrows. 'The way you live your life? I very much doubt it.'

By the time they got downstairs, Helen had gone; the door to Alf's room was wedged open with a patent dress shoe, there was a cup of tea on the dressing table and Alf was lying on the bed, head hanging over the edge, moaning miserably. During her absence he had managed to get his shirt off, which was now lying in a damp, crumpled heap on the floor.

'We need to turn him over and get his trousers off,' said Cass.

Andy laughed. 'I wish that we'd met under different circumstances,' he said, catching hold of Alf's free arm. 'I . . .'

Cass looked up at him. Andy shook his head as between them they flipped Alf over onto his back.

'I feel sick,' moaned Alf, as Andy undid his belt.

'If he's got a thong on, I'm out of here,' said Cass, as Andy wrestled with Alf's fly.

Andy laughed. 'You won't be alone.'

Fortunately Alf was a boxer man, and once they got his socks and shoes off and eased him into the shower, Andy said, 'Why don't you go and get ready – we'll be fine here, won't we, Alf?'

Alf, still in his boxers, was sitting slumped on the floor of the shower. He was as pale as cream cheese and had his eyes closed as the water played over him.

'Would you like your tea in there?' asked Andy.

At which point Alf retched. Cass looked at Andy, who shook his head and waved her away. 'Go on, I'll be fine. What time does he need to be downstairs?'

'Seven thirty.'

'Okay – what time are you on?'

'After the interval, we need to be there by half eight.'

Andy grinned. 'Piece of cake . . .'

Which was how around half an hour later Cass was standing in front of the bedroom mirror, taking a long cool look at her outfit. The dress she'd brought along for their concert was midnight blue, off the shoulder and fitted her like a glove. A tight, sexy glove. To go with it she was wearing diamante drop earrings, choker and matching evening gloves. Underneath, Cass wore very little, as the dress was boned like a kipper and once zipped in nothing was going anywhere. She turned right and left to admire the effect and smiled.

She had put her hair up into a pleat, and then teased tendrils out to frame her face. Cass grinned at her reflection. Not bad, not bad at all. She had just got the merest hint of a tan, which gave her a healthy outdoorsy look.

She was just collecting together her bag and shoes when there was a knock at the door. Cass checked her watch; she'd still got loads of time.

'Who is it?' she called warily, checking her earrings as she headed over to open the door.

'Me,' said Andy, framed in the opening. 'Wow,' he said appreciatively. 'You look fantastic.'

Cass reddened. 'Thanks – and thanks for helping me with Alf earlier. I don't know what I'd have done without you.'

Andy shrugged. 'Don't mention it.'

'How's he doing?'

He's a lot better. He's had the tea, shower, the whole works.'

'Sick?'

Andy nodded. 'Uh-huh, but we don't need to dwell on that, he's more or less okay, a bit fragile but not too bad. Also, I wanted to let you know that I've got a flight. The airline rang me about fifteen minutes ago – they've had a cancellation, so I'm just going next door to finish packing.' He glanced towards his room. 'I just wanted to say thank you . . .' He took a deep breath. 'You've been great and – I wanted to tell you, this is not who I am. You're really not seeing me at my best.'

Cass laughed. 'It's all right. Really.'

Andy shifted his weight. 'I was thinking maybe when you get home, that maybe I could take you out to supper some time, to say sorry. Or maybe thank you – I'm not sure which yet.'

'There's nothing to say sorry or thank you for,' said Cass automatically. And then she grinned. 'Just get Amelia out of my house and then maybe I'll take you up on that.'

She sensed he didn't want to go and, oddly enough, she didn't want him to go either.

'Well, I'd better be off,' he said unnecessarily. 'I wanted you to know that I'm not usually like this.'

'So you said – but it's all right.'

He shook his head. 'No, it's not all right. I don't want you to think badly of me. I'd like . . .' Andy was looking increasingly uncomfortable. 'I'd really like to see you again.'

Cass stared at him, wondering if she had heard him properly. 'Andy, I'm flattered, but it's not a great idea. You're upset and things have been shit just recently but the bottom line is you're off limits – you're a friend's bloke. That's not what friends do.'

'She is sleeping with someone else.'

Cass sighed. 'Fiona is still my friend.'

'You're right. Sorry, I didn't mean to offend you . . .' Now he looked uncomfortable.

'You didn't.'

'If things were different,' he said.

'But they're not,' said Cass.

'Okay, well I hope it goes well tonight. Break a leg.'

Cass laughed. 'That's just what my mum said.'

Or at least that was what she was planning to say the instant before Andy leaned forward and kissed her. She should have protested or slapped his face or told him he was a bastard or something but what she actually did was kiss him right back and realised that it was what she had been longing to do since they'd met. The idea took her by surprise and she pulled away, hoping she could pretend it hadn't happened.

'Well,' Cass said hastily, trying very hard to regain her composure. 'Goodbye. I hope you have a good flight.' And with that she slammed the door shut, her heart beating like a snare drum.

Cass leant against the wood, hands flat, forehead pressed hard up against the spyhole; reddening, embarrassed, stunned – *bugger, that was such a stupid thing to do – god, how crazy was that?* And all the while she could hear her heartbeat hammering in her ears.

After that, time seemed to speed up. Cass finished getting ready, picked up all her bits and hurried downstairs to meet up with the rest of the gang for a quick warm-up. Alf and the rest of the basses were there. Alf was peaky and apologetic – but then again, so were the rest of them.

Alan began the warm-up with the words, 'I'm not going to give anyone a lecture, we're on the clock here,' and with that, he lifted his hands to bring them to order. An instant later they began to sing.

Halfway through the opening song, Fiona pushed open the door to the hallway and hurried across to join them. She looked flushed and lovely in an old gold strapless evening dress, her carefully styled hair so straight you could use it to calibrate lasers. She didn't quite meet anyone's eye as she slipped into place alongside Cass, murmuring apologies, straightening her dress and joining in with the first number. Once they'd got through the warm-up and rehearsal, Alan glanced at his watch. 'Right. It's just after eight, we need to make our way down to the amphitheatre. No one, and I repeat *no one* is to drink anything stronger than water – do I make myself clear?'

A murmur rippled around the hall.

Fiona sniffed and pulled a compact out of her handbag. 'What's all that about? Seems a bit harsh. I mean, we're hardly children, are we?' Cass looked across at Alf, who appeared to have decided not to answer on the grounds that he might incriminate himself. What it told Cass was that, wherever she'd been all day, Fiona hadn't been anywhere near the rest of the choir. Alf belched damply into a clenched fist.

Fiona pulled a heavy brocade wrap out of the bag she was carrying. 'I need to talk to you,' she said.

'I really have to go,' Cass said warily, looking at the stream of singers who were already heading out the door. The last thing she wanted was a scene in front of everyone.

Fiona looked contrite. 'Please Cass, I wanted to apologise.' When Cass didn't reply, Fiona continued, 'You know how bad things have been between me and Andy – it's not your fault all this blew up now. I just wanted to say that I'm sorry. I thought that you and him were – well, you know . . .' She grinned self-consciously. 'I should have known better really.'

Given the whole *ordinary* thing, from their last conversation, Cass decided she would pass on finding out what that meant, but Fiona was on a roll. 'We've been friends for a long time and I know you're not like that. And let's be honest, you're really not his type. Andy likes his women to be more – more—'

'Psychotic?' suggested Cass.

Fiona laughed, 'Don't be silly – he prefers them more . . .' She made a funny wriggly gesture with her hands and then smiled and did a little head flick. Not a strand of hair moved; the unwary might lose an eye on hair that coiffured and crispy. 'Well, you know,' she concluded.

So this was what passed for an apology on planet Fiona.

'Right, great – okay, well thanks for that, but I need to be going,' said Cass, picking up her bag.

'Wait,' said Fiona, catching hold of her arm. 'The other thing that I wanted to let you know is that I'm not flying home with the rest of the choir. Well, not permanently anyway, I have to nip home to sort things out at some stage, obviously. Anyway, I've already told Alan. The thing is, Geno has asked me to stay in Cyprus with him – actually he asked me to marry him, and stay – we're going to get married, Cass . . .' The words disintegrated into a high-pitched girly giggle and she held out her hand. On it was the ring-pull from a drink can. 'It's not a real ring, obviously, and I know it's happened quickly, but god, it was just so romantic, we're going shopping for a proper engagement ring as soon as he gets some time off. I am so excited, I had to tell someone. I'm going to ring my mum and dad and tell them later. I'm hoping they'll come over for Christmas. I know they'll love him – I mean, he is just *so* lovely!'

Cass stared at her. 'Fee – this is crazy. You've only known him a couple of days,' she said before she could help herself. 'I mean, you're not seventeen . . .'

Fiona's expression hardened. 'All the more reason to grab things when they come along – and anyway, you can hardly say anything about things being quick. Remember I came up and practically caught you at it the day we arrived.'

'Fee, that isn't what happened at all. For god's sake be sensible, don't throw everything up for a holiday fling.'

'This isn't a fling,' protested Fiona. 'Geno is different. I mean, sometimes you just have to go with your instincts.'

'This is crazy, Fee.'

'I knew you'd say that, but I don't care what people think, I mean sometimes you just know, don't you?'

Cass sighed. And sometimes, Cass thought, you just knew when to save your breath.

'Cass, please just be happy for me for once – he went down on one knee. It was just so romantic. And he wants children straight away – we're going to go and look at houses just as soon as his money comes through; apparently he's got some investments that mature later this year.

Meanwhile there is this villa a bit further down the coast that he's renting and he says that we can live there for the time being – you know, just till we find somewhere.' Fiona was babbling on.

'So have you spoken to Andy yet?'

Fiona pulled a face. 'And the point of that would be what? I mean what is there to talk to Andy about? I still don't know what's going on with him but to be honest I don't care any more. He said it was over – for god's sake you were there. No, I've had more than enough and I've given him enough chances. No, my life is out here with Geno now. A fresh new start.

We're going to go looking at villas as soon as he gets a few days off. We're thinking of buying off plan; you get a really good deal and he's got this friend who's just got permission for a really classy development out near Coral Bay. And I'm going to need a job obviously, well at least until we get married; this developer might need someone in the office, showing people around, that kind of thing. I'm so excited; say you're excited for me. Say you're pleased for me.'

Cass hesitated just long enough for Fiona's hysterical grin to cool down to a frown. 'You're thinking that this isn't going to work, aren't you? You're thinking it's all happened too fast. Aren't – *aren't you*?'

Cass opened her mouth, considering what the right reply was, when Fiona cut her short.

'You know what, I know what's going on here – you're jealous,' she snapped. 'All on your own with the kids and that junk shop, and no man – I can see exactly why you're jealous. You don't want me to be happy, do you?'

Aware that she was being railroaded by an expert, Cass

didn't rise to the bait. 'Not at all, I really truly hope that it all works out for you,' she said, and then, turning fast, hurried to catch up with Welsh Alf, a back-marker amongst the little procession of basses.

'Wait, wait,' said Fiona. 'Come back. There's just so much I want to tell you, about his family and what the wedding is going to be like. You will come, won't you?'

By this time Cass had slipped past Alf, sold Fiona the dummy and body-swerved past a posse of tenors who had linked arms.

'Bitch,' Fiona hissed, but by the time Cass heard it, she was on past the sopranos and was almost neck and neck with Alan and a very pallid Mrs Alan.

'Thanks for your help this afternoon,' said Alan as she fell into step alongside him. 'God knows who else could have handled Alf.'

An image too far. 'Don't mention it,' Cass said, and truly meant it.

And then they were on their way, the singers in all their finery, walking out along the sea front, under the strings of lights flickering and swaying and twinkling in the gin-clear waters of the harbour. In the distance they could hear the other choir singing.

And as they walked, Mrs Alan explained how she had taken the basses out on the Cyprus Gourmet Tour, just to keep them out of the bar, joining instead an afternoon sampling the traditional tastes of Cyprus, except that she had reckoned without the plentiful supply of wine with every dish and the local liqueur, a variation on grappa, which she was certain one of the guys on the coach had added to the fruit punch.

And she still didn't feel at all well.

When they reached the marquee dressing room, the interval had just begun, which was perfect for a last-minute warm-up. And then finally the stage manager came over to guide them on, and they settled into formation and then in single file, as they were led out onto the ancient stone stage at the base of the great rock tiers that made up the ancient Roman theatre.

Cass gasped. The stage was lit with oil lamps and, for a second, as they stepped out of the darkness into the ring of light, Cass hesitated, overawed by the sense of occasion and place, knowing that they would be singing in a theatre that had been there for almost two thousand years. Their voices and their songs would join echoes that went back through history.

Cass felt her heart fluttering with excitement. Down in the front row, the judges looked up in anticipation. The crowd had settled back into their seats after the break and you could almost feel the hum of expectation in the air. Slowly the noise in the arena was fading to a shared breath, a murmur and then silence.

Cass closed her eyes for an instant, letting the smells and the sounds and the feel of the place wash over her. This was what they had come to Cyprus for, to sing in this ancient space. One night centre stage, not sharing it with anyone else, not singing anyone else's repertoire or sharing the glory. And, though the arena at Kourion might be grander and take five times as many people, tonight this crowd was there for them.

Cass shivered; she could pick out faces she recognised out in the gloom. Bekya and Alya, Geno and Nick, George the American and his family, other people she had met at the workshops for the combined concert – and for an instant she could have sworn she saw Andy sitting at the back.

And then at the front of the stage Alan, resplendent in full evening suit, signature monocle and white bow tie, lifted his hands, drawing their attention to him. In an undertone he gave them their notes and mouthed the count, one, two, three, and they were in and singing the opening number, and as the harmonies rolled away from the main tune, weaving and supporting and plaiting their way around the melody, Cass smiled and the audience and the faces vanished as she heard the voice of the choir, rich and three-dimensional, rise up and roll out over the crowd, held and amplified by the ancient tiered rock.

The sound was so stunning, so perfect, so complete that Cass almost stopped singing. Around her she could see the rest of the choir smiling and then the music caught up with her, and she was back, lost in the melody, carried along on the tune, and knew that she was smiling too.

Alongside her, even Fiona seemed focused, and when the first number finished the applause began like rifle fire, before swelling to a roar and then, almost before they could take it in, Alan was giving them their next start note and they were off again into the next number.

And as she sang it occurred to Cass that finally all the stress and fuss of the last few weeks was over, maybe not in a way that anyone had planned but it was over; Andy was flying home, Fiona was staying behind. There was just Amelia to deal with and then everything was done and dusted, and life would finally get back to normal.

The All Stars' set seemed to be over in the twinkling of an eye. All that rehearsal, all the planning, the travel, the waiting, the highs and the lows and before she knew it

Alan was announcing the final piece and then their encore and then as the final note echoed and faded and slipped away into the starlit night, the second choir stepped up to join them on the stage and the crowd got to its feet and clapped. And clapped and clapped until Cass's ears hurt. Even after they had done another encore, the crowd kept applauding them until finally the stage manager waved them off and they processed, exhausted but high as kites, back into the marquee, where the crew was breaking out bottles of champagne. Cass had no idea what the judges had made of it but everyone else seemed to have had a great time.

As Cass took one of the glasses of champagne she stopped, almost mid-stride, overcome with a flash of compassion for Fiona. This wasn't a night to hold onto bad thoughts and hard grudges, they went back too many years as friends not to share this high spot together, but when Cass turned round to find her Fiona was already gone, presumably already off to meet up with Geno. Cass felt a wave of regret that the week should end like this. She had a feeling that this was the end of the road as far as their friendship was concerned. So much had changed over the last few days.

The following day was the final day of their trip. At around six they were bussed up to Kourion for a celebration supper and the final joint concert, which was great, but somehow for Cass it meant far less than the night before when the choir had sung for Paphos and their friends and family, and also people they had met on the trip and buddied up with from other choirs.

'Okay folks,' said a man with a megaphone as they

climbed down from the buses. 'We need to get you all into position for a sound check – just follow the stewards – and remember all the way through this we'll be filming fly-on-the-wall stuff, so keep on smiling, because it could be your face up there on that screen. Now let's move it.'

Cass crocodiled after the others towards the tents erected as dressing rooms, relishing the buzz of excitement in the air.

By necessity the arrangements for the joint concert were far more formal – a song from each choir and then their combined repertoire, the cameras recording it all for posterity, but it wasn't the same. And there was no sign of Fiona.

Even when Perry Hulme got up to announce the winners of the choral competition, Cass felt a sense of anticlimax – they hadn't made the top five but, as Alan said, first year out they hadn't expected to.

The top five choirs had a chance to sing all over again so the film crews could get some extra footage, before the overall winner – the gospel choir – was announced.

The applause had barely died down before Perry was inviting them all to join him and his tireless team in Texas the following year. And then they all stood in the rich blue of the Cyprus night and sang the final song together, holding hands, their voices rolling out as one across the glittering waters of the Med, carried on the warm night air. Cass felt the prickle of tears in her eyes.

So, on Sunday morning, Cass stood her case outside the door to her room and looked back inside. The shutters were open, the bed turned back. It felt as if she had been in Cyprus for an age. So much had happened, so many things had changed. She had hoped to see Fiona before they left, but it was Nick who appeared at the open doorway to help take her bags down to the waiting coach.

'Geno tells me that your friend Fiona is staying?' he said as they made their way downstairs.

Cass nodded. 'Apparently, and if you're thinking about sharing your thoughts about that, please don't.'

'Not a word. Cross my heart.' He grinned. 'And what about you?'

Cass laughed. 'Me? I can't wait to get home. I took a look at the forecast on Teletext this morning: apparently it's bitterly cold with freezing fog and scattered sleet showers.'

Chapter Fifteen

It was raining when Rocco picked Cass up from the coach station. As she walked towards him he hurried over and threw his arms around her. 'Good to see you, how was the flight? See, we ordered you some welcome-home weather,' he said pointing skywards.

Cass grinned and pulled her coat tight around her shoulders, delighted to see him. 'You shouldn't have gone to any trouble – it was around twenty-four in Cyprus when we left, clear blue skies,' she said. 'How's mum?'

'In the kitchen basting the fatted calf when I left her,' he said, dropping Cass's bags into the boot. 'She seems to be under the impression they don't have food abroad.'

Cass climbed into the passenger seat and yawned. 'It's so nice to be back. It feels like I've been away for ages. How have things been here? You and mum been ok? Have you sorted out Amelia?'

Rocco looked sheepish.

'Please – tell me she's gone.'

'We've tried, Cass, but your mum was worried about where she'd end up.'

Cass nodded, trying hard to disguise a flicker of frustration and annoyance.

'I'm sorry,' said Rocco.

'I know, but I can't help feeling angry about it – not with you . . . I can't believe she just showed up, expecting me to take her in.'

'And you're angry with the pair of us for letting her in?'

Cass laughed dryly. 'Well, yes. I can't believe either of you are that bloody gullible. But hey-ho – we'll get it sorted. Anyway, enough about that, tell me what else has been going on. Sounds like you've cleared half my stock – I'm dying for a cup of tea.'

Rocco hugged her again. 'Nice to have you back.'

Even in the driving rain, the shop looked warm and inviting. Cass dropped her bags at the back door, taking it all in, relieved to be back – the girl in *The Wizard of Oz* was right: there really was no place like home. For a few seconds before familiarity clicked in, she saw the place with fresh eyes and smiled. The lamps were lit in the windows. Everywhere looked cosy and colourful and, it had to be said, thanks to her mother, extraordinarily tidy.

As the hall door opened, Buster burst through, wagging and whining and delighted to see her, while the cat – which had followed the dog to see what the fuss was about – marched off as soon as he clapped eyes on her, backside swaying from side to side, tail up as a protest for being abandoned to people who were ruining his life by feeding him tuna steak and letting him sleep on the beds.

Her mum was a yard behind the animals – smiling broadly, arms open, wearing Cass's stripy blue apron over her jeans and an elegant cream sweater. 'Welcome home,' she said, eyes bright with tears. 'Oh it's so lovely to see you. We've missed you, haven't we Rocco? I rang the boys

301

and told them you'd landed safe and sound – I said you'd ring them later.'

Cass, held tight in Nita's arms, couldn't help but laugh. 'Mum, I've been to Cyprus not Siberia.'

Nita sniffed as she pulled away. 'Yes, but you're home now. Come on through, I've got the kettle on and Rocco's made some lemon drizzle cake. You look wonderful – you've really caught the sun. Have you lost weight?'

Minutes later and they were upstairs in the kitchen, with the kettle on and dinner in the oven. As they talked, Nita backhanded a stray tendril of hair off her face, the gesture such a blast of childhood memory that it brought tears to Cass's eyes.

Rocco handed Cass a mug of tea. 'There you go,' he said with a smile. 'So you had a good time then?'

Cass nodded. 'Not bad. But it's lovely to be back.'

There was a funny little pause and then Nita said, 'I thought I'd do us a proper Sunday roast: beef, Yorkshires, all the trimmings.'

Her mum and Rocco glanced at each other.

'And have you invited Amelia?' said Cass lightly, standing the mug down on the table.

Nita looked sheepish. 'I couldn't bring myself to just throw her out. She's got no one else and nowhere else to go to.'

Cass nodded. Not that she believed Amelia for a minute, but she believed in her mum's inherent good nature. Not wanting to spoil how good it felt to be home, she nodded some more.

'It's all right,' she said, 'I'm sure we can sort this out. Is she upstairs?'

Rocco nodded. Her mum opened her mouth to say

something, maybe an apology, maybe an explanation, but Cass, holding her smile, waved the words away. 'I won't be a minute, and I'm not going to cause a big scene,' she said, and before anyone could say anything else, headed upstairs to the spare rooms on the top floor.

Climbing the stairs, Cass wondered how best to play it. Should she shout? Rant? Reason? As she stood outside the door, she hoped that when it came to it, instinct would prevail. Cass tapped on the door and waited. There was nothing from inside, not a noise, not a peep.

Cass knocked again, and this time from somewhere in the room came a peculiar little scurrying sound, a sound that reminded her of hamsters and mice.

'Amelia, this is Cass, your dad's friend. I know you're in there,' said Cass evenly. 'You might as well open the door. I've got all day.'

There was a funny mewling sound from inside and Cass, tired from the flight and bored with the game, pushed open the door. The room was in darkness; in the wedge of light from the doorway she could see the blinds were drawn tight, although the smell inside the room was almost luminous.

'Bloody hell,' Cass gasped, holding her breath and reaching out for the light switch. She flicked it on, nothing happened. She tried again, still nothing so, picking her way through a maze of boxes and piles of clothes, Cass headed over to the bed and flicked on the bedside lamp. The lamp cast a pool of light in the gloom. Cass looked around and sighed.

The room was complete chaos. Every flat surface was littered with papers and clothes, books, magazines and bottles, takeaway cartons, bags, mugs and bowls and plates and cartons of milk, and here and there between the debris were candles, wedged into bottles and fixed to saucers in puddles of melted wax. Cass looked around with a growing sense of horror. How could someone do this inside a week? The room smelt of sweat and cigarettes, unwashed feet and cheap perfume, all mixed in with an odd hamstery smell.

Curled up on the bed under the duvet, Amelia peered at her from over the very edge, her dark eyes huge and glistening in the lamplight. Her hair was a haystack and she was as pale as tallow – she reminded Cass of a startled bushbaby.

'We need to talk, you and I,' said Cass, trying to ignore whatever it was crisping and crunching under her boots.

Amelia whimpered and blinked in the lamplight. It seemed to take a long time for her to close her eyes.

'Well?' said Cass, crossing her arms over her chest in a way she had seen her mother do a thousand times.

'I don't feel very well,' Amelia said.

'Oh really.'

Amelia sounded just like one of Cass's sons when they were trying to skive off school and Cass found herself caught in a peculiar time warp, heavy with maternal *déjà vu*.

'No, I really don't feel well,' said Amelia.

Cass looked at her as Amelia, tiny hands clenching the edge of the duvet, dropped it far enough so that Cass could see her face. She was even smaller than Cass remembered, with great big dark circles under eyes that were too bright to be healthy. Her skin had an odd waxy look. Instinctively Cass reached out to touch her. Amelia's skin was hot and damp and oddly clammy. And then she whimpered and Cass stared at her. Unless Amelia was Oscar-winning material, she really was in pain.

'Where does it hurt?'

'My stomach, it really, really hurts,' Amelia gasped. 'I can't move.'

'Are you bleeding?'

'No, no I'm not,' she whimpered, biting her lip as one huge tear rolled down her chalk-white cheek. 'But I feel terrible. Am I going to die? I am, aren't I?'

Cass stared at her, torn between anger and concern. 'No, you're going to be fine,' she said quietly. 'Just don't move, I think we probably need to get you to hospital. I'm going to go downstairs and ring for an ambulance.'

'I'm frightened,' Amelia said in a tiny, fretful voice.

Cass sighed, suddenly overcome with compassion for the poor lost little creature. 'Don't be, everything is going to be okay. Just lie still – they'll be here soon, I promise.'

Amelia looked grateful and then rolled over onto her side, curling up into a tight ball.

The ambulance arrived in under half an hour. One of the men looked at Amelia's room with an expression close to pity, as they lifted her gently onto the stretcher. 'Nightmare at this age, aren't they?'

Cass started to explain that Amelia was a squatter rather than her daughter but decided she was wasting her breath. 'Where are you taking her?'

'The QE, I'd imagine: state she's in they'll most likely admit her. Might be an idea if you could bring a bag up later?'

As soon as the ambulance doors had closed, Cass went

back inside, arms wrapped tight around herself. Nita and Rocco were in the kitchen waiting anxiously for news. 'Is she all right?' said her mum.

'They think she'll probably be kept in. I'm going to ring her dad and then see if I can pack a bag for her out of all the junk she's got stashed upstairs.'

'Her dad?' said Rocco, which made Cass realise she hadn't told them about Andy.

'Andy,' Cass said. 'He came home early.'

'But I thought . . .' Nita began.

Cass held up a hand. 'It's a long story. I'll just pack Amelia a bag and then I'll tell you all about it.'

Her mum shrugged. 'Fair enough. Do you need any help?'

Cass smiled. 'No, just food.'

Upstairs Cass stood in the doorway of the room where Amelia had been sleeping and rang Andy.

'Hi,' she said.

'Cass?'

'Yes.'

'You're back. I'm really glad you rang.' He sounded genuinely pleased to hear from her. It seemed almost a shame to let him know the real reason for her call.

'Andy, I'm afraid this isn't a social call. It's about Amelia.'

'Ah right. I was going to come round and see you – I've already talked to her. Now I know you're home, I'll pop by. I promise—'

'Andy, she's been taken to hospital, with abdominal pain. She looks really ill.'

Cass heard Andy's breath catch in his throat. 'Really – God – okay – when?'

'About fifteen minutes ago. I went up to see her as

soon as I got home. She looked terrible. Anyway, I called an ambulance and they've taken her off to hospital.'

'Oh – okay. Is there anything I can do?'

'She'll need a bag with a few things, nightdress, toothbrush.'

'They're keeping her in?'

'That's what the ambulance driver said.'

'I haven't got any of her things here,' he said, sounding anxious.

'Don't worry, I have,' said Cass, ruefully looking around the spare room. 'If you want to pop round and pick up some stuff for her, there is plenty to choose from.'

As soon as she had hung up, Cass took the roll of bin bags she had brought upstairs and started clearing up. It was amazing just how much mess one person could make in a week.

As Cass worked she could pick out the inviting fragrance of Sunday dinner as it cooked downstairs. She heard Buster barking and grumbling when the doorbell rang but, immersed in trying to claim the room back, she ignored it and carried on working. Amelia had written phone numbers on the wall above the bed. The dressing-table drawers were full of empty fast food cartons, dirty mugs and bowls and shredded sweet wrappers, so very carefully peeled and rolled up that at first Cass thought maybe it was a mouse nest.

'Your mum and dad said you were up here. Do you want a hand?' Andy said, making her jump. He was standing in the doorway staring in at the chaos.

Cass handed him an empty bin bag. 'Actually that's my mum and her fancy man, but it's as broad as it's long. I'm putting anything that isn't rubbish in that holdall.' She pointed to a bag on the bed. 'I've already put a couple of tee-shirts and stuff in a little bag for you to take to the hospital.'

'Thanks,' he said, stepping into the room alongside her. It felt odd having him so close. 'I'm really sorry about this,' he said, picking up a pile of magazines and sliding them into a bag.

'I don't want you to tell me how sorry you are,' she said, fishing a pile of polystyrene trays out from under the bed. 'I just want you to do something about it.'

'I've rung up a couple of housing association places locally – and the council.' He folded up a sweater and dropped it onto the bed alongside the bag, which for some reason infuriated Cass.

'Can't you put it in the holdall – I mean, what does it take?' Cass snapped. He looked at her as if she had punched him. Cass paused. 'Forget I said that. I'm just so pissed off with this. Look at the state of it.'

He stared at her. 'I'm sorry. Look, I can help sort this out – pay for any damage. I didn't mean for this to happen.'

Cass shook her head. 'I know you didn't,' she said, softening. 'It must have been a real shock for you finding out about her.'

Andy nodded. 'It's changed everything – the trouble is I don't know how to help her or how to make things right, or what to do now. I've never been a parent.'

Cass laughed. 'Welcome to the house of fun. You need to go to the hospital and then ring her mum and let her know where Amelia is.'

'And then?'

She laughed. 'Andy, what you do next isn't anything to do with me.'

'I know.'

Andy sat down on the bed, fiddling with the lace of a well-worn high-top trainer. 'What she wants is a daddy who loves her unconditionally and does all the things that dads do. She wants one who picks up the bills and puts a roof over her head and pays her an allowance and makes up for all the years he missed.'

Cass stared at him. 'Andy, that only happens in films. She is playing on your guilt, and I don't know what to say or what the answer to this is but I'd start by talking to Amelia's mum if I were you.'

'I haven't spoken to her since before Amelia was born.'

'Then it's about time you did. She was the person who didn't tell you about Amelia – she's got her own reasons and until you talk to her you've got no idea where Amelia got her ideas from; or, come to that, what her mum told her about you. You have to ring her.'

Andy looked uncomfortable. 'I know, but the problem is I have no idea who she is, Cass, and not in some kind of hippy way – I don't remember her at all. And trust me, I've spent hours, days, weeks, trying to put her face and a name together. It's not like I was putting it about, but I was certainly no angel – I had my fair share of one-night stands and—'

Cass held a pink mobile phone out towards him. 'I don't need to know – I found this on the floor.' She scrolled down the menu till she found an entry that read, 'mum'. Cass handed him the phone and a piece of paper. 'Here, ring her – I wrote down the details of the hospital.'

'Thanks,' said Andy, heading out onto the landing. Cass nodded and turned away, pulling the bedroom door to behind her so that he could have some privacy. Part of him wished that she would stay.

He tapped in the phone number and waited, wondering what he should do if he got an answer machine. Should he leave a message? Hang up?

'Hello,' said a voice at the far end of the line.

'Hi, is that Liz? This is Andy,' was how he started the conversation.

'Oh hello – I wondered when you would ring,' said the voice at the end of the phone. The voice was flat and noncommittal and there was nothing about it that reminded Andy of anyone in his past or any mad passionate snatched moment. Had he called her Elizabeth? Or was it Lizzie back then – or maybe Beth?

'I suppose you've got a lot of questions,' she said.

'No, not at the moment. Well yes I have, obviously, but actually I rang to let you know that Amelia's been taken into hospital.'

'Oh for god's sake, what now?' said the woman called Liz with the voice he didn't recognise. 'That girl is such a bloody drama queen.'

'Well I don't know exactly, but I thought you ought to know. I'm going to the hospital now with a few things for her.'

'She's living with you?' said the woman incredulously.

'No, no she's not, she's –' he looked back through the crack of the door at Cass, who was still sifting the detritus of Amelia's life – 'she conned her way into staying at my friend's house.'

The woman laughed but didn't sound at all surprised.

'I wondered if you wanted to meet me there?' said Andy.

'Sorry?' said the woman.

'At the hospital, where they've taken Amelia, we could

talk. There are a few things – a lot of things I'd like to talk to you about. I mean, I had no idea Amelia even existed. I didn't know – all these years.' The words felt like dry straw in his mouth. 'Well, you know.'

And for a moment Andy wanted to say, *Why didn't you tell me, why didn't you let me know before now, have you any idea what finding Amelia after all this time is like? What it has done to me?* But he didn't; instead he said in a very even voice, 'So shall I see you there?'

There was a long silence at the far end of the line. 'I'm not sure,' she said.

Andy felt a wave of frustration. 'She's ill.'

'So she says,' said the woman. 'You've got no idea what she's like.'

'Actually Liz, I think I have. But the bottom line is that at the moment she is in hospital, she's not well and she needs you. Did you know that she was pregnant?'

'Oh, for Christ's sake,' snapped the woman. 'Let me get a pen. Whereabouts is she?'

Andy glanced at the sheet of paper Cass had given him and read out the address of the hospital and the phone number. When he looked up, Cass was there, handing him a cup of tea.

'Do you want me to come with you?' she said.

'Are you serious?' he said, gratefully.

Cass nodded. 'Uh-huh, Amelia's going to need her stuff and, besides, I want to check she hasn't got one of my house keys with her.'

Andy laughed. 'Okay.'

Amelia's stuff, when it was peeled away from the rubbish and the junk, packed down into a holdall, a cardboard box, a suit carrier and a drawstring bag full of dirty washing.

As they carried it downstairs to the kitchen, Nita was busy basting a joint of beef. 'How long do you think you're going to be?' she asked, spooning oil and the juices over the meat.

Cass shrugged. 'How long till dinner's ready?'

'I'm about to put the potatoes in.'

'Okay, well, save me some.'

Nita straightened up, red faced, hair curling away in the heat from the oven. 'Cass – I'm not sticking your dinner on a plate in the microwave. It was meant to be a welcome-home supper.'

'I know, but I want to sort this out. I'll eat it when I get home,' said Cass, pulling her coat on.

'In that case I won't put the potatoes on till you get back then. Will you be stopping, Andy?'

He looked from face to face until Cass put him out of his misery. 'What she's saying is that you look like you could do with a good meal. Would you like a roast dinner – think carefully before you say no. She'll probably clock you if you turn her down and she always cooks enough to feed an army.'

'It certainly smells good,' said Andy.

'So that's a yes then,' said Cass's mum, sliding the joint back into the oven. 'Give me a ring when you leave the hospital.'

The doctor they saw was holding a clipboard. Cass suspected it was to add some much-needed gravitas. He looked about twelve, and was all kitted out as if he was off to a fancy-dress party, with pens, stethoscope and a little torch in his top pocket. She was tempted to say, 'So you've come as a doctor, have you?'

'So,' he said, looking down at his clipboard and pushing his trendy oversized specs back as he did, 'you're Mr Cummins.'

'No, I'm Andy Sharpe.'

'Right,' he spoke slowly and deliberately. 'And you're—'

'Amelia's father.'

'Okay.' He ticked something on his clipboard.

Modern families must be a nightmare, thought Cass, who up until that point had been reading the public health notices on the waiting room wall.

'And you're . . . ?'

Cass, shaken out of her trip through glaucoma, diabetes, sexually transmitted diseases and the breastfeeding clinic, looked up. 'Sorry?'

'Ms Cummins?' he suggested.

'No, although I think she might be on her way. I'm a friend of Mr Sharpe's.'

'Right, well in that case, Mr Sharpe, we've admitted your daughter and are prepping her for theatre.'

Andy's colour drained. 'Is it the baby?'

The doctor looked mystified and ran a finger down his notes. 'I don't think so. We have reason to suspect Amelia may have appendicitis.'

'Did you know she was pregnant?'

Now it was the doctor's turn to look pale. 'It's not in my notes but I'm sure that my colleagues—'

Andy moved a step closer. 'Ring them.'

'I'm certain . . .'

'It's not on your clipboard, is it?'

'Well no, but . . .'

Andy picked up the phone hanging on the wall and handed it to him. 'Now,' he said, in a voice that didn't invite contradiction.

The man did as he was told. Cass watched Andy as he firmly, politely took control. Given the state of play it was impressive; seeing him in action with Fiona, Cass had begun to wonder if he was always such a pushover – the answer was, apparently not.

A little while later they were taken upstairs into a small anteroom to see Amelia. She was already dopy and un-focused from the effects of the pre-med, a cannula in the back of her hand. There was a nurse hovering nearby, with a porter waiting to take the trolley down to the theatre.

Amelia's hair was tucked up under a disposable blue cap; she looked tiny and pale and terrified and, as Andy took hold of her hand, Cass was aware that she had no right to be there, no part in this, but she stayed.

'How are you feeling?' Andy murmured.

Amelia smiled sleepily. 'Better now I'm here.' She winced. 'Thanks for coming.'

'I've rung your mum and . . .' He stopped speaking and very gently stroked a stray lock of hair back off her face. 'You're going to be all right,' he said softly. 'And when you're out of here we're going to start over. Do you understand?'

Amelia nodded and Cass felt her eyes well up with tears.

The nurse eased her way into the emotional space between them. 'We've got to go now,' she said quietly. 'They're ready for her in theatre.'

Andy touched Amelia's hand and for a second held onto her fingertips as the porter pushed the trolley away into the corridor, and then they were gone. And in the room

314

was a space where the bed had been that was as raw and empty as a tooth socket.

Andy sighed. 'I'm going to go and ring Amelia's mum to see if she's on her way.'

Cass nodded and sat and waited in the little room, with Amelia's bag on her knee, until Andy came back with two paper cups of tea. She kept remembering what it had been like when Neil had been in hospital, waiting for tests, waiting for news, waiting and waiting until she felt as if she couldn't wait any more.

'I didn't know whether you took sugar,' Andy said, putting his hand in his pocket to produce a handful of sugar straws and a couple of little plastic sticks. Cass shook her head and then he sat down alongside her on a grey plastic chair and they both waited.

'Thanks for coming with me,' Andy said. 'I really appreciate you being here.'

Cass smiled. 'I just wanted to make sure you took all her stuff home with you.'

He laughed, which was the effect Cass had been hoping for.

'There is no part of me prepared for this,' said Andy. 'It wasn't that I didn't want kids. It's just that I was never in the right place with the right woman to start a family.'

Cass took a long pull on her coffee. 'Still time,' she said.

Andy snorted. 'I don't think so. Not now, I don't fancy chasing around after my kids on a mobility scooter.'

'You're not that old.'

'You know what I mean. The moment's past.' He paused. 'Amelia appearing out of the blue, all grown up, knocked me for six. I should have told Fiona, shouldn't I?'

Cass shrugged. 'Every life is haunted by the list of things we should have done.'

He sipped his coffee. 'Do you think I ought to go and ring Liz again?'

'Did you get her last time?'

'Just the answer machine.'

'Maybe she's already on her way. Where's she coming from?'

'Just outside Cambridge.' He glanced down at his watch. 'I'll give her another half an hour and then ring again.'

And they waited, and waited and waited some more. And Andy rang Liz while Cass went to get more tea. And the time seemed to slow down so that every minute was ten and every ten an hour. Cass yawned. The air in the hospital was heavy and dusty and seemingly without any oxygen. She was exhausted.

After what seemed like an eternity the door opened and a big bluff man, dressed in a tweed suit, came in. He was carrying a sheaf of notes and said, 'Just wanted to let you know Amelia's fine – damn good job you brought her in when you did. Any idea how long she had been like it?'

Cass looked up. 'No, I'd just got back from a holiday.'

He nodded. 'Kids – well, it could have been a lot worse.' And he sort of smiled, although Cass suspected it was purely politeness. 'And the baby appears to be fine too,' he said when he saw Andy about to speak. 'But we'll be keeping her in and keeping a close eye on her for the next few days.'

'Thank you,' said Andy. Cass could hear the relief in his voice. 'Can I see her?'

'Of course. If you wait here, she'll be back on the ward in a little while, although you probably won't get much sense out of her.'

Andy shook his head. 'No change there then.'

This time the man laughed with him. 'My daughter's just the same.' And then he was gone.

And so they waited some more and every time the door to the side room opened Cass wondered if it was Amelia's mother arriving, but it wasn't. First it was a nurse bringing the bed back, and then it was a nurse with a porter and then Amelia on a trolley, and they lifted her onto the bed and then once she was settled the nurse and the porter left and Andy got up and so did Cass.

Amelia was asleep although the colour was creeping back into her cheeks and she looked less pinched and pale. Cass could almost see the tension easing in Andy's shoulders; gently he ran a finger across Amelia's cheek and for a moment or two she opened her eyes and looked up at him, eyes barely focused, and smiled.

'Dad,' she said in a hoarse whisper.

'It's all right,' he said and then her eyelids fluttered closed and Andy tenderly pulled the sheet up a little higher around her shoulders.

Cass smiled to herself; it was touching, even though there was something charmingly staged about it too.

'See you later, baby,' murmured Andy.

Cass followed him, quietly, not quite on tiptoe, and for a second as she looked back towards the bed she could have sworn Amelia was peering out at the two of them under half-closed lashes. Cass smiled and shook her head.

They walked back down the corridor in companionable silence and then Andy said, 'Maybe Liz will show up later. Maybe she got caught in traffic. I mean, I'm assuming she drives – maybe I should give her another ring. The mobile she gave me was switched off.'

Cass touched his arm. 'Maybe you should come home and have something to eat. Liz will either turn up or she won't – and if Amelia's going to be in here for a few days there will be time enough to talk to her. You don't have to do it now.'

He looked up and then said, 'You're right. But given my track record, I was thinking maybe there was no time like the present.'

Cass laughed.

As they got to the main entrance, Cass pulled out her mobile. 'Anyway, my mother would be devastated if I showed up without you. You saw her put the roast in . . .'

They drove back to the shop in almost complete silence. Cass didn't like to ask him if he had spoken to Fiona, or what he was going to do about Amelia or Liz or anything else come to that. There was no subject that was entirely easy or painless to talk about, so they said nothing.

Finally, as they drew up in front of the shop, Andy said, 'I can't thank you enough.'

Cass smiled. 'My mother's cooking is good but it's not that good.'

'You know what I mean, today, in Cyprus – the last few weeks have been tough. I don't know what I would've done without you.'

'Come on, let's go and eat,' said Cass. 'My mum's Yorkshire puddings can cure anything up to and including bubonic plague.'

Upstairs, Nita had laid the big table in the kitchen and there was wine and they wanted to know all about Cyprus and the concerts and the hotel, and Buster was excited and pleased to see them back.

While they talked, the smell of the beef and the roast potatoes filled the house. And then the boys rang to see what kind of time Cass had had, and she had to tell the story all over again.

Suddenly they were all laughing and talking, and for a moment Cass looked across the table and discovered that Andy was looking at her; as their eyes met, he smiled. When her mum finally handed round the overflowing plates, Cass felt like she had come home at last.

They had apple pie and custard for dessert, eaten in the sitting room in front of the fire. Rocco had baked it, full of thick slices of dessert apple, laced with cloves and cinnamon and custard so thick, so creamy that you couldn't pour it but had to spoon it over the pie and watch it melt with the heat.

It was late when Andy finally said he had to go. He seemed reluctant to leave and Cass felt reluctant to see him go. After all the thanking and the goodbyes, as they got to the door Andy turned, and Cass felt her heart do a funny sideways two-step.

'Thank you,' he said, eyes alight and glittering in the half-light. He moved a little closer. 'I was wondering . . .'

Cass waited, not altogether sure what he was going to say, wondering if he was going to lean closer and kiss her good night, kicking herself for thinking it – kicking harder when she realised she wanted him to.

'What?' she asked softly.

'Well – this is really hard for me to ask.'

'What?' Cass pressed.

'I wondered if you'd come . . .'

She waited, was he going to say *out with me, out to dinner, out to the theatre*?

'I really have to talk to Liz about Amelia, and I was wondering if you would come with me.'

Cass felt her jaw drop. 'What—?'

'It's probably too much to ask. Sorry.' And then he was haring out of the door as if the devil himself was after him.

'No, wait,' said Cass, stepping out into the street, pulling her cardigan tight around her shoulders. 'Why do you want me to come with you? I don't understand. It's such a private thing.'

Andy stopped, stuffing his hands into his pockets against the icy chill of the wind. 'It was crazy, sorry. Thank you for supper. Tell your mum it was wonderful.'

And then it was all awkward and uneasy. What did they say next? 'I should be going,' said Andy, but he didn't move.

'Me too,' said Cass, shivering.

'You should go in,' he said. 'You'll catch pneumonia.'

Rooted to the spot, Cass nodded. This was the moment after which they might never see each other again, and Cass couldn't quite work out why that mattered. Andy turned his collar up, lifting his shoulders against the dark, cold night.

'Go in,' he said. 'It's too cold for you out here,' he said, his voice low and intimate.

Cass nodded. 'Let me know how Amelia is, won't you?' she said. 'Call me,' she said, wondering if it sounded desperate.

And now he nodded. 'Thank you for supper.'

'Don't mention it,' said Cass, and then he was gone.

Back inside it was warm and light and the cat had re-appeared to help with any annoying beefy leftovers and

Rocco was snoozing in front of the fire, Buster alongside him. Her mum was in the kitchen scraping plates.

'He seems very nice,' said Nita, as Cass joined in with the clearing up.

Cass smiled. 'He is.'

'But?'

'But it's all way too complicated.'

'Ah. So what happened with him and Fee?'

'What is this, the Spanish Inquisition?'

'I'm only asking,' said her mum, eyes and voice full of mischief and fake indignation. 'I need to know.'

'It's over. I think it was probably over a long time ago really. Fee's stayed on in Cyprus with some guy she met on holiday.'

Nita look incredulous. 'No? That girl is such a fool. Here, put this in the dishwasher, will you? So, is Andy going to ring you?'

Cass sighed in exasperation. 'Andy wants me to go with him to meet Amelia's mum.'

Her mum nodded, and scraped a few choice morsels into the cat's bowl. 'Ah,' she said.

'What is that supposed to mean?'

'Well he obviously values your opinion. Amelia clearly had a complicated upbringing. She didn't seem to know anything about Andy until quite recently – and her mother sounds like a peculiar woman, although who can tell? Obviously Andy didn't know about Amelia either, so maybe what he wants is a witness, a friend, someone who can help him get it all straight in his head.'

Cass stared at her. 'So you think I should go?'

'That wasn't what I said.'

Cass started to stack the plates edge on, aware that it

didn't take very long at all for them to slip back into the role of mother and child.

'Let's be honest, Amelia is a total fruitcake,' said her mum, turning to catch Cass's eye. 'Aren't you just the slightest bit curious about what her mother's like? I know I am.'

'So you want me to go with Andy because you're nosey?'

Cass's mum lifted an eyebrow. 'Pretty much nails it . . .' and then she paused and laughed. 'And what? You're not nosey? I could be just the excuse you need.'

Cass, feeling caught out, looked away. 'No.'

'Fair enough, in which case don't go. Can you pass me the dishcloth?'

'But . . .'

'But?'

'Well, I'd like to know Amelia's okay.'

'Because?' said her mother.

'Because I'm a good human being,' said Cass.

Cass's mum laughed, at which point Rocco, who had clearly been earwigging, came in wearing a big grin. 'I think you should go,' he said. 'I really like him. Presumably he hasn't got a purse?'

Chapter Sixteen

Although it was nice to be home, the next couple of days seemed a little anticlimactic. Once Cass had taken a long hard look around, a visual stock-take of what had been moved, what had been sold, Rocco helped her bring a few things out of storage. And life – albeit with Nita and Rocco still in residence – was back to normal. By mid-week, Cyprus seemed a long, long way away. Nita had sent her down to open the shop with a mug of good coffee and a slice of Rocco's trademark lemon drizzle cake for company; with them staying, Cass felt a bit like the Saturday girl.

The roof was almost finished and the terrace ready for cocktails, and Rocco had promised they would be out by the weekend. Cass was torn between wanting to have her life back and missing having the two of them there – if nothing else it was great having someone to cook for her.

Stacked on the desk was the morning's post. Cass pulled up a stool and started to work her way through the heap, sipping coffee as she sorted.

Early in the week, particularly at this time of the year, trade was pretty slow; if people did come in, they were most often there to browse, or get out of the bad weather, so she barely moved when the shop bell rang.

'Hello,' said a familiar voice.

Cass looked up in surprise. 'Andy?' she said.

He smiled, one hand tucked behind his back. 'I brought you these,' he said, producing a great big bouquet of scarlet peonies. Cass knew they must have cost him a fortune at this time of the year.

Cass stared at them. 'God, they are lovely,' she said, 'they're my favourites.'

He laughed, 'I know. I asked your mum last time I was here.'

'Thank you, they're beautiful. How's Amelia getting on?'

'Not bad. I've rung and been up a couple of times to see her and she's doing really well – she'll be out in a couple of days, they just want to keep an eye on her because of the baby. And I think I may have found her a housing association flat: someone is going in to see her tomorrow.'

'That's brilliant.'

A silence opened up and when they spoke again they both started speaking together. 'I was going to . . .' said Cass. 'I'm going to . . .' said Andy.

And then they both laughed and Andy said, 'After you.' And Cass said, 'No, after you, please.'

'The hospital want to know where Amelia's going to stay once she's discharged. She can't really look after herself for the next couple of weeks and I can't have her at my place because I'm at work, so I'm going to go and see Liz later today.'

'Today? Does she know that you're coming?'

'I rang her and told her that we needed to talk. She hasn't been to the hospital yet . . .'

Cass nodded. 'So what time are you going to pick me up?'

She saw Andy do a double take. 'You'll come with me?' he said with a broad smile.

'Yes,' said Cass. 'If you still want me to come, that is?'

'Yes, that would be good.' He reddened. 'How about seven? I said I'd nip in and drop some things off for Amelia first and then I could come round and pick you up after that?'

Cass nodded. 'Okay.'

'Well in that case, see you later,' Andy said.

Cass laughed as he backed out of the shop. 'Are you going to leave the flowers?' she said, as he reached the door.

'God – yes of course, sure – sorry, what an idiot,' he blustered, looking down at the bouquet he was holding; and then Andy left and Cass watched him leave and as she did she realised that she was still smiling.

'So, what do you wear to meet a new friend's old flame, the mother of his surprise daughter?' asked Cass, looking at her reflection in the mirror on the door of her wardrobe. She was holding a jacket up against herself.

Cass's mum was sitting on the end of the bed, drinking a mug of tea, along with Buster and the cat; they were all watching Cass work her way along the hangers. 'So Andy's a friend now, is he?' said her mum.

Cass pulled a long brown wool dress out of the wardrobe. 'Could be, might be, who knows?' She turned left and right, trying to gauge whether the dress said all the right things. 'When did he ask you about the flowers?' she said, trying to make it sound casual. The peonies were currently in a huge lead crystal vase on the pine wash-stand at the end of her bed. They looked fabulous.

'While he was helping Rocco clear the table. You're not going to wear that brown thing, are you? It makes you look like a Carmelite.'

Cass slid it back in onto the rail amongst the others. 'What about this?' she said, holding out a long biscuity-coloured skirt. 'With the cream V-neck jumper you and Rocco bought me last Christmas. And maybe boots?'

'Better, although if I'd have known you could shut the shop up early for a fashion crisis, we wouldn't have bothered staying open till five thirty every night.'

'It was almost five.'

Her mother laughed. 'It was four thirty. Do you want me to make you a sandwich before you go?'

Cass narrowed her eyes. 'When exactly will your roof be finished?'

'Oooo meow,' said Nita. 'Do you want ham or cheese?'

Cass, holding the cream sweater and skirt up against herself considered for a few seconds. 'Both,' she said. 'Oh, and are there any crisps?'

Cass wasn't altogether sure what she was expecting from Liz Cummins: all kinds of possibilities presented themselves as she and Andy drove through the bleak open countryside towards Cambridge. Liz lived in one of the satellite villages on the edge of Cambridge's green belt and, as they got closer to their destination, Andy and Cass fell into an odd expectant silence.

They'd been chatting on the way there, skimming the surface of each other's lives without going very far into the darker, more painful corners. They'd talked about Cass's sons, and the shop, and Andy's job and what he might do if it went under, and it had been easy, and then the words faded until now there was only the sound of the car engine and the fen wind blowing outside.

'What was the name of the street?' asked Cass, leaning forward to peer out into the gloom.

'Church Lane. It must be around here somewhere, that's the church up there on the left,' Andy said, squinting slightly and pointing out into the gloom. 'The house is called The Beeches. It can't be much further. According to the directions it should be up here on the left . . .'

'There,' said Cass, pointing at a Georgian house set back a little off the lane. 'Is that it?'

The house was square with tall rectangular windows either side of the front door. The woodwork was painted black or perhaps dark green: it was hard to tell in the jaundiced yellow cast of the solitary streetlight. If there were lights on inside then there were none visible from the road. On the ground floor, heavy curtains were closed tight against the night. There was no sign of any beeches, but the nameplate that hung on the gate did say that this was their destination.

Andy cut the engine and they sat quietly, as if waiting for the sound to die away. Neither of them moved.

The house had cast-iron railings framing a tiny front garden that had suffered horribly in the icy cold grey blow of the Fenland autumn. The climbers around the front door were as bare and twisted as old wire, and the planters flanking it were full of rotting leaves. There was a galvanised scraper mat in front of the doorstep, and beyond that, under the lee of a little porch, a coconut fibre mat that looked damp and dead.

Cass shuddered. 'Is this it?' she asked.

Andy nodded. 'According to Liz's directions.'

They both sat for a little longer. 'You don't have to come in if you don't want to,' he said, buttoning up his jacket. His voice betrayed something close to nervousness.

Cass bent down to pick up her gloves and handbag, making a show of being businesslike. 'Silly to come all this way and not to go in,' she said briskly. 'I'm sure it will be fine.' No one needed to tell her that she sounded exactly like her mother. 'You ready? Shall we go?'

'Okay,' he took a deep breath. 'Let's get it over with.'

And with that they were out of the car. The wind was bitter, making Cass gasp as it snatched at her breath. Ahead of her, Andy opened the gate and headed up the front path, Cass close behind, shivering, hoping that Liz didn't plan to keep them hanging around outside too long.

As they reached the door it swung open. 'I thought it was you,' said a female voice from inside, in the shadows. 'You'd better come in. Wipe your feet.' And for an instant Cass felt lost and awkward, wondering what she was doing there and why on earth she'd come. But Andy waited for her to catch up. 'Liz, this is my friend, Cass,' he said, holding out an arm to guide her inside.

'Oh right, oh well in that case you'd better come in as well then,' Liz said.

Liz, the woman in the doorway, was small boned and thin as a cane, no more than maybe five feet tall with stringy shoulder-length grey-blonde hair, which was pulled back away from her face under an Alice band. Cass could see where Amelia got her looks.

Liz was dressed in a sensible brown tweed knee-length skirt, a white blouse under an Aran sweater, thick flesh-coloured tights and a pair of flat brown shoes, a pair of glasses strung around her neck on a gilt chain. She had the look of a sickly scout mistress from the 1950s, Cass thought. Given her dress sense, she ought to have been a sensible handsome country woman, but her slightly crazed eyes gave her away.

The hallway was barely warmer than the lane outside.

'Better come through into the kitchen, it's snugger in there. Terrible place to keep warm, my parents didn't believe in central heating. I suppose you'd like a cup of tea.' She spoke well, in a high-pitched, tightly clipped middle-class voice and made wanting tea sound like an unreasonable demand.

Inside, the large hall was dominated by a staircase, and a broad passageway with rooms off to either side. The whole place was dark and cold and smelt of joss sticks and frying, stale cooking smells and old damp dogs.

As they made their way into the back of the house, Cass could pick out paintings and furniture pushed up against the walls, things covered in Indian throws, and rugs hung with bells, and all around a pervading smell of dogs. As her eyes adjusted to the gloom she could pick out the chew marks on the furniture, the signs of digging and clawing and the places where wet tails and fur had been dragged across the peeling paintwork.

'You don't mind dogs, do you?' Liz said, without waiting to hear the reply, and then she pushed open the kitchen door as if there was some resistance, which there was.

From behind it sprung half a dozen dogs ranging in size from what looked like a large collie-cross down in various stages to a noisy yapping excited Jack Russell. The noise they made was overwhelming.

'Back, back,' Liz said, flapping the pack away with her hands and then, turning to Andy and Cass, said, 'Come in and sit down, just ignore them, they'll soon settle.' All around them the dogs barked and jumped and yipped and nipped, so by the time Cass had made it to a chair by the kitchen table she was exhausted.

Liz pushed a kettle on to the Aga. Andy stood just inside the kitchen door, looking round, looking at Liz and Cass and the dogs.

'Well,' said Liz, not quite meeting anyone's eye. 'What would you like, tea or coffee? I've got Earl Grey if anyone would prefer. Or something herbal? I think I've got some camomile.'

Cass looked anxiously at Andy; she couldn't second-guess what he was thinking, his expression resolutely neutral.

On the kitchen table, alongside a tray filled with the paraphernalia of tea- and coffee-making, a pot and a tea cosy, and half a dozen chipped and stained mugs, was a large tartan photo album, a green leatherette one and an Oxo tin in which piles of photos were stacked edgeways on. Cass had to fight the temptation to get them out, the urge to look so great it made her fingers itch.

And as if sensing her curiosity, Liz said, 'Help yourself,' with a wave of the hand. 'What are they if you don't look at them?' And then turning towards Andy said, 'Would you like to look at the photos? I got them all out for you.'

On the Aga the kettle was coming back to the boil, spitting droplets on the hotplate, skating and hissing across the surface like mercury.

'Why,' said Andy quietly. 'What are they of? The good old days?' The tone in his voice was so odd that Cass looked up at him.

'Oh yes,' said Liz, apparently oblivious. 'And there are lots of when Amelia was little, when she was a baby, her christening, when she went to nursery, her first day at school. Why don't you get them out?' she said to Cass.

'To be honest with you there is no way I want to look at all the years I missed,' Andy said, still standing by the doorway. 'Why didn't you tell me about Amelia before?' he continued in the same low, even voice. 'Why now? One phone call twenty-odd years ago and I'd have had the chance – the choice, to have been there – to have shared them all with you.'

And Cass realised that what she had heard in Andy's voice, however carefully controlled, was anger and frustration. Finding Amelia had changed his life forever.

'So, would you like tea or coffee?' Liz asked, her voice as even as if he had asked her the time of day.

'Well?' demanded Andy.

'I really don't feel there is any need for this to be unpleasant, do you?' Liz said, setting the kettle back on the stove and picking up the teapot. 'I mean, we're all adults, water under the bridge and all that. It was all a long time ago now.'

Cass stared at Liz, wondering what that was supposed to mean.

'Why don't you just sit down and take a look at the photos. She was the most beautiful child.'

Nobody touched them.

Andy started to pace up and down the kitchen while Liz made a show of making the tea.

'You see the thing is,' he said, 'I've got a real problem with all of this, Liz, because I don't know who you are. I've got no idea. And before you say anything, I don't mean that in some sort of metaphysical hippy way: what I mean is that I don't remember you at all.'

Liz laughed. 'Well trust me, Andy, I remember you very well.'

331

'That's just it,' said Andy. 'I don't trust you. I had expected to come in here and see you and hear your voice and for it all to come rushing back. And you know what? There was nothing – nothing at all.'

'Well you can hardly blame me for that,' said Liz lightly. 'It's not my fault you can't remember. It was a mad time. Crazy. We were all smoking and drinking—'

'Okay, okay, tell me when we slept together or screwed or whatever euphemism you'd like to use. I'd like to know, when did we conceive Amelia? Who were we friends with – who remembers? Who remembers me and you?'

Liz shot Cass a look, and Andy waved the unspoken protest away. 'She's my friend, I want her here.'

'Well, we used to hang around with lots of people.'

'Who?' demanded Andy, still without raising his voice.

'Kat and Mike and Julia and Finn, and then there was Jack – Gill, Colin—'

'Now you see, that's the thing – them I do remember,' said Andy. 'So how long did we go out for? Where did we meet?'

Liz put the teapot down. Close up, Cass could see that her hands were shaking.

'What is this, some kind of interrogation? It was all a long time ago now,' she protested.

Andy's expression was hard as stone. 'Where?' he repeated.

'All right, we met first time at one of Pablo's parties, we didn't go out for very long. We used to drink in the Taps.'

'Okay, so I know Pablo and the Taps, but how long is not very long?'

'A month, two months,' said Liz lightly.

Cass stared at her. Andy shook his head. 'You see, I don't

332

believe you. I was no angel and I've had my fair share of one-night stands over the years. But I would remember a month. I would certainly remember two months and I've spent hours and hours, *days* trying to work out when Amelia was conceived.'

Liz set the teapot down, straightened her back and tucked her chin in. 'What exactly are you trying to say to me, Andy?' she said.

'It doesn't take a degree to work this out, Liz. Amelia isn't mine, is she.' It wasn't a question so much as a statement. Liz bit her lip and blinked. Fascinated, unable to tear her eyes away, Cass watched.

'Why don't you just take a look at the photos?' Liz said, pinning on a strange false smile. 'Please, Andy, why don't you take a look? She was such a pretty baby.'

'But not my baby,' said Andy flatly.

Liz opened her mouth to speak, fingers now knotting themselves around and around each other like rope.

'Or would you rather I asked Amelia to take a DNA test?' said Andy.

It was as if Andy had thrown a switch. Liz swung round, eyes bright with tears, face contorted with anguish. 'Please don't do that,' she said. 'Please. You have to understand how much I love you,' she said. 'I've loved you from the moment I first saw you at the Taps, I always knew we were meant to be together, me and you. You were with someone else but I knew she wasn't anyone important. I wanted it to be me – it should have been me.'

'But it wasn't you,' said Andy, his voice still level and icy calm.

A huge tear rolled down Liz's face. 'One of the men who worked in the bar invited me when Pablo had a party.'

She stopped and wiped her face. 'You have to understand, Andy, in every true sense of things Amelia is yours. All yours – I gave up my life, my career, everything to bring up your daughter.'

Andy sighed. 'Look Liz, I'm sorry, but this isn't going to wash. I think you need help. I don't know what the hell is going on here but let's just be straight about this, Amelia isn't my daughter, is she?'

For a moment Cass thought Liz might bluff it out, but then her face crumpled, the tears rolling down her cheeks unchecked. 'No, no she isn't, but she should have been. I love you, Andy,' she said. 'I've always loved you – I've always told everyone you were the only man for me. I told Amelia. I said that you were a very special man, but that we couldn't be together. And that I understood and she would too. It was such a little lie to begin with, but it got out of hand, and once I'd told her I couldn't take it back. I told her that you were kind and loving – I said that you'd have made a good father.'

Andy was ashen. 'So what happened?'

'One day she told me she wanted to meet you. I suppose I should have known it would come eventually. I didn't think she would be able to – but she's clever and then there's the Internet and I'd told her things about you, where you used to work, things like that – she said you weren't hard to find. She said she thought it was fate.'

'So why didn't you tell her the truth then?'

'How could I?' sobbed Liz. 'How could I tell her that I'd been lying all those years? Did she show you the photos? I took some at one of Pablo's parties, oh and out on the river. And when she was little . . .' Liz turned her attention to the tin full of photos. 'Let me show you. I had some copies made, so you can take them home.' She wiped her face with her sleeve, sniffing.

'What did you think would happen when she found me, Liz? Surely you must have known this would happen. What did you think I'd do – just roll over and assume she was mine?'

'But she should have been, Andy. That's what I've been telling you. She should have been.'

Andy held up his hands. 'Liz, please, you've got to stop this.'

But she couldn't. Edging towards hysteria, she started to pull photos out of the tin, first one at a time and then by the handful.

'I always thought that eventually I'd meet someone else and, even though they weren't you, that they'd take Amelia and me on, but then Mummy and Daddy were ill and I moved back home and it just never happened. I suppose you became a sort of myth. My hero . . .' A huge tear rolled down her face. 'What am I going to tell Amelia?' she wailed.

'How about the truth?' said Andy.

Liz glared at him. 'How can I, after all these years? I can hardly tell her I had a one-night stand with some cabby who took pity on me, can I? Can I?'

Any pretence of calm or, come to that, sanity was rapidly dissolving with the tears, the dogs were barking, the wind was howling. All they needed now was some wailing and gnashing of teeth and it would be a night straight out of a Victorian melodrama.

Cass stood up; enough was enough. 'Come on,' she said to Liz briskly, 'sit down, you're upsetting the dogs, and this is doing no one any good at all. Andy, pass me that kitchen roll and pour the tea.'

Without a word he did as he was told. Cass handed Liz a couple of sheets of tissue. 'Now blow your nose and pull yourself together. Whatever happened before, Amelia's your daughter and I know she loves you – and she needs you now. She's not well, she's had an operation and she's going to have a baby—'

'She is such a drama queen,' said Liz, without a hint of irony.

'It doesn't matter what she is, she is still your daughter. What you did to her and to Andy is cruel but you can still put it right. She needs your help,' said Cass.

'She isn't the only one who needs help around here,' said Andy. Cass shot him a look, while Liz sobbed miserably.

'You need to go and talk to her, she needs your support. And she needs to know the truth. Please Liz.'

'But what about Andy? And me?' protested Liz. She swung round to Andy. 'Amelia told me that when she met you that she knew straight away – she said that you were lovely, Andy. You see she loves you too. She knew, she just knew instinctively as soon as she saw you.'

'What did she know, Liz?' asked Andy.

'That you were her dad, of course. That party at Pablo's we kissed under the mistletoe and I just knew then that all the waiting was worth it. All those months and months of waiting. And then you went off with what's-her-name but I knew it wouldn't last. That's why I went off with the taxi driver: I wanted to make you understand what you were missing – make you jealous. I thought you moving back so close was a sign. I thought you'd come back for me, for us . . .'

Cass caught hold of Andy's arm. 'We need to go,' she said in a quiet voice. 'We're not getting anywhere with this.'

Andy shook his head. 'This is insane. She's fucked the last six months of my life up and – from what I can see – all of Amelia's. I've been going through hell trying to remember her, worrying about Amelia, trying to work out what my responsibility to her was, how I should handle it. What I should do and say and take on. And now it all turns out to be a lie. The thing with Fiona came to a head because of this, the way I've looked at everything; my whole life has been changed because I thought I had a daughter.'

He turned to face Liz. 'You need to go and see someone before you fuck the next generation up too. Amelia needs you to be there for her and she needs you sorted and sane. You need to go and see her, tell her the truth – sort this bloody mess out before anyone else gets hurt. What you have, the two of you, isn't dependent on me or some imaginary father.'

Liz was pale and emotional. 'You can't tell me what to do. And I can't tell her. How can I tell her that you're not her dad? She loves you.'

'She doesn't know me. If you don't tell her, Liz, I will,' said Andy.

'You wouldn't,' she gasped.

Andy didn't reply. Liz sniffed back the tears. 'We could have been so good together.'

Andy shook his head. 'Liz, I didn't know you when I walked in through that door. I've never known you.'

He pulled a sheet of paper out of his pocket and put it down on the table next to the piles of photos. 'This is the ward Amelia is on, the phone number of the hospital and the address.' He pulled a pen out of his inside pocket and scribbled something else. 'Those are the visiting hours.'

337

'What about the dogs? I can't leave the dogs,' said Liz, looking at the baying yapping pack.

Andy offered Cass his hand. 'Come on,' he said. 'I think we should go.' Cass didn't resist and followed him out across the kitchen, glad of the feel of his fingers wrapped tight around hers.

'But what about your tea?' pleaded Liz. 'And the photos. You should at least look at the photos while you're here.'

But they were already out in the hall, halfway to the front door, dogs yapping and giving chase as Liz followed them. 'I love you,' she said as Andy jerked open the door and they hurried down the path towards the car.

Cass's last sight of Liz was her standing in the doorway waving frantically, trying to persuade them to come back inside. A mile down the road, and well away from the village, Andy pulled over into a lay-by and for a few seconds sat and stared out into the wild Fenland night.

'There are times,' he said, 'when I wish I still smoked. Are you okay?'

Cass looked across at him. He was ashen, hands gripping the steering wheel. 'I'm fine,' she said. 'How about you?'

Andy shook his head. 'Numb. When I walked into that house I'd expected all kinds of things. I expected to meet someone I'd forgotten, someone I'd had a fling with, something. I'd assumed there would be some sort of recognition there. Something . . .' He stopped.

'I've spent the last few months getting used to the idea that I've got a daughter, that I'm a father. Picking through my memories, changing all kinds of givens in my life. And now I discover that it's some kind of weird obsessional fantasy. I thought I was going to be a grandfather,' he laughed. 'And now I discover that it's a lie, all of it – smoke and mirrors. Mind you, meeting Liz helps me understand why Amelia is like she is. Mad as a badger.' He smiled grimly. 'You fancy a coffee? I could really do with one. I saw a fast food place just up the road.'

So there they were, sitting either side of a Formica table, on benches that were screwed to the floor, drinking coffee out of cartons, watching a family argue over who had broken the free toy, and who had been good, a situation remedied by an under-manager who swept in like Lady Bountiful to hand out another small plastic man with a wand.

And they watched in silence as people ate and toddlers screamed and bikers came and went and finally Andy said, 'The trouble is I don't feel I can let her go, she needs me.'

'Amelia?'

Andy nodded. 'She waited all her life to find a father and now, thanks to her mum, he's someone who never existed. And okay, so she is difficult and complex, but you can see why and it's not a reason to give her up.'

'She'll know that you're not her dad though.'

Andy shrugged. 'And I'll know that she's not my daughter, but it doesn't matter, does it?'

Cass smiled. 'I suppose not. How about Liz?'

Andy grimaced. 'I've got no idea, but I'll think of something. Oh, and while we're on the subject of how weird my life is: I had a phone call from Fiona last night.'

Cass nodded; there was nothing she could think of to say, although she was relieved that Fee had rung Andy and not her.

'She thinks that maybe she's made a mistake.'

Cass felt her jaw drop. 'She's only been out there a little while,' Cass said incredulously. Surely lust had a longer shelf life?

'She thinks this Geno is after her money, apparently. He says he's got some kind of bond – I think it's supposed be an inheritance – coming out but there's no sign of it . . .'

'Sounds dodgy to me.'

'Me too. She says she wants to come home – and see how he reacts when she tells him she's leaving.'

Cass hesitated, drawing a stir stick through a coffee spill. 'So, do you feel you can't let her go, because she needs you?'

'Fiona?'

Cass nodded, not quite trusting herself to speak.

'Would you mind?' he asked, eyes holding hers.

Cass waited for a long, long minute before replying. 'Actually, I would,' she said softly.

Andy smiled. 'I was planning to ask if you'd like to go out to dinner with me some time. I was worried that you'd still think I was off limits.'

'It depends on what you said to Fiona.'

'I told her the truth, that our relationship had been over a long time before she met Geno, and that I'd been a coward not to talk to her about how I felt – and of course if she needed help then I'd be there, but that we haven't got any kind of future together.'

Cass stared at him. 'And what did she say?'

Andy grinned ruefully. 'Not much, and nothing I'd care to repeat, and then she hung up.'

Cass nodded. 'So did you get to tell her about Amelia?'

Andy shook his head. 'No, I didn't get the chance, but I will. So would you like another coffee?' he asked, rattling the empty paper cup at her.

Cass smiled. 'I thought you'd never ask.'

Read on for an exclusive preview of Kate Lawson's
next book *Mother of the Bride* . . .

Chapter One

Molly Foster was standing on the quay at Wells-next-the-Sea beside the radio car, where a man dressed as a bear was juggling rubber herring. Alongside him was an Elvis impersonator in a white jumpsuit and rhinestones and a woman called Linda, who knitted jumpers from the yarn spun from the fur of her three Newfoundlands – encounters that were all in a day's work for a presenter on a local radio station.

Molly had one half of her headphones pressed to her ear and the other half off so she could hear what was happening on the quay. The last track had played out and Airwave Anglia FM's station jingle was coming to a close. Ready with the mike, all the while nodding and smiling inanely at her guests, giving them the thumbs up and holding eye contact so they didn't wander off, Molly was waiting for the moment when they went live to air.

'You okay? All ready?' she mouthed. Everyone nodded in unison – all except Elvis who curled his lip and said, 'A-huh-huh.'

'Here we go,' she said.

Phil, the broadcast assistant, really should be covering the sheep-dogging, but instead – thanks to some technical glitch – he was hunched over in the back of the radio car, fiddling with the control panel. The radio car was a converted people carrier with a retractable radio mast that the station used for outside broadcasts, painted in the station's livery – an unmistakable mix of orange, pink and lime green.

She hoped that what she could see billowing out of the car door was steam from Phil's coffee and not smoke.

Meanwhile in her ear, her producer Stan, back at the studio, was about to cue in her next caller. The music faded out at which point Molly said, 'Great track that. Perfect for a sunny day by the seaside – speaking of which we're here live in Wells-next-the-Sea today as part of our Great British Summer Days Out series, visiting all those great places we have right here in Sunny East Anglia and we've got some fantastic guests lined up for you during today's show.

But first of all on line one we've got Maureen from Little Newton, who wants to talk about – what is it you're talking to us about today Maureen?'

'Death,' said Maureen in a monotone. 'I want to talk about how it felt when my cat Smokey died.'

'Right,' said Molly, pulling faces at Phil, who had stopped fiddling and was currently sitting on the step of the radio car, busy flirting with two teenage girls in bikinis. Apparently nothing had been on fire.

'I'm sure that we all feel very sorry for your loss, Maureen – I know that my pets are very important to me – but we were hoping that you were going to talk to us about your memories of the local fisher fleet—'

'Smokey loved fish, particularly the heads,' said the unstoppable Maureen. 'We used to save them for him. Little tinker used to stuff them down the back of the sofa if you didn't watch him. Stank the place out. I had him

344

cremated last March. Fourteen he was. I've got the urn here with me – he loved the radio. Not you but that other chap, the one with the glasses, what's his name?'

'Right,' said Molly, waving now, desperately trying to drag Phil's attention away from the wriggling jiggling giggling girls and back to the job in hand.

From somewhere close by she could hear a mobile phone ringing with a distinctive Laurel and Hardy theme, a theme downloaded by her live-in lover Nick as a joke; it was her mobile phone. This was the ultimate no-no. On TV and on radio, before you go on air you always check that your mobile is switched off and if you're not sure that it's off you take the battery out, except of course hers was ringing and it seemed to be getting louder.

'I've been having grief counselling,' Maureen was saying. 'And we held a séance – he's still here you know. Him and Timmy the rabbit . . .'

'We're lucky enough to have Ken Barber with us here today,' said Molly, plunging into the abyss, all the while praying that someone back at the studio would have the good sense to pull the plug on Maureen.

To her right the bear man was mid-flow. 'Ken is currently working his way around the coast line of Great Britain staging a one-man show to raise public awareness about the state of the British fishing industry – which I have to say probably doesn't sound like much fun until you see Ken's act for yourself. Now for the listeners at home Ken, let's just describe what you're wearing, shall we?' At which point Ken growled.

Molly sat bolt-upright in bed, sweating hard, gasping for air, her heart pounding in her chest. Close by her mobile phone kept on ringing.

'Y'go-na-getthat?' said Nick, half-asleep, sniffing and fumbling around in the dark.

'You're fine, it's all right, go back to sleep, I've got it,' Molly said, picking up the phone that was not only ringing but glowing and flashing on the bedside cabinet. She felt around for her glasses. According to the alarm clock it was two o'clock in the morning, which brought her to full consciousness like a glass of cold water in the face.

In her experience, very little good news ever came in at two o'clock in the morning. Molly blinked, wondering who the hell it was and focused in on the caller display. It said 'Jessica', her daughter, which made Molly's heart lurch.

'Jess?' Molly said anxiously. 'Are you all right, baby? What's the matter?' She couldn't quite keep the panic out of her voice. Two o'clock in the morning and her daughter was phoning home, did that mean a car accident, a fire, theft?

'Mum – hello – hello?' Jess sounded drunk. 'I knew that you'd be up. We've got some brilliant news – we wanted you to be amongst the first to know. Max has just asked me to marry him and I've said yes. I've said yes, Mum. *I'm getting married –*' The last few words were a shriek of pure delight followed by giggling. It sounded as if Jess was being spun around – which she most probably was – and then Molly heard Jessica say, 'Here, you talk to Mum – just say hello. Yes, yes just say hello – She wants to talk to you –'

Which wasn't strictly true, mainly because Molly hadn't quite caught up yet and was still a little way back down the emotional road where she was relieved that neither of them were in hospital. But Max came on the line anyway and said in that deep dark self-assured voice of his, 'Hi there Molly – hope we didn't wake you. Jess is insisting that we ring everyone – she wanted you to know straight away.' He paused and then added as an afterthought, 'Mum.'

Molly closed her eyes wondering what to say, but before any words came out Jess was back on the line all squeaky and excited and full of joy. 'Isn't it fab? I am just *so* excited. Max went down on one knee and everything and he'd already got the ring and it fitted. It's like this little diamond flower in white gold and all these cute little coloured stones and it was just so romantic. God, there is so much to do; we were thinking Christmas? Sleigh bells, reindeer – maybe we should all fly everyone out to Lapland, what do you think? I mean what are the chances of there being any decent snow in England? And you know I've always loved snow, mind you maybe we could hire one of those machines. Is that a bit naff? Oh isn't it exciting, mum? If we had snow I could have one of those fur-trimmed hoods and a long cloak and the page-boys could wear tartan waists coat. Maybe we could have it in Scotland – oh they could wear kilts then – What do you think? Aren't you going to say something?'

Molly opened her mouth to speak but there still weren't any words in there, which was odd because Molly was renowned for always being able to find something to say no matter what – which was why she was on the radio, that's what they paid her for.

'Mum? Are you still there?' asked Jess sounding a little anxious, and then presumably to Max, said, 'I think she might be breaking up.'

Never a truer word was spoken, thought Molly and then finally she found her voice and said, 'well, well done you – both of you – congratulations. That's brilliant. I'm really pleased for you both. It's just a bit of a surprise that's all. I mean why so quick? I mean December? It doesn't really give us much time to . . . Oh my god, you're not pregnant, are you? I mean not that I mind or anything but—'

Jessica, giggling, cut her short. 'No, of course I'm not pregnant, Mum, at least not yet. Although I think Max is quite keen on the idea.'

Molly heard them both laughing then and felt her face redden.

'It all seems just a bit sudden, that's all.' Now her mouth was in gear Molly couldn't stop it, and it was saying all those things that her mother would say – none of them particularly helpful or positive. 'Have you rung your father yet?'

'No, he and Marnie are still away on a cruise at the moment. We've just emailed them. And then tomorrow morning first thing we're going to ring Max's parents, they won't be up tonight. You don't sound very pleased,' said Jess.

'I am sweetie. Really, I am. I'm just a bit shocked. You know me, it's not often that I'm speechless.' Molly laughed, trying hard to recover her composure. 'It's all come as a bit of a surprise. I hadn't realised that it was that serious.' Inwardly Molly groaned – that was *exactly* what her mother would say.

'Well it is,' said Jess defensively. 'And I thought you'd be pleased for us.'

'I am darling – very, really – I couldn't be more pleased. Really.' It sounded like a lie. 'What about Jack, have you rung him yet?'

Jess snorted. 'Not yet. Every time I ring my little brother's phone it goes to voicemail. I think he's trying to avoid me.'

'I don't think it's you Jess, I think it's Pippa.'

'No! She's not still after him, is she? Are you serious? They split up months ago. She must be mad—'

'I think that is the general consensus – he says it feels like she's stalking him.'

'God, shows how long it is since I've talked to him, mind you she *must* be desperate if she's stalking Jack. You know I always liked her, she seemed such a nice person – anyway I'll leave him a message.'

Alongside Molly, Nick was slowly coming to. It always took him a while. He had switched on his bedside lamp and blinked myopically in the light, looking for all the world like a well-loved, extremely handsome hamster.

'Everything all right?' he mumbled while feeling around for his glasses. Nick was gorgeous but very short-sighted, which Molly always thought was a real bonus for the older woman. Molly suspected that in this light, without his glasses, she was just a warm, feminine, glamorous, soft-focus blur, which was how she would have preferred to stay.

'It's Jessica,' she said, covering the mouthpiece.

Nick nodded. 'She's all right?'

'She's getting married.'

Nick flinched. 'Bloody hell. Tell her I love her very much but she's mad – and Max must be certifiable if he's taking her on.'

'Here,' said Molly handing him the mobile. 'Why don't you tell her yourself?'

And then she got out of bed and headed for the bathroom, looking back en route at Nick who was laughing now, and even though he was only half awake was saying all the right things and offering congratulations and jokes. Not for the first time Molly marvelled at her good fortune at finding a man like Nick after all these years, a man who loved her and her children – who repaid the compliment by loving him right back – and who loved her in ways so numerous and so palpable that she couldn't imagine what life had been like without him.

In the bathroom Molly took the time to compose herself, brush her teeth and her hair and think about what she should be saying to her only daughter. Jessica had been going out with Max for maybe six months, which wasn't that long, but plenty long enough to know if it was going anywhere – and Molly's impression up until that point had been that it was going nowhere at all.

Although, maybe she had misread it. When they first started dating Max had taken Jess to Barcelona and Paris for weekends away. City breaks seemed to be the thing that people did now instead of going to the pictures.

In the time they'd been together Jess had brought Max to see them maybe two or three times at most, once for a barbeque, once for Sunday lunch. Jessica was twenty-four and Max was older, closer to forty – although Molly hadn't taken that much notice of quite how close because she hadn't thought he was staying around that long. He had struck Molly as tall and charming and a little too polished and worldly-wise. And if she was honest, Molly would have said she wasn't all that keen on him, although wild dogs and thumbscrews wouldn't have dragged that out of her at this precise moment.

Last time they'd talked about him, Jess had come over on her own to drop off her dog, Bassa, for the weekend and they had gone for a walk together over the common, while Nick had cooked lunch. It couldn't have been more than a couple of months ago.

'*Max is lovely. He knows how to treat a woman and he's always buying me things chocolates – and flowers – and knows what wine to order. You should see his house – he's got this fabulous cat called Choux – he's a chocolate Burmese I think. And he's got a great car . . .'*

Molly had sensed a *but* coming but hadn't said anything and instead held her tongue, because it's common knowledge that if you say anything negative about your children's friends or lovers – even if they are busy pretending to be grown ups – your children just hung on in there to spite you.

So Molly had nodded and said, 'He seems nice.'

And even as she was saying it Molly knew that it was mostly because it meant that Jessie was probably finally over Glenn, who had gone off to do something important in America and broken her heart, and relief that Jess hadn't gone back to the boyfriend before that who used to shred beer mats and tissues into little nests of paper tape, and that despite being her first real love Jess had decided not to accept the invitation to go on holiday to Goa with Beano, who was lean and lovely with limbs like a daddy-long legs, and who everyone loved but who drank, smoked and snorted his way through life with an enthusiasm that startled even the most robust of observers.

And now she was getting married. Molly couldn't help wondering if Jess had had any idea Max was going to propose, after all it was very sudden, but she couldn't quite bring herself to ask.

Back in the bedroom, Nick was still cracking jokes on the phone, asking about Jess and Max's plans and saying all the right things. As Molly crept back to bed he said, 'Anyway darling, here's your mum. We'll have the champagne on ice waiting for you both when you come back – yes, yes see you soon – and well done. Love you too.'

He made it all sound so easy.

'Hello,' said Molly to Jess. 'And congratulations darling. I'm so pleased for you. Whereabouts are you now?'

'On the beach at St Audrey's Bay – you know the place where we used to go camping when we were kids? Bassa loves it – he keeps running in and out of the water, barking. Max said that we needed a break and that he'd take me anywhere I wanted to go and this was it – isn't that romantic? It's just like when we used to camp here. And the tide's coming in and we've got this funny old blanket out of the car – and it is just so beautiful.' Jess sounded so young and so wistful and so full of love and hope. Molly felt her eyes filling up.

'Can you hear the sea, mum?'

Molly sniffed. 'Yes, I can hear it. I'm so happy for you, baby.'

And then there were a few seconds of silence in which Molly could hear Jessica breathing. She remembered cradling her in her arms when she was a newborn and watching those tiny baby breaths, remembered marvelling at her tiny perfect eyelashes, letting tiny baby fingers curl around hers, in awe of something so new and so perfect, in awe of the huge responsibility she had just taken on, the act of trust of this tiny little creature coming into their lives. She remembered the sensation and smell of Jess as she snuggled in close, and a tear broke free and rolled down over Molly's cheek.

'Oh Jess,' she whispered. 'You're all grown up, aren't you?'

And then Jessica said softly, 'Please don't make me cry mum, I've been really good and I don't want to end up looking like a panda.'

'Right,' said Molly, backhanding the tears away and making the effort to pull herself together. 'Sorry. So if this wedding is going to be in December then we'll need to get together and start planning as soon as we can really.

It doesn't give us very long – and a lot of places will already be booked up for Christmas.'

There was a crisp little silence on the phone and then Jess said, 'Mum, I'm not just having my wedding in any old place.'

'No, of course not, baby, and that wasn't what I said. It's just that a lot of places will be busy at Christmas. Look, why don't you come over as soon as you get back and we'll talk about it. We need to start getting things organised as soon as possible. Make lists—'

At which point Jess giggled again. 'Oh yes – I've just got so many ideas. This is going to be *so* exciting.' Her voice raised an octave or two. 'Anyway we'll be home on Friday. We'll come to see you over the weekend. Love you lots. See you soon.'

'I love you too,' said Molly and meant every word. 'And congratulations. And don't get cold down there . . .'

'We won't,' said Jess.

When Jess had hung up Molly slipped back under the duvet and Nick slipped his arms around her. 'My baby is going to get married,' she sniffled.

Nick grinned. 'It could be worse,' he said. 'She could have been ringing to tell you, you were going to be a granny.'

'I don't know how I feel about this. I mean we don't really know anything about this Max.'

'You don't have to,' said Nick. 'Jess knows what she's doing. She's a sensible girl.'

'Is she?' said Molly, feeling the tears welling up. 'I've never organised a wedding before. What exactly does the mother of the bride do?'

'I've got no idea.' Nick pulled her closer. 'But by the look on your face, mostly cry and panic?'

Molly poked Nick till he yelped in protest and then snuggled up alongside him. 'I'll look on the internet tomorrow. There'll be something on there.'

'I'm sure there is. And someone is bound to do a book, but just don't go getting any ideas,' Nick said, gently stroking the hair back off her face. 'Before you say anything *we're not getting married*, all right? So don't ask.'

'Oh, spoilsport,' said Molly, relishing the sensation of his arms around her. 'We could have a double wedding. Me and you, Jessica and Max.'

Nick raised his eyebrows. 'I can't see Jess wearing that one, can you?'

Molly laughed. 'No, me neither but all my friends think it's high time you made a respectable woman of me.'

'It'd take a lot more than getting married,' Nick said with a grin. 'And besides I like what we've got. If it ain't broke don't fix it, is what I say.'

'They want to buy hats.'

'Uhuh and now that Jess is getting married they'll have their chance, now turn over and let's get some sleep.' Nick reached out and flicked off the lights.

'You're all heart,' said Molly.

'I know. Where are you working tomorrow?' asked Nick.

'Wells-next-the-Sea,' said Molly. 'We've interviewing some guy who is single-handedly trying to save the British fishing industry. Apparently he uses comedy to make his message more interesting—'

'Uh-huh, the herring juggler in the bear suit,' said Nick, sleepily.

'That'll be the one,' said Molly. 'How did you know?'

'You were talking about him in your sleep.'

* * *

The following day was hot and sunny. Lots of people showed up to see the radio show going out live and no-one growled or went on about cat death, not once. Three hours on air flew by.

'And now it's bye-bye from me, Molly Foster and the rest of the crew over here in sunny Wells, and back to Karl our news reader in the studio for the latest regional and national updates. Hi Karl, what's the weather looking like in Norwich?'

'Not as nice as Wells by the sounds of it, Molly. And I really envy you those fish and chips. Here is the round-up of today's news headlines, followed by the weather forecast from Sasha for everyone across the rest of the region.'

Through her headphones, Stan's voice came up over the sound of broadcast. 'Great job – we got a brilliant response – the phone lines were really buzzing here. You're coming back in?'

'Uhuh. I'll be bringing the car back and we've got a meeting with Rob at three – or had you forgotten?' Molly said, smiling and turning her attention to her guests as she unhooked the backpack for the radio mike and headphones and gave them to Phil. He'd started to stow the kit away the second Molly had started the handover back to the studio. 'I just need to thank the guys who were on the show.'

'Sure thing – catch you later.'

Molly turned to her guests and the little impromptu audience that had gathered around the radio car. 'Thanks for all your efforts, you were brilliant – great show, we've had lots of calls. Well done,' she said warmly, shaking hands and paws and smiling, signing autographs and handing out pens and balloons and various other station freebies to anyone who wanted it.

Phil meanwhile, was busy rolling up cable and putting

away the PA system, as well as retracting the giant aerial, which very slowly slid down into the body of the car like a giant periscope all clad around with a curl of gold cable.

'Ah, showbusiness,' he said, as Molly handed out another autographed paper sunhat to a small child with a horribly runny nose and what looked like it might be impetigo.

'Thanks for coming,' said Molly, ignoring Phil. 'And I hope you have a lovely holiday.' The little boy skipped away, all smiles and snot, to rejoin an exhausted-looking young woman in a sundress who, along with a bad case of sunburn, had a baby on one arm and was heavily pregnant. Molly caught herself staring; the young woman looked a lot like Jessica.

Another five years or so and it could be. Molly swallowed back a tidal wave of tears and dropped the give-aways back into a plastic stacker box.

'You are extremely cynical for one so young,' she said, sliding the box into the back of the car.

Phil grinned, apparently taking it as a compliment. 'You should have told everyone that Jess was getting married on air – I bet we could have blocked the phone lines, nothing people like better than a bit of romance. Oh now there's an idea – we could run it on the show, do a countdown to Jessica's big day. We could run a competition – I can see the strapline on the website now, *Be a bridesmaid at Jessie's Big Fat Norfolk Wedding*. You want me to bring it up at today's planning meeting?'

Molly fixed him with an icy stare. 'No, we could not and no, you're most definitely not to run it by anyone in the planning meeting. Okay? First of all not everyone in the family knows yet and secondly it's private. Who wants the world and his wife watching you making wedding plans?'

Phil sniffed. 'Oh come off it, anyone who is anyone these days. We're all obsessed with it. Who's marrying who, what they're wearing, who's invited, who isn't, and who's likely to have a fist-fight break out over the canapés. And the bride's dress.'

Molly held up her hands. 'Phil, stop it, you're scaring me – you're meant to be a boy. Boys hate weddings.'

'It's not me, it's my girlfriend and all her friends. Our whole flat is stacked with celebrity magazines, who's got fat, who's far too thin, who'll never love again, who's had lipo, who would die rather than go under the knife. Who's a love rat . . . I can't help it. I never used to read that kind of crap, I was strictly an *Autocar* and *What-Hifi* guy, but it gets into your blood – it's addictive. To be honest the weddings are a bit of light relief.'

'Okay, okay I get the picture.'

'So why not talk to the management, see if you can't make it into a feature?'

'Have you got no shame?'

'Not much, why? It would be great. You could probably wangle all kinds of freebies.'

'What you mean? When my daughter and future son-in-law kneel down at the altar rail instead of having price tags on the bottom of their shoes they'll have little signs saying, "*sponsored by Linda's Luxury Buffet Services*"?'

'Well, it's an idea. And you could invite all the famous people you know. Get the paparazzi there—'

'I don't know any famous people, Phil,' said Molly, heaving one of the PA speakers into the back of the car.

'Yes you do. You've interviewed loads.'

'Yes, but there is a big difference between interviewing them and inviting them to your daughter's wedding.'

357

'Says who? There was that bloke off *The Bill*, oh and that girl who was on *HOLBY CITY*, some of the guys at Norwich City Football club, Delia – oh and that really famous artist bloke who got some kind of big international prize – the one with the red hair who bought a summer place down on the salt marshes.'

Molly raised an eyebrow. 'Just remind me not to have you as Master of Ceremonies on the door announcing the arrivals, "*Oh look, here's the woman who used to be the best friend of the one that's getting married.*"'

Instead of being offended Phil grinned. 'Oh wow, does that mean I'm going to get an invite?'

'Oh, for goodness sake.'

'The thing about all those people though is that they're famous and they'd add a certain something to your wedding.'

'That's right Phil, a security nightmare – and lots of photographers elbowing my family out of the way so they could get a good shot of some bird with a trout-pout and a spray-on tan. The bottom line is that I don't know them and I don't want them at Jess's wedding.'

Their conversation was going on around the familiar rigmarole of packing away. Usually it didn't take very long at all but then usually Molly's daughter wasn't getting married. In Molly's recollection, Phil had never been this talkative in the three years she had worked with him.

'You got on with them really well.'

'That's what I'm paid to do Phil, I got on with that clown in a bear suit but it doesn't mean I'm going to invite him round for tea . . .'

'So where is Jess having her engagement party?'

Molly looked up from the box of electronic oddments she was currently packing away under a seat. 'What?'

'The engagement party – I mean presumably Jess is having one, isn't she?'

Aware that she had her mouth open Molly closed it fast and said, 'Phil I only found out about them getting married last night. I don't know *what* she's having yet, or come to that where or when.'

But Phil was on a roll. 'When my sister got married they had this big engagement party – mum and dad put an announcement in the *Times*. And then there were the stag nights and hen nights – and then my parents organised some sort of meet and greet dinner party for the groom's family so we could all meet up and get acquainted before the big day—'

Molly decided that she had heard quite enough. 'Fish and chips?' she said, nodding towards the parade of shops that fronted the little harbour.

Phil grinned. 'I thought you'd never ask. You want me to lock up or do you want me to get them and we'll eat them out of the paper?'

'We'll eat in,' she said.

Phil nodded and finished off the lock down, while Molly put on a bit of lipstick and dealt with the after-effects of headphone hair.

'My sister ended up using a wedding planner,' said Phil as they headed off across the car park. They had fallen into step and crossing the road joined the queue outside French's chippie, where holiday makers were two abreast, waiting to get inside and be served.

'Do we have to keep on about the wedding?' asked Molly. Her stomach was rumbling, she was tired and they still had to make their way back into Norwich to drop the radio car off before going on to the management meeting.

'I was only saying,' said Phil. 'They asked me to be an usher. We all had cravats and cummerbunds that matched the bridesmaids' dresses.'

Molly settled into line. 'This wedding planner, was it a person or a wall chart?'

'She was called Cheryl and she did all the arrangements at the hotel where my sister had her wedding. She was very keen on themes.'

'Who, your sister?'

'No, this Cheryl. She had a whole book full – my sister brought it home – pirates, princesses, wenches.' He grinned. 'And that was just for the civil partnerships.'

Hunger was making Molly's attention wander towards a family who were making their way past the queue with their chips and crisp battered cod. The fish and chips were unwrapped and sprinkled with salt and vinegar and the aroma made her mouth water. Ahead of her people very slowly shuffled forward. It took her a moment or two to realise that Phil was still talking.

'My sister picked this one Cheryl had done before called Spring something or other – there were a lot of daffodils involved and a lamb.'

Molly decided not to ask whether the lamb was gambolling up the aisle with a ribbon round its neck or on the buffet in slices. What was obvious was that she really needed to get down to some serious research. Getting married seemed to be a damned sight more complicated than it used to be.